**Two brand-new stories in every volume...
twice a month!**

Duets Vol. #33

Featured authors are Liz Ireland, who creates
"sassy characters, snappy dialogue and
rip-roaring adventures..." says *Romantic Times*,
and talented new author and
Golden Heart finalist, Jane Sullivan.

Duets Vol. #34

Popular writer Tina Wainscott "is back and in a big
way," says *Romantic Times*, making her Duets debut.
Sharing the spotlight is Barbara Daly,
well-known for her wonderfully wacky tales.

Be sure to pick up both Duets volumes today!

The Sheriff and the E-mail Bride

"Don't you ever just want to do something foolish and impulsive?" Shelby teased.

Sam almost pointed out that foolish and impulsive had probably landed her in single motherhood, but he didn't.

"Occasionally," he admitted carefully. "Uh...last week I went to Fort Davis on a whim. Got that Pooh rattle for you."

"Uh-huh." She sounded unimpressed.

"I don't know what you want me to say. Impulsive?" He shrugged. "I guess I'm not sure what you mean. Is there something impulsive you'd like to do?" *For instance, kiss?*

Her face lit up. "Oh, yes!"

"What?" he asked, a little too eagerly.

"I'm *dying* to turn on your siren, Sam."

For a moment he thought this was some kind of big-city sex talk. Then he noticed that Shelby was *not* staring at him with reciprocating lust, but was eyeing the control panel on his dashboard.

She wanted to turn on his siren. Literally.

For more, turn to page 9

"Sorry, Jason. Date's over," Matt growled.

"But I was thinking about kissing Kay good-night," Jason said.

"Think again, buddy."

In one smooth move, Matt grabbed Kay's arm, pulled her from Jason's grasp and hauled her into the house.

Matt slammed the door, locked it, then flipped off the porch light. Jason tried the door, then started banging. "Hey! Open up!"

"Matt!" Kay gaped at him. "What are you doing?"

Ignoring her protest, Matt slid his hands along either side of Kay's neck, his fingers cradling her head. Every bit of desire he'd suppressed for the past several weeks welled up inside him until he felt like a volcano ready to blow.

"You want a kiss," he whispered.

Her gaze fell to his lips, hovered there a moment, then rose to meet his eyes again. "Yes."

"From him?" Matt gave a nod toward the door. "Or me?"

"You," she whispered. "It's always been you."

For more, turn to page 197

HARLEQUIN DUETS

ISBN 0-373-44099-5

THE SHERIFF AND THE E-MAIL BRIDE
Copyright © 2000 by Elizabeth Bass

STRAY HEARTS
Copyright © 2000 by Jane Graves

All rights reserved. Except for use in any review, the reproduction or utilization of this work in whole or in part in any form by any electronic, mechanical or other means, now known or hereafter invented, including xerography, photocopying and recording, or in any information storage or retrieval system, is forbidden without the written permission of the publisher, Harlequin Enterprises Limited, 225 Duncan Mill Road, Don Mills, Ontario, Canada M3B 3K9.

All characters in this book have no existence outside the imagination of the author and have no relation whatsoever to anyone bearing the same name or names. They are not even distantly inspired by any individual known or unknown to the author, and all incidents are pure invention.

This edition published by arrangement with Harlequin Books S.A.

® and TM are trademarks of the publisher. Trademarks indicated with ® are registered in the United States Patent and Trademark Office, the Canadian Trade Marks Office and in other countries.

Visit us at www.eHarlequin.com

Printed in U.S.A.

The Sheriff and the E-mail Bride

LIZ IRELAND

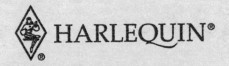

HARLEQUIN®

TORONTO • NEW YORK • LONDON
AMSTERDAM • PARIS • SYDNEY • HAMBURG
STOCKHOLM • ATHENS • TOKYO • MILAN • MADRID
PRAGUE • WARSAW • BUDAPEST • AUCKLAND

Dear Reader,

Welcome to Heartbreak Ridge, the setting for *The Sheriff and the E-mail Bride*, which is the first book in my LONE STAR LAWMEN trilogy. Heartbreak Ridge is a small town with a long history of ill-fated romances; it's also the home of Sam, Cody and Cal, three handsome badge-carrying heroes who are determined to buck the odds and find love.

I'll admit I have a special fondness for the place. Having just moved to Oregon in the past year, writing about Heartbreak Ridge allowed me to revisit my old home state whenever I felt a little homesick for the land of barbecue and big hair.

In *The Sheriff and the E-mail Bride*, Sam Weston is a man who thinks he's very up-to-date and progressive, till the woman he's been romancing online turns up on his doorstep eight months pregnant! I hope you enjoy, as I did, watching Sam try to deal with this peculiarly modern predicament while his town is abuzz with old-fashioned gossip. And watch for Cody's story in September's Duets #35, *The Deputy's Bride*, and then Cal's in Duets #38, *The Cash-Strapped Cutie*, available in October 2000.

Best always,

Liz Ireland

1

SHERIFF SAM WESTON took a swallow of the artery-clogging special at the Feed Bag Diner and listened with a long-suffering ear to his cousin. Jim Loftus, as usual, was in a lather over the problem that had plagued him for a decade: his crumbling house on Heartbreak Ridge.

"Don't know what we're gonna do, Sam," Jim said. "The place is plum falling apart. It's a quandary."

Sometimes it felt as if Sam hadn't eaten lunch in peace since Jim had inherited that white elephant with no plumbing from Sam's uncle many moons ago. He wished to heaven Jim would find another topic of conversation. Hoping that he would find another place to eat was pointless, since the Feed Bag was the one and only dining establishment in Heartbreak Ridge.

Every day Sam waffled between undying loyalty to his small hometown and total exasperation, yet he couldn't imagine living anywhere else. Only sometimes...

Sometimes he wished Heartbreak Ridge was just a little bit *different*. A restless feeling had been plaguing him lately, making him want to change his life. Drastically. And maybe he would. That's why he was out of uniform today and why he'd taken some time for himself here and there. In fact, thanks to a woman he'd never met named Shelby Waterbury, he was ninety-nine point nine percent sure he would do something about his situation—good enough odds to make Jim's relentless moaning about that overblown shack of his just a hair easier to take.

"It's your house, Jim."

His cousin's doughy face scrunched unhappily. "It might be mine on paper, but it's the old Weston homestead, Sam. I'd think you'd care more about what happened to your heritage."

It took all Sam's muscle power not to roll his eyes. The illustrious Weston heritage—a tumbledown monstrosity perched on the side of a cliff! "Take a wrecking ball to it."

Jim winced. Much as he complained about his uninhabitable hovel, he couldn't abide anyone else criticizing it. He sent Sam a wounded look. "You shock me, Sam. You really do. You know I'd as soon take a wrecking ball and aim it at my own heart. Yes, my own heart."

The building in question was the house Jim was going to fix up for his bride-to-be…before he discovered that his fiancée was two-timing him with a banker over in Fort Stockton. As far as Heartbreak Ridge romances went, that kind of disappointment was par for the course, but poor Jim never had seemed to get over that one cheating woman. And the incident happened ten years ago.

"Why don't you move into it?"

Jim made a show of looking heartsore over the very idea, though Sam figured the real reason his cousin wouldn't consider moving into the place had less to do with his broken romance and more to do with the house's lack of amenities. For instance, a roof.

"Then sell it."

At that suggestion, Jerry Lufkin, the proprietor and sole chef at the Feed Bag, choked. "*Sell* it?" he repeated, aghast. "Who in their right mind in this town would buy that ramshackle place? Why, a sneeze would blow it down!"

Now that Jerry had jumped into the conversation, the diner suddenly came alive with speculation. Amos Trilby, the pharmacist, shouted out, "That property oughta be condemned, if you ask me."

"Nobody asked you," Jim hollered back.

Merlie Shivers, Sam's secretary at the sheriff's office, didn't hesitate to toss her two cents' worth in from a couple of tables back. "*Condemnation* is too kind a word for what should happen to that place."

Jim whirled on his bar stool, offended to the core. "Heck, all she needs is a coat of paint and some TLC."

"And a sucker," Amos drawled.

Jim puffed up for a moment before deflating in concession. He shrugged. "But where am I going to find a sucker? Heartbreak Ridge isn't exactly a boomtown."

The statement was met by somber nods of acknowledgement all around.

"The other day Doyle was tellin' me he couldn't scrounge up another worker to sack groceries at the Stop-N-Shop," Jerry said.

"And we lost two people just last week."

Ted Jenkins's fix-it shop hadn't been making enough money, so he and his wife, Mary, had finally decided to pack it in and move to Houston, where their children lived, which left Heartbreak Ridge's population at sixty-two and falling. "I'm going to renumber the sign this afternoon," Sam said. As sheriff, one of his many municipal duties was to make their declining population official.

"Say…"

At the tentatively spoken word, everyone looked up from their plates. Cody Tucker, Sam's nephew and deputy, wasn't normally the talkative type; in fact, he was famously shy. When he butted into a conversation, people listened.

Cody pinned his dark-blue gaze on his uncle. "Couldn't Jim advertise on the Internet?"

In Heartbreak Ridge, Sam was known as the authority not only on the law, but also on practically anything that whiffed of progress. He owed this reputation not so much to his expertise in technology as to the fact that Heartbreak Ridge was a throwback to the Stone Age. To call the town backward was almost a compliment; the twentieth century, never mind the twenty-first, had rushed by the old berg like a Thoroughbred at the finish line.

Sam considered the matter for a moment. "It's true. You can look up what's for sale anywhere on-line."

Jim's face lit up with glee as a world of potential suckers opened up to him.

Merlie laughed. "Why sure! If Sam can find a sweetheart on the computer, Jim, then I'm sure you can find somebody to buy that thing you call a house."

Suddenly, the place was so quiet you could hear a pin drop, and Sam suddenly felt as if all eyes were on him. What did Merlie know about his on-line romance anyway? He hadn't told anybody in town about Shelby Waterbury!

Then again, as he glanced around at the speculative and knowing grins he was receiving from all corners of the Feed Bag, he was instantly reminded that there were no secrets in Heartbreak Ridge, only delusions of privacy.

"Tell us about your sweetheart, Sheriff!" Amos called out.

"We hear she's a real humdinger!"

"Dallas girl, ain't she?"

How did people find out this stuff?

Cody's face reddened, indicating that he, too, had done a little on-line spying. "I guess I might have just happened to glance at your computer screen once or twice, Sam."

"Just happened?"

In his brown deputy's uniform, the blond-haired, blue-eyed kid looked like a Boy Scout as he nodded. He even crossed his heart. "I swear."

Well, they did share a thumbnail-size office. Sam sighed, hating that Shelby Waterbury was now in the public domain. But what could he do? The cat was out of the bag; in fact, it had apparently been frolicking about town for some time now.

"What does she look like?" Jerry asked, all eagerness.

"He doesn't even know what she looks like," Merlie barked sharply. "Can you imagine? The two of them have been writing each other for months!"

"No kidding," Amos said. "How long exactly?"

"Since last Christmas," Merlie said.

"Is that right, Sam?"

Sam laughed. "Why ask me? Merlie and Cody have all the information."

Everyone chuckled except Merlie, who did have the grace to look just the slightest bit shamefaced, though she stuck out her chin stubbornly. "Can't help what I accidentally see on the screen when I'm shuffling paper in that mess of an office, can I?"

"You're always telling Merlie that she should use the computer more, Sam," Jim teased.

"Yeah, you can't hold some tech-friendly eavesdropping against her."

Sam smiled. He would have to be careful not to read Shelby's e-mail at the office anymore. Thank heavens today was his day off, and he could invite Shelby to visit Heartbreak Ridge from the privacy of his own home. "You'll be happy to know that Merlie and Cody's information is dead-on accurate. Shelby and I have been e-mailing for about six months."

"E-mailing for six months?" Jerry deadpanned, flipping a burger. "Lord-a-mercy, that sounds serious!"

"What color's her hair?"

Sam shrugged. "Dunno."

Jim looked aghast. "You've been romancing some woman since Christmas and you don't even know her hair color? What's the point of that?"

With that attitude it didn't surprise him that his cousin's one big stab at romance had been a disaster. "Because, you lunkhead, Shelby and I write about more important things...like books we've read, and what we're thinking, and what's going on in the world."

"Okay," admitted Jim, "so you know all about the beautiful stuff she thinks. But what if she's a dog?"

"I'm not looking for Pamela Anderson Lee."

He doubted there were many beauty queens drumming up husbands on the Internet, anyway. His gut told him Shelby was an honest, kind person, and her e-mail made him laugh. The fact that she was a dog lover, and mentioned wanting to raise a big family in a small town, meant more to him than a pretty picture would have. After all, his nephew Cal had married a real good-looking city woman, and she'd fled from Heartbreak Ridge after three scant months. Sam was thirty-five years old—fast approaching his Geritol years, in his panicky estimation—and after all these years of waiting, he was searching for a life companion, not a beauty queen.

What he wanted was a middling pretty, competent, entertaining woman to make his life complete. Fanny Farmer with a funny bone.

"Say, Sam," Jerry said, "you were in East Texas just last fall for that convention. Why didn't you look the little lady up then?"

"Haven't you been listening?" Merlie shot back. "He didn't know her last fall."

"Oh, yeah." Jerry scratched the bill of his green John Deere cap with the handle of his spatula, as if jogging his memory.

"So, when are you two gonna get hitched?" Amos asked.

"Land's sake, he hasn't even clapped eyes on 'er yet!" Jim brayed.

Sam stood, eager to escape all this speculation. Truth was, he was still too bowled over by the way things were going with Shelby to feel comfortable about letting other people in on the deal. Sometimes he felt like he and Shelby Waterbury were practically soul mates. He'd told her things that he would never have been able to admit to a woman in the flesh.

Jerry sent him a level glance. "Sounds like you're taking a big chance, Sam."

"Especially considering where you come from,"

Merlie pointed out, voicing the sentiment that couldn't be tiptoed around much longer. Ominous silence met her statement.

Heartbreak Ridge hadn't earned its name from happy endings. The town was named for the bluff where Sam's own great-great-grandfather, Thelonius Weston, settled at the turn of the century after his wife had run out on him. Jim's house stood—barely—down the hill from Thelonius's two-room cabin, and everyone knew what had happened to Jim's marriage plans! Then there was Cal, who rented the original cabin after he'd endured the same heartbreak as Thelonius. And it wasn't just the Weston clan that suffered these love catastrophes. Everyone in town had a hard-luck love story to tell. Merlie's husband had died when she was twenty-three. Amos Trilby had been through four divorces. Jerry was a woebegone bachelor, despite running the most successful business in town. And Cody…that boy was so shy, chances were slim to nothing that he would ever work up the courage to ask a woman for a date, much less get himself married.

Maybe they were right. Maybe romance was doomed in that town.

Sam grimaced when his usually rational thoughts embraced such nonsense. "That's ridiculous superstition!" All towns had their problems. Despite the gloomy moniker, there was no reason to believe Heartbreak Ridge was more unlucky in love than any other place.

Jerry sucked in his breath. "It isn't superstition, either. Look at poor Amos over there."

Amos of the four divorces gave Sam a long-suffering look that indicated more than Jerry's greasy food was causing his heartburn.

Nevertheless, Sam wasn't convinced. "What about my parents? They were happy."

"And they died when they were in their thirties," Cody gently reminded his uncle.

Sam frowned. Evidence did seem to mount up, but that still only left them with a circumstantial case. As a reasonable, forward-thinking person, he refused to believe that there was something in the air here that caused perfectly happy lovers to spat, spouses to cheat, or divorce attorneys to circle the town like buzzards over a day-old carcass.

But as a citizen of Heartbreak Ridge, he wasn't taking any chances. "Even if the town's love affairs are doomed, I've taken steps to ensure that won't happen with me."

To his chagrin, the room erupted in roars of laughter.

"Oh, steps!" Jerry hooted.

Merlie ribbed her dining partner. "The sheriff's been using the scientific method to find himself a foolproof bride."

Sam waited for the jeers to die down before explaining. "First, Shelby's from out of town, and immune to our local mumbo jumbo. And unlike some I could mention, I didn't fall for Shelby based on looks. More importantly, I've gotten to know her these past months. She's not fickle, or deceitful. And just to safeguard against small-town panic, I've told her all about this place, down to the tiniest crack in the sidewalk, so she knows what she's getting into."

"Does she know about monotony?" Merlie asked. "Having to look at the same old faces day after day after day? No offense, but there *are* days when I get sick of the sight of you people."

Jim laughed. "How about feeling like your life is an open book for the enjoyment of sixty-two other people? Make a mistake at lunch, the whole town talks it over at dinner."

Amos nodded. "'Sides, we've got one restaurant and no movie theater. She know what that's like, Sam?"

Jerry added, "Heck, if you want to buy a book that's not in the lending library, you have to drive thirty miles to get it."

Sam pursed his lips, refusing to give in to their gloom. "I've got one word for you people. *Amazon.com.* The whole world's at our feet now, even way out here. Why, you can get anything you want on the Internet!"

"Wives included," Merlie deadpanned.

"When you live in a town whose dwindling population practically puts us on the endangered species list, what choice is there?"

Jim nodded. "He's got a point there. I might have to look into this Internet business."

Merlie clucked her tongue. "I hope the good Lord's lookin' over the earth the day Jim Loftus gets let loose on the World Wide Web!"

As soon as the laughter died down, Sam asserted, "All my efforts aside, there's absolutely no reason to believe that some silly town jinx will enter into the equation at all."

"Hope so, Sam," Amos said.

"Yep," Jerry agreed. "It'd be a fine thing to have a romance work out around here. Yessir, it sure would."

"Let's not kid ourselves," Merlie cracked. "It'd be a miracle!"

Sam plopped two dollars down for a tip and strolled over to the shoe box to pay his tab. Behind him, the noisy bell above the door jangled, indicating that a customer wanted in. The space at the entrance was tight, so Sam scooted back to hold the door open so it didn't crush him as he let the stranger in.

And what a stranger!

The minute the pretty redhead appeared at the door, all eyes were glued on her, including Sam's. For one thing, she was a knockout. Hair the color of raging fire spilled in spirally curls around a face that was like something out of a fashion magazine. She had perfect cheekbones with a dusting of freckles, full lips turned up in a tentative, charming smile, and knockout green eyes that twinkled with liveliness. Sam's breath caught in his chest, even before he'd gotten a gander at the rest of her. Miss Redhead put a whole new spin on the word *curvaceous*. Beneath her practical jean jumper stood the most shapely pair of legs he'd seen in quite some time. She was slender without being anorexic like so many twenty-something women were these days. In fact, just the opposite. Her breasts were full, the arms poking out of her tight T-shirt were just this side of plump...and as for the rest of her, there was only one word to describe it.

Pregnant.

Sam squeezed around to help her, getting a heady whiff of flowery perfume. "Here, let me give you a hand," he offered.

She was carrying an oversize purse and not managing too well as she waddled through the door, though for a woman in her advanced stage, she was doing better than you might expect. Sam took the woman's arm, feeling a shameful rush of awareness when his hand sank down on the soft flesh.

Sweat beaded at his temple, and just as soon as he'd ushered her through the door he dropped her arm like a hot potato. Good grief! He had to go home right away and write that letter to Shelby. If he was having reactions like this to pregnant strangers, he needed a woman more desperately than he had reckoned!

He grabbed a fiver out of his wallet and slapped it on the counter, in a hurry to get out of there, but of course, Jerry's attention—like everyone else's—was riveted on the redhead.

"Can I help you, young lady?" Jerry asked with more eagerness than Sam had seen on the old guy's face in a dog's age. It took a special woman to sidetrack the proprietor from cold hard cash.

The redhead smiled anxiously, her gorgeous green eyes scanning the rapt crowd. Sam had never seen eyes quite like hers. Two soft pillows of green that made him think of cool spring mornings…

What you need is a cool shower, a voice inside his head mocked.

And then she spoke. "Maybe…"

That was it. One word from those pink lips, and Sam was officially, unequivocally smitten. Her voice was soft yet clear, with a slight Texas drawl that held more than a hint of humor. And as he stared into her face, he couldn't help noticing that the corners of her lips were tilted up in a wry grin. Something about her face and that voice made him forget all about middling pretty Shelby Waterbury and what kind of books she read and the fact that she'd always dreamed of raising a family in a small town. He bet Shelby didn't have entrancing green eyes and hair a man itched to run his fingers through.

"You lost?" Jerry asked her.

That red hair shimmered in the dull light as she shook her head. "No, I'm looking for somebody."

"Well, you've come to the right place, missy. There aren't many somebodies wandering around Heartbreak Ridge, so between us in here, we know 'em all."

"Good." The woman darted her green eyes around the small room. "I'm trying to locate a man named Sam Weston."

A hush fell over the room.

The woman shifted uncomfortably. "Is something wrong?"

For a moment, Sam thought it was just the blood rushing up to his ears that made him unable to hear anything. Then he noticed everyone in the place staring at the two of them standing side by side.

Had she said...?

Even Merlie was dumbstruck; in fact, she looked as if she just might choke on one of Jerry's greasy cheeseburgers. Amos's bottom lip had almost disappeared into his chin, and Jim, who normally would be sizing up any stranger solely in terms of mortgage loan potential, was gawking at the woman with the most puzzled expression on his face. Cody was silent and his cheeks were bright red, but that was normal behavior for him when faced with a stranger, especially a female.

Finally Jerry cleared his throat and spoke, with a curt nod of the bill of his green cap. "Sheriff's right beside you, ma'am."

Those green eyes turned on him, and Sam felt as if his cheeks were as rosy red as Cody's. Because as he and the woman gaped at each other like characters in a silent movie, there was suddenly no doubt in his mind, no doubt at all, who she was. And worse, he was positive that every person in the room also knew that he was finally, after six long months of nothing but e-mails, meeting Shelby Waterbury.

Her face paled and her red brows darted up curiously. "Sam?"

Shelby…saying his name. It was a moment he'd dreamed of for months. Only everything was wrong. This Shelby was too young.

This Shelby had siren looks that would stop traffic.

This Shelby was pregnant!

2

SHELBY PERCHED uneasily on her swivel chair and peered around the sheriff's small office. With two desks—one for Sam and one for his nephew, the deputy—the room was crowded, but the old high ceiling and wide windows looking out on Main Street made it feel bigger than it was. The place certainly didn't feel like any police station she knew and, unfortunately, she'd known at least one more intimately than she cared to admit. Only the computer on Sam's desk hinted that the Heartbreak Ridge police station had changed since 1950.

Sam shifted uncomfortably in his squeaky chair. "May I offer you something to drink? Cola? A cup of coffee?"

She smiled at Sam's offer. "I can't drink caffeine."

Puzzlement appeared in his blue eyes, then the creases fell out of his forehead and he glanced down at her swollen abdomen, or so visibly tried *not* to glance down that it was tantamount to the same thing. "Oh." He cleared his throat. "Well, um, I think we've got some lemon-lime here...."

He swiveled so quickly back toward the minifridge hidden in the corner that he banged his knee on the side of the desk, then tried to suppress a wince.

For some reason, her sudden arrival seemed to be

making Sam Weston as nervous as a frog in a frying pan. And maybe she shouldn't have come, except…

It felt so right! The little town was just as Sam had described it in his e-mail, from the one-street Old West town setup that looked out over a strange, breathtaking sea of hills and bluffs, right down to the plainspoken Heartbreak Ridge inhabitants she'd encountered in that crazy diner that smelled of grease and pine cleaner. Sam's e-mails had allowed her to visualize it all, from Jerry's green cap to Merlie's cat glasses and overalls right down to the dusty ruts in the gas station parking lot that Sam said became like small lakes in springtime. Every detail stood out like a tribute to Sam's descriptive powers…except Sam.

When it came to himself, Sam had been too modest by half. The man was… Well, he was a hunk. He had a dark, rugged look about him—just like Dylan Mc-Dermott, the man on that legal show she used to love to watch in the days before she became embroiled in real legal troubles of her own. Back when facing jail time was only part of the lives of people far removed from Shelby.

She brushed the unpleasant thought away and focused on Sam's blue, blue eyes. Somehow, without knowing their specific color, she had expected Sam to have kind eyes, and he did. She knew so much about him, everything from the important to the trivial. Like how he'd lost his parents when he was little more than a kid, and lived with his older sister through his teen years. How he'd humiliated himself performing a magic act in his junior high talent show. How he'd always wished he could have gone on to graduate studies in history, but had felt duty-bound to earn his living, especially since every male ancestor since the turn of the twentieth century had worked in law enforcement. She knew that he'd read *Where the Red Fern Grows* five times when he was a kid, that now he favored biographies but loved funny movies. She knew that driving rains made him feel sad because it had rained hard the day they had buried his parents, and that more than anything else he loved his nephews Cal and Cody, even though Cody was hard to get to know and Cal was just plain ornery. She not only knew that his dog, Sadie, liked pigs' ears and exhaustive ear scratches, but also that when she got into the garbage Sam sometimes couldn't bring himself to reprimand her.

She'd expected Sam's kind blue eyes like she'd expected to see Althea's Nail Boutique nestled right between Trilby's Drugstore and the Western Auto. The thing she hadn't expected was his formidable height—the man was six foot three if he was an inch—his chiseled-in-granite jaw, and his physique that hinted at a gym somewhere in town even when she knew for a fact that Heartbreak Ridge didn't have one. She'd always heard that men you met on the Internet were mostly the computer geek type, and that would have been fine with her. After what she'd been through, a soft-spoken nerd with a biography habit would have hit the spot. That's even what she'd been hoping for.

James Arness here was throwing her for a loop.

She shifted in her chair, growing uncomfortable herself. Sam's gaze might be kind, but his nervous manner was telling her things she didn't want to hear, like that her sheriff wasn't exactly tickled pink to see her. In fact, his dumbfounded expression when he first figured out who she was back in the diner was enough to let her know that their fragile long-distance relationship had just been blown apart like a doomed planet in a sci-fi movie.

She could only imagine what was wrong. Maybe he expected someone prettier...or richer—he'd certainly looked askance at her old wreck of a car filled up with boxes and suitcases. Or maybe he'd simply hoped she'd remain a cyber-presence in his life.

Her heart sagged in disappointment in her chest, but she tried hard not to show it. Looked like she'd goofed again—invested her emotions in exactly the wrong person. Although, God knows, this wouldn't be the first big blunder of her life.

She smiled in spite of herself. "I guess I should have told you, huh?"

His lips flattened into a scowl. "That might have helped."

A little surprised by his curt tone, she lifted her shoulders innocently. "But I promise you I had no idea myself."

His dark brows raised in disbelief.

"It just happened," she explained.

He released a sputtering, incredulous laugh. "Just how do you reckon that?"

"Haven't you ever just... Well, done anything in the heat of the moment before?"

His level stare was as merciless as his tone was skeptical. "Oh! Is that what happened?"

"Well, yes." For a moment, Shelby had an ugly flashback to her old inquisition days, of harsh florescent lighting, insistent, ugly questions, and inky coffee. The truth—and chocolate—was all that had gotten her through that terrible time. Maybe it would work its magic again. Although Sam's office was much less intimidating than the Tarrant County Jail had been, his demeanor was becoming as hostile as those other lawmen, and even though she wasn't facing prison time, she felt the stakes now were much higher.

"After all that you said in your last e-mail about Heartbreak Ridge, I decided on the spur of the moment that I had to see the place for myself." She reconsidered for a split second. "No, that's not right. I felt *compelled* to see it, to see you. I guess I didn't want there to be a big buildup."

His gaze zoomed in on her stomach. "I'd say the build up has been pretty substantial! More than I ever knew."

At his flat tone, she blinked. It was almost as if he intended a double meaning. "I beg your pardon?"

He let out a gruff laugh that was practically a snort. "Lady, do you really think right now I'm wondering why you decided to pay me this little visit?"

Her lips parted and she gaped at him, uncomprehending. She'd hoped that he would feel flattered that she'd come. Apparently, that wasn't the case. In fact, from the rigid set of that Dick Tracy jaw of his, she would almost say he looked a little angry with her, something she didn't understand at all. "I thought you might be."

Sam popped out of his chair and began pacing, shaking his head. Then he stopped and raked a hand through his thick dark hair, which, now that she looked at it more closely, had a few flecks of gray. She laughed—to herself, she thought.

His intense gaze zoomed in on her. "Do you find something amusing?"

At his tone, she sobered immediately. "I was just

thinking that it's true what they say. Men *do* look more distinguished with some gray hair.''

Like a shot, his hand dropped down to his side and he glared at her self-consciously. Was the sheriff sensitive about his age? That was something she hadn't expected! She had to force herself to suppress another grin.

"Is something bothering you, Sam?"

"*Bothering* me?" he repeated, aghast. At what, she couldn't fathom.

"You seem...uncomfortable," Shelby continued, trying to break through to whatever it was that had him in such a snit. "If there's something on your mind, I wish you'd just come out with it."

He gawked at her as though she were speaking gibberish. And she was beginning to think that maybe she was. This conversation wasn't making any sense. Unless...

Dread struck in her heart. "Oh, dear!" She tilted her head and asked softly, "I've really, really goofed, haven't I?"

"That's one way to put it!"

Her shoulders sagged in disappointment. "I've heard about things like this happening, but I never expected it to happen to me."

His brows drew together. "Expect what to happen?"

"To be taken in by an Internet Casanova." When his jaw dropped—playing Mr. Innocent—she folded her arms. "That's what's happened, right?"

"*What?*"

"After all, I don't really know you," she said, a horrible possibility suddenly dawning on her. "You might be a married man!"

"I am not."

"Then maybe you're one of those guys who romance multiple women on the Internet with no intention of ever making a commitment to one of them." Both possibilities hurt more than she would have expected. "Somehow I thought that we were more intimate than that."

"We were!" Sam puffed up in offense. "I mean, I *thought* we were. Lady, where do you get off calling me a Casanova?"

She shrugged. "Well then, what is it, Sam?"

He looked dumbfounded. "You're obviously the one who's had something going on on the side!"

The accusation cut Shelby to the core. She pushed herself out of her chair—with great effort—and stood toe-to-toe with Sam, arms akimbo. "What are you implying?"

"I'm implying nothing." He gritted out a laugh. "I'm saying flat-out that you're *pregnant,* Shelby, and not just a little bit, either."

They glared at each other for a long minute before Shelby could even think to speak. The man had to be bug crazy! How could he be bringing up that subject at this late date?

"Well, of course I am." She forced her voice to remain calm.

At her simple affirmation, he crossed his arms over his chest. "Well?"

What did he want her to say? "My due date's in three and a half weeks."

His gaze didn't waver. "And you waited until now to tell me this? Showing up on my doorstep unannounced so I couldn't back down?" She couldn't believe her ears. "I told you right away that I was pregnant."

"No, you didn't."

"I'm sure I did."

"When?"

She mentally sifted through the hundreds of missives they'd sent each other, harkening back to some of their earliest correspondence. "Well...when you were telling me about your golden retriever, Sadie, and you asked me if I was all alone, I know I told you about Jack."

"Uh-huh."

There. Encouraged by the first point they'd agreed on since meeting, she rushed ahead. "And that I was having trouble with him, because I was getting sick a lot."

"So?"

So? She huffed in frustration. "So that was one of our first e-mails, Sam, when I told you about my baby!"

"Jack..." the sheriff's jaw dropped open "...your... *baby?*"

"What did you think?"

Red streaks stained his cheeks. "And later when you went to the doctor and discovered that Jack was really a Jackie, that was a real doctor?"

"Of course it was!" she retorted, offended. "I know I've been hard up for money, but do you think I'd risk my baby's health on a quack?"

Dumbfounded, the sheriff looked down at her stomach again, and not with what she would call a rapturous expression. "Then this..."

Her hand flew instinctively, protectively, to her baby. She smiled. "Sam...meet Jackie."

She'd imagined this moment a million times. The man she loved—or had convinced herself she loved for all these months—finally meeting up with the baby that, despite all she'd been through, meant so much to her. The scene with the imaginary Sam had played out myriad ways in her mind. But never had the Sam of her daydreams woodenly stuck out a hand, then, after just the briefest of touches to her belly, recoiled as if he'd just touched a slimy slug.

His face paled, and he opened his mouth to speak, then swallowed. He began backing toward the door, shaking his head. "I..." His words cut off for a second while he gulped down a breath. "Will you excuse me for a moment, Miss Waterbury?"

He didn't wait for her permission to whirl on his boot heel and flee to the outer room. His secretary was almost flattened when the door flew open; apparently Merlie had had her ear to the keyhole. No telling how she'd interpret what she'd heard. Shelby wasn't sure how to interpret it herself; troubling questions swirled in her mind.

Sam hadn't known she was pregnant. Who had he thought Jackie was?

And how could the mere thought of her baby make Sam, a grown man, look as if he were going to faint?

And was the relationship formally, officially over when the man she thought she had come to Heartbreak Ridge to marry suddenly started calling her *Miss Waterbury?*

MERLIE CACKLED. "You thought her baby was a dog?"

Sam would gladly have sunk through the floor rather than face his secretary's gleeful ribbing, but there was just no escaping it. "Would you mind keeping your voice down to a gentle holler?"

Unfortunately, Merlie's oft-used vocal chords didn't know the meaning of *subdued.* "How in Sam Hill did you come by this asinine—excuse me, canine—assumption?''

Sam shrugged, realizing that he now understood, intimately and completely, the meaning of the word *idiot*. ''We were discussing Sadie, and then she started writing about Jack. I thought it was a poodle or something. Haven't you heard women refer to their pets as their babies?''

Merlie's lip curled. ''You're asking the wrong woman. I call Tubb-Tubb the money drain. That old feline is gonna eat me out of house and home someday.''

Sam sighed. He felt like a damn fool. And now that Merlie knew about the little misunderstanding, it was only a matter of time before the rest of the town found out about it. He would be a laughingstock...but even humiliation was secondary to the crushing disappointment he felt in the pit of his stomach that Shelby wasn't... Well, she wasn't Fanny Farmer, that was for damn sure.

She was young. Beautiful. A single mother-to-be.

It just seemed so strange that she wouldn't have mentioned her pregnancy more often, or more explicitly! And yet Shelby didn't seem to be the type to try to sucker a man into marrying her to provide a daddy for a kid who'd been fathered by some other man. And genuine shock had registered on her face when he said he didn't know about the baby.

Sam sank lower in the metal folding chair by Merlie's desk, the one usually reserved for offenders being booked.

Merlie *tsk*ed at him. ''Folks in town aren't gonna believe this when I tell them.''

Great. Already he had to think about the gossip mill,

which in Heartbreak Ridge was the only thing that moved at warp speed. "I'd prefer it if you didn't say anything about what you've heard here today."

Merlie laughed. "Why? It'd be better than what people were speculatin' about at the Feed Bag after you two left."

"What were they saying?"

"Well, mostly that maybe you weren't on the up-and-up when you said you'd never met Shelby before."

"But they saw us meet—we didn't even recognize each other."

"That's what Jim pointed out."

"At least someone has a little sense."

"Oh yeah? Jim was the one who was wondering maybe if there wasn't such a thing as on-line insemination."

Sam buried his head in his hands. "Oh, Lord."

"Have to admit, Sam, it looks like something screwy's goin' on. But I wouldn't worry about what they're sayin' at the Feed Bag half so much as what you're going to say to that woman in there about thinking her fetus was a poodle."

"I'm not going to tell her that."

"Isn't she going to wonder?"

Sam shot a glance through the old leaded glass door and saw Shelby still gazing curiously around his office. Every time he looked at her, he felt a little more disappointed. True, she was more beautiful than an Internet wife-hunter had the right to hope for. But she was so *young*. Couldn't be more than twenty-five! Why would a beautiful young thing like her have to scour the Internet for dates? It seemed to him that a woman who looked like that would have to beat men away with a club. The whole setup was suspicious.

And then there was this baby.

"Did she actually think I was going to welcome the opportunity to be a father to someone else's kid when I don't even know her?"

Merlie's gaze skewered him with mirth. "You knew enough to tell everybody at the Feed Bag that you were going to marry her, as I recall."

"But that was before..." Before he'd seen her and felt this disappointment of not getting what he'd expected. Shelby didn't look like a small-town type, a woman who would be happy in a town where people were so desperate for entertainment that they actually viewed PTA meetings as fun and looked forward to Sunday morning church service the way other people looked forward to an evening at the theater.

And yet there was another feeling tugging at him, one he wasn't comfortable with, either. Raw desire. Hunger he hadn't felt the likes of since he was just a randy youngster. Looking into those green eyes and at that long red hair and those shapely legs made long-forgotten hormones gallop through his system like a stampeding herd of wild mustangs. It made him forget all about wanting a soul mate and a life's companion, and instead turned his thoughts to how good it would feel just to have a wild, wonderful fling.

But then his gaze always strayed down to that baby. And he was shocked that he could think that way about a woman on the brink of maternity. A protective instinct kicked in that he wasn't sure was compatible with either desire or disappointment.

Only one thing was crystal clear in his mind. All in

all, Shelby Waterbury was more trouble than he'd ever imagined taking on.

Merlie chuckled. "So much for avoiding the pitfalls of a normal Heartbreak Ridge romance, Sam. Looks to me like your scientific method just got you the surprise of your life."

Sure enough, all his careful planning had backfired. After six months, he knew absolutely nothing about Shelby Waterbury—nothing that really counted, as it turned out. For surely if he had known that she was pregnant six months ago, he never would have struck up an e-mail correspondence with her.

Would he?

Lord, he was in a conundrum. How was he going to tell Shelby that he didn't want to pursue this relationship further without feeling like a heel? Then again, why should *he* feel like a heel? She was the one who came sashaying into town eight month's pregnant! But if was true that she had told him about the baby—given him obstetric updates, apparently—then who but he was to blame for the surprise he felt?

Merlie shot him a look that was both comical and sympathetic. "For a man who prides himself on being careful, you sure gummed this up, didn't you?"

He straightened defensively, then realized she was right on the money. He had gummed up everything. Now how was he going to get out of this sticky mess?

Before he could reply, the inner office door opened and Shelby marched into the middle of the room. Reflexively, Sam stood, watching her warily. Her pretty face turned up to him, her expression a mask of determination. Heaven help him, he hoped she wasn't going to make some kind of embarrassing scene right here in the middle of the office. Merlie was here, and no telling who would walk in next. If the woman was going to break down crying or something...

She took a deep breath. "Sheriff, I think we'd better call it a day."

Sam blinked.

Call it a day? The words were exactly opposite from the ones he'd expected. And Shelby's eyes were completely dry. Instead of tears, they shone with resolution.

He opened his mouth to speak but no words came out. Of course she was right—hadn't he wanted to tell her the very same thing?—but at the same time, his gut told him she was being rash. After all, they'd been correspondents for a long time.

Or was he uncomfortable because she was giving him the brush-off, and not the other way around?

Don't be a fool, she's letting you off easy, the voice of reason admonished. Sam let out a breath he hadn't known he'd been holding, although now he realized it had been hitched in his chest since Shelby had strolled into the Feed Bag. He'd been handed a hell of a problem, but now the problem was toddling off of her own accord. He might be a laughingstock, but it wouldn't be forever. Heartbreak Ridge would forget. Eventually.

"I'm glad you feel that way," he said at last. "I suppose that's the only reasonable thing to do."

"We obviously misunderstood some things about each other."

Sam nodded. Then he frowned. What could *she* have misunderstood about him? He'd been completely on the up-and-up!

Quickly, she reached her hand out. "No hard feelings?"

For some reason, he didn't know what to say. If anything, he'd anticipated resentment from her. And though she was leaving on her own, even exonerating him as best she could, he *still* felt like a heel.

Especially when he stared down at her hand. That hand didn't seem to go with the rest of her. From her abundant luxurious hair and her round cuddly appearance, he might have expected pampered hands with long, manicured nails. But Shelby's nails were cut short, almost too short, and one or two looked ragged. The skin on her hands was dry and scratched in places. They were hands that had seen work, and worry.

And, he realized suddenly, they were the hands that had typed messages he had stayed up nights reading over and over. Messages that he sneaked illicit work time to respond to. Those weary fingers had typed words that made him feel as excited as a kid inside, words that occupied his mind when it should have been thinking about more important things, words that made him laugh when he wasn't even aware he was thinking about Shelby at all.

That breath hitched in his chest again, and he forced himself to grasp her hand and shake it. The moment their skin touched, he felt a surge of desire...and at the same time, it seemed as if part of him was seeping away, the hopeful part that had lived in dreams for the past six months.

Maybe that was for the best. What had those dreams gotten him? What had their e-mail told them about each other? Writing letters hadn't conveyed even basic facts, like a pregnancy. Or more elusive facts, like how Shelby possessed the power to arouse him with just a smile and a handshake.

He cleared his throat. "No, no hard feelings." The words came out as a bare rasp.

He was half relieved, half regretful when she pulled her hand away again. "Good," she said, her chirpy voice relaying none of the inner conflict, none of the bowled-over-with-desire feeling that he was experiencing. "Then I guess there's only one more thing that you can do for me."

He forced a smile, even though his stomach knotted nervously at both the statement and the ever so slightly mischievous glint in her eye. "What's that?"

"Tell me where I could find a place to stay."

To get this far west from Dallas, Shelby must have been on the road since at least yesterday morning. Naturally she wouldn't want to drive all the way back east tonight. "There are a couple of places on I-10 to stay. Motels, mostly, but they're not bad."

Shelby's auburn brows drew together. "There's nothing closer?"

She must be really tired if she didn't want to drive even thirty miles, which, in terms of West Texas distance, was nothing. "Last hotel in Heartbreak Ridge closed in 1952. Now it's the Feed Store."

"Oh, right." Shelby considered this for a moment. "Then there's no place I could find a room? I'd be glad to pay for however long I stay."

Why would she be so determined to find a room in town? And that phrase, *however long I stay,* wasn't sitting well with him. Her car had been full of boxes, he recalled now. "But you're going right back to Dallas," he said, "aren't you?"

"Dallas?" She laughed. "Of course not!"

"But that's where you live."

She shook her head. "Correction. That where I *lived*."

He was baffled. "But...?"

She grinned up at him, her arms folded serenely over her belly. "Is there some law that says I can't move to Heartbreak Ridge, Sheriff?"

He almost asked her to repeat herself. But there was no way he could have heard her wrong. "*Move?* To Heartbreak Ridge?"

She nodded, still smiling.

Little beads of sweat began to gather on his forehead. She couldn't intend to up and settle in his hometown! It didn't make any sense. "I thought you said we should call it a day."

Green eyes stared at him placidly. "But I didn't say a word about leaving town."

But of course she would leave town! "Maybe you don't understand, Shelby. Heartbreak Ridge isn't the type of place a person just moves to. In fact, it's more like a place people move out of. I was just going to downsize our population sign this afternoon."

She grinned. "Well, now you can add one person to it. Me!"

Good lord, she was serious! "Nobody in their right mind would move here for no reason at all."

"But I have a very good reason. I need a place to raise my baby," Shelby said simply.

Sam tossed his hands in exasperation. "And out of the whole U.S. of A. you can't think of a better place than *this?* Not that I don't love his town—heck, most of the time I'm its biggest booster—but facts are facts. Heartbreak Ridge is not a Mecca for commerce and development...or for single mothers."

In fact, Shelby would be the first of those.

If he expected his words to make her back down, he was mistaken. "I could think of a million places, but Heartbreak Ridge is the only place I know."

"You just got here," he pointed out.

"But you told me all about it, Sam." She turned, gesturing out the window. "And you did such a wonderful job! I didn't realize it until I drove into town, but in my heart I felt I knew every brick, every bush, every person. In my imagination I had packed my bags and moved long before I ever set any hopes on our relationship."

Terrific. Undermined by his own accurate prose!

"Regardless of how things have turned out between you and me, Sam, I love this place."

"But you just can't pick up and move!"

She shrugged. "I already did. My car's loaded with my stuff, and I gave up my apartment."

He was flabbergasted. "You intended to turn your life upside down on the basis of some e-mail?"

"A lot of e-mail," she corrected.

"All right, a lot." And, a little voice in the back of his mind reminded him, he had also been on the brink of turning his own life topsy-turvy. Even so, he hardly knew how to begin to tell her how foolish that was, especially in her condition! Who would take care of her? She hadn't mentioned much about her family back in Dallas, but she was bound to have more of a support network there than she would have here. There was no place for her to live here. And where would she work? *Could* she work? From the looks of things, she might go into labor any second.

His frantic questions must have been written all over

his face, because she laughed and reached over to pat his arm reassuringly.

"Don't worry, Sam."

Again, her slightest touch was like a jolt to his system. "But—"

"I'm not your responsibility," she insisted.

But of course she was! "Whose fault is it that you're here?"

"Mine." She shook her head, only half smiling now. "And if you think this is the worst mistake I've made in my life, you couldn't be more wrong."

Sam wanted to argue with her, but she seemed so calm, so sure of herself. So opposite from the way he felt! He didn't like this situation at all. Here he'd thought she was going to leave him in peace to lick his wounds, but it turned out he wasn't being let off the hook at all! Everyone in town knew why she'd come here—thanks to his own foolhardy pronouncement—and as long as Shelby remained in Heartbreak Ridge, there would be a reminder of his folly, of how his e-mail bride gambit had backfired. He would be *on* the hook, and for who knows how long?

And there was something else rubbing him the wrong way. He still couldn't believe how beautiful she was, and he wasn't comfortable with it, either. The fact that one look into her sexy green eyes could make his nerves sizzle, that her merest touch affected him like an aphrodisiac, that her moist pink lips tempted him to throw caution to the wind and ask her to stay, to stay at his own house even, to be his wife... Well, these didn't strike him as healthy responses, given the situation. A reasonable man couldn't let himself be directed by lust, but if Shelby Waterbury stuck around Heartbreak Ridge, his attraction to her was bound to cloud his reasoning sooner or later.

If she left, he would have been able to forget her and get back to normal. But now...

He returned to the most concrete argument against staying in Heartbreak Ridge. His ace in the hole. "There's nowhere for you to stay here."

"Oh, yes there is."

Both of them turned to Merlie, who Sam had almost forgotten was sitting there. He was shocked she'd been able to keep her lip buttoned this long. From the gleeful grin on her face, he could tell she'd been savoring every word of the conversation. "You can stay with me, hon," she told Shelby in an almost maternal tone. "I've got a spare room in the back of my house with its own bathroom, even its own door."

Sam was taken aback. "You've never had a boarder!"

Merlie stuck out her chin at him stubbornly. "Never was no one in town before to rent to, but as I was listening to Shelby here, it suddenly occurred to me that I could earn good money with that extra room. Something's got to keep Tubb-Tubb in cat food, and it sure won't be the wages I earn here pushing papers for you." She flashed a friendly smile at Shelby. "Like cats, don't you, hon?"

Shelby nodded eagerly. "Oh, thank you, Ms. Shivers!"

"How the heck did you know my last—?" Merlie looked over at Sam and it apparently dawned on her. When Shelby said she knew everybody in town, she wasn't kidding. Merlie waved her hands as she focused again on Shelby. "I don't even want to *think* about what else he may have told you 'bout me. Just call me Merlie, and I'm sure we'll get along fine.''

Now that she'd gotten a toehold in his community, Shelby brimmed with enthusiasm. ''I can pay, and clean, and take care of things around the house for you.''

''Said I wanted a boarder, not a wife,'' Merlie cracked. ''Why don't I take you over to take a squint at the place before you go promising me a pot of gold?''

''I'd love to see it!''

Merlie glanced over at Sam in a way that was more command than question. ''Sure you can look after everything here for a while, boss man?''

Sam lifted his shoulders. ''Of course, but...''

Cody slid through the front door just as Merlie was gathering her purse and escorting Shelby out. One glance at Shelby and the young man's cheeks turned scarlet. He tugged his hat off his head and nodded in her general direction.

''Hasta la vista,'' Merlie shouted back at them through the door.

Shelby whirled on her heel and smiled big at Sam. ''See you around, Sheriff.'' Her fingers trilled at him as she waved goodbye.

Sam barely managed a nod.

Cody was all excitement after the door had closed behind the two women. ''You mean she's staying? Are ya'll gettin' married, Uncle Sam?''

Uncle Sam! As if things weren't bad enough, he had to have some fresh-faced kid calling him a name that made him feel like a gray-haired old geezer with a beard.

Sam sank down wearily into Merlie's chair. His muscles ached liked he'd just been through a pitched battle. ''Yes, she's staying...and no, we're not.''

Cody's smile faded. "Then…?"

"The population of Heartbreak Ridge just increased by one," Sam informed him, burying his head in his hands.

"Two," Cody reminded Sam. "Don't forget ya'll are about to have a baby."

The misguided reminder made Sam's heart sink. It was going to take a heap of explaining to set Heartbreak Ridge straight on this one.

3

FOR ONCE in her life, Shelby felt she'd landed in cotton.

Though Merlie's house was decorated with the accumulated stuff of a lifetime lived in one place, she was tidy, and most of all, her house was a home, the kind of place Shelby had always dreamed of living in. Knickknacks and keepsakes were stacked everywhere, pictures covered every inch of wall space, and the furniture had the well-worn appearance of treasured family pieces. Everywhere Shelby looked, she saw Merlie's personality. The refrigerator was cluttered with magnets of all descriptions, some of them holding down old photos with curled edges or yellowed newspaper clippings. An enormously fat yellow tabby cat—an animal Merlie insisted was a stray she was just keeping until the rightful owner came along—nestled on the couch next to a sampler pillow embroidered elaborately with the phrase, You Must Have Mistaken Me for Someone Who Gives a Damn. The sight made Shelby laugh, and when Merlie laughed with her, she felt right at home.

Home. Not a word that exactly tripped off her tongue. Growing up, her mother had moved them often, usually to smaller and smaller apartments. Shelby had vowed that when she was an adult, she would find a better place to live than a shoe box with no privacy, maybe someplace with a yard, even. But every meager clerical position she'd scrounged up for herself had driven home how difficult it had probably been for her mother, a waitress, to provide single-handed for a daughter even as poorly as she had.

Here in Merlie's back room, Shelby had more privacy than she'd had in her Dallas efficiency with its paper-thin walls. And for the first time in her life, she had a yard surrounding her, and a porch with an old-fashioned porch swing.

Lying on it that night, Shelby looked up, used one leg to push the swing forward, and sighed. What bizarre gene was she carrying that got her into situations like this one? Picking up and moving to Heartbreak Ridge probably wasn't the wisest thing she could have done, but what choice did she have? All the way here, she'd told herself over and over that she wasn't running away. She'd never run away in her life. She was just *extricating* herself from the humiliating dead end her life in Dallas had become, and providing her baby with a future worth living in, in a town where she might grow up and feel she belonged. And somehow, no matter how sour things had gone with Sam, her gamble had worked.

Lord, she was pooped. All that driving must have done a number on her, because she felt stiff and crampy all over. But as the swing arced its gentle path, she could see a jillion stars, fat and low and bright in the night sky, and she felt all her aches and pains slip away. One of the great things about living so far from a population hub was this magnificent nighttime display, Sam had written months ago. Now that she was actually underneath it, she experienced a warm glow of satisfaction. It made her think of that old song about the stars belonging to everyone. She even hummed a bar of it to herself, about how the best things in life are free.

Amazing. How long had it been since she'd been able to relax, really relax? During what she referred to now in her mind as simply *the nightmare,* she hadn't had a moment's peace. Every waking moment—which was practically one hundred percent of the time, since she hadn't been able to sleep much—had been consumed by fear, worry and self-recrimination. *What was going to happen to her? How would she be able to survive? Why had she been such an idiot?* Her worries had been as pointless as they were relentless. Like a gerbil running on a wire wheel, they got her nowhere. If only she'd known someone she could talk to...

That's where Sam had come in. A social worker had introduced her to the Internet as a way to find information about her pregnancy, and while she had discovered a wealth of information there, she'd also discovered she could meet people. People who maybe wouldn't hold her past against her. Even a kindly sheriff in a tiny town who couldn't possibly know what a fix she was in.

Had she been deceitful? Sam couldn't even guess how much. Sure, she hadn't mentioned her pregnancy very often, mostly because she figured it wasn't the sort of thing a man would want to have a woman writing to him about, but she'd told him absolutely zilch about her disastrous relationship with Clint Macon, and the trial....

But if finding out about a baby had turned him off, imagine if she informed her Andy Taylor-of-the-Internet that she had been booked for fraud?

Besides, her life was so completely about the baby, and about the troubles surrounding Clint, that she wanted to reserve one little corner of her time for something else. For reflecting on the good things in life, its possibilities, and the fact that she could still connect with another human being.

Headlights shone through the darkness. Merlie's house was a comfortable quarter mile outside the town of Heartbreak Ridge, which, Shelby had learned long ago, was itself a few miles down the mountain from the actual geographical place called Heartbreak Ridge. She could hardly wait until daylight to go exploring. Having spent her entire life in Houston and Dallas and San Antonio, where there were plenty of cocktail bars for her mother to work in, she had never experienced mountains. She liked the way it got cool at night—so cool she'd had to put on a sweater even in June.

She hoped the approaching car was Merlie's, so she could ask what sights she should hit the next day. She wanted to take a day off to see the area before she started job hunting.

When a truck pulled into the yard instead of Merlie's old Buick, Shelby shot up to sitting. Suddenly, the distance from town didn't feel so cozy. She wished Merlie hadn't gone out for her poker night, leaving her all alone.

Boot steps sounded in the darkness, then, almost when he was stepping into the light of the porch, Shelby made out Sam's tall form. At the top step he stopped, leaned against the porch railing and tipped his hat. "Settled in?"

She wasn't fooled by his relaxed demeanor; the air between them crackled with tension. Just looking at the man made Shelby sit up a little straighter, breath a little deeper, and hope… Yet she couldn't allow herself to get too carried away by his looks. She doubted he had come here to help her unpack.

"Yes, I am." *And I'm not leaving,* she added silently with a determined smile.

The sheriff shifted, studied his boots, and cleared his throat. "I see."

Shelby didn't wait for more hemming and hawing. "If you came to try to run me out of town, Sheriff, you're out of luck. I've already paid Merlie for a month."

He frowned and looked up at her, almost as if she'd wounded him. "That's not why I'm here, Shelby. I don't know why you're so defensive."

She laughed. "Because when I arrived, I saw that look in your eye."

His face screwed up quizzically. "What look?"

"The one that made you look as if some parcel service had just delivered the wrong package. You were already worried about how you were going to send it back."

He smiled. Damn, he was good-looking. Not that it mattered. Part of what she'd liked about Sam was that she had no idea what he looked like. After all, good looks and a sinful smile had nearly ruined her. In fact, if she'd known Sam was even better looking than Clint Macon, and that his blue eyes could make her heart feel like it was turning to mush, she might have shut down her e-mail account and never logged on to a computer for the rest of her life.

She sighed. "Okay, I'll bite. What are you doing here?"

"I don't know if I can explain it. I guess..." He poked back the brim of his hat, and when he spoke again, his voice dropped. "This was about the time I used to do it."

Do it? His nervous manner made her feel suddenly

edgy. Maybe she didn't know this man at all. He could be some sort of psycho.... "Do what?"

He shot her a hurt glance. "E-mail." His tone indicated that she should have known right away what he was talking about.

She let out a sigh of relief. "Oh, good! I was worried you were going to say 'bury the bodies' or something like that."

Only the slightest of smiles hinted that he found her joke amusing.

She had never given much thought to what time Sam had written e-mail. "I didn't know you had a schedule."

His dark brows drew together. "You never noticed?"

She lifted her hands. "Sorry."

He looked amazed. "When did you...?"

"Whenever I could get to the library. That's where I accessed my e-mail account."

Her answer surprised him, apparently. "Don't you have a computer of your own?"

She laughed. "Me? Good grief, no!" That was a good one. "I was just working temp jobs before I came here. Most days I barely had enough money to keep gas in my car, never mind splurge on luxuries like computers." Of course, now she had more money than ever before, but that was only because she'd had a garage sale at her apartment and sold everything she could possibly get rid of. She knew she'd need the money to resettle.

He peered at her as if the Grand Canyon yawned between them instead of a few feet. Her lack of funds, apparently, was another thing he hadn't known about her.

Shelby felt so nervous under his intense gaze she pushed off with her foot and began to swing, which she

immediately regretted because for the first time she noticed that the chains made an intolerable squeaking
sound.

"Let me ask you this," Sam said after a few moments
of rusted metal serenade. "This afternoon you said that
we had misunderstood each other."

She nodded.

"What did you mean?"

She laughed. "You have to ask? You obviously had
no idea that I was pregnant. I'm beginning to wonder if
you actually read my messages at all."

"Of course I did," he said, offended.

"Then what did you think? What *could* you have
thought?"

"I thought…" He looked down and shrugged. "Well,
what does it matter now? My question is, what could
you have misunderstood about *me?* I was completely
truthful with you."

Shelby shot to standing. His words indicated that he
still thought that she had lied about the baby, which was
both wrong and insulting, even if she had omitted telling
him about that other little matter. She crossed her arms
and glared at him. "You apparently misled me every
time your fingers touched the keyboard."

"What?"

She paced furiously—or as furiously as she could
manage carrying forty extra pounds around with her.
"You gave the completely wrong impression. You're
not at all what you seemed in your letters!"

His jaw clamped reflexively. "How did I seem?"

"Kind," she snapped. "The type of man I wanted to
spend the rest of my life with, to have children with."
When his gaze fled south, Shelby laughed bitterly. "Not

just this baby, but others. I had all sorts of cockeyed dreams about living out in the country and having a big family, and I was fool enough to pour them out to you. I thought that was what *you* wanted, too, but I can see I was wrong. Just the thought of one baby has made you want to run me out of town on a rail.''

''Now wait a—''

Shelby had no intention of letting him defend himself. She'd been fairly calm and philosophical about the matter all day. As she'd said, worse things had happened to her. Much worse. But if Sam thought he could drive out here with the sole purpose of playing the wounded party and making her feel small, brother, was he wrong! ''You painted yourself as the kind, avuncular type, Mr. Loves Dogs and Little Kiddies, a man who cared about everyone.''

''I do!'' he interjected.

''Oh, I know,'' she said, ''when the locals wanted to kick the children of illegal immigrants out of the school, you went to the school board meeting and said that the community needed to educate *all* its children. You've won over people who didn't think the town needed a lending library. You're a great one for causes. But maybe you're also the type of man who puts on a generous public face but can't handle personal crises so well.''

''After one day I don't think you're in a position to judge me,'' he replied stiffly.

She stopped pacing and stood toe-to-toe with him. ''One glance was all it took for you to judge me and decide you wanted me out of your life. But don't worry, Sheriff. I said I'm not your responsibility, and I'm not.''

''But if you stay here...''

"Aha!" She chortled. "I *knew* you were trying to drum me out of town."

"I am not."

"Maybe you would be more comfortable if I wore a scarlet *UM* on my chest?"

"*UM?*"

"Unwed Mother."

"Listen," he said, bristling defensively, "your having a baby out of wedlock is fine. I'm as liberal as the next man—more, even—but—"

"But you wonder if I'll really be happy here," she finished for him, nodding knowingly. "The old not-in-my-backyard attitude rears its ugly head."

His mouth dropped open comically. "You've got me all wrong."

"I know. You're only concerned about my welfare."

"That's right. How are you going to live?"

"I've got enough money scraped together," she announced proudly, although *enough* was a relative term. The proceeds from the garage sale wouldn't last forever, even in a place where rent was next to nothing and colas were still forty cents.

"And what about after that's gone?"

She lifted her head proudly. "I'm accustomed to working."

"Where?" he asked. "Who's going to hire an obviously pregnant woman?"

His questions stung, mostly because they were the same questions she'd been anxiously asking herself for months. Maybe she *had* come to Heartbreak Ridge hoping Sam would rescue her from a difficult predicament. And maybe it was even more difficult to accept that her thin hope had been busted when she actually met the man. But she certainly didn't expect him to help her out now, when he obviously viewed her about as favorably as a severe case of anthrax.

"I've managed to work and support myself my entire life, and I have no doubt that I can continue to do so now, but the one thing I don't need is some finger-wagging man standing over me all the time predicting failure." Exhausted, Shelby sank down into the porch swing again, but forced herself to remain straight-backed even though she suddenly felt like doubling over.

Sam frowned. "Are you okay?"

"Of course!" she retorted with as much spirit as she could muster. "Haven't I told you that I'm not your responsibility? I can take care of myself."

"I don't doubt it."

She took a deep breath. Then another. "...always have... I'm sure I'll be...just fine...."

"Maybe," Sam drawled, "but I have to tell you, you look green."

Oh, God! Shelby leaned back, tense with pain, and realized suddenly what was happening. Cold fear seized her, and she clamped a hand down on Sam's arm, not about to let him leave her now for a single second, no matter how infuriating he was. "If you do want to help, there *is* something you could do for me, Sam."

He blinked at her worriedly. "What?"

She swallowed. "Deliver my baby?"

A DOOR OPENED down the hall and Sam leapt to his feet. Lucky thing his legs moved, because his mind was frozen in panic. When Dr. Burnet appeared down the corridor, Sam's booted feet skidded toward him down the shiny, newly polished tile of the county hospital.

Lloyd Burnet turned to Sam with a big grin. "Sam, you old son of a gun! Why didn't you tell anyone?"

"Oh, well..." Sam wasn't sure if he could explain it all right here in the hallway. He couldn't say he cared to, anyway, just this moment. He was too worried about Shelby. "Is she okay, Lloyd?"

"Course she is. Should be over pretty soon now." Lloyd chuckled and tapped his stethoscope on Sam's chest. "You just calm down, Papa."

Sam rolled his eyes. "You can cut the Papa bit. Why is everything happening so quickly? I thought she was going to have the baby in my pickup truck!"

Lloyd's lips turned down in a practiced, professional frown. "Quiet labor. It happens sometimes. Most likely she's been dilating for some time now, and just didn't realize it. Maybe there's been some upheaval in her life...?"

Moving across the entire state would certainly qualify as upheaval, Sam thought.

"You can put on scrubs and come in now," Lloyd continued, turning to go back into the surgery.

But Sam's boots were rooted in place. *"In?"*

Lloyd nodded. "Most fathers want to witness the births nowadays."

"Oh, but—" A wave of queasiness struck him, just before another, stronger wave of amazement. "They do? *Why?*" Just driving Shelby thirty miles in the truck had nearly done him in! He was still clinging to the edge of his very last nerve.

The doctor laughed. "You'll see when you get in there. She's already asked for you several times."

"For *me?*" Sam repeated, astonished.

"Who else?"

"I don't know...."

That was the problem. Sam suddenly felt as if he were being swept up in someone else's life. It couldn't be his own. In the few hours since Shelby had arrived, his every minute had been consumed by that woman—what to say to Shelby, how to convince Shelby to leave town, how to deliver Shelby's baby....

Why was all this his problem? Shouldn't someone else be here getting into scrubs to hold her hand?

"Come on," Lloyd said, taking him by the arm. "I'll show you where to go."

"Oh, but..." Sam hesitated. On the drive over, Shelby had appeared to be in a lot of pain. She hadn't screamed or cried—he'd almost wished she had. He wasn't sure he could stand watching more of that quiet agony now. "I, uh, better call Merlie."

Lloyd chuckled. "What would you want to do that for?"

"She'll want to know." Sam wasn't sure if he was just babbling out an excuse or he was really making sense. "She and Shelby live together."

"Baby's about to come, Sam."

As if to punctuate Lloyd's words, a short sharp cry came from the other side of the swinging double doors. Shelby!

That sound was all the impetus it took to propel Sam's boots toward the scrub room, where a nurse slapped a gown, gloves and mask on him and poked him into the surgery. Lloyd, who'd just minutes before had been doing his hale-fellow-well-met routine out in the hallway, now stood somber and concerned over Shelby. The whole scene was like something out of *ER*. Nurses bustled about with instrument trays and patient charts, and in the middle of it all was Shelby, bathed in sweat and breathing heavily in a ragged manner that positively panicked Sam. It might look like she was having a baby, but it sounded like she was having a heart attack!

The nurse who'd escorted him in handed him off to another nurse who led him right to Shelby's side. Despite her rough breathing, she turned her head toward him and grinned as she exhaled. Even in the middle of labor she still somehow managed to dazzle him. "Sam! You're pale as a sheet."

He swallowed. "Are you having trouble breathing, Shelby?"

She laughed. Amazing. "That's Lamaze, you ox!"

"Oh." He'd heard of it, but he didn't know what it was. What he didn't know about pregnancy and childbirth could fill the *Encyclopedia Britannica.*

"I'm supposed to have a coach, but I'm trying it solo." She drew in another deep breath.

"Is there anything I can—"

Before he could finish, a contraction overtook her and she bore down, gritting her teeth, her grin turning to a grimace in nothing flat. Her hand reached out toward him and he took it, nearly felled by her linebacker grip.

"One more push, Shelby," Lloyd coached. "This is it...."

"It?" Sam's voice came out a squeak. How could this be *it?* He wasn't ready!

But Shelby was, apparently. Her hand nearly crushed his and she let out a cry that sent chills through him. Suddenly, nurses closed in tightly around Shelby so that Sam could barely see what was going on. He just saw the exhausted relief on Shelby's face and knew it was all over.

"You did it!" he said excitedly. An inexplicable rush of excitement overtook him, as though *he'd* just delivered a baby.

Shelby didn't share in his jubilation yet. "Why isn't she crying?"

On cue, the baby let out a wail to end all wails, and Lloyd pushed through the nurses to hand the tiny baby over to her mother. Shelby beamed as her daughter was placed on her chest. "Look at her!" she exclaimed in awe as she hurriedly counted fingers and toes. "Isn't she perfect?"

Sam was hard-pressed to disagree, or say anything for that matter, at the sight of Shelby's rapt face as she inspected her new creation. A lump the size of Mount Rushmore had settled in his throat, making speech impossible. He reached out and gently nuzzled the brand-new human being with his finger, unable to believe what he'd just taken part in. A birth. This morning Shelby had been just an idea to him, words on a screen, and now they'd been through childbirth together.

She glanced over at him. "Now that she's here, I'm not sure Jackie's the right name for her, are you? She looks more like a Maud or a Lucy to me. Or Lily. How about Lily?"

Sam tilted his head, wondering. She just looked like a newborn baby to him—messy, misshapen and somehow magical. Strange to think a whole new life was just beginning, a personality being formed starting this very second.

"We're going to take her into her room now, Sheriff," one of the nurses said.

"I'll go with her."

"Mrs. Weston needs rest."

Shelby's eyes widened, and she looked from Sam to the nurse in alarm. "Oh, I'm not Mrs. Weston!"

The nurses and Lloyd turned on Sam, their faces a mix of curiosity and recrimination.

Shelby laughed and gave her daughter a quick kiss on the head. "Didn't you tell them we weren't married, Sam?"

"I, um, didn't have time."

The nurse who'd spoken before marched forward, nudging Sam out of the path of traffic as two others took hold of Shelby's gurney. "You may see your daughter in the nursery, then, Sheriff Weston."

Sam shook his head sheepishly and Shelby laughed again. She seemed to be enjoying this way too much. "Sam's not the father, either," she explained.

Lloyd was surprised. "He's not?"

"Goodness, no! How could he be? We're just e-mail buddies."

The head nurse nodded. "That *would* be a medical miracle!"

Sam chuckled listlessly along with the others. He didn't know why, but it suddenly seemed awkward to be there, more awkward than it had been during the actual delivery. Then there had been drama to focus on; now everyone was distracted by the fact that he didn't belong there.

And strangely, as they began wheeling Shelby away, a part of him wished he *did* belong. He felt let down, shut out, like a player who'd just scored a touchdown but wasn't allowed in the locker room to celebrate.

Lloyd came over and patted him on the back. "Well, Sam, it was a good thing you did, being here for that young woman."

Sam smiled. "Is there anything more I can do?" He couldn't believe it was all over. Shelby would probably sleep for the next twelve hours, but he was too keyed up to sleep himself. In fact, he didn't want to leave the hospital at all.

"Have you called Merlie yet?"

Suddenly, Sam remembered. When Shelby had gone into labor, Merlie had been at her poker night, but she'd probably be home by now. It wasn't even midnight yet, he discovered when he looked up at the clock by the phones.

After five rings, Merlie answered. "Hello?"

At the sound of the familiar yet groggy voice, Sam felt a surge of excitement. "Merlie, I wanted you to be the first to know. We've just had a baby!"

There was a long, skeptical pause on the other end of the line. "Who the hell is this?"

"It's Sam!"

"Oh." Merlie chuckled. "I thought maybe I had a crank caller on my hands."

"Shelby had her baby! A girl," Sam told her, speaking a mile a minute. "She's going to name it Lily."

"I was wondering where that woman got off to. I was considering calling your pager number when I fell asleep on the couch. Is Shelby okay?"

"Fine."

"Are *you* okay?"

"Of course!"

Merlie laughed. "Sounds like you're ready to start passing out cigars."

Sam frowned into the receiver, suddenly struck speechless. The odd thing was, he *did* feel like passing out cigars, or setting off fireworks, or tossing confetti.

Something. Maybe it was just all the excitement. "I just thought you'd want to know," he grumbled. "Looks like you've got another new boarder."

"Uh-huh," Merlie said. "And it looks like you've got a crush on the woman you were trying to run out of town."

"That's ridiculous," he said to Merlie before he hung up.

Ridiculous. He repeated the word to himself as he stood in the hallway, wondering what to do next. Just because he'd helped out a woman during a time of crisis didn't mean that he had a crush on her. Shelby still didn't belong in Heartbreak Ridge, and now that she had a newborn on her hands, she would probably want to get her money back from Merlie and go home, where her people were.

Where the father of her baby probably was, whoever the worthless rascal was.

Sam frowned, worried by the way his fists clenched in dislike for a man he'd never met. But where was the guy, anyway? And what had happened?

It's not your problem. She's not your responsibility.

Thank heavens! Shelby herself had absolved him of responsibility for her, so he didn't have to worry about feeling like a varmint when he went his own way and got on with his life without her, which he fully intended to do very, very soon.

But first, he wanted to check on Lily.

4

"SAM, you look like a zombie."

Sam forced his dazed glance up from his computer screen. He'd been sifting through new-mother Web sites since before dawn, and now his eyes had a hard time focusing on the blur that was Merlie. "What did you and Shelby have for breakfast?"

His secretary raised her brows with interest at the unexpected quiz. "Same thing I've eaten for the past forty years—eggs, bacon, buttered toast and black coffee."

Sam winced. "Cholesterol, fat, more fat and caffeine. A nutritional disaster."

Merlie plunked down her purse. "It's called food. Get over it."

All morning he'd been reading about what nursing mothers should be eating; none of Merlie's offerings even came close to an optimum diet for a new mom. Although it shouldn't have surprised him. In Heartbreak Ridge, chicken-fried steak passed as health food.

"How much coffee did you two put away?" he asked Merlie.

She grinned. "You want the answer translated into cups, or pots?"

He ducked his head as if fending off a mortal blow. "Are you trying to poison that little baby?"

"Lily didn't have any, unless she sneaked a cup on the sly."

"Very funny. But I'll have you know, every sip of coffee Shelby ingests goes straight to that baby's system!"

Merlie rolled her eyes. "I'd never have pegged you for a nutrition counsellor. Not after the specials I've seen you inhale at the Feed Bag."

"That's different. I'm not nursing."

"I'm beginning to think you would if you could." Merlie tilted her head and leveled a curious glance at him. "What's up with you, Sheriff? In the past week, you've boned up on this maternity stuff so much you could probably pass the midwife's exam. You have baby envy, or are you just trying to figure out some reason to see Shelby again?"

"Neither." He hopped out of his chair. "I'm just concerned, is all."

"Shelby's told you that there's no reason for you to be."

"Oh, that's fine." He practically hooted. "A lot of sense she has, running clear across the state the day she's about to give birth. A foolhardy act like that doesn't exactly show a laserlike sense of reason."

Merlie folded her arms across her chest. "So *you're* going to reason for her, I suppose."

"Why not? I'm the sheriff of the town, aren't I? Shouldn't I have some interest in what's going on?"

"What's going on is one thing. That just makes you a good lawman. What everyone's eating is something else. That makes you a kook."

He lifted his chin. "If it weren't for me, Shelby would never have come here."

"That's true. But that doesn't mean she wouldn't have had her baby two weeks early anyway, or that you need to monitor her diet. Land's sake, Sam, you aren't responsible for that."

He frowned and rocked back on his boot heels. He was tempted to make an argument, but Merlie did have a point. Shelby had as good as told him during the five times he'd just happened to drop by the hospital while she was there that he didn't need to worry about her and little Lily. And he wouldn't have…except how could he not worry when he kept getting these reports about Shelby guzzling coffee and packing away bacon? He bet Shelby wasn't even taking vitamin supplements, and Lord knows she wouldn't see a whole grain or raw vegetable while she was living with Merlie. The woman ate like a trucker!

"You can surf the Web till you're waterlogged, Sam. I'm not going to change my chow just because of what some Web site says," Merlie scoffed.

"Even if it's good for you?"

"Good grief, you sound like a Richard Simmons infomercial."

"It's just common sense."

"Pretty soon you're going to be recommending virtual food. Thanks, but I'll stick with the old-fashioned kind."

He grabbed his hat off its nail by the door and smashed it on his head. "I'll be back in a minute."

Merlie nodded. "Tell Shelby hi."

"I'm not going to see Shelby," he snapped back.

At least, not right away. He had somewhere else to tag first.

At the Stop-N-Shop, he took his time, going down the list he had scribbled while on-line. He loaded up his cart with every kind of dairy product he could think of—goodness knows, Merlie didn't even acknowledge the existence of yogurt. Yoplait probably sounded like a foreign conspiracy to her. Not sure which flavor Shelby would prefer, he scooped up one of each. Next he loaded up on juice, everything from humdrum orange to guava-strawberry, since he didn't know what she'd prefer in beverages, either. In fact, when it came to the minor details of life, he realized he knew very little about Shelby, which shouldn't have been surprising, since one minor detail he hadn't picked up on was that she was going to have a baby.

But it did surprise him. How could he know so little about a woman he'd practically considered a soul mate?

He picked up some vitamins, some whole-grain bread, rice, and some different soups and broths of the low-salt variety. Plenty of fresh vegetables. Unfortunately, when he turned down the diaper aisle, things got a lot stickier. The baby wipe issue wasn't as cut-and-dried as it had appeared to be on the Internet—there were different kinds to choose from—although he did manage to select a package and feel fairly comfortable with his choice. But that was just a warm-up for the truly mind-boggling questions to come. Which diapers should he buy? The row was crammed with diapers, practically as far as the eye could see. Whoever knew there were that many babies in Heartbreak Ridge? He inspected every brand in every size, shape, fastening technique, and new absorbent fabric until his head started spinning.

He was jolted out of his nappy stupor by the crash of metal against metal. With an apology on his lips, he whirled to move his already overloaded cart and found himself looking at one of the people he least expected to see at the grocery store.

"Cal!" His tone didn't begin to hide his surprise.

His nephew, his devilishly handsome Brad Pitt features hidden beneath a month's growth of beard, smiled at him. More specifically, he smiled at the economy-size pack of Huggies superabsorbent diapers Sam held self-consciously in the crook of his arm. "Sheriff."

Cal's tone always managed to sound just the slightest bit mocking, which could be disconcerting to strangers. But having worked side by side with his nephew for several years, Sam considered his feathers immune to Cal's ruffling. "What brings you down the mountain?"

Few had seen Cal since he'd resigned as deputy and retreated up to the cabin above Heartbreak Ridge right after his wife left him. Disillusioned with people in general and women specifically, he'd announced that he wanted to become more self-sufficient, and hotfooted it to the wilderness.

"I came down for a few supplies."

Both men looked with interest down at each others' carts. Cal's spoke volumes about the pioneering hermit life-style he'd adopted. Half his cart was heaped with a six-month supply of beer. The other half was loaded with cans of beans, flour, cornmeal, coffee, lightbulbs.

Sam laughed. "Maybe that's what Grizzly Adams's cart might have looked like if he'd had a Budweiser habit."

Cal ignored the joke and pointedly gazed into Sam's cache of nutritional goodies. "Heard you up and had yourself a baby."

Sam rolled his eyes. "*I* didn't."

"Really? That's not what they're sayin' at the Feed

Bag.'' His meaningful glance at the large pack of baby wipes in Sam's cart bespoke a hearty skepticism.

''They're a bunch of gossipy hens over there,'' Sam said. ''Shelby is just a...''

''Fiancée?''

''A *friend*,'' Sam insisted. ''Some woman I met over the Internet.'' Although something in him bridled at this impersonal description.

Cal sighed, and his expression turned back to the mournful look it had worn ever since Connie had left him. ''And now she's got you trapped. Isn't that just the way.''

''I'm not trapped,'' Sam corrected. ''I'm just helping her out.''

''Uh-huh.''

His unruffleable feathers fluttered uncomfortably. ''The poor woman's all alone in town.''

Cal frowned. ''I thought she was living with Merlie.''

''Well, she is. But besides Merlie, she's alone.''

''Uh-huh.''

''Would you stop saying that?'' And in that skeptical tone! Lord, it was annoying. ''Believe me, it's not what you're thinking. I told Shelby the day she came here that a relationship between us was impossible.''

''Sure. And now you're buying her multivitamins.''

Sam felt his cheeks turn red. ''Just this once,'' he said. ''Just so she won't be on my conscience.''

Cal nodded. ''I see. If she'd been deprived of her eight essential vitamins and iron, you just wouldn't have been able to sleep at night.''

''Something like that.'' Smart aleck!

But when he looked in Cal's eyes next, his nephew wasn't sneering. Instead, he again wore the expression of the walking wounded. "I used to feel that way about Connie—that her every breath was my responsibility. I would have done anything for that woman."

But Connie had ditched him. The woman he'd fallen head over heels for on a trip to San Antonio, who had sworn that she'd always wanted to live in the country and would be happy there for ever and ever, had spent three months in Heartbreak Ridge and then run fleeing back to her old city life, leaving his nephew bereft, a mere shell of his former self. Granted, Cal had never exactly been Mouseketeer perky, but now he seemed hermetically sealed in lover's gloom. Cal believed he'd never find a woman to live in Heartbreak Ridge with him, and he loved this place too much to leave.

Sam ached to help his nephew somehow, but what words of encouragement could he offer? Ms. Right hadn't appeared in his life, either.

Only Ms. Waterbury. And her baby.

"Why don't you come back to work, Cal?"

Cal looked at him long and hard. There was gratefulness in his gaze, and patient humor. "You already have a deputy."

Sam thought of Cody—hardworking, earnest and woefully ill-equipped for the job. Cody's shyness made him loath to pull anyone over to give them a speeding ticket, especially anyone he knew personally—and who in Heartbreak Ridge didn't know everyone else? Whenever they had somebody in the tank overnight, Cody apologized endlessly to the poor prisoner, so that even the most harmless old drunks were ready to plan a jailbreak just so they wouldn't have to listen to all his groveling. And though Cody had trained as a policeman, Sam had never actually seen him draw a gun; frankly, he couldn't imagine it.

"Let's just say we're lucky Heartbreak Ridge is a peaceful place."

Cal's brows rose and he stroked his scraggly beard. "Isn't he doing a good job?"

"Of course," Sam answered. "He's careful and honest and doesn't do anything anybody could fault him for...."

His nephew nodded, catching on. "But it's like having Gandhi for a deputy?"

Sam laughed. "His heart's not in it. We both know that. He just got trained cause he felt compelled to follow in some harebrained family tradition."

"I noticed you didn't shun the harebrained family tradition, Sheriff."

Sam shrugged. "Cody's different. He just isn't willing to admit it yet."

"Well, when he does, maybe I'll come down the mountain again."

"You could come down now," Sam assured him.

The darkness that passed over Cal's expression pierced Sam. "No, I couldn't, Sam. Not yet."

After working his way slowly through the checkout— the Stop-N-Shop was still operating with seventies retail technology, a fact Sam always noted with dismay—Sam jumped into his sedan and headed out to Merlie's... which was also Shelby's. How long would that last? How long could Shelby really be intending to stay?

He assumed it wouldn't be long. Once the newness of the setup wore off, no doubt she would want to return to Dallas, like any number of women before her. Heartbreak Ridge wasn't the entertainment capitol of the world by any means. Once most people got a taste of the isolation, they couldn't take it. And like Cal's exwife, Connie, Shelby had said she'd been raised in the big city, places like Dallas and Houston. That's what he'd been worried about most when he was thinking about proposing to her.

Proposing to a stranger! Now he couldn't believe he'd ever been contemplating such a rash thing. Too much computer terminal glow must have been fuzzing his reasoning.

He was barreling along the road, half lost in thought, when he came upon a sight that made him slam on the brakes.

Shelby, in a field. Her blinding beauty appeared suddenly, as if rising out of the blanket of grass and wildflowers around her like Venus rising out of the sea. Her long curly red hair sparked in the morning sun, and she wore a loose blue cotton sundress that draped her newly diminished body in a way that tantalized more than told. Her back was to him—she must not have been paying attention—but even without seeing her beautiful face, he was dazzled. He got out of the car, shutting the door quietly so he wouldn't disturb her, and began crossing the field.

When he was halfway across, she made a quarter turn, and he gasped. It wasn't just her beautiful profile that took his breath, or the fact that Lily was hanging around her in a homemade reverse papoose, lending Shelby a mother nature Madonna radiance. No, what really captured Sam's attention—causing that gasp of horror—was the Hershey bar she was munching absently as she took in the view.

Chocolate! Empty calories and stimulants! No nutritional value whatsoever. *Was she out of her mind?*

And now that he thought about it, what was she doing this far out of the house? She was just home from the hospital, and still recovering from giving birth, which was more of an ordeal than he ever would have guessed. She should be in bed—or at least somewhere close to a phone!

Cellular phones weren't really considered too practical around here—they tended to be out of range of any company's signals—but maybe he should look more seriously into the matter.

He stomped the rest of the way down the hill, not capturing Shelby's full attention until he was nearly stepping on her. "Sam!" she breathed in surprise, her voice half high, half husky. Her green eyes looked up at him, dewy and sweet.

Her slender hand clutched the offending chocolate bar, but it wasn't the candy he was focused on anymore. It was her eyes, staring up at him as if he were the person she most wanted to see in the whole world. He grinned, and an answering smile quirked her full lips, which were pink even without a trace of lipstick.

Forgotten were the deleterious properties of chocolate. When she snapped off a piece of the candy bar and popped it into her mouth, all he could do was stare at those full lips and imagine how the sweet chocolate melted in her mouth. Watching Shelby while she savored the confection somehow seemed like a sensual experience.

He put the kibosh on his wayward thoughts and once again confronted that dangerous attraction to her that seemed to overwhelm his normally reasonable nature.

He shouldn't be thinking about Shelby this way! She was a new mother…of someone else's child. He was just trying to help her, not get involved in some kind of tangled relationship.

He brought his gaze down to Lily, who was blinking in seeming wonderment at the world around her, much as Shelby had appeared to be doing before he interrupted. Unable to stop himself, he reached out and chucked her on her dimply chin, noting that the baby looked much better than she had in the hospital. Recently wrinkled and wizened, she was now growing into her skin, and instead of being mottled red as she was in the hospital, she was a healthy Gerber baby pink.

Shelby smoothed her hand over her daughter's downy soft brown hair. "When I looked out the window this morning and saw all these beautiful wildflowers on this hillside, I had to bring Lily out to see it, to understand why I moved us out here."

It was a beautiful view, made even more so by Shelby herself. Standing so close to her, a hint of her clean fragrance, mixed with Lily's baby powder scent and wildflowers, made him almost dizzy. In that moment, he had a wild impulse to kiss her. He saw himself taking her into his arms in a Valentino-style dip, her red hair spilling toward the earth, and tasting her warm, sweet lips.

He shifted uncomfortably as his tight jeans began to seem a little tighter. Good lord, he needed to hold on to his sanity! He'd just come out here to deliver some vitamins.

Lily kicked her legs fitfully, making him smile. The problem of fitting a baby into his overwrought romantic scenario dampened his ardor somewhat.

"Lily can't see," he said. He doubted she could understand the concept of moving across the state yet, either.

"What?" Shelby looked down at her daughter with panic. "What do you mean?" She waved a hand in front of the baby's face.

Sam chuckled. "No newborns can see," he explained with authority. "That is, they can't focus clearly on objects very far away. Say, fifteen inches."

Her eyes widened in surprise at his expertise, then she looked back down at Lily, who was slapping her tiny fisted hands in the air like a shrunken George Foreman. "Oh!" She sounded a little disappointed. "I wanted her to see how pretty our new home is. It's much nicer than any of the places I grew up, that's for sure."

Where had *she grown up?* Sam wondered suddenly. Cities...but beyond that, he didn't know. Where had she gone to grade school, had her first date, graduated from high school? It all just added to the growing pile of things he didn't know about the woman he'd thought he knew well enough to marry.

One thing he did know, however, was that a woman expecting a baby didn't pick up and leave her home without some kind of reason. What had been the impetus for such a drastic move? He tried to believe that Shelby was speaking the truth, and that she just wanted a change in her life, but what about the father of her child? And friends...surely she had some. Did they know where she was, and would they be worried?

He leaned back on his heels. "I don't know what kind of arrangements you and Merlie have with the phone, but if you need to call home for any reason, you can always take care of that down at my office."

Her lips turned up in a smile. "Thanks, but I really don't have anyone I need to get in touch with." She watched the surprise register on his face. "Does that seem strange to you?"

He shrugged, trying not to sound too judgmental. "Everybody has loose ends."

She laughed. "Maybe, but mine have been fraying at the edges for quite some time. No one's looking for me, if that's what you're worried about."

"Even…" He swallowed, then finished in a rush, "Well, what about Lily's father?"

Her smile evaporated like a dewdrop on a Dearborn heater. "That's one loose end that was snipped clean."

"Oh. I thought maybe you had some folks somewhere…or some place you called home."

"I've never had that." She shook her red ringlets from her face, lifting her chin. "Till now. I know it irks you, Sam, but Heartbreak Ridge is for me. I'm here to stay."

"It doesn't irk me," he said, realizing he did sound rather annoyed. "You plan to stay with Merlie?"

"Until I can find a place of my own. A home, like hers. I've told you not to worry, Sam, and I mean it."

He wished she'd stop saying that! If he didn't know better, he'd almost think Shelby was using reverse psychology on him. Because the more she told him not to feel responsible for him, the stronger his urge to step in and try to fix her problems became. "Finding a place could take a while," he warned. "Rental property isn't plentiful here."

Shelby's brow furrowed. "Merlie asked around town the other day, and one man's already called about selling me a place."

If she couldn't even afford a computer of her own, what kind of house could she afford?

The answer hit him like a ton of bricks. *Lord have mercy!* "This man who called you...he wouldn't happened to be named Jim Loftus, would he?"

"How did you guess?"

"Believe me, it wasn't difficult!"

She tilted her head, curious. "Do you know him?"

"Know him! He's my cousin, I'm ashamed to say."

"Why ashamed?"

"Because he's conning you, Shelby. That house he wants to sell you is a plumbingless, lumbering shack that's about to fall off the mountain."

Disbelief registered on her face. "But he told me it was a historic home."

Sam snorted. "He's right. The place is ready to become history at any moment."

Her green eyes darkened as his words sank in, and those creases in her forehead deepened. Suddenly, he regretted blurting out the information about Jim in such an incredulous tone, as if she'd been a fool to believe the man. Shelby had been through a lot in the past week, and through it all she'd managed to keep her chin up.

But now that selfsame chin dimpled as her lip twitched. Tears sprang to those dewy green eyes, and she looked choked with frustration. Her head shook, her clasp on Lily tightened, and Shelby—cool, headstrong Shelby Waterbury—released a strangled sob and dissolved into a puddle of tears.

SHE FELT like a damn fool. Not so much for believing Jim Loftus's offer of a dream house where she could raise little Lily, but for crying in front of Sam Weston. She never cried!

But she was on a tear now. No dainty sniffling for her, either. No sirree, Bob. Her shoulders were heaving, she could barely see out of eyes nearly swollen shut, and the salt water just kept flowing. The pipeline had burst.

Sam, who was just an amorphous blob to her watery eyes, shifted uncomfortably in front of her. After several minutes, he looked as if he might be reduced to tears soon, too.

"I'm sorry," he said for about the hundredth time. "I didn't mean to make you cry."

"That's okay. You can't help it if your cousin's a con artist." But the thought of being tricked into believing that she was going to be able to buy a beautiful house on a mountain just made her feel all the more gloomy.

She'd known it was too good to be true. What she had in her purse—a couple thousand bucks—might seem like a mint to her, but it wouldn't put a down payment on a phone booth, never mind a house. But Mr. Loftus had sounded so positive and reassuring on the phone this morning! She was obviously from a big city, he'd said, since she didn't know about real estate in the country. Too much property and not enough people, he'd continued, had driven prices down to the point where everyone could own their own homes here. He'd met her skepticism with laughter, and even offered to drive her by the place this afternoon.

She'd spent the entire morning lost in dreams. A historic two-story house, just like the ones in *Architectural Digest*. Rooms galore. A yard—a whole field!—all her own. She could have big dogs and grow eight varieties of zucchini like Martha Stewart, and run barefoot through her own carpet of wildflowers in the spring. So much space and freedom was nearly beyond her imagining, but she'd taken to the idea of it like a mouse takes to cheese.

And then came Sam to tell her that what she'd really swallowed was sucker bait.

The trouble was, he hadn't told her anything that she hadn't already known deep in her heart. She made a Herculean effort to quit crying. "I don't know why—" her shoulders shuddered "—I'm reacting this way."

Sam patted her gently on the shoulder, something that just made her want to weep more, because more than anything, she hated being the object of pity. He probably thought she was a weak idiot, that she wept all the time, when in reality she'd been through a whole lot worse than this with dry eyes.

"It's okay," he told her calmly. "It's just your progesterone level dropping."

The bizarre comment threw her. Her head snapped up. "I beg your pardon?"

"Your hormones," he explained sagely, tipping his Stetson back a bit and squinting in the sunshine. "Your estrogen and progesterone levels have dropped, causing mood fluctuation. In other words, your hormones are running amok."

She gaped at him.

"Chocolate doesn't help, by the way," he added.

Maybe hormones running amock explained her overheated reaction to Sam, too. Though, on second thought, she doubted it. The way the man filled out a work shirt and a pair of jeans would be a hormone rush inducer under any circumstances. But where did he get off telling *her* about progesterone, and whether she could eat chocolate or not? "You seem to know an awful lot about pregnancy for a man who makes a living handing out speeding tickets."

If he was offended, he didn't show it. "I've been reading up."

"So have I, for nine months. This isn't just postpartum depression, Sam." She didn't add that she'd had a short bout of that already. Sitting in the hospital bed, she'd had plenty of time to anguish over what kind of mother she would make for Lily, what kind of home she could provide the newly arrived apple of her eye. Wallowing in feelings of inadequacy was hardly a productive way to kick off Lily's life, however, so she'd tried to look to the future more positively. Talking to Jim Loftus had made her embrace the possibility—at least for a few hours—that home sweet home wouldn't be a refrigerator box.

"Could your cousin's house really be as bad as you say?"

Looking as if he feared risking opening the floodgates again, he nodded reluctantly. "We can go take a peek at it, if you'd like."

She had to see the house; it had been the focus of too many of her hopes today just to dismiss it out of hand. Besides, what if this was just another attempt by Sam to discourage her from staying in Heartbreak Ridge? She couldn't let him influence her too much, but neither did she want to be with some sleazy salesman while she was eyeballing the property. She hated leaning on Sam for help, but it would definitely be advantageous to view the house with someone who would remind her that indoor plumbing wasn't an outrageous feature to expect in a home.

"Okay," she said. "Lead the way."

When they climbed into the police sedan she looked back in surprise at the number of groceries he had in the back seat—the man either loved to eat or shop or both! Then she saw the diaper label sticking out and groaned. "Oh, no! Sam, you shouldn't have."

"I couldn't help myself," he replied. "I know you don't want me to feel responsible for you—and I don't, I really don't—but will it hurt to accept a few bags of groceries?"

Her eyes widened. "Those are *all* for me?" There were four overstuffed bags there! It was the most extravagant gift she'd received since the weekend Clint discovered the Quality-Value Channel—and those decorative *Gone with the Wind* plates had made a lot of money back at her garage sale. She felt like crying again, maybe because this was the most concern for her anyone had shown since her pregnancy had begun. It was nice to know someone cared, even if that same someone wanted to run her out of town.

"It wasn't that much," Sam said, seeing her hesitation. "And I wanted to do something for Lily."

Shelby gazed down at the baby, who still seemed more miracle than human to her. Right now she was zonked out in deep sleep, probably induced by the rhythm of the moving car. She smiled. That rascal Sam. "I guess you've found my Achilles' heel."

He looked at her questioningly. "Lily?"

She nodded. "I can refuse her nothing."

"You'll spoil her," he warned.

He'd probably read all sorts of tracts on child-rearing, too, she speculated.

She had to laugh. "Good. To me, that sounds like a

privilege...at least for now. In a few years—say, when this precious little angel transmutates into a teenager whining for a tattoo or a nose ring—I might rethink my total indulgence policy.''

Sam also laughed as they drove up a steep, winding road. Having been raised in the flatter landscape of East Texas, Shelby wasn't used to looking at drop-offs out the car window and found herself clawing her armrest more than once. But finally Sam pulled the car off the main road onto a rutted dirt lane that jostled them enough to remind Shelby that she'd recently given birth just a week ago. She shifted against the discomfort, and in another moment, they were on a sort of plateau, and she gaped in delight at the sight before her.

Gorgeous was the only word to describe the vista from Heartbreak Ridge. The spectrum of green around them was a contrast to the brown, almost desertlike vegetation she'd driven through on her way to the Davis Mountain Range in West Texas. The view of mountain wilderness stretched out before them across a canopy of clean, fragrant air. Plentiful green grass and oaks and juniper trees dotted the landscape. At higher elevations, she could see tall pines blanketing the mountain, serving as a rich verdant border between the earth and the blue, blue sky.

She was in love.

''Oh, Sam! It's beautiful!'' She could hardly contain her delight. She jumped out of the car and spun on her heel, excitedly looking past an old barn to try to catch a peak of Jim Loftus's house. There it was, a little further up the mountain, a tiny rustic cabin; it was cute, but hardly the two-story structure Loftus had described to her on the phone. Sam was right—what a liar Jim Loftus was!

"Is that it?" she asked.

He nodded. "I'm afraid so."

She frowned, swallowing her disappointment but looking at the matter realistically. How much could she expect for the little money she had? "Well...it's not as bad as you'd led me to suspect, Sam."

His eyes widened in surprise, then he squinted into the distance. "It's not?"

She shrugged. "Why don't we drive up and take a look?"

Now he was squinting at her. "Shelby, I'm not talking about the cabin up the hill. I'm talking about the house right in front of you."

House?

Her gaze focused on the barn. Actually, she'd assumed it was a barn because it looked so cavernous and decrepit—she'd never seen a house in such bad shape! The wood plank boards siding the house were weathered far beyond a gray—they were nearly black, and even moldy green in parts. Whole sections of roof shingles had collapsed into the second floor, and at just that moment she spotted a brown squirrel scampering into one of the holes, now obviously an oft-used rodent doorway.

"I'll be!" Sam's voice sounded impressed. "Jim's done some work on the place!"

She gaped at him in astonishment. "You mean *improvements?*" Judging from the exterior, a lit match might be the most useful improvement.

He nodded. "There's a new pump handle, and a new front door. See?"

She saw, and she wasn't exactly overwhelmed. Once the shock wore off, frustration began to take its place...and despair. Good heavens, was this the best her money could buy? This crumbling overgrown shanty made even the dreaded refrigerator box of her imagination seem like the Paris Ritz.

"So much for that dream." She released a sigh of resignation. Maybe it was high time she stopped living on her silver-lined fantasy cloud and dropped back to earth.

"You don't want to go in?"

She shook her head. There were limits to how much reality she was willing to absorb.

Sam shifted from one boot to the other. "Well...there are other houses, you know. I don't know what you can afford, but..."

His obvious discomfort made her ashamed for moping. She straightened her shoulders. "It doesn't matter. I'm paid up at Merlie's for a while yet."

He gazed at her so long and hard that she finally had to turn away from his dark eyes, distracting herself by fluffing Lily's fine hair.

"I could drive you around some of the surrounding towns, if you like," Sam suggested.

She lifted a brow. "Other towns? Still trying to get rid of me?"

His face colored. "Heartbreak Ridge is small. There aren't any other places for sale."

But I wanted to live in Heartbreak Ridge! She had to keep herself from stamping her foot like a petulant child. Sam was trying to be generous...she guessed. Yet his plan to show her houses worked very well with his intention to push her out of Heartbreak Ridge. "You've got better things to do than play real estate agent, Sam."

"Well, it doesn't have to be right now. We could do it later."

"How much later?" she asked.

Their gazes met and held. Eyes of pure blue trapped

her in their intensity. Sometimes Sam seemed so kind, and at others he seemed desperate to push her away. Yet for some strange reason, just at that moment, she felt like taking a step forward, standing up on tiptoe, and pressing her lips smack against his. She had to smile to keep from following up on the impulse. It was ridiculous! And yet what woman could resist being up here on a mountaintop with a handsome man with devastating blue eyes, with just the earth and sky and Lily as witnesses to whatever indiscretion he and she wanted to commit?

A few novel indiscretions tripped across her imagination before she managed to get a hold of her reason. Good heavens! The man barely tolerated living in the same town with her. Would she never learn?

Sam swallowed. "Well, how about tonight?"

He didn't look sure about asking her at all. And she knew she shouldn't feel the kick in her pulse rate at having him ask her. "All right."

Slowly, a smile pulled up at his lips. "It's a date then."

"Oh—"

He frowned. "I mean—well, not a date, mind you—"

She shook her head in agreement. "No, no."

"Just a—"

"Of course." She grinned, pleased that the man's feelings were as tangled in confusion as hers were.

Which meant maybe the sheriff wasn't so set on getting rid of her after all.

5

"OH!" Shelby cried out, laughing. "You got me right on the lips!"

Sam's mouth felt bone-dry. Until that moment, he'd never been envious of a dog, but watching Sadie and Shelby frolicking in the grass, he could honestly say he would have gladly switched places with his pup.

Shelby let out a shriek as the two roughhoused, then freed herself long enough to look at Sam accusingly. "You never told me Sadie was a golden retriever with the soul of a pit bull!"

In response, the canine in question, with paws in the pounce position, butt straight up in the air and tail swishing crazily, let out a playful growl.

Sam chuckled. "The soul of a kitten, maybe."

He luxuriated in the deep green of Shelby's eyes for a moment before catching himself. It was so easy to lose his common sense in Shelby's company. She was quick to laugh and easy to get along with, but still he didn't quite understand how to deal with her.

He looked down at Lily, asleep on the blanket in the shade next to him, and patted her back gently. A casual observer of this scene might think they looked like a happy family on a picnic instead of the confused cluster that they really were.

Shelby popped a grape in her mouth. "Penny for your thoughts, Sam."

"They're about the only things left you can get for a penny, probably."

"Well, at least something's within my budget." She smiled. "But don't think that I didn't notice that you evaded my question. What were you thinking about?"

He hesitated. "I guess I was wondering how you would take something I brought for you."

Those green eyes sparked with interest as she scooted closer to him. "A surprise, Sam?"

He shrugged, unable to take his eyes off her face. Maybe it was the hair that drew his attention, or the pert nose, or her naturally pink full lips. Or perhaps it was simply that he was still expecting to find some indication of what she was doing in Heartbreak Ridge written in her eyes—something she'd never explained to his satisfaction.

"You shouldn't do anything more for me. You've already done so much!" She gestured toward the tablecloth that held the remains of a small, wholesome feast. "All this food…it must have taken hours to prepare."

He shrugged modestly. To absolutely no one would he admit that he'd worked all morning trying to get the modest meal just right. He'd never known cooking—even a simple pasta with chicken—could involve so much blood, sweat and tears. The spinach salad had been a snap, of course, but the muffins were more of a challenge. Not to mention, until yesterday, he'd never even owned a muffin pan. Feeding Shelby was broadening his horizons, cooking wise.

"You're turning into a regular Julia Child," Shelby noted.

He smiled immodestly. "I'd prefer Wolfgang Puck, if you don't mind."

She laughed. "Anyway, I'm grateful. My only regret is that there won't be any leftovers for Sadie."

The dog's ears perked up.

"Sadie snacked all morning on snatches of chicken."

"Okay then, I regret nothing. But honestly, Sam, I don't know why you're doing all this for me. I've told you time and again you don't owe me anything, and it can't be that you're bored, or lonely."

He raised a brow. "Why not?"

"Because...well, because—please don't take this the wrong way—but you're too much of a stud muffin to be lacking for company."

He nearly fell off the blanket. *Stud muffin?* Is that what she thought? He would never have guessed from their conversations, since she usually spent about half the time telling him he shouldn't do things for her, shouldn't come around Merlie's so often, shouldn't spend too much time with her.

Before he could think of any response, she rushed on. "Actually, I'm shocked that a man like you even had to go looking for a lady friend on the Internet."

He shrugged. "In case you haven't noticed, single women aren't exactly climbing out of the woodwork in Heartbreak Ridge. Most of them hightail it for the city at the first opportunity."

She sighed. "I can't imagine why! Why, I think this is about as close to heaven as I've ever been."

He shook his head. She certainly sounded sincere, but could he believe her? Had she been here long enough to judge how much she really liked it?

She blinked at him. "So what is it?"

"What's what?"

"The surprise. Is it dessert?" she asked, licking her lips so temptingly that he was sorry he didn't bring dessert, empty calories be damned.

Of course the thought that a kiss would make just the perfect ending for their alfresco meal skipped into his mind, and was hard to dismiss. Shelby's face was turned up to him, her cheeks catching snatches of sunshine. It would have been so easy to lean down and press his lips to hers....

For a moment, time seemed to stop. Those lips parted. Maybe his did, too. He could hear his pulse pounding in his ears, loudly, insistently. And then Sadie barked.

The two of them sat up straight, turning to watch Sadie tear across the field after a rodent or something.

Sam reached into his back pocket and pulled out the article he'd brought for Shelby. He suddenly felt more hesitant than ever to give it to her. "I, uh, clipped this for you. I found it in the paper this morning and thought you might be interested."

She took the clipping, unfolded it, and read quickly. Pink blotches stained her cheeks, but Sam didn't know when they'd appeared there, or what had caused them. Had she known that he was thinking about kissing her? Would she have wanted him to kiss her?

When she looked up at him, her eyes weren't overflowing with love, but flashing with anger. "Sam, this is an article on Pittsburgh."

"I know."

"Pittsburgh, Pennsylvania."

He nodded. "The writer speaks very highly of it. I thought you might be interested."

"Oh!" She laughed. "I see. All the house hunting we

did last week was just a preamble to trying to get me to look for a house a thousand miles away!'' She looked away from him. ''Thanks a lot, Sam. That *was* quite a surprise!''

He suddenly felt embarrassed, almost ashamed. ''It's just a suggestion. I thought maybe you might be interested in places far away. You came here, didn't you?''

''Because I knew Heartbreak Ridge like the back of my hand! Pittsburgh isn't a small town, and besides, I don't belong in Pennsylvania. I've never lived outside Texas.''

He shrugged, eyeing her closely. ''I thought maybe a whole different state might be a good thing if you were trying to run away from something....''

She swung toward him. ''Who said I was running from anything?''

''You sold everything you owned and jumped in a car and left home, Shelby. You have to admit there's something odd about that.''

She hopped up and planted her hands on her hips. ''I've never run from anything in my life,'' she declared hotly. ''I moved because there was nothing left for me in Dallas, and I wanted a different place to raise Lily, someplace where you just don't feel like an anonymous face in the crowd. You seem to think having a town with only sixty-two people is a drawback, but have you lived in a city where you were one of five million?''

He shook his head.

''I'd count the day I looked up and saw the number sixty-four on that population sign as the happiest day of my life, Sam, because I'd know then that Lily and I were acknowledged members of a community, for keeps. Don't you see? I moved here because I thought Heartbreak Ridge would be a warm, welcoming town, which it has been, except for the sheriff.''

At that accusation, he got up, too. ''I've done my best to help you.''

She hooted. ''To help me get out of town.''

He folded his arms, trying to speak from a point of reason, not emotion. His emotions were involved in such a confusing tug-of-war anyway, that he doubted he could make much sense. Part of him wanted to pull Shelby into his arms and kiss the daylights out of her; the other part wanted to throttle her for being so impulsive and whimsical, so unreasonable.

''All right, I'm sorry,'' he said. ''I won't clip any more articles.''

''Thank you. You don't have to do anything for me, Sam.''

''There you go again,'' he said wearily.

She laughed. ''But it's true. You seem to have a knight-in-shining-armor complex that makes you want to come to the rescue of new moms in distress, but can't we just be friends? Normal, ordinary friends?''

He shrugged. ''That mean you don't like me cooking for you?''

''I swear to you I'll get along fine cooking for myself. I always have. In fact, if you come over to Merlie's some night, I'll fix you my super deluxe grilled cheese sandwich special.''

He tilted his head, frowning. ''If you let me grill it with a tomato in it, that would provide a good antioxidant.''

She let out a strangled croak of frustration as she bent down to start gathering up their picnic things. ''You're hopeless, Sam!''

Hopelessly torn, he feared.

MERLIE STOOD in the doorway, hands buried in the deep pockets of her overalls. "Did you know Doyle Stumph has a yen for our Miss Waterbury?"

The question, though directed toward Cody, sent Sam shooting out of his chair. Then, self-conscious at having been so obviously eavesdropping, he scratched his head, pretending to have jumped up for a reason entirely other than Doyle Stumph's crush on Shelby, and strode over to an old file cabinet, where he rummaged aimlessly as the conversation continued.

"He's even asked her out on a date."

Sam's hands stopped cold on a hanging file folder from 1972. *Date?*

"No kiddin'," Cody said. He leaned back in his chair and looked over to where Sam stood frozen by the file cabinet. "Did you know about this, Sam?"

Though he strained to sound casual, his voice came out a few octaves higher than usual. "Um, no..."

"Well, then you couldn't have been payin' much attention at the Feed Bag lately," Merlie said.

"I haven't been going over to the Feed Bag."

The fact was, despite Shelby's protestations that she could cook for herself, every chance he'd had he'd been driving over with more lunches for her—baskets of tuna sandwiches or the pasta salad recipe he'd found in the issue of *Modern Maternity* he'd sneaked out of the library. His repertoire was growing. All Wolfgang Puck jokes aside, he was getting to be a whiz in the kitchen, if he did say so himself.

Though they were still on a friends-only basis, he'd thought Shelby had been enjoying his company.

"Well, it's like this," Merlie explained. "Every day at the Feed Bag, Doyle treats me to a game of twenty questions, all about Shelby. What does she like to do? Like to eat? What kind of perfume does she wear? What TV shows does she watch? Good Lord, you'd think that my sole purpose in life was to report on Shelby Waterbury trivia!"

Sam didn't care if Doyle knew whether Shelby watched *The Simpsons* or not. He was still caught up with the date business. "Doyle asked Shelby out on a *date?*" he asked, still astounded. "What on earth for?"

Merlie put her hands on her hips. "Maybe to have someone to hold his popcorn at the movies," she said sarcastically. "What do you think?"

Poor Doyle. He'd been a loner so long, it was hard to imagine him longing for a sweetheart.

"How did he take it?" Sam asked.

"Take what?"

"Shelby's rejection."

Merlie laughed. "She didn't say no, Sam. They've got a date."

For the second time in the span of five minutes, Sam was stunned. He tried to picture forty-year-old, potbellied, balding Doyle Stumph out with Shelby and felt himself getting more and more outraged. Why hadn't Shelby told him Doyle was pestering her? "I've never heard anything more outrageous! Doyle has no call asking Shelby out."

"Why not?" Merlie asked.

"Well, for one thing, she barely knows him."

Cody scratched his head. "How's he supposed to get to know her if he doesn't ask her out?"

"He's not!" Sam response came out more hotly than

he'd intended. Doyle Stumph, owner of the Stop-N-Shop, was a lifelong bachelor who'd never shown interest in any woman since Vita Teller moved to Amarillo to take care of her sick mother, and that was seven years ago. Why was he suddenly so interested in Shelby?

The obvious answer echoed in his mind like a taunting refrain. What man in his right mind wouldn't be interested in Shelby?

Sam frowned. "This is the first I've heard of any of this. I have half a mind to go ask Doyle myself and see if you two aren't pulling my leg."

"Why?" Merlie asked. "Is the man trespassing on your territory, Sam?"

Sam practically tripped standing still. "Of course not. There's nothing but friendship between Shelby and me."

"That's not what they're sayin' down at the Feed Bag," Cody noted.

Merlie cackled. "Mercy, no. Tongues haven't wagged this hard since Lew McLeroy started using Grecian Formula."

For a moment he forgot that he wasn't supposed to care what a bunch of gossipy old hens were reporting. "What are they saying?"

"Well, a lot of people have been seein' you two around town. Clyde saw ya'll sitting in a field one time around noon, and he said it looked like you were having yourselves a romantic picnic."

"There wasn't anything romantic about it," Sam said, ignoring the memory of nearly kissing Shelby, a memory that had been on his mind almost nonstop since that day. "Can't two people just eat lunch together without arousing all sorts of suspicions?"

Merlie shook his head. "Then a lot of people's been

seeing you two driving together. Parking in places where no one's living.''

He rolled his eyes. "I'm helping her house hunt, is all.''

"I told everybody that was probably the case,'' Merlie said. "Leastways, if you two were really of a mind to have a romantic hoo-ha, you could always just hole up at your house. Can't nobody see your house from the road. It would be a complete secret.''

"There are no secrets in Heartbreak Ridge,'' Sam reminded her.

"Well, not from me,'' she agreed.

"Not that we're having a hoo-ha anyway,'' he muttered.

"Is that true, Uncle Sam?'' Cody asked. "Cause Leon down at the drugstore said you just bought a big new bottle of Old Spice, and when we asked Amos about the purchase, he confirmed it.''

"Well, for heaven's sake, what's wrong with Old Spice?'' Sam bellowed self-consciously.

Cody shrugged. "Nothing.''

"It's the same stuff I've been using since I was fifteen.''

Sam looked over at Merlie and she was grinning like a mule eating briars.

No one was buying the story that he and Shelby weren't having some kind of romantic fling, which made him wonder. "If everybody thinks Shelby and I are involved, why's Doyle asking her out?''

Now that he thought about it, he felt almost betrayed. He and Doyle sometimes played cards together!

"Doyle took a long time working up his courage, and that's a fact,'' Merlie explained. "He was worried what you might think. Also, he was worried that he's too old for Shelby.''

"He is," Sam said.

Merlie's jet-black brows arched. "He's only five years older than you, Mr. Whippersnapper."

"He looks older, though," Sam grumbled, praying it was true.

His secretary rolled her eyes impatiently. "Be that as it may, poor Doyle might never have worked up the courage if Shelby herself hadn't gone into the grocery one day to pick up some cookies."

"Cookies?" He nearly slapped his head in frustration. Had he taught her nothing?

Merlie nodded. "High time, too! I was getting run down on that rabbit food you keep bringing over to the house." She shuddered. "Anyways, Shelby went into the Stop-N-Shop, and wouldn't you know it, Leila the checkout girl was on break. So Shelby, armed with her cookies, walks up to the checkout stand, which at the moment was manned by Doyle. Lovestruck Doyle rang up the cookies and took Shelby's money, but his hands were so sweaty from being next to his lady love that his fingers slipped on the cash register keys. Then he dropped the money and had to lean down and pick it up. Made a real bumbling oaf of himself.

"Meantime, while he was leaning down Shelby did him a favor by hitting the cash drawer key, which turned out to be not such a favor at all, because when Doyle straightened up with the money he hit his head smack against the drawer and ended up with a nasty cut. So then Shelby felt guilty and ran to aisle four for an extralarge bandage while Doyle stood there embarrassed because his old egghead was bleeding, but then Shelby slapped an ouchless pad on it and told him how sexy she always thought Yul Brynner was and how she'd watched *The King and I* at least thirty times, and then Doyle just blurted out did she want to go out Friday, and she said yes.''

"*Friday?*" That was tonight!

"Yep," Merlie said. "And you should see the snazzy little dress Shelby's going to wear. It's a real cute red number. Says she hasn't been able to fit into it since Lily came along."

Shelby, out in a red dress, with *Doyle?* Every new detail just added to his pain. "What about Lily?" he asked indignantly. "She just can't leave the baby home alone."

"I'm baby-sitting," Merlie replied. "I rented a tape of *The Fugitive,* so it's just going to be Lily, me, those cookies, and Tommy Lee Jones."

Cody frowned. "You'd better be careful about those cookies. I've heard babies aren't supposed to have chocolate."

"That's right. Babies and dogs," Sam murmured absently. He was still thinking about Doyle.

"Babies, dogs, what the difference? Right, Sam?" Merlie said, winking.

Cody turned to Sam. "If you don't want Doyle to go out with Shelby, why don't you just go talk to him, Sam?"

"Who says I don't?"

Merlie nearly fell out of her chair. "You! You've been squealing about how unworthy Doyle is ever since we mentioned his name."

"Well, I can't tell him that." Sam lowered himself into his chair. "I suppose he has as much a right to go out with Shelby as anyone else has,'' he allowed grudgingly.

"Especially since you keep insisting that there's no romance between you and Shelby," Merlie said. "A young pretty woman needs a little spark in her life."

Cody scratched his head in wonder. "Could anyone honestly imagine sparks shooting off Doyle Stumph?"

"She never mentioned anything to me about sparks," Sam said. Even though he felt them, plenty, whenever he was around her. Heck, every time he looked into her eyes it was like the Fourth of July going off inside him— he couldn't be the only one feeling the electricity!

She'd even called him a stud muffin. And yet she was going out with Doyle, who didn't resemble any kind of muffin. More like a day-old bagel.

The same push-me-pull-me set of emotions that had been tugging at his insides since Shelby's arrival nearly tore him apart now.

"Lucky thing Doyle's a man of strong resolve," Merlie muttered, not entirely to herself. "Otherwise, no telling how many lonely Friday nights Shelby would be spending in this town!"

SHELBY TWIRLED in her red dress, pleased with how she looked for the first time in what seemed like the longest nine months of her life. Though she still pooched in places she never had before her pregnancy, this was definitely an improvement from feeling like the *Hindenburg*.

And she was going out on the town!

She laughed, not sure how that phrase translated in the language of Heartbreak Ridge but eager to find out if there were signs of nightlife anywhere. In fact, she was flattered, almost giddy, that any man had asked her out.

Even if she was a little disappointed that the man wasn't Sam.

Of course, Sam *had* asked her out—countless times. Out to drive by houses. Out to shop for things for Lily. And, most of all, out to lunch because he was worried she wasn't eating right. She'd gladly downed enough rubbery pasta salad to choke a horse, just to be with him. But no matter how many houses they looked at, how much pasta she consumed, something about her time with Sam made her feel as if she were butting her head against a brick wall. He was willing to allow her to get just so close to him and no further. And yet he didn't seem to want to leave her alone, either. No matter how many times she told him that he shouldn't worry his stubborn head about her and Lily, he kept coming back with groceries and little toys and terrible noodle salad.

And then he'd suggested she move to Pittsburgh!

With his ability to induce sexual frustration, the man should be labeled a danger to society. He'd never asked her out just for the heck of it, just to have fun, just because he wanted to be with her.

Sam's hot-and-cold attitude was enough to make any woman lose confidence, and Shelby didn't have an ample supply of that quality to begin with. Still, there was something between them. Whenever she looked into his eyes, her pulse raced a little faster. And occasionally she caught him staring at her with something that looked suspiciously like hunger in his eyes.

She'd spent nearly a month ogling Sam's perfect bod. Nearly a month staring into those blue eyes that made her want to shimmy right up to him and whisper sinful sweet nothings into his ear. Nearly a month driving and shopping and lunching in a state of pure unrequited lust. Was there something wrong with her? Weren't new mothers supposed to shy away from sex? You'd think after what she'd been through, the last thing she'd want to think about was doing the wild thing with any man! You'd think that she'd have learned not to let her hormones leapfrog common sense, and common sense told her that Sam was never going to let her into his life.

The man was a walking, breathing puzzle. He wasn't put off by Lily; he seemed to worship her. In fact, sometimes she wondered if he didn't look forward to visiting her baby more than herself. Maybe the problem was that he still couldn't get over that she'd arrived on his doorstep pregnant with another man's child.

Maybe she just wasn't the type of woman he was looking for.

Obviously she wasn't. Sam hadn't even tried to kiss her, and in her experience, there wasn't a man on earth who wouldn't take any excuse to cop a feel or a grab or a wet smack on the lips. Granted, she hadn't been dealing with King Arthur calibre men, exactly...but surely Sam was no saint, either. They had been alone together plenty of times, not counting the presence of Lily, whose eyesight he swore hadn't developed yet anyway. If he'd had the slightest bit of interest in her, wouldn't he have at least attempted a peck on the lips? Or even the cheek? Heck, at this point she would have been flattered by some illicit hand-holding.

She sighed, trying to put thoughts of Sam out of her head...at least for tonight.

"Well, snap my garters!" Merlie chimed in from the

doorway, startling her. "Don't you look like a million bucks!"

Shelby's brow puckered and she peered into the mirror with unexpected worry. "You don't think I'm overdressed, do you?"

Merlie considered. "Well, Doyle isn't exactly Cary Grant, but what man doesn't appreciate a skimpy red dress and a little leg? He'll be the envy of the Dairy Queen."

Shelby laughed. "Is that where people go here?"

"Mmm. If they're lucky."

"And if they're unlucky?"

"Last man I went out with treated me to an endless night at the game table of the Chugalug out on the highway. So I guess you could say it's a toss-up between Dilly Bars or dominoes. But don't worry if you find the entertainment options around here a little on the dull side," Merlie assured her. "You won't be the first."

Shelby shook her head. "Any social life seems like a whirl of gaiety to me. Believe me, after what I've been through, I'm grateful for any sliver of fun I can get."

Merlie leaned her hip against the doorjamb and studied her with interest. "What exactly *have* you been through, Shelby?"

Shelby flinched, and her face turned pale in the mirror. It was never her intention to give that much about her past away to Merlie, who from Sam's description was practically the town crier when it came to gossip.

Ugly snippets nipped at her memory. An interrogation room in a police headquarters. A courtroom of hostile glares. Nights spent pacing through her apartment feeling utterly friendless. She'd thought she'd run far away enough to escape those terrible thoughts, that the past was safely behind her.

She attempted a nonchalant little chuckle. Dwelling on misfortune would get her nowhere; talking about it would serve no purpose, either. "Oh, you know, the same sob story as a million single mothers. I got dumped."

She didn't add that she also nearly got dumped in the slammer.

Merlie's expression oozed sympathy. "Hush my mouth, Shelby. I didn't mean to bring up bad memories."

Her kindness just added to Shelby's guilt.

"You didn't. Everything's turned out for the best. Honestly. I've got Lily, and the chance to make a new start. Some people never get that much."

She went over to the crib where Lily was sleeping and picked up her baby. In the hospital, she'd been terrified that she'd drop her or make some other horrendous mistake, but now those fears had abated. She'd also been afraid that Lily would remind her of Clint; that, also, hadn't turned out to be the case.

Thank heavens.

"I think I'll take Lily out to the porch for a swing before I go."

If there was one thing Lily liked more than riding in a car, it was the to-and-fro motion of the swing. Even its infernal squeak affected her like a lullaby.

Merlie smiled at them with an expression that was the closest thing she had to sentimentality. "If she happens to wake up, you might ask her if she wants popcorn with her movie." She gave the baby a closer squint. "On second thought, she might be more the Milk Duds type."

Shelby laughed. "Right now, she's just the milk type, period."

"While you're waiting for Doyle, I think I'll call my Aunt Hildegarde in Chicago," Merlie said. "I haven't talked to her in a long while."

The evening was turning cool as the heat of the day relented to a more merciful mountain breeze, and Shelby lowered herself into the porch swing feeling the same love of her new home as she'd felt her first night here. That night seemed long ago now, but slashes of feeling came clearly back to her…like how she'd felt about Sam when he'd strolled up the porch stairs and stared at her through the darkness. Those sexy blue eyes could melt icebergs. For a moment as they'd locked gazes she'd hoped…

Well, she'd hoped what she'd secretly hoped a thousand times since that night, if she was honest with herself. She'd hoped that Sam had changed his mind and wanted her as much as he'd seemed to all those months they'd been writing to each other. Which was absurd. Upstanding pillar of the community Sam Weston, and Shelby Waterbury? The woman whose highest achievement in life had been as administrative assistant to a creep?

She laughed, as if the past two years were a clever joke on herself. Laughter had been about all that had kept her going these past months. Laughter, and the prospect of having Lily, and Sam's e-mail.

Sam again! She had to get him out of her mind, once and for all.

She faced forward and swung with her foot so resolutely that Lily fidgeted in her arms. And as she swung she tried to force her thoughts to look forward to her night with Doyle Stumph and all the fun they were going to have out on the town.

DOYLE STUMPH'S FACE was a study in confusion as he stood in the jailhouse and attempted to explain to Sam exactly what had happened.

"I was just drivin' along normal like—leastways, I thought I was—when all the sudden I see the flashing lights behind me. Gosh, Sam, I didn't even realize I was speedin' until the moment Cody pulled me over and informed me I was going sixty-three in a sixty mile an hour zone."

Sam tipped his hat down to hide his surprise. "Three miles over the speed limit, huh?"

He looked over his nephew, who was suddenly immersed in processing nonexistent paperwork. Cody's cheeks practically glowed red. "Like you always say, Sam, the law's the law."

"It's not all Cody's fault, Sam," Doyle said. For once they had a prisoner who looked even more depressed than Cody did for putting him there. And no wonder. One minute Doyle had been headed for a hot date; now he was looking at a night in the cooler. "Cody wouldn't have kept me at all, I'm afraid, if I hadn't blurted out that I'd just come from...the Chugalug." The way he told him the name of the highway tavern, you'd think he was confessing to mugging old ladies.

"Said he'd had a rum and Coke," Cody announced as if imbibing this particular beverage were tantamount to high crime.

Doyle nodded miserably. "You know I haven't been out on a date with a woman since Vita left town, Sam.

And I was talking to Merlie earlier today, and she mentioned that I might take some liquid courage."

Uh-oh. A clearer picture of what was happening formed in his mind.

"Not that my predicament is Merlie's fault, either," Doyle added quickly.

Sam looked at Doyle—the very man he'd been seething about all day long—and managed to work up some sympathy for him.

Now that he was safely behind bars.

"Did Cody ask you to use a Breathalyzer?"

Doyle shook his head. "He said he'd overlook it this time if I came to the jail to sleep it off. I think that was pretty nice of him, don't you?"

Sam crossed his arms and cut a knowing glance at Cody. "Very generous," he agreed, then looked back at Doyle. "I guess you're stuck here for the night."

"That's okay." Doyle appeared a shade less gloomy. "I'm sort of relieved, to tell you the truth. But I'm a little worried about Shelby...."

Sam doubted she'd be crushed with disappointment. "Oh, don't worry about that. Merlie's rented a movie and got her popcorn popper out."

"I think he means he's worried about what Shelby's gonna think," Cody said.

Doyle nodded miserably. "I can't just leave her there waiting."

"Well, heck, why don't you call her?"

Cody jumped up, nearly hurling himself over the old black phone in a linebacker tackle. "He already used his phone call to phone his ma."

Sam blinked in astonishment. What was this? *NYPD Blue?* He could count on the fingers of one hand the number of times they'd stuck by the old one-phone-call rule. "Well, let's just let him have a second call."

"What kind of precedent would that set?" Cody set his chin in a rigid clench.

"Who's going to know?" There were only the three of them in the jailhouse.

"You always say there aren't any secrets in Heartbreak Ridge, Sam. Doesn't he, Doyle?"

Doyle nodded. "Yeah, he does."

Cody crossed his arms. "There."

There what? All denying Doyle his second phone call did was keep them from informing Shelby that she was waiting for Godot. She was probably watching the road right now—and getting plenty steamed by this time, if his guess was correct.

"Maybe you'd better call her yourself, Sam," Cody suggested, shuffling through some papers on his desk. "I'm busy."

Suddenly, Sam understood all.

Sly Cody! He might be shy around women, but he apparently didn't pussyfoot around when it came to playing matchmaker. He'd probably tailed poor Doyle all night hoping to catch him the instant his foot touched the accelerator just a little too hard. Sam shook his head and shot his nephew a glance to inform him that the jig was up, then picked up the phone and handed it through the bars to Doyle.

"Don't be intimidated by Deputy Dawg over there," he said. "Go ahead and call her."

As Doyle dialed, uncle and nephew engaged in a battle of glares. Cody seemed as put out that Sam wouldn't take the bait as Sam was disappointed in Cody for using his badge to engage in personal business. The surprising thing was, Cody didn't look a bit guilty. It made Sam wonder whether that old saw about a criminal's heart beating beneath every lawman's uniform didn't have a whiff of truth. Cody struck him as the most honest man alive, but even he seemed to have a mischievous streak.

Further evidence was that his own heart, which was supposedly dedicated to honor and justice, lifted perceptively when Doyle slammed the phone into its cradle. "Darn it all, the line's busy."

"Could be Merlie on the telephone," Cody said with suspicious assurance. "She might be on the phone with her aunt Hildegarde."

"Aunt *who?*"

Cody shuffled more paper. "Hildegarde, from, um, Cleveland."

In the twelve years he and Merlie had worked together in their two small rooms, Sam had never once heard of this person. She'd never even mentioned knowing anyone in Ohio!

"Her aunt talks a blue streak," Cody said. "Might not be done gabbing till midnight."

Or until I show up at her house, Sam thought. He should have guessed Cody and Merlie would be in cahoots over this Shelby business.

"You'd better go over there, Sam," Cody said.

Sam pursed his lips to keep from snickering. "I had a feeling that would be your next suggestion. Why don't you go yourself?"

His nephew stared at him through round, innocent eyes. "You don't expect me to leave a prisoner, do you?"

"Won't you go, Sam?" Doyle pleaded. "It kills me

to think of her out there at Merlie's house, all dressed up and nowhere to go.''

Sam balked.

Cody glanced up at him with carefully feigned casualness. "Yeah, you heard what Merlie was sayin' about her dollin' herself up in that little red dress.''

Sam didn't know whose groan was louder, his or Doyle's.

"That *sexy* little red dress,'' Cody added pointedly.

Sam let out a sigh of resignation, resenting the joy that leapt in his heart at the prospect of seeing Shelby, especially in the garment under discussion. He shouldn't feel this way about her. He shouldn't be raring to jump into his car and speed out to Merlie's. Most of all, he shouldn't be thinking that he even had Doyle's blessing to take his place for the evening.

He wasn't going out there on any kind of date. He was just going out to deliver a message.

"I'll be back,'' he told Cody and Doyle.

"We'll be here,'' Cody said, and Sam detected more than a hint of triumph in his smile.

6

"WHY, look who's here. It's the sheriff!"

Merlie widened her eyes, clapped her hands together, and generally did a bang-up job of pretending that Sam was the last person on earth she'd expected to see standing on her porch this evening.

"I called earlier, but the line was busy," he replied.

"Merlie was on the phone with her aunt."

Shelby was standing before him in that red dress Merlie had been describing earlier. Now that he saw it in the flesh he realized that even his overheated imagination hadn't done it justice. Besides being an eye-catching fire-engine red, the clingy material fitted her curves in all the right places, dipping down low enough in front to leave him a little less to guess about than heretofore. Sam shook his head, trying to clear it. *You're just here to deliver a message—and you're not delivering it to her breasts.*

He forced his gaze over to Merlie, who was fairly twinkling at him. "That would be dear Aunt Hildegarde, I take it?"

Merlie nodded, not looking the least bit remorseful for telling a whopper. "Aunt Hildegarde from Chicago."

"Really? Cody told me she was living in Cleveland."

Merlie winked. "The sly old bird gets around."

"Not as well as some sly old birds get around the truth, I'll bet." Sam waited for some sign of shame from Merlie, received none, then turned back to Shelby. "I'm afraid I've got some bad news."

Her green eyes blinked in surprise at his sudden shift in tone, and her lips parted. "Oh, no—is it about Doyle? Did something happen to him? I never thought that was the reason he was late!"

She was practically hopping up and down in panic; Sam waved his arms to calm her down. "Don't worry. The Don Juan of grocers didn't meet with an accident." After Shelby had deflated with relief, he added, "He met with a patrol car."

Her brows drew together, and she planted her hands on her hips. "He got a ticket? That's why he's an hour late?"

"He got a ticket coming out of the Chugalug and is being held in the jail till morning."

Merlie's widened eyes and sharp intake of breath were so realistic Sam almost believed her shock. "That Doyle! I'm surprised at him."

"I'll bet you are, Miss Meryl Streep."

Shelby listened to the interchange with obvious confusion. "What about Doyle? How is he?"

"Just like you'd expect. He's sitting in the jail cell apologizing all over the place."

Shelby shook her head. "Oh, I feel terrible."

"You'd feel even more terrible if you'd gotten into a car with a fellow who'd been tying one on," Merlie reminded her.

Shelby nodded. "Well, I guess that leaves me with the night wide-open...."

When she smiled at Sam, green eyes sparkling like

jewels, his arms quaked with the effort it took not to reach out to her and show her just how he'd like to spend her newly freed up evening. Looking into her eyes, he almost believed a passionate embrace would be welcome. But Shelby had never indicated she wanted his attentions; most of the time she treated him as though he were a benign sort of pest. Besides that, all the books he'd read said that new mothers usually didn't think about intimate matters.

Although one book he'd read said that in some unusual cases, a new mother might crave sex....

Shelby's dewy parted lips beckoned his glance.

"Sorry I can't stay," he rasped out, ready to bolt off the porch before he did something he might regret, like ravish Shelby right there in front of Merlie. "I told Cody I'd be right back."

He was almost down to the last step already when a cry sounded—and it wasn't Shelby boo-hooing over his not being able to stick around. It was Lily. She lay nestled in the corner of the porch swing, which to her obvious displeasure had stopped moving. Sam leapt back up the stairs, almost instinctively, to aid the crying child.

"Poor Lily!" he cooed, unable to resist the opportunity to pick up the tiny bundle. It still amazed him that he had been present at the moment of her birth. That coincidence gave him a connection to Lily that he'd never felt with any child before.

"You're better with her than I am," Shelby joked.

Merlie hooted. "He oughta be—he's read so many child care books he could put T. Barry Brazleton out of business if he had a mind to."

"Sheriff turned baby care expert," Shelby mused as

she looked down at Sam and Lily rocking. "That would be quite a switch."

"You wouldn't think so if you'd seen some of the guys we keep overnight in the jail. Sometimes it seems as if I've been a baby-sitter for twelve years."

"Would you like something to wet your whistle, Sam?" Merlie asked. "Coke? Iced tea? It's a nice evening. You two could sit here out on the porch... together."

"No, thanks." Sam busily inspected Lily's tiny fingers to make sure they were all there. As always, they were. In response, Lily stared up into his face. "I can't stay," Sam said, though he was riveted to Lily's gaze and made no move to leave.

"I wish you could," Shelby said.

Sam looked up at her in surprise and tried not to get carried away with the first thought that popped into his head—namely, that Shelby *was* one of those unusual sex-craving mothers.

God knows, he was quickly turning into a sex-craving lawman.

He tried concentrating on Lily's button nose. "Did, um, Lily like the Pooh rattle?"

The last time he'd been in Fort Davis, he hadn't been able to resist picking up a few items at a store called L'il Darlins.

Shelby nodded. "Oh, yes, it's one of her favorites now, right behind the caterpillar."

He'd purchased the caterpillar a couple of weeks before.

Merlie appeared in front of him with a soda and a bottle of formula. "Here. I brought you both a bottle."

He took the soda pop gratefully and propped the formula bottle for Lily. "Thanks, Merlie, I wish I could stay." He self-consciously looked up at Shelby. "To play some more with Lily."

Merlie put her hands on her hips. "Have you forgotten? *I'm* supposed to be playing with Lily this evening."

Shelby laughed. "You two sound like kids in a school yard arguing over who's Lily's best friend."

Merlie harrumphed indignantly. "Can you blame me? All day I was looking forward to baby-sitting Lily, cooling my heels, and watching a movie. Now I'm entertaining guests."

Sam frowned. "I'll be out of your way just as soon as Lily finishes her drink."

Merlie came forward and took Lily from him. "I have a better idea. I'll take care of Lily so you two can skedaddle."

"Oh, but—"

"We can't—"

Shelby and Sam spoke at once, then stared at each other.

"I *was* looking forward to going out..." she admitted.

Sam shook his head. "I wouldn't want anyone to think that I was involved in arresting Doyle."

She lifted a hand to catch an unruly red curl blowing across her cheek. "Why on earth would they think that?"

Merlie and Sam exchanged a quick glance. They both knew what Shelby didn't—that all the town believed Sam still considered Shelby his girlfriend. He didn't, of course, but battling public opinion in Heartbreak Ridge was right up there with fighting city hall in terms of successful outcomes, and if word got out that he was seen driving around with Shelby right after Doyle got tossed in the clink on the night of his date, he'd never hear the end of it.

Of course, if the result was that people like Doyle stopped asking Shelby out on dates...

He shook his head. "No reason."

She smiled. "I know. Why don't we get something to bring to Doyle in the jail? The poor man's bound to be hungry."

Sam was about to firmly state his objections to that plan when Merlie began poking both Shelby and him down the steps. "That's a good idea, Shelby. What a little do-gooder you are. Don't you think it's a good idea, Sam?"

"I don't know..." Sam muttered, slamming his hat onto his head reluctantly. Mostly, he didn't know if he could control himself alone in a car with Shelby. And even if he could, the last thing he wanted to be thinking about was picking up dinner for Doyle.

And what did it mean that Shelby was so all-fired eager to visit Doyle in the jail? Could she be more serious about the man than anyone had guessed? Maybe her and Doyle's fateful Oreo encounter wasn't such an impromptu affair after all. In fact, maybe it was a carefully choreographed seduction! Shelby certainly didn't need much prodding to get into his police car. Also, she'd seemed very upset at the idea of Doyle getting into an accident.

He opened her door and then crossed to the driver's side. Over the top of the sedan, he saw that she was still standing there, frozen like a statue. "Something wrong?"

She blinked. "I just realized. You're the first person to do that for me."

He tilted his head. "What the heck are you talking about?"

"Opening the car door for me. I've always seen it in the movies, but you're the only man I've known to do it in real life."

"Oh, well..." He wasn't certain whether to be proud or embarrassed by his antiquated manners. "Maybe we've seen the same movies."

They got in and he headed instinctively toward the Dairy Queen, the nearest restaurant that was open.

Then, about five minutes down the road, the inevitable happened. Shelby dissolved into a panicky puddle of maternal remorse.

"I should never have agreed to this!" she exclaimed. "What if something happens to Lily? What will Merlie do?"

"The same thing you would do, only she'll probably be a lot calmer."

Shelby looked wild-eyed out the windshield, holding the door handle as though she might leap out of the moving car and run back to Merlie's. "Turn the car around, Sam!"

"Why?"

"I should have written a list for Merlie to follow. I didn't even tell her where binkie is!" she exclaimed, referring, he knew, to Lily's favorite blanket.

"Will you relax? She'll find binkie." He tried to soothe her with his newfound expertise. "Believe me, what you're feeling is perfectly normal. The first separation creates even more anxiety for the parent than it does for the child."

Far from calming her, this revelation only seemed to panic her anew. "You think Lily's anxious, too? What if she cries and cries and Merlie regrets ever having agreed—"

"Shelby! It's okay. Merlie knows how to handle a crying baby. Besides, if you don't start getting out sometimes, it won't be good for either you or Lily."

Shelby sent him a wry sidewise glance and crossed her arms, resigned to the fact that he wasn't going to turn the car around. "Thank you, Dr. Spock." She flopped back against the car seat in frustration. "I should never have agreed to go out."

"I was wondering about that myself...."

"About what?"

He practically snorted. "Your decision to go out with Doyle Stumph."

"What's the matter with Doyle? He seems perfectly nice to me."

"I didn't mean there was anything the matter with Doyle. But now that you mention it, you have to admit that you're a mismatched pair."

She flipped her red hair. "Why? You said Doyle was nice. Do you think I don't deserve someone nice?"

He'd never dreamed she would take his observation that way. "Of course you're nice enough. I was speaking on more superficial terms."

"What?"

He let out a ragged breath, certain she was being purposefully obtuse. "For one thing, Doyle's not exactly what anyone would call an Adonis."

"So? I think he's cute."

Cute? Doyle? Now it was his turn to be astonished. "He's bald!"

She shrugged. "Not completely."

"He's got a paunch like one of Dr. Seuss's Sneetches on the beaches that I was reading about to Lily."

Her eyes narrowed. "I thought Doyle was a friend of yours."

"He is."

"Do you always refer to your friends in terms of unflattering cartoons?"

He flinched guiltily. "I was just trying to be objective."

"Well, subjectively, I would say he's cute, not in a *GQ* cover model way, naturally, but in that solid American citizen way."

"Your solid American citizen is in jail," he reminded her.

Albeit put there by solidly unethical methods.

"You know what I mean. I don't want flashy looks anymore. Believe you me, falling for a handsome face has brought me nothing but trouble."

The comment gave him pause. It was the first time she'd alluded to her former life, and maybe to the man who was Lily's father. Had he been just a handsome face, or had he broken Shelby's heart? Curiosity heightened in him to the point that he practically itched with it. He scratched his chin and tried to keep his mind out of something that was none of his business.

Doyle, however, he considered fair game.

"No matter what Doyle looks like, you have to agree that he's way too old for you."

"How can you say that? He's your age."

He drew back in offense. "Good Lord, how old do you think I am?"

She shrugged. "I haven't given it much thought."

"I'm thirty-five, a good five years behind Doyle!"

She laughed. "You don't have to be so prickly about it. I like older men."

"Apparently. But fifteen years…"

"What about nine years?"

"Nine years is nothing to sneeze at, either. I notice you didn't tell me your age during all our e-mails."

"You never told me yours, either," she retorted. "Besides, I didn't think it mattered."

"Of course it matters."

"Do you mean to tell me that if you'd known I was twenty-six from the start, you wouldn't have even bothered to correspond with me?"

"That's exactly what I mean."

"That's ridiculous!"

"Is it?" He'd been through the math a million times. "When you're my age, I'll be pushing fifty!"

"That's a bit of an exaggeration. And do you really mean that you would let nine measly years stand in the way of a meaningful relationship?"

"When Lily graduates from college, I'll be a card-carrying member of the American Association of Retired Persons."

She laughed. "You seem to have given this some thought."

"Just in passing. But a woman just shouldn't shrug away facts."

"And a man shouldn't be so choosy that he ends up with only his golden retriever for company."

Ouch. Was she right? Had he been too choosy?

There were several women who had gotten away from him over the years. Or, more specifically, there were women who'd become fed up with his trying to decide, in his rational and forward-thinking way, whether he really wanted to settle down with someone who talked too much—incessantly, actually—or a woman who had a feral beast for a mother, or a woman who had an Imelda Marcos-type shoe fetish....

"Okay, so maybe I've been a little picky over the years. What's wrong with that?"

She shook her head. "In thirty-five years, you've never found a woman who you were sure was the one? Or at least made your heart do flip-flops every time you looked at her?"

He looked over at Shelby and, oddly enough, his heart flipped. In fact, it did a flip elaborate enough to put Mary Lou Retton to shame.

But was that enough? Was her heart flipping, too?

Had it flipped for Lily's father? That was a sobering thought.

"Heart flops don't seem to be the grounds for a solid partnership," he observed.

She tossed her hands in front of her. "You're hopeless."

"How?"

"Don't you ever just want to cut loose and do something foolish and impulsive?"

He almost pointed out that foolish and impulsive had probably landed her in single motherhood, but he didn't. He wasn't even sure that was the case. Besides, she was talking about him now, and the fact was, he was curious. Did she want to do something foolish and impulsive with *him?*

"Occasionally," he admitted carefully.

"What?"

He shrugged. "Well…last week I went to Fort Davis on a whim. Got that Pooh rattle."

"Uh-huh." She sounded unimpressed.

"I don't know what you want me to say. Impulsive?" He shrugged. "I guess I'm not sure what you mean. Do you have something impulsive you'd like to do in your head at the moment?"

For instance, kiss?

Her face lighted up. "Oh, yes!"

"What?" he asked, a little too eagerly.

"I'm dying to turn on your siren, Sam."

For a moment he thought maybe this was some new kind of big-city sex talk. Having Shelby *turn on his siren* did have a vaguely sensual sound to it. Then he noticed that, no, Shelby was not staring at him with reciprocating lust. She was eyeing the control panel on his dashboard.

She wanted to turn on his siren. Literally.

He couldn't say that he wasn't disappointed, but when he looked over at Shelby's face, any thought of refusing her request dissolved. And, he remembered with some pride, his car had quite a siren, and it had just been put in.

"Madame, your impulsive wish is my command."

SHELBY STUCK her head out the window of the moving car and listened to the crazy blare of the siren as she and Sam cruised down the dark country road. Maybe it was the realization that she was free to ride in a cop car for fun, not for real. Maybe it was because the cool night air felt good on her cheeks. Or maybe it was because she feared she was falling in love with Sam Weston without much hope of having him love her back. She let out a long lusty whoop that was half teenage silliness, half heartfelt howl at the moon.

From inside the car, Sam laughed.

"Sadie likes to do that, too," he called out to her.

She grinned and poked her head back in. "You want me to stop? I wouldn't want to confuse you, since you seem to get people and puppies confused sometimes."

His jaw dropped, then snapped closed. "Merlie shouldn't have told you about that."

Shelby laughed. "I thought it was funny, Sam. And if you'd told me up front why it was you were so shocked by my pregnancy, it would have been a lot easier for me."

"I guess I just felt too foolish to admit to that blunder."

She shot him a sideways grin. "I can't imagine why." At his rueful look, she cracked up. "Honestly, Sam, when we first met, I thought you must have been completely repulsed by me." She tapped her fingers against the armrest and looked at him curiously. "Of course, maybe you were."

"Hardly."

She grinned. "What did you think, Sam? Was I at all what you envisioned?"

His lips thinned to an inscrutable line. "No."

She tilted her head, trying to read his profile. "Why?"

"You were pregnant!"

She clucked her tongue. "Besides that! I'll admit that when we were writing, I had a very clear mental picture of what you looked like—completely wrong, of course."

Sam's face turned to her with a healthy curiosity. "What did you think?"

She chuckled. "Well, I was sure you were a pale,

spindly sort of fellow with glasses, naturally, because I just assumed you were a computer geek. You had stooped shoulders, pasty skin, and lank brown hair. But of course I knew you were a sheriff, so I put a little Gary Cooper swagger into the mix, too.''

He didn't look too happy with her preconceived notion of him. "Great. Bill Gates with a badge."

She shrugged. "To tell the truth, I was a little disappointed when I got here and discovered how good-looking you were."

His brows raised. "You would have *preferred* a geek?"

She shrugged. "Maybe I'm just insecure. Maybe I just thought a geek would prefer me."

"That's ridiculous! Any man would be out of his mind not to think you were attractive."

Now *that* got her attention. "Was I what you expected, Sam? You must have had some idea in your head of what I would look like."

"Not really. I guess I really wasn't thinking clearly at all."

Hmm. Every time she thought they were going a step forward, Sam took two steps back. The man could give an eel a run for its money in the department of slipperiness. Like the long, tall Texan of the old cowboy movies, Sam just didn't give much away when it came to his emotions. On the surface, aside from the occasional glint in his handsome blue eyes that never failed to get her hopes up but inevitably led to nothing, she wouldn't have guessed that he cared for her at all.

And yet she couldn't forget that his actions told a different story. For a month he'd been her faithful companion, he'd plied her with food and helped her get through the rough patch of being a new mother. By the amount of time he'd spent boning up on parenthood, you'd think he was ready to step up to the plate of dad-dyhood himself. He'd even tried to help her find a place to settle.

Of course, he seemed to prefer to find her a place in another town, or better yet, another state. And she knew from his e-mail that he was the avuncular type, so maybe he just looked on her as a silly young thing he had to take care of. He'd said their ages were too far apart…and yet he'd reeled off their age difference barriers as if he'd given the possibility of a relationship between them quite a bit of thought. That was one indication that he was interested in her.

What she needed, however, was solid proof.

Suddenly, she decided she couldn't put up with his Hamlet-style indecision a moment longer.

"Sam!"

He glanced over at her, startled. "What is it?"

"Pull over!"

Sensing her urgency, he veered the sedan onto the shoulder of the road. "For heaven's sake, Shelby, what's wrong? Are you still worried about Lily? I told you—"

"No, it's something else." She turned to him, looking deep into his blue eyes and trying to keep an iron grip on her courage.

As she gazed at him, Sam tilted his head, looking increasingly uncomfortable. He glanced at the dashboard panel and flipped a switch. Outside the car, the siren kept blaring. He fiddled some more with the controls without success.

She put her hand over his, and he almost jumped in reaction. "Never mind the noise, Sam. Kiss me."

He flinched—surely not a good sign.

"What?"

"Kiss me. Think of it as another impetuous thing I want you to do."

His gaze searched her face until he honed in on her lips. Then he murmured, "I never could resist a challenge," and took her in his arms.

His mouth came down on hers and Shelby felt almost dizzy when she felt the firm pressure of his warm lips on hers. She'd dreamed of this moment almost as many times as she'd dreamed of winning the lottery, but never in her imagination had the mere touch of skin against skin practically dissolved her into a warm puddle. She thought *she* was the one taking the bull by the horns here, but now her driver's seat position was seriously in question. As Sam kissed her, she felt both languid and nervous, both jittery and completely self-assured in his arms. Half of her wanted to bolt out the door, the other half wanted to stay until they'd used up every molecule of oxygen in the parked car.

"Shelby," he whispered.

That husky voice. His simple utterance of her name could make her quiver with desire.

He turned slightly, gaining better access to her mouth, and then his tongue mingled with hers. She moaned and sank into his embrace like an exhausted person sinks against a down pillow. This felt so right, so wonderful, so necessary after all this time. She threaded her hands around the nape of his neck and pulled herself closer, closer, until she was pressed tightly enough against him to feel the rock solid firmness of his chest. No feather pillow there.

"You taste wonderful," he murmured, bestowing enticing little kisses on her cheeks, her closed eyelids. She shivered, and he gazed into her eyes.

"Don't stop," she whispered.

He tipped her chin up again and showered more attention on her lips, this time accompanying it with a wonderful back massage that rendered her boneless. His hands caressed their way down her back to her hips, tilting her so that she could feel exactly how the kiss was affecting him. The hard pressure against her leg started an urgent churning deep inside her, and she moved against him, knowing it was dangerous but unable to resist turning up the heat.

He groaned, and suddenly, the timbre of the kiss changed from a simple experiment to a testing of both their limits. His hand teased the hem of her skirt at her thigh, pushing the thin, shimmery material up inch by sensuous inch. In return, her hand slowly snaked down the collar of his shirt, playfully fingering each button on his chest before popping it open. Her lips followed close behind, tasting the salty sweetness of each newly exposed area of skin. Sam smelled of leather and aftershave and something she could only describe as all man.

They'd skipped a few stages. There had been no pecks on the cheek, no simple good-night kisses on Merlie's doorstep. Instead, they were jumping with both feet right into purely sexual territory, and doing a pretty thorough job of it, too. It was happening too fast, she thought, but how could she stop what she had secretly craved for so long?

She raised her head and tilted her lips against his again, losing herself in their languid warmth.

So lost was she in the kiss that at first she almost didn't hear the tapping.

Sam pulled up, startled.

"What's that?" she asked, peering into his deep-blue eyes until her addled brain processed that someone was knocking on their window.

They both turned. It wasn't just one someone, it was two someones. Shelby could barely make out their faces through the fogged glass of the car windows.

Cheeks aflame, she hopped off Sam's lap and scooted to her side of the seat, quickly doing what she could to set her clothing to rights.

Sam rolled down the window, which not only revealed the curious faces of Amos Trilby and Jerry Lufkin peering in at them, it also let in the blast of the car's siren.

Amos and Jerry didn't bother to conceal their curiosity. "Somethin' the matter, Sam?" Jerry hollered over the noise.

Sam fiddled nervously with the controls on the dashboard. "Can't get the blasted thing to shut off." Red-and-blue lights strobed when he flicked a wrong switch.

"How 'bout that red one?" Amos asked.

Sam stared unseeingly at the panel. "Which?"

"The one that says Siren," Jerry observed.

Sam had punched it before to no avail, but when he did so now, they were greeted with sudden, deafening silence.

"Phew," Jerry said. "That'd drive a person out of his mind."

The four of them sat blinking at each other in the near darkness. Unfortunately, Shelby could tell by the grins on the two men's faces that it hadn't been dark enough to hide what had just been happening in that car.

Not that the fogged windows weren't a giveaway as old as time.

Out of their minds. Maybe that could explain what had just happened. Or maybe it wasn't so crazy after all.

"Well, guess you two are all right," Jerry said.

"Yeah, don't mind us. We just saw you here and worried you might be in a clinch." He grinned. "Um, I meant in a *bind.*"

His companion laughed. "But we feel better knowing you're making out okay, Sam."

Amos chuckled, then smiled at Shelby. "Sure are!"

And by seven o'clock tomorrow morning, everyone at the Feed Bag would know how well Sam and Shelby were making out, too.

"SEE, the thing you gotta remember, Shelby, is that it isn't nearly as bad as it looks on the outside."

Shelby shifted in the worn red leather booth, duly noted the barely concealed guffaws coming from the bar, and leveled a skeptical gaze on Jim Loftus. She hadn't intended to reopen negotiations over the house on Heartbreak Ridge, but the moment she'd stepped through the Feed Bag's door, Jim had started pestering her. "It looks pretty bad."

"Course it does. The old place is nearly a century old. Why, we all sag a bit when we're that old."

Merlie, who was seated at the bar reading a newspaper and pretending not to be eavesdropping, cackled. "Some of us started sagging earlier than that. And I'm not just talking about myself."

Jim shot her a look. "I know you'd like to keep your boarder from becoming a homeowner, Merlie—"

Merlie hooted at that insinuation. "Land's sake, Jim. Shelby wasn't born yesterday. The sheriff drove her up to the place weeks ago and it scared the wits out of her. Now you're trying to tell her it's not as bad as it looks?"

"Well, it's not. The inside has a certain...timeless charm."

"Oh, sure," Amos snickered from two booths back.

"Peeling wallpaper and small rodents. Veeery charming."

Jim's face turned cherry red and Shelby tried to hide a smile. "I'm just not sure, Mr. Loftus," she said before the Feed Bag's patrons could provoke the man further. "The price is certainly right...."

The price was seven thousand dollars. No other house she and Sam had found came anywhere near being that cheap. Granted, Jim's house appeared uninhabitable right now, but if she pitched a new roof and made some minor repairs...

Well, it was probably the only house she could afford. And the truly frightening thing was, she honestly believed Jim could be talked down.

As she was considering the matter, the door's bell sounded and Sam walked in. She knew it was him even before she saw him; maybe it was the familiar sound of his boot steps, or the way the hairs on the back of her neck prickled when he was near. There he was, in the flesh, and when she saw him, her mouth felt bone-dry. She took a slurp of cold diet soda and tried to lower the mercury on her sexual thermometer to the point that she could at least pass for a composed adult.

Sam obviously didn't see her at first, but after an awkward silence in the café and pointed speculative glances between them, his gaze soon honed in on her. He smiled and nodded politely, apparently in an attempt to appear casual, too. But even at his innocent, impersonal gesture, Shelby's cheeks flooded with heat, and she couldn't seem to take her eyes off him. So much for keeping that mercury down! Memories of his arms around her and their wonderful kiss were too fresh for her not to take a moment to appreciate how handsome he was. Just looking at him made her wish they were alone on the side of the road again.

Or at least under the delusion they were alone. The grins going around the Feed Bag clearly indicated that though only two people had discovered them last night, everyone had heard about their romantic roadside interlude.

"Have a squat at the bar, Sheriff," the proprietor said. "Looks like most of the booths are taken."

"At least the one he's probably interested in," Shelby heard someone behind her joke.

She strained to focus her attention on something else besides Sam. Out of the corner of her eye, she could see him sitting down at the bar stool nearest her, which pleased her, since there was one on the other side of the bar that he could have chosen. She wondered if he was hoping to talk to her...or maybe he just wanted to get a peek at Lily, who had nodded off in her portable car seat in the booth next to Shelby.

With concentrated effort, she turned her attention back to Jim. "What were you saying about the house?"

"House!" Sam piped up before Jim could even speak. "Are you still shopping that thing around?"

Jim addressed his cousin impatiently. "It's a house, not a thing."

"It's a residential *Titanic,* is what it is. A disaster waiting to happen."

"It is not," Jim brayed defensively.

"No, the disaster already happened," Merlie interjected. "When it comes to that house of yours, Jim, the iceberg's done been hit."

Jim's face went red with frustration as he looked back

at Shelby. "It's no wonder you received a bad impression with my cousin as your tour guide."

Sam laughed. "I didn't even have to show her the place, Jim. She took one look and practically ran screaming in the opposite direction."

"That's an exaggeration," Shelby said, in deference to Jim's feelings. As eager as he was to unload his heap of a house on her, he also seemed to have some residual affection for it. She'd never had a home, so she could only imagine how difficult it would be to part with one, especially one with so much family history.

"Tell you what," she told Jim. "Why don't you show me the house yourself this time, and if I'm still interested afterward, then we can come back here and talk."

It sounded as if Sam might just choke on his coffee. "You go up on that mountain, he'll weasel you into buying it for sure."

Jim looked duly offended. "Will you mind your own business?"

"This is my business," Sam retorted.

Shelby straightened, turned, and stared at Sam as his statement was greeted by a silence pregnant with speculation.

He cleared his throat. "What I mean to say is...as sheriff of this town, I can't just let you run around cheating people."

Shelby let out her breath. For a foolish moment, she'd hoped Sam was about to proclaim his love for her right there in the middle of the Feed Bag—not the most romantic of places, surely, but it would do in a pinch. And the way her hormones raced around Sam, she was definitely feeling pinched.

But no, while she was going out of her mind about

him, he was still harking on responsibility—and not even his responsibility toward her, in this instance, but his duty toward the town.

Why did she feel as if she'd just received a demotion?

Jim let out a war whoop. "Since when has the sheriff's department handled real estate oversight?"

"Since now." Sam said, standing. He drained his coffee cup, slapped two dollar bills on the counter, and slammed his hat on his head. "Let's go."

Jim balked. "I resent this, Sam. I'm not trying to hoodwink your little lady here."

Shelby folded her arms, waiting for Sam to announce to the café that she was not his "little lady." When he didn't, she tamped down the zip of pleasure she felt at what was probably a simple omission on his part and gathered up Lily and her things. "I can handle this, Sam," she assured him.

He automatically grabbed the handle of Lily's portable car seat. "Humor me."

On the drive up to Heartbreak Ridge, during which Shelby rode with Jim while Sam tailed them in his police cruiser, Shelby tried to look at the situation rationally. She knew the house was a wreck. It might be cheap, but the repairs required to make the place habitable would probably double the cost. She should take Sam's advice and rent in one of the towns nearby.

But "nearby" in West Texas terms was still a good half hour drive from Sam. As ashamed as she was to admit it even to herself, she had to acknowledge that one of the chief reasons she found Jim's nightmare of a place so appealing was its proximity to a certain sheriff with eyes like Paul Newman's. Experience told her she shouldn't base important life decisions on a man who hadn't made her any promises. Actually, experience taught her not to trust any man. After all, Clint had promised her no less than undying love and an expensive convertible.

But here she was, flying up a mountain to consider tossing her money into a ruin, all because a man's front-seat kiss had given her a few thrills.

Okay, maybe more than a few. Sam's kisses had left her wanting more—a whole lot more.

On Heartbreak Ridge, Jim hadn't unlocked the front door before Sam began giving his own tour of the house's flaws, as if they even needed to be pointed out. Shelby wasn't an expert on construction, by any means, but even she could see that a floor that sagged in the center like a worn-out mattress didn't indicate the strongest of foundations.

"Look at that!" Sam exclaimed.

Jim's effort to make a good impression wasn't helped by the fact that the light rain of the night before had managed to leave a swampy puddle right in the middle of the living room. "That's just a roof problem. Anyone can tell that the roof needs fixin'."

"I always wanted a swimming pool," Shelby joked.

Both men turned to her and glared—Sam because he obviously didn't think she should be making light during such a solemn occasion as house hunting, and Jim because he apparently didn't appreciate her attempt at levity. But what did the man expect? His living room looked like Lake Erie.

To alleviate some of the tension, she turned, pretending not to notice their disapproval, and made a big fuss over the chandelier in the center of the room. "How beautiful!"

Or it would have been if it didn't have a thick layer of dust covering each piece of glass.

"Can we turn it on?"

Sam vaulted the water like a Thoroughbred at a steeplechase and hurled himself at the light switch. "Don't touch the light switches. The wiring in this place will probably light the whole place up like a torch."

"I've never heard such foolishness," Jim insisted, brushing Sam aside and flipping the switch.

After Sam's dire prediction, Shelby couldn't keep herself from flinching, and she squeezed her eyes closed, half expecting the house to detonate.

Instead, nothing happened. Nothing at all.

Sam clucked his tongue. "That's fine."

"Power company must have cut me off," Jim grumbled.

"More likely the squirrels did," Sam replied.

Shelby tried to keep an open mind, she really did. And she was encouraged by several features of the house, which had its original ceramic tile in the downstairs bathroom, several more cute light fixtures, big airy rooms, and a wonderful stone hearth by the fireplace. But when she reached the kitchen, a layer of grime kept her from seeing clearly what condition the counters were in, and she didn't dare open up a cabinet for fear of what might jump out at her. After all, there was no guarantee that the scratching noises she heard coming from the walls were the sounds of cute little squirrels.

She tugged Sam's sleeve. "If on the off chance I do

buy this place, I'll definitely want a cat," she said. "Maybe I'll ask Merlie if Tubb-Tubb has any relations."

"You might want something fiercer than Tubb-Tubb," Sam advised. "See if you can rent a panther."

Shelby carefully tested the first step of the staircase. The wood squeaked under her foot, but it seemed strong enough. Tentatively, she continued. The second step was a little stronger, though she was extremely careful for another five steps...which was probably why on the seventh she fell straight through the staircase into the hall closet below.

"Shelby!" Sam was by her side in a flash, taking her hand and pulling her up from the rubble of the fallen stairs. "Are you all right?"

Not waiting for an answer, he swung her up into his arms and picked his way out of the debris. Jim was hovering outside the closet, his face as white as a sheet. No doubt he was envisioning lawsuits. "Is anything broken?"

Shelby laughed. "Yes. My confidence in those stairs."

She had one thing to thank Jim for now though. All morning she'd craved the sensation of being back in Sam's arms again, and now, thanks to Jim's rotten wood, here she was. She looked up at Sam, admiring his strong jaw and a profile worthy of a classic Greek statue, and felt her pulse quicken.

"That fall nearly scared me to death," he said. His voice had that husky quality to it again, igniting a slow burn inside her.

She licked her lips. "I think you'd better put me down, Sam." Before she made a fool of herself.

Sam looked uneasy with the idea. "Are you sure you're okay?"

"I won't know until I stand on my own two feet."

Reluctantly he set her down. The concerned look on his face as she took her first few steps amused her. No one had ever cared more about the state of her health. Didn't that mean that he cared about her, too? Why wouldn't the stubborn fool just break down and admit it?

And a few moments later, he had the opportunity to do it in private. Jim seemed so embarrassed that his grand tour had turned into such a debacle that he roared back down the mountain without even offering her a ride. Sam didn't seem the least perturbed to load her and Lily into his police car, which she took as a positive sign, too.

Darn it! He liked her, his kisses made her weak in the knees, and he loved her daughter. As far as she was concerned, all systems were go. If their relationship were a spacecraft, their romance would already be in orbit. Of course, she could have told him a few things about her unsavory past that would have made him sit on the launching pad. But he couldn't possibly know about those things.

"I don't understand you, Shelby," he scolded gently. "Wouldn't it be better for you to rent a nice place than own a shack?"

"I want Lily to grow up knowing what it's like to live in her own home. I want her to feel rooted in a community and not consider herself just an apartment squatter."

He sent her a narrow-eyed, sideways glance. "Is that how you felt growing up?"

She'd told him a little of her nomadic childhood, but as always, she tried to make light of it. "My mother was definitely a hunter-gatherer as opposed to a cave dweller. And mostly what she hunted was cocktail bars where she could get work."

That was another thing to appreciate about Heartbreak Ridge. No sleazy girly bars in sight to remind her of her family's illustrious past.

No, there was just one sexy sheriff to remind her of her frustrating present. They'd been in the car alone together for several minutes now, and he hadn't sent her one sly wink or a knowing grin—anything that would indicate that their relationship had undergone a seismic shift last night. Maybe he was one of those men who thought kisses meant nothing, she thought despondently.

"Jim's just taking advantage of you."

"It's no big deal. I need a house, he had a house to sell."

"I've told him repeatedly not to pester you with his sales pitches."

"Wait a second." She turned to him, surprised. "You *what?*"

Sam's jaw twitched. "Jim can be as hard to shake as a tick."

"But I was looking for a house, Sam. I hope you didn't warn anyone else off."

"No one else in town has a house for sale, anyway."

"But if they did, you'd tell them to stay away from me."

"Well now, I'm not so sure about that."

She felt almost wounded by his words. "Sam, I know you mean well, but you really need to start butting out of my affairs."

He brayed in displeasure. "Since when have I been guilty of butting in?"

"Since the day I arrived in town," she snapped. "You tried to discourage Merlie from taking me in. You made it clear to me that you wanted me to go. You've attempted to prevent me from settling in Heartbreak Ridge, even to the point of trying to get people not to show me property."

He sputtered in dismay. "Just that one house—and it's a mess!"

"Well, a mess is practically the only thing in my budget. And, on top of everything, you seem dead set on making sure no man in town goes out with me, even though you don't want to yourself."

"*What?*"

"You know what I'm talking about," she scolded. "Last night, with Doyle? Merlie didn't seem to think it was such a coincidence that he was waylaid by your deputy."

Sam appeared so surprised by her statement that he nearly veered the cruiser right off the mountain. "Of course she didn't—she and Cody were in cahoots. I had nothing to do with the whole scheme!"

"Humph."

He sighed. "Well, I'm sorry. I didn't know your date with Doyle meant that much to you."

"Of course it did! He was the first man here to show a real interest in me. And say what you will about him, his intentions don't seem to teeter-totter about like someone else's I could mention.''

"I've always tried to be straight with you, Shelby."

She shook her head. "As far as I can tell, the only thing about me you like is Lily. So at least for her sake I wish you would let me get on with my life here in Heartbreak Ridge.''

"Well, for heaven's sake! I wasn't trying to stop you.''

She leveled a skeptical glance on him. "Not that I don't appreciate all the things you've done for Lily, and for me, Sam, but I really need to start getting back on my own two feet. It just doesn't look good for the whole town to think that we're some kind of item when we aren't.''

He slammed on the brakes when they came to a stop sign. "Since when do you care what everybody thinks?''

"It means a lot to me to have a good name in this town, which I certainly can't do if I'm going to be known as your...your *property*,'' she said for lack of a better word. It had a slightly dramatic ring to it, but maybe it would get her message across.

Yet even as she looked up at him, she half wished that he *would* somehow claim her as his...because he cared for her. Having him butt into her life because he loved her would be entirely different than him doing so out of some throwback sense of honor.

He sputtered indignantly. "B-but *you* were the one...''

She glanced sharply at him. "Who what?''

"Who instigated that kiss last night. If that's what

you're worried all the jaws are flapping about, I had nothing to do with that.''

If she hadn't been so shocked, she would have laughed. So much for him claiming to care for her!

Nothing to do with it? Was he kidding? ''Was that your identical twin I was kissing last night?''

''Don't be silly.''

''Silly is your trying to deny that you weren't present when our hands were all over each other last night. It's true I asked for the kiss, but I wasn't holding a gun to your head, and once things were underway, you certainly weren't beating me away with a stick.''

His face could have given a canned beet a run for its money.

''Be that as it may...''

She tossed her hands in the air and cut him off with a groan of irritation. ''I really don't want to discuss this anymore.''

''For Pete's sake, you were the one who brought it up.''

He stepped on the accelerator and they drove in stiff silence. Shelby was grateful to note that they were fast approaching Merlie's house. The tension in the car made her squirm; she should never have brought up the subject of that kiss. His answer had been stunning in its ability to humiliate and depress her in equal measure.

''You can just drop me off,'' she said.

And when he did, without even insisting on carrying Lily inside the house, that was more depressing still.

''HAD A FIGHT with Shelby?''

Sam scowled. After a frustrating verbal bout with

Shelby, he was in no mood to hash it out with Merlie. He immediately headed for his office, but a simple thing like a shut door was no obstacle for Merlie. She barged right on in after him.

"I had a feelin' you were going to muck everything up." She sighed. "After me and Cody worked so hard to get you all set up, too."

He buried his head in his hands, realizing that there was a dull ache starting in his temples. "Do we have any aspirin?"

"Drugs aren't what you need. You need a wife. You need Shelby."

"She's the one that started this headache."

"See? You two complement each other perfectly. She's a headache and you're a pain in the rear."

His lips thinned. "Very funny. You didn't by any chance barge in here with anything constructive to say, did you?"

"Naturally. I never barge for nothing."

"If you're going to give me advice about Shelby, or tell me I shouldn't have butted in with her buying Jim's house—"

She crossed her arms and cut him off sharply. "You might consider why she wanted to buy that house, dumb cluck."

He remembered the rodent noises and the dust and the trapdoor stairs. "I can't imagine."

"To be near you! Though heaven knows why. You keep pestering the girl and then telling her you really don't want to be around her. It's no wonder she's confused and ready to burst." She grinned. "Did she tell you off good?"

"Passably."

Merlie nodded with satisfaction, then frowned. "And you probably argued right back and at just this moment she probably thinks it's hopeless and is wondering if she should just turn tail and go back home."

"I seriously doubt *that* will happen."

"But what if it did? What would you do if she just packed up and moved back to Dallas?"

At the question, a coldness shimmied up his spine. "Why would she do that?"

"Because she's probably sick of butting her head against the brick wall that is Sam Weston. What's the matter, Sam, isn't she pretty enough for you?"

"Of course she is. She's beautiful. But she also has a temper like a mongoose!" He shook his head. "Do you know how many times she's tried to push *me* away? All she ever tells me is that I'm not supposed to help her. The one time she decided to go out for a romantic evening, it was with Doyle Stumph. She's the one who's confusing matters."

"That kiss last night didn't clear things up for you?"

He frowned. That kiss. Now that he recalled it, it seemed like something out of a dream. He'd never been so carried away, not even as a randy teenager. But then he'd never known a woman's lips to be so intoxicating. If Jerry and Amos hadn't shown up, he didn't know what would have happened.

And what if they hadn't stopped. What then? If they had made love, would she have professed love for him, or would she have considered it a rash, impetuous mistake?

Merlie shook her head. "Sam, I think you're trying

to reason out something that knows no reason. Haven't you ever heard that old expression, 'He who hesitates is lost'?''

As he thought about the possibility of Shelby leaving, a cold chill ran through him. Was it possible that she could really do that—simply drive away, disappearing as quickly as she had appeared?

More important still, could he possibly let her?

No! The answer was as insistent and resolute as it was frightening.

Merlie shoved her cat glasses up the bridge of her nose and nodded curtly. ''I'll get you those aspirin, Sam. You're looking a mite poorly.''

8

WHEN HE ARRIVED AT Merlie's door the next morning, Sam had his hat in hand, a ring in pocket, and Sadie and a picnic basket in the back seat of his car. He wasn't going to bungle this important moment.

Unfortunately, the first thing he'd noticed pulling into the drive was that Shelby's car wasn't there. He rapped on the door until Merlie shuffled forth to answer it.

Still in her aqua-blue quilted satin bathrobe that looked as if it had been imported from 1962, she eyed the bouquet in his hand warily. Then she grinned. "Honey, you shouldn't have!" she exclaimed, taking the flowers from him.

He good-naturedly wrestled the flowers away from her. "They're for Shelby. Where is she?"

One of Merlie's eyebrows arched with interest. "She didn't tell you?"

Sam froze. "Didn't tell me what?"

Merlie hesitated. "Want some coffee, Sam? I've got a fresh pot."

Sam tilted his head. Merlie didn't beat around the bush unless something was very wrong. A bead of nervous sweat popped out on his brow. What was going on?

"You two must've had one heck of an argument," Merlie said, turning and heading into the house, leaving him no choice but to follow. "Worse than you let on. Last night that girl was mad as spit."

"That's why I'm here this morning."

"Well, you're too late. She's gone already."

The words stopped him in his tracks.

She'd done it, then. The image of Shelby in her car flying down the interstate, dashing angry tears from her eyes, flitted through his mind. He'd driven her away. Shelby. Lily. The best things to happen to him in his entire life—gone in an instant. Maybe he should jump in his car and try to catch up with her. How much of a head start could she have on him?

"When did she leave?"

"'Bout six-thirty this morning."

Three and a half hours. She might be a long ways ahead of him now, but if he hurried…

He was so busy calculating how fast he would have to drive to make up for a three-and-a-half-hour lead, he almost missed the sound of Lily crying. At first he thought it was the television. But when he ran into the next room, there she was in her crib, kicking her bootied feet in the air toward him. The sight of her brought a gasp of surprise from his lips. Next to her lay Tubb-Tubb, zonked out sleeping, which, now that he thought about it, was all he had ever seen Tubb-Tubb do.

Merlie rolled her eyes. "If you're going to start lecturing me on letting Tubb-Tubb sleep in the crib, Sam, I—"

He shook his head. "Shelby left her baby?" He couldn't believe it!

Merlie stared at him as if he were nuts. "Course she did. Doyle doesn't want a kid around."

At that moment, the earth seemed to stop rotating. *Doyle!*

So much for Shelby driving down the highway dashing away tears of heartbreak and solitude! That son of a gun Doyle, waiting until he and Shelby had a fight and then horning in when she was vulnerable! "Doyle? She never even let on…"

All she'd said was that she thought Doyle was "sort of cute." Sort of, not even definitely cute! What kind of foundation was that for a relationship?

Merlie shook her head. "Shelby warned me you'd be mad. Guess she was right."

Sam crossed his arms over his chest in an attempt to rein in his explosive sense of anger and loss. "Why? Why did she do it?"

Merlie shrugged. "She said she had to do something. She got lonely and restless just sitting around by herself all day."

Here he thought Shelby was a mature woman, a caring mother…

He looked at his watch. "Six-thirty? Where would they be now?"

Merlie blinked. "At the Stop-N-Shop."

Naturally! He was surprised Doyle felt a need for a wife at all, since he was already married to his grocery store. Sam clapped his hat firmly on his head and stomped back toward the door. "Guess I'll go congratulate her!"

"She'd appreciate that, Sam," Merlie said behind him.

As an afterthought, he turned and gave the bouquet to Merlie. "Here. You might as well take these after all."

She sent him a deadpan stare. "Gee thanks, Sam. I'll always treasure this moment."

How she could joke at a time like this was beyond his comprehension. He left the little house in a huff, jumped in his car, and peeled out of the dirt drive. All the way back to town, he stewed. Shelby...lost to him forever...to Doyle of all people!

He should have figured out a way to keep that guy in jail!

The ring in his breast pocket might have weighed three hundred pounds, his heart felt so heavy. Sadie, too, looked especially mournful now, her sad brown eyes sympathetic as she propped her snout on the armrest in the back seat. Seemingly sensing his mood, she knew instinctively not to wriggle restlessly and poke her head out the window as she usually did.

He had to force himself to stay calm. He wasn't going to make a scene. He wasn't going to hurl accusations or play the part of the jilted lover.

Lover, ha! He and Shelby had barely made it beyond pen pal status. Yes, he'd helped deliver her baby and, yes, they'd shared the most passionate kiss he'd ever been a partner in, but what did that mean?

His heart sank a notch further as the answer came to him. It meant he was going to be one heartbroken sheriff.

He pulled into the Stop-N-Shop and marched toward the automatic doors. When they swooshed open, he found himself face-to-face with Doyle, and all his best intentions flew out the window. He glared down at him.

Doyle's eyes bugged. "Hiya, Sheriff."

"Hello." His voice came out so gritty it sounded as though he'd just swallowed Padre Island.

"What's the matter?"

"You tell me."

The grocer swallowed. "I don't know...."

"What are you doing at work today? Can't you take a day off even on special occasions?"

Doyle's face contorted in confusion. "The only thing special today is the price of watermelons, Sam."

Sam tensed. The man didn't call marrying Shelby *special?*

Or maybe they hadn't even gotten married. Maybe he'd just jumped to that conclusion because marriage was on his own mind. But maybe Doyle thought that because Shelby was a single mother and desperate for company that they could just shack up. That thought managed to rile him up even more.

Doyle sent him a sickly grin. "I haven't been speedin' lately, Sam, if that's what you're worried about."

"Haven't you?" Sensing gossip in the making, several shoppers had pulled their carts up just close enough to witness the drama, but Sam was beyond caring. "According to what I've heard, you've galloped ahead of the pack and snatched Shelby."

He nodded. "Gosh sakes, *she* was the one who insisted on this, Sam, not me."

"Oh, right! You had nothing to do with it," he growled. "I don't know what's going on with you two, but you better pray it's on the up-and-up, because if you're doing anything cheap—"

Doyle flapped his hands in front of him. "Nothing cheap about it! I'm payin' her same as I paid Elda."

"Paying her!" Sam frowned, his brain still stuck in the groove Merlie had placed it in—namely, that he and Shelby were lovers. His mentioning Elda made Sam think he might be mistaken. Elda had been seventy, and not exactly a hot little number, when she'd retired as Doyle's oldest employee.

Employee...

He looked toward the checkout stand, where Shelby stood, her luscious figure draped in a boxy, bright-blue apron that read Doyle's Stop-N-Shop—Thanks for Stopping By! Sam met her stunned, disapproving stare and felt his face pale.

Shelby was Doyle's new grocery sacker!

She rushed forward, putting herself bodily between the two men. "Mind if I take my break, Doyle?"

Her boss shrugged. "Suits me."

She didn't wait or beckon Sam. She merely turned on her heel and stormed out of the grocery store. With a sheepish shrug for the assortment of customers who had witnessed the scene, a group that pretty much encompassed the gamut of gossip groupings in Heartbreak Ridge, Sam turned and followed her.

In the parking lot, Shelby tapped her toe impatiently as he approached her. "Sam, are you crazy?"

He lifted his hands in a gesture of innocence. "What?"

"Stomping into the grocery store as if I needed your permission to go to work, that's what!"

He groaned inwardly. This little scene would just fit perfectly into Shelby's idea that he was trying to control her life. "That's not what I was doing," he argued. Then, unable to help himself, he added, "But while we're on the subject, what the heck do you think you're doing?"

"Earning money."

"But what about Lily?"

"Lily's the reason I'm here."

"But you're a new mother. You need to be at home looking after her. All the literature—"

"Your vaunted ideas of motherhood aren't going to keep my child in diapers, Sam. It's past time I rejoined the real world and went to work."

"And who's going to look after Lily all day, Tubb-Tubb?"

She pursed her lips. "Merlie said she would today. Tomorrow I'm starting her in day care."

"Day care!"

Shelby waved her hands frantically. "Please don't start spouting more statistics at me, Sam. I've thought this all through on my own, pros and cons."

"You want Lily raised by strangers?"

"Not strangers, Sam. Ona Simpson lives in McMillan, just down the road. Everybody knows her."

Her choice of baby-sitter took a little of the wind out of Sam's sails. Ona Simpson was the widow of McMillan's Presbyterian minister, and probably one of the most trustworthy people in the world. Still...

"You'd better let me take care of this."

Shelby let out a huff of frustration, although what she had to feel annoyed about was beyond his imagining. *He* was the one who'd been through a scare this morning. He was the one stepping into this situation without warning, and now had to figure everything out right here on the spot.

"I don't want you to take care of anything, Sam. Haven't you been listening? You don't have to bully people or take on responsibility or put yourself out in any way on my behalf."

"How much are you making per hour?"

Her lips thinned. "Six dollars an hour."

"Six dollars!" The seemingly paltry sum sent him into a flurry of rapid-fire calculations. "For an eight-hour shift, that's less than fifty dollars a day! For a five-day week you wouldn't even earn $250."

She crossed her arms and sent him a patient grin. "You should give up the law, Sam. A mind like yours belongs at MIT."

He scowled. "Once you pay Merlie for the rent and Ona Simpson for taking care of Lily, what will be left?"

She tapped her foot impatiently. "That's what I mean by reentering the real world. Six dollars an hour is the real world, Sam. It's not some ideal in your head about nurturing or my dreams of Lily having the perfect life. Maybe the best gift I can give her is to see her mother behaving responsibly."

Sam sighed, and suddenly remembered why he'd set out to find Shelby this morning in the first place. So much had happened to throw him for a loop! He took a breath and gathered his thoughts. Thank heavens he had the answer to all their problems, including both heartbreak *and* six dollars an hour!

"Shelby, I think we ought to get married."

There.

Shelby blinked up at him, uncomprehending. The joyous grin he was waiting for her to break into never materialized.

"You *what?*"

He wasn't certain he could put it more succinctly, so he repeated himself. "I think we ought to get married."

Instead of answering, she shook her head as if he had just suggested something completely addle brained. In fact, she looked vaguely insulted.

"What's the matter?"

Her cheeks stained red, and her eyes flashed with fury. "Everything! You! Yesterday you acted as if even kissing me was an egregious mistake, and today you suggest marrying me so I won't have to put Lily in day care."

"I was going to ask you even before I found out you had a job," he said defensively.

She tilted her head and leveled a disbelieving gaze on him.

"I was," he said. "I even bought you some flowers, but I gave them to Merlie when I thought you'd run off with Doyle."

Shock registered in her eyes. "You thought *what?*"

Sam shrugged. "It was just a misunderstanding, is all."

She laughed. "Sam, you need to do something about these little misunderstandings of yours. First you thought my baby was a poodle, then you thought my job was a marriage."

He couldn't argue with her there. But whose fault was all his confusion? Before Shelby arrived in his life, he'd been perfectly levelheaded. Since she'd come to town, he couldn't be certain which side was up. "The important thing is, I'm relieved you're still free."

She grinned, but it wasn't exactly the sort of grin that made his heart hum a merry tune. "That's right. Because you *think* we *ought* to get married."

He was beginning to see his mistake. "Okay, okay, maybe I could have put it better...."

"*Maybe?*" She crowed. "Neanderthal man could have put it better by clunking me over the head and dragging me to city hall by my hair."

He remembered the ring and pulled it out of his

pocket. "Here, I brought you this. It was my mother's engagement ring."

For a moment, Shelby's defensive shell cracked as she stared wide-eyed at the simple pearl ring surrounded by tiny diamond chips. It wasn't an overwhelmingly ornate piece of jewelry, but its age and its history spoke his intentions more sincerely than the most expensive jewel at Tiffany's could have.

"Oh, Sam," she whispered reverently. "I couldn't wear your mother's ring."

"I want you to," Sam said.

"But..." Her gaze darted helplessly from his face to the ring.

Whatever hesitation she had, he was determined to overcome it. Maybe he hadn't been the most romantic pursuer these past weeks, but what had all his efforts been for if not because he loved Shelby?

He stepped forward and pulled her into his arms. "I've wanted you to wear that ring since before I'd ever even seen you, Shelby. When I would see your e-mail in my in-box, my heart would race like a teenager's with his first crush. I've wanted you for my wife for months, and since I met you I've been torn up inside, wondering how things would work out between us. But now—"

"Oh, Sam!" Her eyes went dewy as he slipped the ring onto the fourth finger of her left hand. When it was snugly in place, he leaned down and touched his lips to hers, intending on a simple peck.

But he should have known, nothing with Shelby was ever simple. She threw her hands around the back of his neck and pressed herself to him until they were as close together as two people could be in public. After the emotional roller coaster of this morning, his resistance was low, and he couldn't help deepening the kiss. Just for an instant, he promised himself.

But in that same instant, Shelby's warm lips and tantalizingly playful tongue made him forget everything but how good she felt. What had he been beating around the bush for? he suddenly wondered. All the past weeks now seemed like wasted time that he could have spent sampling Shelby's lips, feeling her full curves snuggled up sexily against him, putting him on the verge of losing control. Everything about her—the apple scent of her shampoo, her soft skin, her curve-hugging blue jeans hidden beneath her apron—drove him to the edge of sanity.

He pulled back slightly. "If we go on too much longer, I'll have to arrest myself for licentious exhibitionism."

She chuckled. "Does much of that go on around here?"

"Not till now." He couldn't force himself to let her go. "You still haven't answered my question."

She smiled. "You never asked a question, Sam. You stated an opinion."

He swallowed. "All right then. Shelby, will you marry me?"

She grinned, and this time his heart definitely hummed. "How's this for an answer?"

She lifted her lips to his and he groaned as he again descended into a sensual fog right there in the Stop-N-Shop parking lot. At first he'd thought they should wait until the weekend to get married. Now he was wondering if this afternoon would be too long to wait.

Fighting his way back to sanity, he lifted his head. "I take it that's a yes."

"A definite yes."

"I THOUGHT I was sending him down to congratulate you on getting a job, not to propose." Merlie grinned. "Now I suppose it's me who should be doing the congratulating."

"Thanks, Merlie." Shelby gave her a hug.

"Are you happy?"

"Off the charts happy, Merlie. I never expected to ever feel this much joy again."

Merlie tilted her head, as if she weren't quite sure how to interpret that last statement.

Shelby blushed, realizing it sounded as if something terrible had happened to her—which it had, but Merlie didn't know that. Shelby was beginning to believe—really believe—that she would finally be able to put the past behind her. She and Lily would have a real home, for keeps. And most important, she would be with Sam.

"When are ya'll tying the knot?" Merlie asked.

Shelby grinned. "If it were up to me, we'd elope tomorrow."

"Elope!" Merlie nearly spat the word.

Shelby blinked. "Well, of course. I don't have any family or friends here…"

Merlie brayed her displeasure. "What's Lily? And what am I—chopped liver?"

"Well, no, of course not. But—"

"Elope, my granny! You can't elope. The whole town's been waiting an eternity to see that sheriff of ours get hitched."

Shelby frowned. "I hadn't thought of that."

"'Sides," Merlie continued, "this is Heartbreak

Ridge. We don't get that many chances to see a romance actually work out right. You two are bucking a trend."

"Oh." Merlie's every word made Shelby a little more nervous.

"And anyway, Sam's from one of the oldest, proudest families around here. Why, everyone will want to turn out for this. Not to mention, you're big news, too. Gotta give people a chance to get to know you."

Shelby shuddered at that thought. "Oh, there's nothing to know, really...."

Merlie let out one of those barks that told Shelby she couldn't be more misguided. "Sam Weston's great-granddaddy was Heartbreak Ridge's oldest settler. Why, he built that house you were thinking of buying from Jim Loftus. Practically the whole town is related to Sam, and now that you're marryin' him, you'll be a part of one of the biggest extended families in these parts."

Suddenly, she felt as if she were under as much a burden as if she were changing her name to Windsor, not Weston. "I hadn't really realized..."

"And not only that, but the Westons have been our lawmen since forever. Sam's granddaddy was a Texas Ranger. His daddy was the sheriff. There's never been a more upstanding, law-abiding family than his. Shoot, I'll bet little Lily here ends up wearing a star on her chest someday."

Shelby attempted to maneuver her lips into at least a limp smile. Suddenly, she felt as if she were an underworld spy infiltrating the law-abiding Weston family. Once someone found out what she'd done, and who Lily's father was, how would that reflect on the squeaky-clean Weston name?

She looked down at the ring on her finger. The pearl

gleamed up at her, pristine and white. Her legs went noodly beneath her and she sank down on a kitchen chair.

Merlie looked at her, alarmed. "Honey, what's the matter?"

"Oh, Merlie. I think I've made a terrible mistake!"

Her friend frowned and touched her arm in concern. "How's that?"

"I can't be Mrs. Sam Weston. Not when…"

She couldn't say the words. How could she tell Merlie all she'd been through before she confessed to Sam? He deserved to hear it from her lips, not from some second-hand source. And knowing Heartbreak Ridge, she had no doubt that if she so much as breathed a word about her past, news would spread faster than she could even dial Sam's number—especially since this was Merlie's poker night!

Sam was coming to visit in a little while. She would tell him then. And maybe she would just have to give him his ring back…depending on how understanding he was of people's involvement in criminal activity.

Merlie's expression lost all its usual traces of humor. "Are you worried because he doesn't know about Lily's father?"

Shelby nodded slowly. "I guess." Clint Macon had been the catalyst for all her troubles.

Merlie smiled. "Well then your worries aren't worth peanuts. Do you think Sam hasn't thought this all through, Shelby? Hell, I imagine he's been wrestling with the idea of your past for weeks now. Would he have asked you to marry him if he still cared about that?"

But he hadn't wrestled with her past in its sordid entirety. Shelby forced a smile. "Maybe you're right...."

"Course I am. Leastwise, I know the very last thing you want to do now is borrow trouble. The thing you should concentrate on now is the future, which means being a bride and having yourself a wingding!"

She'd always wanted a church wedding, Shelby realized. But warm fuzzy dreams of a long white dress and a flower-festooned church and a long honeymoon had dropped off her imaginative radar a long time ago. The last year had been so filled with anxiety, schoolgirl ideals of flower girls and bridesmaids would have been as frustrating as a jailbird dreaming of an unmarked car and an open highway. A festive occasion like a wedding was so far out of the realm of possibility it was only painful to think about.

And yet here she was, nearly a bride. "Apparently, I'm not going to get off without a wingding of some kind."

"Heck, no. But I wouldn't worry about it, honey. Sam's so eager, he's probably done most of the planning already." Merlie glanced at her watch and hopped up. "Oops! Gotta go or I'm gonna miss the first hand."

She disappeared, leaving Shelby to wonder how she should proceed. Do as Merlie said and not borrow trouble? Tell Sam now? If so, how, exactly, should she bring the subject up? *All wedding plans aside, Sam, let me tell you a little story about fraud....*

Before she could think of a more palatable alternative, Sam's headlights shone through the window. In the next second she heard the sound of a car door slamming, then his footsteps. Though just moments before her heart had been heavy, Sam's imminent presence boosted her spirits. Maybe that's what real love was—being comforted by a man's presence no matter what difficulties were roiling inside you.

She opened the door and immediately found herself on the receiving end of a long, lingering kiss.

"That's quite a hello," she whispered when they were finally forced to come up for air.

"You're quite a fiancée," he replied in a husky, sexy voice that made her knees feel weak beneath her.

He grinned, took her hand, and led her inside. Of course he had to inspect Lily in her crib in the living room, but after he'd performed his usual safety check, he turned back to Shelby. "How about Saturday?"

She blinked. "What?"

"Saturday—you and me, and the preacher."

His grin held such boyish enthusiasm that she couldn't help taking a shine to the plan. "Oh, Sam, how wonderful! Merlie was talking about a big wedding."

"Of course!"

She tried to hide her disappointment at his response. "How many people could be planning to come to a wedding on two days' notice?"

"Shoot, practically the whole town besides Earnest Stubbs. Earnest has a funeral in Fort Davis."

So that meant sixty-two minus one people there to witness her vows. The prospect of having that many eyes focused on her caused a lump the size of a boulder to form in her stomach.

"Not having second thoughts, are you?"

Actually, she was on her seventieth thought by this time. But with Sam's arms wrapped protectively around her, and those earnest blue eyes locked with hers, it was hard to express her doubts. If she loved a man this much, wanted him this much, there had to be a way for things to work out. Besides, what had happened had been nearly a year ago. A year. How could something that happened that far in the past come back and nip her happiness in the bud now?

"No second thoughts," she said, and she made a conscious decision then and there not to live in the past, or to hang her tail between her legs and behave as though she didn't deserve this happiness, this fresh start, this miraculous love that had come her way. "Except maybe about what I'm going to wear," she joked. "Coming up with a wedding dress in two days might be a tall order."

"If you showed up at the church in a bikini it would be okay by me."

"Would it?"

She was so close to him she could feel his laugh rumble through his chest. "In fact, no. I'd want to clobber the first man who looked twice at you."

She clucked her tongue. "I'd save my punches if I were you. Whoever it was would probably be gawking at my stretch marks."

He waggled his brows sexily. "Talk like that could make a man lose control."

She tossed back her head and laughed. "Oh, Sam, I love you!"

He pulled her closer. "And I love you, Shelby Waterbury."

His eyes darkened, and she knew he was going to kiss her again. She held her breath, feeling pure electricity as his lips drew closer. Every time they kissed, it felt as if she were spinning out of control; all her best intentions fled out the window. No man had ever affected her so wildly, not even Clint.

She gasped, horrified that Clint's name could enter her mind now. Then again, maybe it had to.

"Oh, Sam!"

He cocked his head, holding her from moving farther away from him. "Are you all right, Shelby? You look like you need air."

She took a deep gulp of it right now. "Sam, do you realize how little you know about me?"

His brows drew together. "Well...we've only really been together a short time. I can't know everything. You don't know everything about me, either."

She laughed. "But you haven't lived the life I have. According to Merlie, you're considered something of a saint around here."

He shook his head. "That's not true."

"An exaggeration, maybe. To me, the term couldn't even be applied loosely." She looked him in the eye and said point-blank, "You've never really questioned me about Lily's father, Sam. Haven't you wanted to?"

He hesitated. "I guess I'd be a liar if I said I didn't. But what does that matter now? You've said that he won't come back into your life, and I believe you. Is there any reason why I shouldn't?"

She looked into the blue trusting pools of his eyes, felt his arms bolster her, and allowed her fears to slip away. *Don't borrow trouble,* Merlie had said. What was Clint Macon to her now, except a man from her past, the past she'd left far behind? If she brought up the whole story now, what would have been the point of uprooting to a town that had never heard of her?

"You're right, Sam. That's one part of my life that's safely locked away now."

In a state prison, as a matter of fact.

When Sam kissed her, lingering doubts slipped away. This morning she would have said that she couldn't love Sam any more than she did, but now, knowing how understanding he was, she clung to him all the more strongly.

When he picked her up and carried her back to her room, she sent him a sly smile. "Aren't you jumping the gun?"

His gaze burned into her so intensely she shivered all over. "We've had seven months of courtship," he said, laying her across the bed. "I'd call that pretty traditional and old-fashioned."

She pulled him toward her. "I have another word for it."

His brows rose in silent question.

"Frustrating."

He grinned as he lay alongside her, idly running a finger down her neck, her shoulder, her arm. Gooseflesh rose on her skin, and she felt raw desire leap to life in her. That same need was mirrored in his dark eyes. "I've wanted you for a long time, Shelby, even before I knew you I dreamed of you."

She grinned. "You liar! You said last night that you'd had no preconceived notions."

"That was the lie," he confessed. "I knew exactly what you'd look like."

"My hair?"

He nodded, running a finger through her hair now as he studied her. "It wasn't like this."

"How was it?"

"Oh, kind of a dull brown, like a horse I had once when I was a kid."

She punched him playfully on the arm. "Very flattering!"

He studied her critically in the dim light. "The eyes I had *nearly* right."

"Did you think they would be green?"

"No, brown. Sort of..."

"Like the horse you had when you were a kid?"

He laughed. "But the body..." He shook his head. "Not at all what I was expecting."

She rolled away from him, lying on her back and crossing her arms. "I'm not sure I want to hear this."

"Hey, don't move away." He chuckled softly, positioning himself over her in a straddle. Desire rumbled through her from the very core of her body. "Is it my fault you're not what I was expecting? That you've got a face that could put fashion models to shame?"

She shivered as he bent to kiss her forehead, the tip of her nose, her lips. When he pulled away, she gritted her teeth against the disappointment. She was raring to go, but he seemed intent on biding his time. "Fashion models? Isn't that going a little overboard, Sam?"

He shook his head, slowly unbuttoning her silky shirt. As cool air hit her skin, sinful thoughts of how to warm herself back up leapt through her mind. Sam unhooked her bra and bent down to tease one rosy nipple with his tongue. "Definitely not Fanny Farmer," he whispered.

She gasped at the husky tone of his whisper.

Then, a second later when his words sank in, she pushed herself up on her elbows. *"Who?"*

He grinned sexily. "Fanny Farmer. That's how I always imagined you—sort of a middle-aged thing, pretty enough, but a little on the dowdy side. You know, what people generally refer to as a *healthy*-looking woman.''

She stared at him in openmouthed astonishment, then fell back laughing. ''Just think what would happen if the man of my imagination got together with the woman of yours.''

''Mmm. I bet Bill and Fanny would produce wonderful offspring. Geeks in aprons.''

They laughed until they were out of breath, and then they kissed, a playful kiss that turned into something much, much deeper and urgent. Shelby felt an unexpected impatience as she helped Sam shed unwanted clothing. They had waited so long, she didn't want to wait another minute for them to be together. Sparks flew; so did shirts and jeans, underwear and socks and anything else in the way. The room became a jumble of discarded clothing and twisted sheets. Rosewater perfume and Old Spice mingled in the air, creating their own heady fragrance.

They moved together, arms and legs entwined, as one. Shelby had never felt both so thoroughly at ease with a man, and so completely unstrung. Every new place he touched lit with fire, until her whole body burned with heat for him. Each word he whispered in her ear set off a new frenzy of desire inside her. And every moment he taunted her, waiting to consummate their love, stretched into a sweet, agonizing eternity.

When neither could wait any longer, Sam looked down at her with such hunger, Shelby felt like a feast about to be devoured. ''I love you, Shelby,'' he said, his raw husky voice working on her senses like a drug.

In answer, she pulled him into her, reveling in the explosion of sensation that ensued. From that moment on she knew she was his, body and soul, for that night, and forever.

———————————

9

THE HAPPIEST day of his life.

Sam grinned as he approached his office. Wasn't a wedding day supposed to be the happiest day in a *woman's* life? Yet here he was, the groom, and he felt about as giddy as a bride. In fact, for the past two days he'd been the one absorbed in the details of getting the ceremony together and inviting everyone to the reception, while Shelby seemed a little dazed by it all. But of course, she barely knew anyone in Heartbreak Ridge, and none of her friends from Dallas was coming in for the wedding. Merlie would be her maid of honor.

In fact, most of the town was more curious about what Merlie would wear to the ceremony than what the bride's dress would look like. Did she have special overalls she brought out for special occasions, people speculated, or was Merlie Shivers actually going to appear in a dress?

The whole town was steeped in a carnivallike atmosphere, which just went to show that hope did spring eternal. Heartbreak Ridge loved a wedding; each one gave them a precious chance to thumb their noses at the town jinx. Everywhere Sam looked now, he saw flowers, balloons and people in their Sunday best. A hand-painted banner draped with bunting announced Good Luck, Shelby and Sam! right across Main Street. For the big bash afterward, Doyle had donated a wedding cake, Jerry was catering, and the elementary school principal had offered the gymnasium as a reception hall. No other building in town would hold the whole community.

With a wedding-day spring in his step, Sam practically danced through the jail area to the back office to fetch the wedding bands, which he had slyly locked away in the jail's safe. The sheriff's office was going to be officially closed during the wedding; after all, Cody was his best man and had duties to perform, like holding on to the ring and making a toast at the reception. Sam was kind of sorry to put Cody at the center of a public ritual since he was so shy, but he hadn't been able to track down Cal on his mountain. His nephew had left his lair, apparently.

Sam crossed the room to fetch the ring out of the safe and was surprised to find Cody sitting in his desk chair, staring at the computer's screen saver. But the most shocking sight was that of Cal standing next to his brother, arms crossed, a glower on his face. This was the most presentable-looking Sam had seen Cal in months; the beard was still there, but at least he was wearing a newly pressed dark suit.

Sam laughed. "Cal, you son of a gun, I should have known you'd make it. How'd you find out about the wedding?"

His nephew's lips twisted into a wry grin. "Junior here sent me a smoke signal."

"What are you doing over here, Cody?" Sam asked. "Don't you know the best man should be over at the church chewing the scenery?"

Cody didn't look at him. "I was worried about that toast I'm supposed to give."

Sam laughed. "Oh, don't fret about that. Just tell everyone that I'm the greatest uncle that ever lived and that should about take care of it."

"It wasn't you he was worried about," Cal said. "It was Shelby."

For some reason, his nephews' behavior was getting on his nerves. Why wouldn't Cody look him in the eye? What was Cal so grim about? "Shelby? Just say that she's the greatest aunt a deputy sheriff could hope for."

Cal cleared his throat. "Cody wanted to get a little more specific..."

Sam crossed his arms impatiently. "Okay, you two, out with it. Have you been reading my e-mail files?"

Cody whipped around. "No, Sam, I swear. It isn't that."

"Well then, what's your problem? You look as if you'd just found out Shelby was a criminal!"

"Good guess, Sam." Cal wasn't laughing.

At Sam's surprised look, Cody swallowed, turned, then pressed a key. The screen saver disappeared, and a story from the *Dallas Morning News* popped up. "You know you always said you could find anything on the Internet...?"

Sam hesitated just a second, then, beckoned by a curt nod from Cal, he stepped forward and skimmed the article. Halfway down the page, he was squinting in confusion. This was an article about some insurance agent who was defrauding his customers by topping off their premiums and taking the extra for himself. The man, whose name was Clint Macon, had very deliberately and deviously preyed on his older customers by sending out notices that their premiums would be raised—money that no one but he ever saw again.

Oh, except maybe one other person: his secretary, Shelby Waterbury.

Cody had typed her name into the search engine and come up with quite a few hits. For months the *Dallas Morning News* followed this insurance scam story very closely, and Shelby, who made for good photos—the sexy redheaded secretary in the center of a scandal—was featured in every column. First the police brought her in for colluding with her boss, then all charges were dropped to secure her testimony against Clint, who was also, the paper gleefully discovered not long after the arrests, her lover.

"The Fraud's Floozy," she was referred to more than once in some of the more salacious articles and editorials.

Sam felt his face burn. Lily's father was no longer a mystery. He was doing a healthy spell in jail. Shelby had done her duty and testified against him.

Was she innocent? In her testimony, Shelby protested that she never knew a thing about the scam, even though she was often the one sending out the letters and taking the checks to the bank. But the most interesting thing to Sam was the fact that when Clint was caught, he was carrying two tickets to South America. One for himself, and one in the name of Shelby Waterbury.

Shelby professed ignorance about *that,* too.

"Did she tell you any of this, Sam?" Cal asked.

"Sure she did," Cody blurted out. His voice was laced with desperate hope. "I bet you're mad at me for bringing up all this stuff you already knew about, right?"

Sam's jaw felt so locked with tension he wasn't sure he could talk. "Sure, I knew."

Cody looked relieved. "I told you, Cal. We should have just kept our noses out of it."

Sam couldn't believe how expertly Shelby had conned him, couldn't believe how foolish he'd been.

"I knew that there was something fishy about her coming here." Sam spoke his thoughts aloud. "I knew it from the very beginning. I just allowed myself to forget it."

Just as he had feared from the very beginning, he had let blind attraction overcome reason.

Cody's face fell. "Then you didn't know...."

Sam's whole world was clattering around him like a building during an earthquake, and there was nothing he could do to stop it. "No. I didn't."

No wonder she'd wanted to start over! With that kind of scandal behind her, he was surprised she didn't try to find a pen pal somewhere farther away, where a man wouldn't have access to her past at the click of a mouse. But where was that place? Bora Bora?

He fumed. What did Shelby think he was? A chump? Maybe she'd been planning this from the very beginning, believing that eventually she would sashay into Heartbreak Ridge and twist him around her little finger. Here he'd thought he'd found the love of his life, and she probably just looked at him as a refuge, the equivalent of the Red Cross for plea bargainers on the run.

Cal looked especially grim now. "Looks like Heartbreak Ridge is living up to its name once again."

"Don't say that!" Cody jumped out of Sam's chair, and when he spoke, his voice was unnaturally bright, and about two octaves higher than usual. "So what if we found a few articles, Sam? It's ancient history!"

"The arrest happened less than a year ago," Cal pointed out. "And the trial was just six months ago."

Six months. "Even when we first started writing e-mail, she never mentioned it," Sam said. "Even though she would have been dealing with the trial."

Cody shrugged helplessly. "Maybe she didn't think…"

Sam's eyebrow shot up. "That it was important?"

His nephew sagged. "I'm sorry. I should have never gotten on the Internet."

Cal shook his head. "You just saved him, brother."

Cody sent one last pleading glance to Sam. His eyes were so filled with anguish Sam almost felt sorrier for his nephew than he did for himself. Cody had done the one thing he most hated to do—he'd gotten someone in trouble. "I would feel awful if this came between you and Shelby, Sam. Why don't you just try to forget it? This doesn't really have to change anything."

Cal was appalled. "You think he could marry her now, without an explanation? You think he could trust her?"

Cody lifted his shoulders helplessly. "She's probably waiting at the church already."

Shelby. Waiting to marry him.

For a moment, Sam was torn between Cal's cynicism and Cody's die-hard live-and-let-live attitude. But the tug-of-war was brief, and he was at last able to reassure his youngest nephew.

"Breathe easy, Cody."

Cody grinned at him hopefully.

"At least now you won't have to give that speech."

"YOU LOOK just gorgeous, honey."

Shelby felt faintly ridiculous as she stood waiting in

the back of the church in her big white dress that she'd gone all the way to Fort Davis to purchase. "You don't think I look like a marshmallow?"

She still hadn't dropped all her pregnancy weight.

Merlie laughed. "No, hon. But I think it'll be mighty peculiar for you to be trailing down the aisle after an old wreck like me. "

Shelby rolled her eyes. Merlie had decked herself out in a real dress for this occasion—lilac tulle—but she obviously felt uncomfortable. "You look great, Merlie. It won't hurt to show Heartbreak Ridge that you actually have legs. Quite nice ones, too."

"Oh, sure. Look at me and most people will think of Betty Grable as Queen of the May. Maybe I should skip down the aisle tossing rose petals."

Shelby shook her head, laughing...which was surprising in itself.

Merlie noticed, too. "Thank heavens! You've looked so shell-shocked all morning I doubted there was a single chuckle to be squeezed out of you."

At the reminder of her nerves, Shelby immediately remembered to be nervous. "Where could Sam be? It's already eleven."

"He had the wedding bands locked up in the jail safe, which is the only safe in town. Fine thing when jailbirds have their possessions better guarded than the rest of us."

Shelby peered through a crack in the door where she could see the backs of the heads of the congregation. A few clusters were whispering; men in suits fanned themselves with hymn sheets. "The natives are getting restless," she observed.

Merlie looked, too. "I guess it does seem criminal to keep people waiting in this heat."

From behind them, they heard a deep laugh. Shelby spun on her heel and found herself facing Sam, impossibly gorgeous looking in his tux. Like a cross between James Bond and Gary Cooper. Looking at him caused her breath to hitch.

And then she frowned. His arms were crossed over his chest and he was leaning casually against the outside door of the church, but the piercing glare in his expression was anything but casual. Or kind.

"If you want to know about what's criminal and what's not, ask Shelby."

Shelby froze. Once when she was a kid she'd fallen out of tree and landed on her back. For a moment the air had been completely beaten out of her. That's how she felt now. Breathless. Dumbstruck.

Merlie didn't have that problem. "What the devil are you talking about?"

Sam folded his arms and pierced Shelby with a hostile glare, and for a sickening moment, she was transported to a place she didn't want to be. A jailhouse, surrounded by cops, plagued by reporters. Labeled, judged, convicted without trial.

"Dallas," Sam drawled in answer to Merlie's question. "An insurance man named Clint Macon, and his secretary, Shelby Waterbury."

Merlie turned and gaped at her.

Shelby couldn't bear it. Here she thought she'd escaped, but now she'd just dragged her old baggage behind her. Even Sam, who in the past days had said a hundred times that he loved her, obviously didn't want to give her the benefit of the doubt, and he was sworn to uphold the principle of innocent until proven guilty. What would the rest of the town think?

As if she had to ask! Sam was the town's favorite son. He was practically the pulse of Heartbreak Ridge.

"Well? What do you have to say?" Sam asked impatiently.

For a moment, Shelby thought she was going to faint. She knew she couldn't speak.

Then she surprised herself, but not by coming out with a plausible answer that would exonerate her at last. She doubted such words existed for such a skeptical audience. She didn't speak at all. She ran.

"Shelby!"

Merlie's voice called after her, but Shelby didn't turn around to look. She couldn't bear to see Sam's face again. She just concentrated on sprinting—which was no easy task in three-inch heels and a floor-length dress with a train. White billowed around her as she hurtled down the aisle, past the altar, toward the front of the church where there was a side entrance. All the while, the train tugged at her, so she grabbed a hank of skirt in her hand and pulled it up. Her veil suddenly felt like a ten-pound weight on her head, so she yanked it off and tossed it away. She threw away her bouquet, too, before making her speedy exit from the church. She could only hope the poor thing that caught it didn't also catch a severe case of bad luck.

Outside the church, Shelby didn't stop running. The thought of Sam, the man who she'd decided was the kindest man alive, glowering at her, kept her legs moving. She might look like a marshmallow in flight, but right now she felt she could have outrun Jesse Owens.

She didn't even run out of breath until she reached

the city limits, which, granted, weren't that far away. Panting with exhaustion, she leaned against the pole of the population sign, struggling to catch her breath…to think clearly…to figure out what to do next.

She looked up at the sign, then blinked in surprise. She could hardly believe her eyes.

Welcome to Heartbreak Ridge, it read. Population 64.

Sixty-four? The last time she'd driven by, the sign had said sixty-two.

As realization hit, tears formed in her eyes. She'd always told Sam she'd wanted to live in a place where she could be counted—and now there she was, number sixty-three, and Lily was sixty-four.

She'd also told Sam she'd never run from anything in her life, but that, she knew now, was a laughable lie. She supposed she'd been running since she was a kid. First, scurrying after her mother. And then, on her own, spinning her wheels until she could find that dream she'd been chasing for so long: that cozy little town where everybody knew her.

She straightened up, dashed a tear from her eye, and staggered back toward Main Street. For better or worse, she was home.

BY MONDAY MORNING, the atmosphere in Heartbreak Ridge was funereal, not festive. The congratulatory banner with its bunting was gone. People in their regular work clothes went about their business a little slower than usual. The only reminders of the would-be wedding were a few flaccid balloons hanging off light poles.

The Feed Bag was dead silent when Sam walked in, and stony stares from his neighbors followed him as he took his place at his customary stool at the bar. Even

Jerry, who usually slapped a cup of coffee down in front of him before Sam could even get situated on his stool, greeted him with nothing more than a curt salute of his John Deere cap. "What'll you have, Sam?"

What would he have? Was Jerry kidding? "Oh, how about a scrambled egg and wheat toast?"

Jerry nodded in concentration, as if this weren't the same order he'd taken from Sam for years.

For a long while, the only sounds in the café were the scrapes of forks against old white plates and occasional slurps from coffee mugs. Sam felt as if he'd suddenly been plunked down in a movie set—*The Stepford Diners,* maybe.

He turned to Amos Trilby, who was usually an endless fount of small talk. Being a pharmacist gave him the edge over everyone else; he was always the first to know who was sick, sleepless or in the family way. "How's it going, Amos?"

Amos lifted his heavy shoulders. "'Kay, I guess." That said, he focused all his attention back on his French toast.

Sam gritted his teeth. The same thing had happened to him at the office this morning. Cody had barely said two words to him, and Merlie had positively given him the cold shoulder. No mention of Shelby. Merlie was probably angry that he'd run her boarder out of town.

Who would have known Shelby could run like that?

The thought of Shelby's flight through the church being the last he saw of her made him queasy. She'd been so upset, a part of him had longed to run after her. His pride, however, forbade it. If she was heartbroken or humiliated, it was her own doing. She'd had plenty of opportunity to tell him about what she was running from.

For instance, before they'd slept together might have been a good time.

But she hadn't explained. Even when he'd asked her to, she'd turned tail and run. He could only hope she'd run clear back to Dallas.

The Feed Bag's door banged open, sending the bell jangle on overdrive. Heads looked up from their oatmeal and pancakes and eggs to see Jim Loftus, red faced with excitement, bustle up to the bar next to Sam. If Jim noticed the tension in the café, he didn't let on.

"Hot dawg!" Jim hooted. "That little lady of yours sure has ideas, Sammy boy!"

Sam paled. Hadn't Jim been in the church Saturday?

Jim suddenly looked around, realizing his error. He put a hand to his lips and shrugged apologetically. "Oops, sorry, cuz. I forgot for a minute that your name was mud around here."

That was putting it mildly! The whole town seemed to hold him personally responsible for the wedding debacle. Never mind he was just saved from tying the knot with someone who'd been dubbed The Fraud's Floozy. A woman fleeing from a church in a white wedding dress drew more sympathy than a guy standing in the back of the church with an indignant scowl.

Plus, they all just plain liked Shelby. No one seemed to think the fact that she'd omitted telling him a serious chunk of her past should mean anything. To Sam's mind, they were all being overemotional and unreasonable.

Jim brightened. "That Shelby—has she helped me out!"

Sam froze. "Shelby? Where did you see her?"

He could only assume it wasn't somewhere far away.

Jim frowned in confusion. "At the Stop-N-Shop, where else?"

Sam's heart sank. Shelby was still here? Merlie hadn't told him that! She'd just gone back to work as though nothing had happened? After creating the biggest scene in Heartbreak Ridge history, she was simply going to stick around and make things awkward for both of them for God knows how long?

He gritted his teeth. "What's she done now?"

Jim held up a piece of paper. "She gave me an idea for what to do with the house. I'm gonna have a raffle!"

This caught the interest of everyone; suddenly the place livened up a bit.

Amos laughed incredulously. "You mean sell tickets?"

Jim swiveled around to face his audience. "Not just sell tickets. Shelby said I oughta get on the Internet thing and advertise in magazines. See, people'll send in a hundred bucks and a little essay about why they'd like the house. Then *I* pick which person wrote the best one—"

This statement was met by jeers. "Since when were you a literary critic, Jim?"

Jim frowned. "It doesn't have to be literary. It just has to be interesting."

Sam frowned. "So you're going to pick some sucker who's never even seen the place and hand the keys over for a hundred bucks?"

"Not a hundred bucks," Jim said excitedly. "Several hundred times a hundred bucks. I'll make a fortune."

"Sounds like a scam to me," Sam said. He didn't say what popped into his mind. *Coming from Shelby, that wouldn't be a bit surprising....* His jaw clenched tight enough to cut barbed wire.

Jim huffed. "How's it a scam when the person's gettin' a whole house for a hundred bucks? Why, the land it's sittin' on is worth ten times that."

"Yeah, but the cost of fixin' the place up is more than a hundred times that," Amos told him.

Jim rolled his eyes. "Well, if you're going to be nitpicky, sure there are a few holes...."

Jerry laughed. "More holes than Swiss cheese, Jim. Besides, what if nobody writes in? Or only ten people do?"

"Well then, I can call it off and send the money back. Or give it away anyway and let it be my tough luck. No one could say I was dishonest then."

Sam shook his head. "It doesn't sound right."

Jim frowned at him. "You're just sore 'cause Shelby thought of it."

The room fell silent again. No doubt everyone was reliving that moment Saturday when Shelby, a sob in her throat, the white dress fluttering behind her, had fled the church. Sam squirmed uncomfortably, growing a hair angrier and more resentful.

This used to be his town. Now he could barely get people to say hello to him. Now he could barely have breakfast without hearing about *Shelby.*

He shot out of his chair and jammed his hat on his head. "Keep those eggs warm for me, Jerry. I'll be right back."

During the few minutes it took him to get to the Stop-N-Shop, he tried to rehearse what he would say. But what was there to say? All he wanted to know was what her intentions were. He would just have to improvise. But when he walked into the grocery store and saw Shelby placidly bagging Nelda Brammer's groceries, his mind went blank. All he could think of was how beautiful she looked. How vulnerable.

Which, of course, was what got him into trouble to begin with. The woman was capable of making him lose track of his better judgment; he knew that now. He came up behind her, close enough that he could smell her freshly shampooed hair.

"I need to talk to you," he announced.

Shelby didn't even bother to turn around. Leila at the cash register did. Astonished shoppers in the store did—and he wouldn't exactly call their expressions welcoming. At the Feed Bag, he'd gotten the cold shoulder from the men. Now he was getting it from the women.

"I'm sorry, I can't take a break right now," Shelby said with a proud sniff, carefully wrapping a plastic bag around a carton of ice cream before placing it at the bottom of a paper sack.

"Shelby…"

She had moved on to Nelda's canned goods now, not letting Sam's breathing down her neck or the curious stares of onlookers break her rhythm one bit.

But Sam wasn't going away. If she wanted another scene, he was plenty happy to give her one. "Okay, we can just talk here."

He sent an awkward glance toward Nelda, whose eyes widened. "Don't mind me, Sam—I'll start filling out my check," she said.

"Your purpose here, Sheriff?" Shelby asked.

That sheriff bit felt like a slap in the face. "I'm just surprised to find you here, that's all."

At his words, Shelby finally turned, her arms akimbo. "Why shouldn't I be? I certainly didn't feel like a holiday. Do you?"

Sam frowned. "No."

"Also, Doyle was a person short, which is why I really need to get back to bagging Nelda's groceries, Sam."

"I guess what I meant was, I'm surprised that you're here in Heartbreak Ridge."

She forced a smile. "Oh, goody! We're back where we started, with you trying to get me out of town. Do you have any more brochures for me today? Any clippings about what a wonderful town Schenectady is?"

"After Saturday I wouldn't have thought you'd want to linger here."

She nodded. "I see. You finally thought you had succeeded—sort of like the sheriffs in those old Wild West movies, pushing the shady lady on the first stagecoach out of town. Strange that you pride yourself on being so modern, Sam. It turns out it's not the twenty-first century you belong in, it's the nineteenth!"

"I just want to know what your plans for the future are."

She grimaced. "If you're wondering whether I'm going to wander around town with a scarlet letter on my chest, the answer is no."

Leila turned away, her shoulders shaking as she attempted to hide a laugh.

Obviously, this wasn't the best time to have a reasonable dialogue.

"I'm done running, Sam," Shelby declared. "I ran till I was pooped, but when I stopped I was standing by a sign that read Heartbreak Ridge, Population Sixty-four. You changed it yourself, Sam, and I sincerely thank you for that. It was the loveliest, most precious present anyone's ever given me. This is where I belong now, and when you belong in a place, you don't have to run away. You stick around and work things out.

"I like the people here, and trust them enough to think that, in time, I'll be able to win their trust again. So if you don't mind, I'd like to start by doing the best job I can here—a goal your presence here isn't helping, by the way."

Sam stepped back. This wasn't at all what he'd expected. Tears, yes. Curt defiance, no.

He should never have changed that sign!

"All right. If that's the way you want it."

"That's the way I want it."

He stood there awkwardly, strangely torn between the urge to throttle her or take her into his arms. She was so unapologetic, and yet her stiff-necked pride and determination almost touched him more than a heartfelt, tearful apology would have. He didn't have any more to say, yet he didn't know exactly how to end the conversation, either.

But Shelby did. She sent him a big, impersonal grin, the perfect Stop-N-Shop employee demeanor. "Thank you, sir, and have a nice day!"

10

"SLOW DAY," Merlie observed.

Sam frowned as he crossed to the water cooler. "They're all slow days."

"Mmm."

And they weren't slow because they were in the dog days of summer. Or because, even at its worst, Heartbreak Ridge would never be called a hotbed of crime. These days were slow because he was here and Shelby was a quarter mile away and he hadn't even spoken to her since the day he'd been at the grocery store.

"Notice you've been taking most of your meals at the Feed Bag, Sam."

He downed a glass of water and nodded. As hard as it was to face his less-than-friendly old cohorts, he'd definitely been avoiding that grocery store. "Back into my old habits."

"Feedin' yourself like a bachelor," Merlie said. "The eatin's better at my house, too, these days. That's one good thing to come out of this breakup—no more noodles and rabbit food. Just red meat and sugar, the food of life."

Sam twisted his lips into a patient smile, refusing to let her words send him into a snit, which they probably would have just a few days ago.

Didn't that prove he was already getting over Shelby?

He turned and went back into his office, where he absentmindedly pushed paperwork for a half hour, until Cody burst into the front room, out of breath.

"Doyle's going to fire her!" the deputy hollered.

Sam shot out of his chair and was at the door in no time. For some reason, he knew instinctively who was being referred to. "When did you hear this?"

"Just now." Cody spoke between gasping breaths. "Apparently, Doyle hadn't learned the details about what had happened to make Shelby leave Dallas, but when he did, he hit the roof."

Somehow, it was difficult to imagine mild-mannered Doyle blowing his stack, but maybe he'd felt as betrayed about Shelby's failure to be frank about her past as Sam had.

But *fire* her?

Cody's face was red and he sputtered as he talked, as if he couldn't get the news out fast enough. "Doyle said he didn't want any jailbird working in his store."

Sam's back stiffened. "That's not even true! Where'd he hear that Shelby went to jail?"

Merlie shrugged. "You know how gossip goes, Sam. After the third telling the molehill's already a mountain."

Sam was taken aback by her attitude. "I'd think you'd be more angry about this. She's your friend."

"Well, sure I'm mad," Merlie retorted. "But what can I do? I don't own the grocery store."

Sam harrumphed indignantly. "The man should at least have come to me for the straight dope! Nobody ever proved Shelby did anything criminal, you know. The charges against her were dropped."

"I've been telling everybody that, even though I wasn't sure," Cody said.

"It's all right there in those articles on the Internet." All of which Sam had pored over a million times since the last time he'd seen Shelby. Reading them closely had given him a lot to think about; maybe more than he was actually ready to absorb. "Doyle should at least try to get the details right if he's going to fire somebody."

Merlie shook her head. "Some people just want to think the worst. You know, suspicious types. No trust."

Sam put his hands on his hips. "Then they're irrational hotheads! Besides, Doyle knows Shelby has a baby to support. How's she supposed to earn a living?"

Cody and Merlie just blinked at him, as if they didn't have an answer to that question. Heartbreak Ridge didn't exactly abound with commerce and job opportunities.

Sam marched toward the front door.

"Where you going, Sam?" Cody asked.

"To talk sense into Doyle. And if that doesn't work, I might knock sense into him!"

AFTER EIGHT HOURS of sacking groceries, Shelby's feet hurt so much that even standing stock-still made it feel as if she were walking across hot coals. She leaned against the counter, trying to rest her feet just a little, when a whole new pain entered her life: Sam. He was marching across the street with a thunderous expression.

She took a deep breath, gearing up for another difficult meeting.

Actually, seeing him couldn't be any worse than not seeing him had been. In its own way, his studious avoidance of her was as awful as his public repudiation of her had been. All these years, she'd harbored fairy-tale dreams of landing in a small town and falling in love with some wonderful man. Her rose-colored spectacles had never allowed her to see the flip side of this paradisiacal setup. For instance, she never imagined how uncomfortable it would be if Mr. Wonderful turned his back on her, leaving her in the midst of sixty-two people who all knew her heartbreak as well as she knew it herself.

That was one thing that really surprised her. She'd fully expected the town to side with their favorite son, but everyone in Heartbreak Ridge, it seemed, had a hard-luck love story to tell, and in the past week, she'd heard them all. Sacking groceries took twice as long as it normally did because she had to listen to tales like Mrs. Ellerby's story of an elopement gone wrong when she was sixteen. Candice Lehigh practically talked her ear off telling her about her second husband, the compulsive gambler who sold the family tractor and skipped town with the proceeds, never to be heard from again. And poor Amos Trilby had been coming by every other hour, using any excuse, buying a soda pop or a single piece of fruit or some breath mints, just so he could tell Shelby another chapter in his endless tale of marital woes.

Everyone had a story; everyone had made mistakes. Everyone was ready to forgive her, in fact, except the one person in town who most mattered to her.

And now he was storming toward her as if his hurt were just as fresh as ever. She stood tall on her aching feet and folded her arms, waiting for him with the fierce determination of a coastal resident preparing for a hurricane. She'd nailed up plywood around her heart and was prepared to weather the coming onslaught.

To her surprise, however, he marched unseeingly past

her and stopped in front of Doyle, who swallowed nervously. Apparently, his nerves were still recovering from his last encounter with the sheriff. "What can I do you for, Sam?"

"Are you going to fire Shelby?" Sam demanded in a fierce voice.

Shelby gasped. What was he trying to do now, make Doyle let her go? She marched up to the two men and inserted herself between them. "Wait a minute!"

Sam shot her an annoyed glance. "I asked Doyle a question." Then he looked back at the man with a hard gaze. "I don't know who you're getting your facts from, Stumph, but let me clear one thing up for you. Shelby was never sentenced to a single night in jail."

"Of course I wasn't!" she interjected.

"She was never convicted of any criminal doings, or admitted any knowledge of any criminal misconduct, Doyle. *Any.*"

"Why, I never said—"

Sam glowered. "Do you know what kind of places those big-city police stations are, and do you honestly think Shelby could have stood up to the grilling they gave her if she was guilty? She's not that type of person!"

Shelby stood gaping at him, almost as amazed as she was confused. It sounded as if Sam were defending her!

But against what?

Doyle didn't seem any clearer on that question than she was. "What do you expect me to say, Sam?"

"I expect you to act like a decent, reasonable human being. Is it Shelby's fault that she believed someone's lies and got caught up in a big mess?"

"No, but—"

Sam reached right over Shelby and grabbed the startled shopkeeper by the shoulder. "Are you so perfect that you can act as judge and jury in a case that the law has already dismissed?"

"Heck, no."

"Then for heaven's sakes, be reasonable! You can't toss Shelby out of a job over an incident that happened a year ago and had nothing to do with you."

Doyle shook his head frantically. "Of course not!"

Sam's Adam's apple bobbed up his throat as he swallowed. "And if you *are* pigheaded enough to throw her out on her ear, you can bet that she'll find another job within an hour, because the whole town's behind her. She's honest, hardworking, and capable, and certainly not dependent on your measly six dollars an hour!"

With that, he turned and marched out of the grocery store just as purposefully as he'd marched in.

Shelby flushed red and felt so stunned she couldn't move.

Doyle continued shaking his head and Edna Grant ran up to share in the drama. "Do you think the sheriff's been drinking?"

"I don't know what to think," Doyle said, scratching his chin. "Mighty peculiar. Someone must have told him that I intended to fire Shelby. Why would anyone do that?"

Shelby knew, of course. Merlie had never stopped conjecturing that she and the sheriff would get together again; apparently, she'd decided to give them a nudge. But after Sam's scene, Shelby just felt shock, and outrage that Sam could march up to her employer and announce that she didn't need her job, when her six dollars an hour was more important to her than ever!

She looked over at Doyle. "Mind if I take my break, boss?"

"No, of course not."

She straightened her shoulders and sped out the door, sprinting after Sam's retreating back until she had almost caught up with him. "Hey, wait a minute!"

He pivoted on his boot heel in the middle of the street. "Yes?"

"I want to talk to you, Sam Weston."

His expression was almost one of surprise. "What about?"

What about? "About what you just said back there!" she said in a blistering tone. "Are you trying to get me fired?"

He frowned. "Of course not. I was trying to save your job."

She laughed. "Save it? You practically turned in my resignation!"

"He was about to fire you."

"No, he wasn't."

"But I heard—"

"You heard wrong, Sam. Doyle said he didn't know what you were talking about."

Sam's face reddened, and for a moment his gaze swung toward the sheriff's office, where the front curtain suddenly pulled closed. He shook his head and breathed out a ragged sigh. "Looks like I was set up."

She crossed her arms, trying to contain a tiny hope that sprung to life inside her. "Looks to me like you've had a change of heart, too."

His gaze narrowed in on her.

"Did you mean what you said back there, Sam?" she

asked. "Do you really think I'm honest, after all you've heard about me now?"

His gaze met hers, and she held her breath, trying not to read too much into the warm expression in those blue eyes. "I meant it."

"Then you don't think I did anything wrong?"

His jaw twitched as he clenched his teeth. "You didn't tell me about it. That was wrong."

She nodded. "I know it was. I wanted to a hundred times, except the moment never seemed right, or even appropriate. I'm such a different person than I was when I met Clint Macon, it hardly seems like me when I remember those days."

"A different person? What do you mean?"

"When I went to work for Clint, I was coming off a string of terrible dead-end jobs. I desperately wanted to make something of myself, to rise above the cheap sort of life I'd been raised in. Clint took one look at me and must've known I was perfect for his needs—young, eager and ready to be unquestioningly loyal in return for getting ahead.

"It's true I didn't know what he was doing, but maybe that was because I didn't want to look too deeply. If I had, I might have realized the reason Clint was romancing me and buying me gifts was so I would keep my trap shut." She laughed bitterly. "He must've really felt cheated when the trial came and he realized I didn't even know what he'd been doing. He could have saved himself a lot of hush money."

"But all this was winding down when we started writing," Sam pointed out. "Why did you never mention it?"

"Because I didn't want to think about it. Would you

want to tell a person you'd just met about the worst mistake of your life? Everything in my life seemed so ugly, I wanted to dream of something honest and beautiful—like this place."

"So you came here."

She nodded. "I was trying to make a fresh start. I didn't want to deceive you, Sam, but I worried the minute I brought up that sordid story about Clint, my mistakes would follow me forever. I didn't want Lily to have to grow up dealing with my stupid troubles dogging her every footstep. I guess I was full of unrealistic hopes."

He nodded. "But when I asked you about it at the wedding, you ran."

She shrugged. "I was scared. You looked so judgmental, so like all the people in Dallas, police and reporters and just plain folks in the convenience stores who didn't know the first thing about me and didn't even want to give me the benefit of the doubt."

His lips thinned, and he said nothing more.

She felt a twinge of disappointment in his silence. "Anyway, I wish you would speak to Doyle. I'm afraid you left him with the impression that I don't need his six dollars an hour."

Sam looked down at her. "Well, do you?"

She put her hands on her hips. "Yes, I do, you big galoot. In spite of what you said, job offers aren't raining down on me here."

"And you're happy at the Stop-N-Shop?"

She tilted her head. "When you're sacking groceries, happiness is a relative term."

He shrugged. "Then I'm not sure I'll talk to Doyle."

She went red with fury. "Sam! I can't afford to lose this job, unless you can think of anything better."

Blue eyes seemed to pierce her very soul. "How about being my wife?"

Shelby blinked in surprise. "Your...?"

"Wife," he repeated, taking her hands in his strong grip. "Shelby, I'm ashamed of myself."

"But why?"

"Because I thought I was being so reasonable, but I wasn't. I let a few newspaper articles get the better of me. Will you ever forgive me?"

"Forgive you?" she repeated, stunned. For an entire week she'd been mentally calling him a hard-hearted, mean-spirited, judgmental old crank. But in the face of his humble apology, those descriptors were light-years from her mind. "Of course I will...if you'll forgive me."

His hands tightened around her arms. "I love you, Shelby—nothing's ever going to change that."

She laughed, for maybe the first time in a week. Lord, it felt good, almost as good as it felt to be in Sam's arms again. "Don't worry, Sam—there are no more surprises in my closet."

He waggled his brows at her sexily, and she felt a familiar shiver of desire snake through her. "No forgotten marriages?"

She giggled. "No."

"No long-lost relatives to show up on our doorstep?"

"Definitely not."

"No tall, dark strangers who are going to whisk you away?"

She held a hand up to his cheek and grinned. "Well...I *have* had a tall, dark stranger in my past...."

His brows lifted. "Recently?"

Her head bobbed up and down. "Very! I think he was some sort of lawman...." She sighed melodramatically. "Alas, I can't remember the details clearly."

Sam's blue eyes glittered sympathetically. "Amnesia?"

"I'm afraid so, only it's a very strange case. The doctors say I'll never regain full memory of this devilishly handsome stranger until he kisses me again. And what are the chances of that happening?"

Sam smiled. "I'd say pretty good."

Without conscious thought, they were in each other's arms, sharing the deepest, warmest kiss Shelby had ever experienced. Of course she'd been lying; she hadn't forgotten a moment of how it felt to held by Sam. He'd been holding her in his thrall all along, and she had never stopped remembering the wonderful night they'd made love. But feeling his lips against hers reminded her that memory could never equal the real thing.

"Let's get married today," Sam whispered. "I'm ready to get this honeymoon underway."

She grinned. "Me, too."

He kissed her again, but Shelby suddenly became aware of a crowd standing outside the Feed Bag, gaping at them. Likewise, people had spilled out of the grocery store and stood on the sidewalk to witness their reunion. Every doorway in town had at least one person standing in it, and from the now open curtains of the sheriff's office, Merlie and Cody beamed their approval.

"Sam," Shelby whispered, suddenly shy. "We shouldn't be doing this."

He laughed. "Why not? We're practically married!"

"But everyone's watching us."

Sam glanced around, nodding happily to everyone he saw. When he looked back at Shelby, his eyes were so full of love she felt her insides melt. Who was she kidding? Anywhere was the right place to kiss this man!

"Of course they're staring," Sam explained. "We're having a romantic reunion in the middle of Main Street, in Heartbreak Ridge, Texas. Might be the first time such a thing's ever happened. How's that for bucking a trend?"

And when they kissed again to rapturous applause all up and down the street, the dappled summer sunlight streaming down on them like confetti, it really did seem to Shelby—and maybe to all of Heartbreak Ridge that day—that a miracle was happening.

Next month, look for #35
THE DEPUTY'S BRIDE,

book two in the LONE STAR LAWMAN
trilogy by talented Liz Ireland.

*Deputy Sheriff Cody Tucker has his hands full
when Ruby Treadwell enlists his help to escape
the scrutiny of her four well-meaning brothers.*

*Ruby wants to experience the wilder side
of life outside Heartbreak Ridge. Little did
she realize that would lead to love and happiness
with shy but sexy Cody Tucker!*

Stray Hearts

JANE SULLIVAN

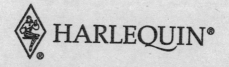

HARLEQUIN®

TORONTO • NEW YORK • LONDON
AMSTERDAM • PARIS • SYDNEY • HAMBURG
STOCKHOLM • ATHENS • TOKYO • MILAN • MADRID
PRAGUE • WARSAW • BUDAPEST • AUCKLAND

Dear Reader,

A few years ago my sister wanted to adopt a cat, so I went with her to an animal shelter in Dallas, Texas, where she chose a lucky little tabby cat from a sea of orphaned felines. Though my heart went out to those animals left behind, the policy of this particular shelter put my mind at ease: Even if an animal is never adopted, he has a home there for life.

Later I found myself wondering what kind of person would make such a promise, and my hero was born—a veterinarian who has dedicated his life to the welfare of stray animals. I loved writing about a strong, sexy man with a heart of gold, confronted by an animal-fearing woman who is sure that a veterinarian is the last man on earth she'd ever fall in love with. But soon they discover that romance can be found in the most unlikely of places—even in an animal shelter!

I hope you enjoy *Stray Hearts.* I love writing romantic comedy, so what better place to have my first book published than at Harlequin Duets?

Jane Sullivan

For my husband, Brian.
Your love and support have
meant everything to me.

The rabbits are just
around the corner!

1

"ARE YOU Kay Ramsey?"

When the stranger called her by name, Kay took the chain lock off her apartment door and eased it open a little wider. The voice belonged to a balding, beady-eyed little guy with the stub of a cigar clenched in one hand and a white envelope in the other.

"Yes," she said warily. "I'm Kay Ramsey."

He handed her the envelope, then gave her a sly smile. "Have a nice day."

He stuck the cigar between his teeth and disappeared down the stairs. Kay took the envelope back into her apartment, where she opened it carefully to avoid smearing her just-polished nails. She pulled out the document it contained, and for a moment thought she was going to be sick.

"Kay? What's the matter?"

Sheila McCann, her across-the-hall neighbor and world-class nail artist, capped the bottle of Peony Pink, set it down on the dining-room table, then plucked the document from Kay's fingertips. She scanned it quickly, her eyes widening as she read. "Robert is *suing* you?"

"Yes! Can you believe it? All I did was get his dogs a lousy haircut, and now he's suing me!"

Sheila raised an eyebrow. "Sweetie, I think it's the *way* their hair was cut that kinda miffed him."

Kay collapsed onto the dining-room chair, wishing her

nails weren't wet so she could hide her face in her hands and pretend none of this had ever happened.

If only she had Sheila's approach to life, she'd be a whole lot better off. If Sheila had been engaged to Robert Hollinger and found him half-naked in his office with another woman, she would have tiptoed calmly through the pile of discarded clothes, grasped him firmly by his excessive chest hair and told him, in so many words, that his after-hours activities had caused her to have an unexpected change of heart about their upcoming nuptials. And that would have been that.

Unfortunately, Kay had approached things a little differently. She'd slipped away from the scene of the crime unnoticed, called a mobile dog-grooming service, and, at her direction, they had rounded up Robert's favorite status symbols—three snooty, prizewinning, slobbering, hyperactive, brainless cocker spaniels—and given them haircuts to her *exact* specifications. And when Robert came home and saw those precious extensions of his manhood looking as if their coats had been run through a blender, he'd gone predictably berserk. She'd felt really good about it at the time. She didn't feel so good about it now.

A major item on Kay's to-do list: *Be more like Sheila.* Right up there with *Get another job before you lose your apartment* and *Never, ever get engaged to the boss,* the latter actually being more like a not-to-do but definitely worth remembering.

"How could I even think of marrying a man who has dogs?" Kay said, fanning her nails to speed the drying. "I mean, how stupid was that?"

"If you'd loved him, you'd have worked it out."

"No way. You know how I feel about animals."

Kay just couldn't help it. She was never so uncomfortable as when a stray dog came bounding toward her or a cat scurried across her path. When she was a kid, her perverted older siblings, Claire and David, had zeroed in on the one thing their timid little sister feared the most—animals—and used them to terrorize her at every opportunity. Intellectually, Kay knew that the worst thing the average dog was likely to do was lick her to death, but she just couldn't reconcile that commonsense point of view with the emotional reaction she had every time she came into contact with anything furry.

"What am I going to do, Sheila? I'm broke. I don't have any money for a lawyer."

"There's always Claire."

Kay was horrified at the very thought. "No. No way."

"She's an attorney. And she'd do it for free. When you're family, you have to do stuff like that—even if you're Claire."

"Maybe I'll just represent myself."

"Against Robert?"

Kay groaned. This situation was getting worse by the minute. What were the odds of both Claire and Robert showing up in the same nightmare?

"You're right," Kay said. "I guess I don't have any choice. I'll talk to her about it tomorrow." Then she squeezed her eyes closed. "Oh, God. This means I'll have to hear the lecture."

"What lecture?"

"The one about how impulsive I am. About how I do stupid things. About how irresponsible it is to be almost thirty years old and not have a real career—"

"You just haven't found your niche yet. Some people take longer to bloom, that's all."

"Well, I'm not doing a lot of blooming as a legal secretary. Why did I let Claire talk me into that? And why did I go to work for Robert, much less get engaged to him?''

''Because he's your family's idea of Mr. Right—which is why you should never listen to your family.''

Kay slumped in her chair, closing her eyes. ''It's going to be horrible, Sheila. By the time he gets finished with me, they're going to take me out back and shoot me.'' She turned to her friend with a plaintive look. ''Will you come to my execution?''

''Stop worrying. It may not be as bad as you think.'' Sheila gave the summons another once-over. ''You know, when it comes right down to it, this is really just a frivolous lawsuit.''

Frivolous lawsuit? Kay felt a glimmer of hope. Frivolous lawsuits usually got thrown out of court, didn't they? She glanced sideways at Sheila. ''Do you think so?''

''Sure. After all, you didn't really hurt the dogs. You just made them…lighter.''

''So you might say this lawsuit is…what do they call it? A mockery of the judicial system?''

''Exactly.''

Kay's mood was improving considerably. ''Then you're telling me Robert could end up embarrassed?''

''Yeah.''

''Humiliated? Disgraced, even?''

''It's possible.''

Kay pondered that for a moment, then decided maybe Sheila was right. No judge would ever take this lawsuit seriously. If Robert insisted on going through with it, he was going to end up looking like a fool, and she'd walk away with her head held high.

Kay settled back in her chair with a sigh of relief. She held out her nails and was pleased to see that the Peony

Pink was still intact.

Maybe everything was going to work out after all.

"THREE THOUSAND DOLLARS? *Three thousand dollars?*"

With the *whap* of the judge's gavel still ringing in Kay's ears, she turned her astonished gaze to the plaintiff's table. Right on cue, Robert gave her a snide little victory smile, and it was all she could do not to cross the courtroom and slap it right off his face.

She spun around to face Claire. "Claire! *Do* something!"

"It's over," Claire muttered, clicking her briefcase shut. "Now let's get out of here before you embarrass me even more than you already have."

Kay followed her sister into the hall of the courthouse. "But three thousand dollars? Just because I got his dogs a stinking haircut?"

"All he had to prove is loss of income as a result of what you did. Without hair on his dogs, he says he can't show them, sell puppies, collect stud fees—"

"But it'll grow back!"

"The judge bought it. That's all that matters."

"I was sure you'd beat him, Claire. I was sure—"

Claire screeched to a halt and spun around, meeting Kay nearly nose-to-nose. "I wasn't prepared. And do you know why I wasn't prepared? Because you didn't bother to tell me the extent to which you desecrated those dogs. I had to find out when the photos were passed around the courtroom!"

Kay shrank away a little and shrugged. "I really didn't think it was any big deal."

"No big deal? You had that grooming service shave Up You into one of the dogs' coats. Why did you do that?"

"It was supposed to be Up Yours. They ran out of dog."

Claire shook her head. "You've got to learn to control that manic streak. It makes people think you're unhinged."

"He cheated on me! It was a perfectly normal reaction—"

"Perfectly normal?" Claire gaped at her with disbelief. "Perfectly normal people yell a little, or throw a place setting of china across the room. They don't pay someone to fire up a small appliance and create graffiti on dogs!"

"Okay, okay." Kay held up her palms. "It was stupid. I was wrong. I should have known Robert would come unglued. I just never thought—"

"That's right. You never think."

Kay stared down at the floor, withering under Claire's blistering gaze.

"You know, Kay, I was beginning to think you'd got yourself together. You finally got a marginal amount of education, a decent-paying job—"

"I never wanted to be a legal secretary in the first place. That was your idea."

"So what would you have done if you hadn't gone to secretarial school? Stayed a waitress the rest of your life? Or maybe you'd have gone back to New York to resume your promising career as an actress? Or returned to your brilliant occupation as a telephone solicitor? Or—God forbid—gone back to that tacky public relations firm."

"Promos-R-Us is *not* tacky."

"Their clients are used car salesmen and exotic dancers!"

Well, okay. So it was tacky. Kay shrugged. "I was just looking for my niche. That's all."

"Niche, my fanny. You *are* looking for another legal secretarial job, aren't you?"

"Yes, Claire. I'm looking."

"Thank God. I was afraid you were going to run away and join the circus."

Kay hated this. She felt her sister's disapproval the same way she'd always felt her mother's. And she knew it was because Claire had turned *into* her mother—a no-nonsense professional woman who put her law career above all else and had little patience for anyone who chose otherwise. All her life Kay had stood on the perimeter of her family, a wandering black sheep beside a snow-white herd of overachievers.

"Excuse me, Kay. I wonder if you have a moment?"

Kay turned to see Robert standing behind her, and her blood pressure skyrocketed. His ultrapolite tone didn't fool her for a minute. "Look, Robert, if you've come to collect your money, forget it. I don't have three thousand dollars."

"Yes, I assumed you'd be a little strapped for cash."

"I wouldn't be 'strapped for cash' if you hadn't black-balled me to every law firm I've applied to!"

"Unemployment is up, Kay. You can hardly blame your unsuccessful job search on me."

That really ticked Kay off. Her "unsuccessful job search" had nothing to do with the availability of jobs. After all, McKinney, Texas, was only a short drive down I-75 from the suburbs of Dallas, where business was booming. She'd gotten interviews for several legal secretarial jobs in the past month, and they'd all seemed interested in hiring her—until they'd checked her references.

"You're blackballing me," Kay repeated. "And if I could prove it, you'd be the one with a lawsuit on your hands!"

To Kay's disgust, Robert merely smiled. "I'll tell you what. Why don't you just forget the money? You don't owe me a dime."

Kay blinked. "Excuse me?"

"You heard me. Forget the three thousand. I'll tell the court it's paid in full."

Kay stared at him, dumbfounded. What was it about this man that scrambled her brain? He'd dragged her through a civil court case, whining about his shaved dogs, and now he says "never mind"?

Claire took a menacing step forward. "What's the catch?"

"No catch, really." He turned to Kay. "All you have to do is agree to perform a hundred hours of volunteer work."

Volunteer work? Now Kay was completely befuddled. Robert's tragically advanced case of ingrown eyeballs made him about as philanthropic as Midas. Sure, he contributed to charities, but only for the professional visibility it afforded him. So why would he trade three thousand dollars for a hundred hours of her time?

"That's it?" Kay said warily. "That's all you want me to do?"

"That's all. One hundred hours of volunteer work—" he paused, "—at the Westwood Animal Shelter."

Kay stared at him, dumbfounded. He might as well have asked her to hang a halibut around her neck and dive into a shark tank. "An animal shelter? You want me to volunteer at an *animal shelter?*"

Claire clamped her hand onto Kay's arm and hauled her backward. "Excuse me," she told Robert as she dragged Kay away. "I have to confer with my client."

Claire pulled her around a corner. Kay shook loose and rubbed her arm. "For crying out loud, Claire! What are you—"

"Take the deal."

"What?"

"You heard me. You're broke. Hollinger says he'll forget the three grand. All you have to do is smile pretty and pet a few puppies. How hard can that be?"

"You know how I feel about animals! I can't go to a place like that!"

"Will you grow up? You're not six years old anymore. The big bad doggies won't get you."

Kay knew her petophobia was irrational, but so was a fear of heights, and nobody made fun of that. Everybody thought you were cold, intolerant or just plain snooty if you didn't rush up to pet a puppy, or let a cat jump onto your lap. And Claire had a lot of nerve giving her a hard time about it, since she and David, at the height of their sibling nastiness, had gone out of their way to turn her aversion into a full-fledged fear. That childhood fear had been tempered somewhat by the rationality of adulthood, but it had never really gone away.

"I can't do it, Claire. Anything but that."

"Look. All you have to do is dress professionally and tell them you have secretarial experience. They'll put you at the front desk and you won't have to get near an animal."

"No. They'd still be too close for comfort."

Claire rolled her eyes. "Will you wake up? Robert is offering you an easy way out."

"Easy for you, maybe. You don't hyperventilate when you flip past a *Lassie* rerun."

Claire put on her I've-had-enough look—the one that made her lips crinkle and her eyes turn into little slits. "It's just a hundred hours, Kay. A lousy hundred hours, and Robert will be out of your life for good. Now, is that really such a big deal?"

Kay expelled a long, weary breath. For the first time since she'd left Robert, she truly regretted flushing her three-carat diamond engagement ring. "Do you really think they'd let me do clerical stuff?"

"Why not? Somebody has to."

Kay tried to look at the situation logically. A clerical job. She could handle that, couldn't she? The cats and dogs would be caged, of course, so it wasn't as if they'd be slobbering all over her. And if she lived up to her end of the bargain, she'd never have to see Robert again.

"Okay," she said finally. "I'll do it."

"Wise decision." Claire grabbed her by the arm again and led her back around the corner. "And keep up that disgusted expression. Let him think he's really getting to you, or he might make it two hundred hours."

Robert leaned against the banister at the head of the stairs, his arms folded across his chest with feigned nonchalance. Maintaining the disgust as Claire requested was hardly an effort.

"Okay, Hollinger," Claire said. "You've got a deal."

"Wonderful!" Robert said, his smile as phony as the caps on his teeth. "I'll phone Dr. Forester at the shelter. He'll be thrilled to have a new volunteer. And since you're such an animal lover, I know the two of you will get along famously."

Kay held up a finger in warning. "Hold on, Robert. I want to see it in writing. I don't want you coming back later and telling me I still owe you money."

"Why, of course. It will be a legal agreement. I'll have my secretary draw up the papers."

"If she can stay out of your pants long enough."

Robert's jaw tightened. Kay knew it had taken him about fifteen minutes to fill her job, and his bed, with a certain little brunette.

"Jealousy is an ugly thing, Kay."

"No, Robert. A forty-year-old man having sex in his

office with a woman young enough to be his daughter—*that's* ugly.''

Robert's eyes took on a nasty glare, and she could see how badly he wanted to bite back. But, as usual, he was the picture of self-control. She knew he'd never let a little thing like an actual emotion cloud his thinking. Instead, he took a single deep breath, stood up tall and tugged on his lapels in a gesture of dismissal. ''I'll send the papers to your office, Claire. I trust you'll handle things from there.''

He turned and strode back across the courthouse lobby. Kay glared at him until the echo of his footsteps faded away.

To think she'd almost married him.

A little over a year ago when she was offered a job at Hollinger & Associates, then found herself being pursued by the big boss himself, it had temporarily disabled her common sense. She'd been blinded by three things: Robert was a successful attorney. He was attractive in an uptight, buttoned-down way. And he was financially secure. In short, Robert Hollinger possessed every attribute she'd been taught, from cradle to adulthood, that you were supposed to look for in a man.

So when she found Robert perusing her legs with far more interest than her resumé, she didn't discourage the attention. They'd started dating, and before she knew it she was reading *Modern Bride* and wondering whether people would snicker if she wore white.

She remembered the moment over dinner at her parents' house when she'd told her family about Robert's proposal. Her father dropped his glass of Scotch, her mother's eyebrows shot up as high as her recent face-lift would allow, and Claire nearly choked to death on an oyster. Then all three of them did in unison something she'd never seen before: they smiled at her. Kay smiled back, and for the first time in forever, she felt like part of the family.

Still, the closer she came to walking down the aisle, the more a warning buzzed around inside her head like a mosquito she couldn't swat away. *But do you love him?*

She'd asked herself that question more than once in the past several months. Too bad she'd never answered it. Then one Tuesday evening it had slipped Robert's mind that he was engaged, and the answer to her question became very clear indeed.

"Listen to me," Claire warned. "Until this thing is over, you've got to stop rattling Robert's cage. I said give him a dirty look, not emasculate him. You're lucky he didn't take back the offer."

"Lucky?" Kay slumped against the banister. She felt like a paratrooper about to be dropped behind enemy lines. The goal was survival. One hundred hours, and it would all be over with.

One hundred hours. It sounded like a lifetime.

"DOC, WE'VE got a problem. Get over here *now*."

Dr. Matt Forester dropped the phone and hurried out the front door of his veterinary clinic, a turn-of-the-century Victorian house on a quiet, tree-shaded street in McKinney, Texas. He leaped directly from the porch to the yard and ran halfway to the sidewalk before the screen door slapped shut behind him. Buddy, a little brown dog who was part terrier, part beagle and part a lot of other things, galloped at his heels.

They dodged a kid on a bicycle and an elderly couple out for a late-afternoon walk as they ran toward the prairie-style house next door, which had been renovated to become the Westwood Animal Shelter two years before. Hazel Willoughby, the seventy-two-year-old manager of the shelter, ruled the place with an iron fist, and Matt knew if there was a problem she couldn't handle he'd better move fast.

Matt skidded through the front door into the ex-living room of the house, which now served as a reception area. A redheaded teenage girl huddled against the far wall, staring down at something on the gray tile floor behind the counter. Hazel held out a pair of heavy leather gloves.

"I'm getting too old for this, Doc. He's all yours."

Matt took the gloves and moved slowly around the counter, his curiosity turning to astonishment as he came face-to-face with the biggest, baddest orange tomcat he'd ever seen.

Hazel peered over the counter. "I thought I'd give you a shot at him before I called the SWAT team."

"SWAT team? Are you kidding? Tear gas and sharp-shooters would only make him madder." Matt pulled on the gloves. "Can somebody tell me why this kitty's so cranky?"

"He's a stray," the redheaded girl said. "He was running loose in my apartment complex. So I put some tuna fish in a carrier and sort of caught him…"

"May I ask why you let him out?"

"Well, he hated the carrier, and he was making a terrible noise, so I thought if I opened the door…"

"Good move. Freedom has done wonders for his disposition." Matt took a step toward the cat, who spat ferociously and planted his rear end even deeper into the corner he'd commandeered.

He crouched down closer to the cat's eye level. "Hazel?"

"Right behind you, Doc."

"Open the carrier. Slowly."

Matt edged forward, hoping to close in on the cat before

he made a run for it, but when the carrier door squeaked open he took off. As he streaked past, Matt lunged sideways and grabbed him around the middle with both gloved hands. The cat scrambled madly, his claws scraping against the tile floor, but Matt dragged him backward with one hand beneath his stomach and the other holding the scruff of his neck.

Hazel turned the carrier on end and wisely backed away. Matt lowered the spitting cat rear end first, but on the way in he managed to hook a hind claw on the edge of the carrier, pushed himself up and swatted Matt across the face. Matt gritted his teeth against the pain, unhooked the cat's hind claw, then lowered him all the way in. He clanged the door shut and latched it, then tipped the carrier back down to the floor.

The redheaded girl took a tentative step forward, a stunned expression on her face. "Oh! I can't believe you picked him up like that! He scratched you and everything!"

Matt yanked off the gloves. He touched his fingertips to his face and saw blood. His ex-wife was right. He should have gone to medical school. He'd be making three times the money and playing golf on Wednesday afternoons. And right now that sounded pretty good.

"I knew I brought him to the right place," the girl gushed. "I couldn't bear the thought of taking him to the pound. He's so nasty I just knew they'd put him to sleep. But you don't do that here...do you?"

"No," he told the girl resignedly. "We try to find homes for all of them."

He picked up the carrier and turned to the reception desk where Hazel now sat, a cigarette dangling between her lips.

"Hazel? A name, please?"

She lit the cigarette, took a long drag and blew out the smoke. "Clyde."

"Clyde?"

"Yeah. Bonnie and Clyde kicked up a lot of ruckus before they got caught, just like this cat here."

Matt maneuvered the cat into an isolation cage, then washed his wound with antiseptic soap. He went to the fridge and shoved aside two bottles of serum and a urine sample before locating the six-pack he was after. He popped a top, took a long swallow, then carried the can out to the back porch.

The hazy brightness of the afternoon had settled into evening, knocking only a few degrees off the July heat. In true Texas style, they'd already had several triple-digit-temperature days, and undoubtedly there were more to come. Matt sat down on the step beside Hazel, who was finishing off another cigarette.

"Get your face cleaned up?" she asked him. "God knows where that cat's been."

"Yeah." Matt tipped up the beer can and took another swallow. "Ungrateful little cuss. I offer him free room and board and he gives me another set of character lines."

"He'll come around."

"I hope I live that long."

Hazel eyed Matt carefully. "It's one more deadbeat dad off the street. That's the point, isn't it?"

"Yeah. I guess it is."

Hazel dropped her cigarette on the step and ground it out with her shoe. "You don't seem real perky, Doc. What's up?"

Matt drained the rest of the beer in a single, long chug, then set it on the step beside him. "The utility bill came today."

"Comes every month."

"Up to now I've been able to pay it."

For a moment Matt felt a tightness in his stomach, followed by the same wave of nausea that passed over him every time he looked at an overdue bill or took in one more animal he might not be able to feed.

"I don't know why you're worried, Doc. With the grant from the Dorland Group—"

"No," Matt said, holding up his palm. "I don't want to talk about that."

"But it's a sure thing."

"Only if I do what Hollinger wants me to. And I'm not so sure that's a good idea."

"What? Letting his ex-fiancée come here to volunteer in exchange for twenty-five thousand dollars? Sounds like a deal to me."

Matt winced at Hazel's bluntness. Maybe it was because she'd made it sound exactly like what it was—a bribe.

Robert Hollinger was chairman of the selection committee for the Dorland Group, a combination of several law firms that pooled their resources to offer grants to nonprofit organizations. Every year they chose one deserving charity and granted it twenty-five thousand dollars. Matt hadn't thought he had a prayer of getting the grant, but he'd applied for it anyway, hoping for a miracle.

Then three days ago, to his complete surprise, he got a call from Hollinger. After a little small talk, he told Matt that he'd recently broken off his engagement with his fiancée, Kay Ramsey. He'd done it in the kindest way possible, of course, but instead of taking it like an adult, she'd sought revenge against him by ravaging his poor, helpless cocker spaniels. To hear Hollinger tell it, she was the lowest of the low—a confirmed animal hater—and Lizzie Borden with her ax couldn't have done more damage to his dogs than she'd arranged to have done with a pair of clippers.

He'd brought a lawsuit against her and won, but in lieu of the monetary damages, he asked Matt, would it be possible for Kay to come to his shelter and volunteer a hundred hours as restitution? At first it all sounded very simple, but as they continued to talk, it became clear that Hollinger's goal wasn't restitution. It was revenge. And it dawned on Matt that if he carried out that revenge, the Dorland Grant was as good as his.

Matt knew he should have called a halt to the conversation as soon as saw where it was heading, but Hollinger kept telling him how impressed he was with his grant application, and what a wonderful community resource the shelter was, and how it would be a shame for it to go under because of lack of financing. He kept repeating that twenty-five-thousand-dollar figure, with his glass-smooth tone and seamless persuasion making it seem as if they were just two old buddies doing each other a favor. By the time it was all over, Matt had agreed to oversee the hard-labor restitution of Hollinger's wayward ex-fiancée, and Hollinger had agreed to use his influence with the committee to ensure Matt got the grant.

"Plenty of other organizations have applied for that grant," Matt told Hazel. "And Hollinger's swaying the outcome."

Hazel made a scoffing noise. "You deserve it as much as anyone, so what's the problem? How do you think most organizations get their funding? By knowing people in high places. One hand washes the other. It's done every day."

But Matt didn't like being the one doing it. Still, it was beginning to look as if the Dorland Grant was his only hope to keep the shelter running when just about everything else in his life had fallen apart. Lately he'd found himself dwelling on the words his ex-wife had tossed at him as she walked out the door for the last time: *Good luck finding another woman who'll put up with all this.*

He lay awake nights sometimes thinking about that as he watched his situation go from bad to worse. As if the expenses of the shelter hadn't been enough, his ex-wife had come out on the winning end of a divorce decree that had stripped him naked. So he'd moved into the second floor above his clinic to keep from paying rent, telling himself it was just temporary. That had been a year and a half ago.

"Think about it, Doc," Hazel said. "We need you." She nodded back over her shoulder. "They need you."

No matter how bad things got, that's what always brought him back around. He was the only thing standing between thirty-some animals and the mean streets, and he couldn't quit now.

"Don't worry, Hazel. I'll do whatever I have to do to make sure the doors stay open."

And in spite of the bills he couldn't pay, the supplies he couldn't buy and the undomesticated tomcats who kept showing up on his doorstep, he meant every word of it.

Even if it meant dealing with Kay Ramsey.

THE FIRST Saturday morning after she made the deal with Robert, Kay stood in the doorway of the Cat Room of the Westwood Animal Shelter, wishing she'd followed her instincts. She should have run screaming from the premises the moment the old lady who ran the place said "cat," but here she was, face-to-face with her worst nightmare: a room full of scary, creepy, menacing felines who, unfortunately, didn't seem to be nearly as afraid of her as she was of them. One or two she might have been able to take. But twenty?

And planted right in the middle of the cat convention was Hazel Willoughby, the geriatric, polyester-clad manager of the Westwood Animal Shelter, holding out the most vile utensil Kay had ever seen—a pink plastic pooper-scooper.

"As I told you before," Kay said, trying to sound level-headed and reasonable, "I have secretarial experience. It seems a shame to waste my expertise—"

"Nope. You'll do what needs doing. And the cat boxes need doing."

No! This can't be happening!

She'd followed Claire's advice to the letter. From her faux gold earrings to her mock leather pumps, Kay was a budget-controlled picture of polished professionalism. Her skirt and blouse screamed *desk job,* but to her dismay, Hazel seemed to have other ideas. Not only did she expect Kay to *enter* the Cat Room, she actually expected her to *clean up* after its occupants. And while she was wearing panty hose, no less.

Hazel continued to hold out the pink utensil, and Kay continued to pretend it didn't exist. "I actually went to secretarial school, you know. Legal secretarial school. I can type, answer phones—"

"Can't do much poop-scooping from the front desk."

"But you don't understand—"

"The longer you piddle around," the woman warned, "the more there'll be to clean up."

Kay didn't doubt that for a moment. As her gaze circled the highly populated Cat Room, a shiver of apprehension trickled down her spine. Most of the animals were roaming free, hunched on carpet-covered perches like vultures, sprawled on the floor or lying on top of one another like piles of dirty laundry. She didn't sweat the sleeping ones. It was the slinking, scurrying, meowing ones that filled her with dread.

Then she glanced at the corner of the room and nearly gasped. A cat that looked like the feline version of a championship wrestler glared at her from—thank God—the confines of his cage. He had orange stripes, a torn ear, muscles like a tiger and an expression of disgust that could peel the paint off walls. An honest-to-goodness nightmare come to life.

Before Kay could fully recover from being stared down by the Godzilla of cats, something furry brushed against her leg. She looked down to see a shifty black feline winding itself around her ankle. She gasped and yanked her foot away, shaking it wildly to dislodge any lingering remnants of cat, then spun around and fled back to the front desk with the old lady in close pursuit.

"Get Dr. Forester over here," Kay said.

Hazel glanced out the window. Kay could see three or four cars still sitting on the street in front of the Westwood Veterinary Clinic, which was housed in a huge Victorian next door.

"Doc's still busy with patients," the old lady said.

"I don't care. I—" Kay stopped, then took a deep, calming breath. "Please. I have to see him *right now*."

If the old lady said no again, it would leave her with only one option: to fall on her knees and beg for mercy. If that's what it took to stay out of that seething sea of felines, she'd do it.

Fortunately, though, the old lady gave up the fight and picked up the phone. After a quick, muffled conversation, she hung up, sneered a little in Kay's general direction, then sat down in a chair behind the counter and stuck her nose into a crossword puzzle book. A wicked-looking Siamese cat jumped into her lap, and she stroked him absentmindedly.

Kay breathed a momentary sigh of relief. She glanced around as she waited, taking in every nuance of the rather unappealing decor. The shelter consisted of a partially renovated, oddly rearranged 1920s prairie-style house in a neighborhood she generally took pains to avoid. She had a passion for older homes, but this place was nothing short of decrepit.

Cheap orange plastic chairs lined the wall of the reception area, which had once been a living room, and beyond that she'd seen a kitchen performing double-duty as a storeroom. The Cat Room had once been a big bedroom, as had the Dog Room. She didn't even want to think about what the other rooms might contain.

Surely the veterinarian in charge of this place would be easier to deal with than the old lady. He was probably some grandfatherly type—she could bat her eyelashes at him and make him feel sorry for her. That kind of ruse really wasn't her style, but it would certainly do in a pinch.

Finally Kay heard footsteps on the porch. She composed herself by squaring her shoulders and smoothing her skirt with her palms. But when the door opened, she took one look at the man who came inside and just about fell off her high heels.

This was Dr. Matt Forester?

2

KAY HAD ASSUMED all veterinarians must be wizened old men with hair growing out of their ears and warts on their noses. But the man who'd just come through the door wasn't in danger of becoming wizened for at least another forty years, and everything on him was growing precisely where and how it was supposed to.

He strode toward the desk. "Hazel? I'm up to my eyeballs over there. What's the crisis?"

The old lady nodded toward Kay. "Meet your new volunteer, Doc."

He turned around, and when he saw Kay he grinned broadly, awakening a whole legion of laugh lines that were proof positive he smiled often. With a quick up-and-down shift of her eyes she took in all six highly attractive feet of him, from his long, jeans-clad legs to his narrow waist, then upward to a faded T-shirt stretched across a broad chest and a powerful pair of shoulders. His dark brown eyes were warm and compelling, drawing her in, and she felt her conviction slipping away. Then she mentally slapped herself back to reality. *Hey, you. He's an animal doctor. A-ni-mal. Remember?*

He stepped toward her, extending his hand. "Hi. I'm Matt Forester. And you're...?"

"Kay Ramsey," Hazel said.

His grin evaporated like a drop of rain on a parched desert floor. Not only did he stop short, he actually took a step backward, his hand falling to his side. He stared at her as if she were a bug under a magnifying glass, and a particularly dangerous species at that.

"Robert Hollinger sent you," he said.

Kay cringed at the mere mention of Robert's name. "Yes."

He looked back at Hazel, who shrugged and turned away, as if washing her hands of the whole issue. She grabbed a pack of cigarettes from the counter. "I'm going out to the back porch for a minute, Doc. Let me know when the coast is clear."

Kay watched the woman leave, and a few seconds later the back screen door slapped shut. Turning, she said, "Look, I don't know what Robert told you, but—"

"He told me you're a true animal lover who can't wait to devote some spare time to a very worthwhile cause."

She detected a hint of challenge in his words, as if daring her to disagree. Kay eyed him warily. Robert couldn't possibly have been discreet enough to tell this man she was an actual volunteer. Maybe it was best to leave that issue untouched.

"Yes. Well." She cleared her throat and tried to look businesslike. "Dr. Forester. I know you must be a reasonable man."

"I'd like to think so."

"Good. Then maybe we won't have a problem after all." She took a few casual steps toward him. He leaned a strong, tanned forearm against the counter and appeared to give her his undivided attention. At the same time, though, he raised a single eyebrow, as if warning her he was long on deduction and short on patience.

"You see, I have secretarial experience. So when it comes to job assignments, do you really think I should be relegated to the back room doing God knows what, when

I could—" Kay stopped short, warning herself not to get carried away. No emotion. Just facts. "I'm sure you can see that the front desk would be a far more logical place for me to work."

"Hazel handles the front desk."

"Yes. I can see that. But I know I could be useful in some sort of clerical function."

"Clerical, huh? Have you ever answered phones?"

"Yes. Of course."

"Greeted people?"

"Certainly."

"Filled out a form with a cat sitting on top of it?"

Kay recoiled a little and crinkled her nose. "Well, not exactly—"

"Given a puppy a bottle?"

"God, no. What has that got to do with—"

"Extracted a kitten from a three-year-old kid who's squeezing the stuffing out of it?"

"Of course not!"

"Well, Hazel can do all those things. Simultaneously. That's why I put her at the front desk and let her run the place. And if she tells you to scrub the floor with a toothbrush and floss between the tiles, that's what I expect you to do."

This was getting her nowhere.

She contemplated telling Matt the truth—that she had this irrational yet very real aversion to animals—but she figured he'd do the same thing everyone else always did. He'd tell her how silly her fear was and shove the animals on her, anyway. She couldn't imagine anyone insisting that a person who was afraid of heights climb a mountain, but nobody seemed to think twice about letting Fluffy jump onto her lap whether she wanted her there or not. Fluffy wasn't like other cats, you see. Surely Kay wouldn't be afraid of *her*. And considering the number of Fluffys in the vicinity right now, she decided maybe she should keep the truth to herself.

In desperation, Kay held out her arms and nodded down at her skirt and blouse. "I'm afraid cleaning up after the cats is really out of the question. As you can see, I'm hardly dressed for that kind of work."

"I've got a pair of overalls in the back. You're welcome to them."

Kay slapped her arms back against her sides. "You have *got* to be joking."

"I never joke about cat-box maintenance."

All at once Kay heard a commotion on the front porch. The door burst open and two teenaged girls rushed in, giggling wildly, dragging behind them two dogs on leashes. Kay watched in horror as one of the dogs, a thousand-pound black monster, took a flying leap onto one of the orange plastic chairs. It teetered for a moment, then crashed to the floor. The dog leaped away, yanking the leash out of the girl's hand, then galloped across the room and sideswiped a coatrack. Matt managed to catch it before it hit the floor, at the same time lunging for the dog's collar. He missed.

Then the beast headed for Kay.

She saw him coming, but getting out of his way was like getting out of the path of an approaching tornado. He planted his paws against her shoulders, pinned her against the wall and lashed his sloppy dog tongue across her face. In those few seconds, Kay thought surely she'd died and gone to hell.

"Rambo!"

Matt hurried over, grabbed the dog by the collar and hauled him away from Kay. Kay flattened herself against the wall, gaping in terror as the hound from hell lunged left and right, trying to free himself from Matt's grip.

"Girls?" Matt said. "Use the back door, remember?"

"Oops," one of the girls said, clearly chagrined. "Sorry, Dr. Forester." She picked up the leash and dragged the dog toward the Dog Room, the other girl following close behind. Once the girls disappeared from sight, Kay heard their giggles explode all over again.

"And latch the cage doors this time!" Then he turned to Kay. "My volunteer dog-walkers." He smiled. "Your new co-workers."

Kay stood frozen for a moment, then slowly peeled herself off the wall, wiping dog spit from her face at the same time. "That's it. I'm outta here."

She brushed past Matt and headed to the front door, intending to clear out of this animal-ridden loony bin and never look back. She yanked the door open.

"So," Matt said, "I guess you've decided you're going to pay Robert the three thousand after all."

Kay froze. She closed the door with a gentle click, then turned around slowly. "So he *did* tell you."

"Oh, yeah. Got a copy of the contract right here."

Matt reached over the counter and grabbed a red folder from a stacker. He opened it and traced his finger down a legal-size sheet of paper. "Yeah. Here it is. D-Day is the third Friday in September. At that point either you've finished working a hundred hours, or you owe Robert three thousand bucks."

Kay's cheeks flushed with embarrassment. "I suppose Robert told you *why* I owe him the three thousand dollars, too?"

"Yeah, I think he did. As I remember, it has something to do with shaved dogs and a court judgment." He looked back down at the contract. "It says here that you're going to volunteer an hour every day after work, and at least four hours on the weekend. Is that correct?''

"Yes," Kay said, squeezing her eyes closed. "That's correct."

The phone rang. Hazel appeared from nowhere to pick it up. She listened for a moment, then looked up at Matt. "A schnauzer just threw up in your waiting room."

Matt sighed, then turned back to Kay with a no-nonsense expression. "Look, Kay. I'd like to stay and chat, but I have a waiting room full of patients I need to clear out sometime before midnight. So here's the deal. Feel free to frown and whine and mope all you want to. But let me remind you that I have final say-so on whether you've fulfilled your end of the bargain with Robert." He leaned toward her and dropped his voice. "And I *hate* bad attitudes."

He fixed his gaze on hers, issuing a cool assurance that he meant what he said. Then he turned and left the shelter, closing the door behind him with a solid *thunk*. Kay looked out the window and watched him jog back to the clinic, a hundred nasty retorts welling up inside her mind. But the second she voiced any of them she had no doubt he'd extend her sentence until she was picking up cat poop and Social Security checks at the same time.

She couldn't believe she'd assumed he'd be more reasonable than the old lady. What had she been thinking? He was a friend of Robert's, and obviously an animal lover. That should have been all the advance warning she needed.

It was his face that had thrown her—that insidiously warm, deceptively open face he'd shown her when he first walked in, with a pair of dark brown eyes you could lose yourself in and a smile that could melt a polar ice cap. But Matt Forester and Robert Hollinger shared a single master plan where she was concerned—to make her suffer—and she intended never to forget that again.

Like a condemned prisoner heading to the gallows, she turned around to face the reception desk. Hazel sat behind it, her arms folded across her chest, a deadpan expression on her weathered face. The pooper-scooper lay on the counter between them.

Kay thought of the Cat Room again, and her heart thumped. She wished she had a choice, but Matt had systematically relieved her of that possibility. She caught the old lady's eye and swallowed hard, barely able to get the words out.

"Dr. Forester said something about...overalls?"

FOUR HOURS LATER Matt escorted his last patient out the door, glad the Saturday rush was over. He peered out the window toward the shelter next door. Kay's car was still parked out front.

When Hazel had called him over to the shelter this morning he'd expected a crisis—a plumbing leak, a rabid dog or maybe just a cat who'd delivered a record number of kittens. Or, God forbid, another Clyde. Instead, all he'd seen was a pretty little blonde standing in the reception area, dressed in a beige skirt and silk blouse, with soft, china-blue eyes and the sweetest, most inviting lips he'd ever seen. All at once he'd had this wild, fleeting thought that maybe his luck had changed, and he'd been sent a beautiful blond angel to help him wade through his mountain of problems.

But it had occurred to him that her expression was hardly angelic. In fact, he'd seen sweeter expressions on junkyard dogs. Then Hazel had told him she was the woman sent here by Robert Hollinger, and from what Hollinger had said about her, Matt knew that the words *angel* and *Kay Ramsey* would never occur in the same thought again.

Buddy trotted over and bumped his nose against Matt's knee. Matt scratched him behind the ears and gave his ribs a solid pat.

"What do you say, Buddy? Think we ought to go over there and see if she survived?"

Together they left the clinic and trotted across the yard to the shelter. As they climbed the steps to the porch, the front door opened and Kay came out.

As soon as she saw Matt she froze, then turned away with a flustered expression and pulled the door closed behind her. Her blond hair was mussed and her expression tired and ragged. Her clothes were rumpled in a way that told him she'd taken his advice and stuffed herself into his overalls. Glancing down, he saw a single slender run in her right stocking traveling from her ankle to her knee, a minor imperfection that did nothing to detract from her legs. She could wear combat boots and those legs would still look great.

Matt stepped aside and allowed her to come down the steps. "So you stayed," he said. "Good for you."

"Don't go making something noble out of this. Contractually I have no choice, remember?"

She tiptoed across the gravel drive in her heels. When she reached her car she slapped her purse on top of the hood and started digging for her keys. The way she was going at it, first pulling out a pack of tissues, then a paperback book, then a handful of pens and pencils, Matt could tell this was going to be a protracted search.

"Need some help?" he asked, walking toward her car. "A bigger keychain? A smaller purse? A quick hotwire?"

"I can manage, thank you."

She finally located her keys, yanked them out of her purse, then crammed the other stuff back in. "Now, if you'll excuse me, I'd just like to go home and detoxify myself."

"Kay. One more thing." He looked left and right, as if checking for witnesses, then leaned toward her and lowered his voice. "Did you really have those dogs shaved?"

"You bet I did." She raised an eyebrow. "Why are you asking? Are you wondering if you should go inside and lock up all the clippers?"

"Believe me, Kay, you running amok with a pair of clippers is the least of my worries. There's not an animal in that place that wouldn't have its appearance improved by shaving."

Kay slid into the car seat, shut the door, then looked back at him through the open window. "Well, then, I may end up liking it here after all. This seems to be the only place I could give a dog a haircut and not get slapped with a lawsuit."

As she backed out of the driveway and disappeared down the street, Matt couldn't help smiling. Exactly who was she mad at—him, or Hollinger? He decided maybe it was a little of both.

He went into the shelter and found Hazel sitting behind the desk filling out paperwork. Beside her sat a little brown-haired girl, maybe six years old. A calico kitten lounged in her lap, and she petted her with slow, reverent strokes. A man he assumed was her father leaned across the counter, writing a check.

Hazel handed the form to the man for his signature, then turned to the little girl. "Gonna take care of her?"

She nodded and cuddled the kitten. "Uh-huh."

Hazel pointed to Matt. "If she ever gets sick, you need to bring her to Doc here so he can make her better."

The little girl looked up at Matt and smiled. The phone rang, and, as Hazel picked it up, Matt introduced himself to the father. Then he grabbed one of his business cards and gave it to the little girl.

"You keep this," he told her. "If you have any questions about taking care of your kitty, you can call me. Okay?"

The little girl nodded. Her dad beamed.

"Doc," Hazel said. "Phone's for you."

Matt picked up the extension in the kitchen. "This is Matt."

"So how did it go? Did she show?"

Robert Hollinger. He'd know that smug voice anywhere. And he was the last person on earth Matt wanted to speak to.

"Yeah," Matt said. "She showed."

"Good. And what duties was she assigned?"

"I don't know. I think maybe Hazel had her helping out with the cats or something."

"Excellent. I think she hates cats even worse than dogs. I assume her duties were…hygienically related?"

"I think she may have cleaned a few cat boxes."

"Perfect. That's perfect. I know what an imposition it is for you to deal with my charming ex-fiancée. But as I told you before, if you do this favor for me, I can absolutely assure you the Dorland Grant is yours."

"Look, Robert. If your organization offers me that grant, of course I would appreciate it. But that's entirely up to them."

"Come on, Forester. No need to be coy about it. You need money for that shelter, and you need it badly. And it seems like such a small favor for such a large amount of money, doesn't it?"

Matt knew he should call a halt to this whole thing right

now, say thanks but no thanks, and keep his self-respect. Instead he said nothing.

"Maybe I didn't make myself clear enough when we made this deal," Robert said sharply. "I want Kay to do one hundred hours of filthy, hands-on work with the most abominable animals you've got. If she suffers, you get the money. Now, do we understand each other?"

Matt looked out into the reception area. The little girl and her father were leaving. The child cradled the kitten in her arms, then kissed her on top of the head.

"Yes," Matt said. "Perfectly."

"Excellent. I'll be in touch."

The line clicked, and a dial tone droned in Matt's ear. He hung up the phone and went back to the reception desk.

"That was Hollinger, wasn't it?" Hazel asked. "Checking up?"

"Yeah." Matt shook his head. "I just don't feel right about all this."

"Kay Ramsey is an animal hater. Hell of a character flaw, if you ask me. She deserves what she's getting."

But Matt didn't like being the one giving it to her. Like it or not, though, he was stuck with her until the third Friday in September. And shortly after that, the grant would be given to the lucky recipient. If he carried out Hollinger's revenge, he'd be the one pocketing that money. Fortunately, it didn't look as if he was going to have to work very hard to make Kay miserable. She was doing a bang-up job all by herself.

He tried to tell himself he was actually doing a good thing. What was so wrong with having Kay clean up after a few cats if it meant he could keep the shelter on its feet? It was a *good* thing he was doing.

So why did it feel as if he'd made a deal with the devil?

3

KAY EASED THROUGH the door of her apartment building and closed it behind her, sure that her landlady and the other tenants could smell her coming.

Mrs. Dalton, the dumpy but endearing English lady who owned the redbrick 1930s building, had graciously decorated the common areas with her own possessions, including an antique painting of horses and hounds, a grandfather clock that chimed the hour and a blue-on-white Royal Wyndham vase that sat on its own little mahogany table at the foot of the stairs. Kay felt as if she was living with the doting grandmother she'd never had. And then she'd met Sheila, and this place had really begun to feel like home.

She carefully skirted the vase and stepped gingerly across Mrs. Dalton's Oriental rug, hoping there wasn't something noxious still stuck to her shoes. As she climbed the wide oak staircase, she repeated the three-part directive she'd issued herself as she left the shelter: *Go home. Take a shower. Burn your clothes.*

As Kay reached the top of the stairs, she saw a note taped to her door. She pulled it off as she went inside, then tossed it down on the dining-room table. She didn't have to read it to know what it contained: a sweet but pointed suggestion from Mrs. Dalton that perhaps she should pay her rent.

Even though her search for a permanent job had turned

up nothing, she'd found a temporary service that had plenty of jobs available and didn't seem inclined to check her references. They were sending her on her first assignment Monday, a six-week-long stint at Breckenridge, Davis, Hill, Scott & Wooster to fill in for a woman on maternity leave. It would be a few more weeks, though, before she'd have enough money to pay Mrs. Dalton. And she *had* to pay her rent, even if she didn't eat. The last thing she wanted to do was lose this apartment.

For years she'd lived in an ordinary apartment complex, with each unit boasting the individuality of a prison cell. Then she'd graduated from secretarial school and started working for Robert, and the resultant leap in salary had allowed her to escape modern mediocrity and step into sixty-year-old elegance.

From the solid oak floors to the French doors that led to the kitchen, to the tiny waterfalls carved in stone on either side of the fireplace, this place oozed warmth and permanence. But the most attractive quality this apartment building had was the No Pets rule Mrs. Dalton enforced to the letter. Kay had been pleased about that when she moved in. She was positively jubilant about it now.

She headed to the bathroom for that much-needed shower, then treated herself to doing pretty much nothing the rest of the day. When seven o'clock rolled around, Sheila breezed through her front door, a bottle of cheap wine in one hand and a package of microwave popcorn in the other. She tossed the popcorn to Kay, who stuck it in the microwave, then grabbed two wineglasses.

"It starts in three minutes," Sheila said, pouring the wine.

"Isn't Jim coming?"

"Nah. He says he hates those 'dumb soap opera miniseries.'"

"But don't you want to spend the evening together? You two are practically still on your honeymoon."

"And this is how you maintain marital harmony. If he doesn't have to sit through this show now, we won't have to fight about it later."

That made sense to Kay. She mentally moved Be more like Sheila to the *top* of her to-do list.

A few minutes later the microwave dinged. Kay dumped the popcorn into a bowl and headed for the sofa with Sheila.

"So tell me," Sheila said, setting down the wineglasses. "How was your first day in hell?"

"I wish it had been hell. Hell would have been a relief."

"What happened?"

"Cat poop. That's what happened."

"Cat poop? And you with the animal thing?" She eyed Kay sympathetically. "Are you okay?"

"I'm going to finish the hundred hours, Sheila. No matter what they make me do. If I don't, Robert gets the last laugh, and I'll still owe him three thousand dollars."

"So why did you get the dirty work? I thought you were going to try to do something clerical."

"The veterinarian who runs the place had other ideas. He's even more impossible to deal with than Robert."

"It's a volunteer outfit. Just tell him you're volunteering to do something else."

"I tried that. Believe me. But he wouldn't budge."

"So is he a grumpy old guy, or what?"

"No. He's a grumpy young guy."

Sheila shrugged. "So what's the big deal? You're a woman, he's a man—"

"He's a veterinarian, Sheila. An *animal* doctor. I'm not about to cozy up to a guy like that for any reason."

"So he's ugly."

Kay rolled her eyes. "No. He's not ugly."

Sheila smiled. "Then he's cute."

Kay stared down at her wineglass. *Cute* wasn't exactly the word for Matt. Looking at him, she knew where the phrase *tall, dark and handsome* had come from. And even while she'd glared at him as she left the shelter, she'd had to keep reminding herself she was supposed to be angry. The memory of those deep, dark eyes and that luminous smile stayed with her all the way home. Matt wasn't the self-important, unapproachable kind of handsome Robert was, but a warm, comfortable kind of handsome that made her want to—

Made her want to slap herself for having such thoughts.

"It doesn't matter what Matt Forester looks like," Kay said, picking up the remote. "He's crabby and stubborn and a veterinarian. Enough said."

Sheila's smile widened. "Oooh. He must *really* be gorgeous."

Kay tossed Sheila a look of supreme irritation, then flipped on the TV. Fortunately, the show was starting, so she didn't have to hear another word about animals *or* Matt Forester.

Dirty Little Lies promised to be the miniseries of the decade, a glitzy blend of intrigue, power, corruption, greed, lust, sex and violence—every ingredient necessary for a truly invigorating small-screen experience—and Kay intended to miss an episode only if the country fell under nuclear attack.

Still, for some reason, Kay couldn't keep her brain focused on the show. All she could manage to think about was Matt, a man who spent more time with animals than Noah himself. What was *wrong* with her?

Then, at the first commercial break, Kay heard an unfamiliar jingle that caught her attention. Her eyes sprang open with an interest she never would have had before today. It was a commercial for something called Super Scoop Cat Litter.

According to the TV mom with the blinding-white smile, Super Scoop made ordinary kitty litter as obsolete as eight-track tapes and leisure suits. Instead of forcing you to dig around in crumbly clumps of soggy litter, with Super Scoop you could pick up the nasty stuff with a single swipe. No smell, no mess.

Kay sat up on the edge of the sofa, spellbound. "Sheila! Look at that cat litter! It's unbelievable!"

"You're losing it, Kay."

"Hey, if you'd been through what I'd been through today, you wouldn't say that."

"Don't they use that stuff at the shelter?"

"Nope."

"Why not?"

"I don't know," Kay said. "But you can bet I'm going to ask Dr. Forester."

AT TEN AFTER FIVE on Monday afternoon, Kay rushed out of the bathroom on the fourteenth floor of the Cauthron Building wearing jeans and a T-shirt. She carried her suit on a hanger over her shoulder and her pumps and panty hose in a grocery sack.

She'd hurried around the corner into the elevator lobby before she realized Albert Breckenridge, her temporary boss, was standing there. He eyed her up and down, his troll-like face crinkling with disapproval.

"This is a place of business, Ms. Ramsey."

Kay let an expression of sudden horror spill over her face. "Oh, I'm sorry, Mr. Breckenridge! I could have sworn it was after five o'clock!" She checked her watch for effect, then breathed a phony sigh of relief. "Oh, look! It *is* after five. Gee, for a minute there, I thought I'd messed up."

Her meaning couldn't have been clearer: *After five, my life's my own, you jerk,* but she'd said it so sweetly he couldn't bite back. He merely raised a single eyebrow, and as if deeming her unworthy of further ocular engagement, he turned his nose up and pointedly dismissed her.

Attorneys. Yuck.

Sometimes Kay wondered why she'd ever let Claire talk her into going to legal secretarial school in the first place. Sitting at a desk all day was no fun whatsoever, and then there was the undergarment thing. Had it occurred to her when she started school that she'd have to spend all day every day wearing panty hose, she'd still be on her last job slinging hash.

Twenty minutes later Kay got out of the car at the shelter. She was amazed at how hot the evening sun still felt. Texas summers were always fierce, and this summer had been particularly brutal, with several days over a hundred degrees already. She stuffed her car keys into her pocket and tossed her purse into the trunk of her car and. If she brought it in, she had no doubt that sooner or later it would end up as a leather chew-toy.

She came through the front door expecting to be met with cool air, but instead she was assaulted by even greater heat, along with an indescribably pungent animal smell that seemed to permeate every molecule of air she breathed. Hazel sat behind the counter, fanning herself with a crossword puzzle book.

"Lord, it's hot in here," Kay said.

"Air's out."

"How do you expect me to work in conditions like these?"

"I don't expect you to. I told Doc the minute you hit the door you'd turn right around and hightail it out of here."

The challenge was as clear as if Hazel had drawn a line across the floor and dared Kay to step over it. Kay met the woman's stony stare. "I have no intention of leaving."

Hazel shrugged as if she couldn't have cared less, but Kay knew better. She was sure the old lady wanted her to leave just so she could run back to Matt and tell him what a whiner she was. And the world would pass away to dust before Kay would give her that kind of satisfaction.

"Ouch! Damn it!"

The sharp, angry voice came from down the hall, followed by the clatter of something metal against the hardwood floor.

"Doc's working on the air," Hazel said.

Matt was here? Kay craned her neck around to look down the hall. Sure enough, protruding from a closet that she guessed contained the air unit, she saw a pair of male legs in ragged cutoff jeans. A very *nice* pair of male legs.

"Does he know what he's doing?" Kay asked.

"He'll get it going again. He always does. Now, if you're sure you want to stay—"

"Quite sure."

"Then I have some cat boxes with your name on them."

"Cat boxes? But I just cleaned them out on Saturday!"

Hazel gave Kay a look that could have melted steel. *I don't like you,* that face said. *Not even a little bit.*

Kay heard bells clink against glass, and looked over to see a woman coming into the shelter with a little boy. To Kay's surprise, Hazel got up quickly and greeted them with an actual smile and a heartfelt apology about the heat.

Face it, Kay. It's just you she hates.

When Kay started in on the cat boxes, she had to admit that coming into contact with the cats today wasn't as bad as it had been on Saturday, as long as she did it quickly and kept a watchful eye out for any cat who tried to break ranks and sidle up next to her. A few of them seemed to be a little light on instinct and acted as if she might actually want to pet them. For the most part, though, they seemed to be content doing what cats did best—ignoring any human who wasn't holding a can of cat food.

Kay felt sweat trickle from her temples onto her cheeks and from her underarms down the length of her rib cage. The smell in the room was incredible, and soon she was certain she didn't smell much better herself. But still she worked diligently, because the last thing she wanted was for that old lady to say she hadn't done her job.

After giving the room a thorough cleaning, she went to the supply closet off the Dog Room to get cat food. By six-thirty she'd finished her work, and as she headed out of the room she heard a low rumble, then a steady hum, and a faint breath of cool air wafted over her. The air conditioner. She turned her face up to the vent and closed her eyes, letting the cool air flow over her.

"Better?"

Kay spun around to find Matt leaning against the doorframe, holding a can of pop. Her heart leaped, then settled into a fluttery rhythm, and at the same time her gaze traveled down his body and back up again, a reflexive action she immediately tried to mask by tucking a sweat-soaked strand of hair behind her ear.

"Yes," she said. "Much better."

That was a lie. Even though the air conditioner was doing its job she felt even hotter than before, and she knew it had nothing to do with the temperature in the room.

Sweat and dirt weren't designed to look good on any

human being, but Matt had suspended that particular law of nature. A smear of grease started at his cheekbone and swept downward, mingling with a five o'clock shadow, then disappeared along the sharp angle of his jaw. His thick, dark hair was damp and unruly, the length of it brushing his collar in the back while several errant strands fell across his forehead. His sweat-dampened T-shirt clung to every inch of his muscular torso, allowing her to form a pretty solid mental picture of his anatomy beneath it. He looked handsome and virile and incredibly sexy. She, on the other hand, felt like a gigantic, smelly, humidity-soaked dishrag.

So what? She was here to work. Period. It didn't matter what Matt Forester saw when he looked at her. But even as she told herself that, she wondered if she had black mascara raccoon rings underneath her eyes.

Matt took a sip from the can of cola he held. "Hazel thought you might not want to work with the air being out."

"Well, Hazel was wrong. If I'm scheduled to work, I'll work." *There, you old bat. So much for your opinion.*

Matt nodded toward the kitchen. "There are a few more sodas in the fridge if you're thirsty."

"No thanks. I'm heading home." She brushed past him.

"Kay. Wait."

She turned back. Matt raised his hand and brushed his fingertips across her cheek. Her heart nearly stopped. She froze, meeting his eyes in one of those endless moments that are only seconds long but feel like hours.

"Cat hair," he said, rubbing his fingertips together.

Kay put her hand to her cheek, the spell shattered. She turned back around and headed toward the front desk, her wildly beating heart compounding her frustration. How could she be so attracted to a man so completely wrong for her?

Matt followed her, and when they reached the desk she pulled her folder out of the stacker. "I suppose I need your initials."

"Sure. No problem." Matt reached for a pen and clicked it open, then turned his gaze back up to stare at her skeptically. "Tell me the truth, Kay. You spent most of this time playing with the kittens, didn't you?"

"I did *not* play with the kittens! If I told you I worked an hour, I worked an hour. I would never—"

She saw too late the devilish sparkle in his eye. "Oh, for heaven's sake," she muttered. "Just sign it, okay?"

He complied, but an amused grin still flickered around his mouth. "You know, you've been doing such a great job I'm considering you for a promotion. From cats..."

Kay looked at him with hope.

"...to dogs."

She yanked the form from his hand. "No, thank you. Whoever has that job can keep it." She stuffed the form back into the folder. "Who *does* have that job, anyway?"

"You're looking at him."

"You don't have any other volunteers?"

"They come and go. After a day of dog poop, they usually go." He tossed a wrench into the toolbox that sat on the counter.

"Speaking of poop," Kay said, "I need to talk to you about the cat litter. It's hardly state-of-the-art."

"Not much around here is."

"Well, it seems to me that it would be much more efficient to use that new scoopable stuff, Super Scoop. I saw it on TV Saturday night. It's clean, it's quick—"

"—and it costs a whole lot more."

Kay was ready for that one. "Yes, I assumed it would

be more expensive. But that's because it's a far better product.''

"Of course it is. At twice the price."

"But that old stuff is such a mess! It takes me forever to clean those boxes. If I had Super Scoop, I could get the job done in half the time. Then I could assume some other duties around here. If I'm more productive, it could end up costing you *less*."

In spite of the convoluted thought process that directed her to that conclusion, she lifted her chin resolutely to stand by her logic. Matt, on the other hand, rubbed the back of his neck as if he was feeling the onset of a major headache.

"Well, that's an interesting theory, but I'm afraid there's only one branch of economics I understand. Price tags."

"But Matt—"

"Forget it. It's more money out of my pocket. On the other hand, your generous volunteer effort costs me nothing."

Kay glared at him. "You really are out to make me miserable, aren't you?"

Matt sighed heavily. "I just need the job done, Kay. That's all. And I need to get it done as cheaply as possible."

"It's only a few dollars."

"A few dollars I don't intend to spend."

Kay didn't get it. What was the big deal about a few bucks worth of cat litter? She glowered at him. "Tightwad."

Matt's eyes narrowed dangerously. "Okay. *That* does it! Come here!"

He started back down the hall. When she didn't follow, he backtracked, grabbed her by the arm and hauled her along. He threw open the door to the utility closet to reveal a metal monstrosity held together with duct tape.

"Now you listen to me. I just spent the past two hours in this god-awful heat playing kissy-kissy with that air unit, begging it to stay running until fall, at which time I'll turn the other cheek and start sucking up to the furnace. So right now I'm hot, I'm dead-dog tired and the last thing I want to do is stand here and justify to you or anyone else how I spend my money." He leaned forward with a look in his eyes that said she'd better be paying attention. "So if I hear one more word about Super Scoop, I'm going to put a diaper on every cat in the place, which you'll be required to change the moment you hear a meow. Got it?"

Too shocked to speak, Kay just nodded.

"Good. I'm glad we've cleared that up."

Matt disappeared down the hall and into the kitchen. A few seconds later the back screen door squeaked open, then slammed shut, leaving Kay staring after him in stunned silence.

"Well, all right," she muttered, now that he was safely out of earshot. "You don't have to get snippy about it."

She headed toward the front door, disgusted that she'd be stuck with that yucky litter for ninety-five more hours. Then, as her hand fell against the doorknob, she had a thought. She stopped and turned back, surveying the shelter, as she played an idea over in her mind. Judging from the way Matt had just come unglued, things around here operated on a very short shoestring with no room in the budget for luxuries. What a perfect setup.

She went to her car, patting herself on the back with every step. She could make the call tomorrow, which meant it might only be a matter of days before she'd be dumping that Edsel of cat litters and using the Cadillac brand. And the best part about it was...Matt couldn't *possibly* say no.

AT NINE-THIRTY that night Matt lounged in front of the TV with Buddy sleeping against his leg. He'd watched the opening episode of *Dirty Little Lies* on Saturday night, but tonight it was a chore to pay attention. He found his mind wandering to Kay.

He'd lost it with her over that stupid cat litter—completely lost it. But if there was one subject he was extremely touchy about right now it was his woeful financial position, and Kay had spoken one word too many. With surgical accuracy, she'd managed to locate and push that one button guaranteed to make him crazy—the money button.

He felt as if he were thirteen again, with his mother working two jobs just to put food on the table for a family his father had deserted. Even though Matt had delivered papers before school every morning and done odd jobs for neighbors on the weekends, they'd still barely been able to make ends meet. And when he'd found that stray dog— that busy little dog who wagged his tail like a windshield wiper and knew how to catch a Frisbee—he'd found out they didn't even have enough money for dog food.

His mother took the dog to the pound. Later he'd found out what happened to animals there who didn't have the good fortune to be adopted, and he swore that someday he'd have enough money to take care of stray animals whether he could find them homes or not. He'd realized his dream two years ago when he'd opened the Westwood Animal Shelter. Only now he wasn't sure how long he was going to be able to keep the doors open. By sheer persistence he'd managed to get that air unit running again, but for how long? With the hundred-degree heat they'd been having, if that unit went out completely he'd have to shut the place down.

He'd gone to the bank yesterday to apply for yet another loan, trying to buy some time. But before he'd even put pen to paper on the application, his bank officer reminded him he was nearly two months behind on his mortgage payment, and that had been the end of that.

Then he thought about the Dorland Grant. All he had to do was keep the thing running long enough for Kay to finish her sentence. The grant money would be awarded, he could replace the air unit…

No. He couldn't depend on that money. Kay might never finish the hundred hours. She might get ticked off and decide that paying three grand beat cleaning cat boxes, and then where would he be?

After the show ended, he clicked off the television and went to bed. Buddy jumped on to the end of the mattress, plopped down and dropped his chin against Matt's foot.

Matt turned out the lamp and lay back against the pillow. The darkness seemed to magnify the silence in the big, gloomy house. The sheet beside him felt cool and empty, echoing the loneliness that settled in his mind like a lead weight. As he moved through his busy life it was easy to shove those thoughts aside, but lying here in the darkness he couldn't deny it.

He imagined reaching beside him, slipping his arms around a woman and pulling her against him, her skin soft and silky beneath his hands, her warmth mingling with his. He could smell her hair, hear her gentle breathing, feel her heartbeat.

Then, as if his subconscious mind was trying to fill in the parts of his fantasy his conscious mind left blank, suddenly the woman he imagined wasn't just any woman anymore.

She was Kay.

His eyes sprang open, and for several moments he stared at the shadows of tree branches dancing against the dingy beige walls of his bedroom.

Kay Ramsey? In his bed?

Was he crazy?

4

IT WAS ONLY HER fourth day at the shelter, but already she felt as if she'd done a life sentence. Two more cats had arrived, a chunky gray tabby and a skittish, fragile-looking tortoiseshell, both of whom ate and pooped with the same irritating regularity as the rest of the bunch.

As Kay popped the top off a cat-food can, she peeked out of the room, and saw Matt coming through the front door accompanied by a woman about her own age wearing a long denim dress and a pair of sandals. In her arms was a dog who was probably the ugliest creature Kay had ever seen. He had a dingy white coat and the broad, angular face of a prizefighter, with a squashed-up body and extra folds of skin in all the wrong places. She figured he was at least half bulldog, but the other half was a mystery.

As they went into the Dog Room across the hall, Matt happened to glance toward the Cat Room and spy Kay.

"Kay? Could you come here for a minute?"

At first she pretended she didn't hear him, but when he repeated her name she put the cat food down and walked reluctantly to the Dog Room.

"Kay, this is Becky Green. She's one of my foster moms. Becky, this is Kay Ramsey. She's a new volunteer. She's going to be helping out an hour or so every evening, and a few hours on the weekend, too."

"That's wonderful!" Becky said, smiling at Kay. "It's *such* a pleasure to meet another animal lover."

Matt gave Kay a sidelong glance, and all at once she felt like a spy infiltrating an enemy camp.

Becky nodded down at the dog. "And this is Chester."

Kay looked down at the misbegotten animal, and for the first time she saw something about him that wasn't right. His paw. His right front paw was…missing.

"Good heavens," Kay said. "What happened to him?"

"His paw got caught in a trap," Matt said. "I tried to save it, but by the time he was brought here the infection was too far gone. I had to amputate. Becky kept him while he recuperated. Now it's time for us to find him a home."

"He's a real good dog," Becky said. "He just doesn't look like much. I sure hope someone looks past the leg thing."

But when she and Matt stared down at Chester, their expressions said that neither of them believed that was going to happen. Kay stared at him, too, and for some reason she felt an uncomfortable twinge in her stomach.

Becky leaned down and gave Chester a big hug. "Gotta go, sweetie. Be sure to smile pretty at the people and someone will take you home for sure."

Chester got all excited at the attention and licked Becky with that big, ugly bulldog tongue. Kay turned to Matt, her nose crinkled with distaste. Matt gave her a warning look, but she just couldn't seem to put her expression back on straight.

"Is something wrong, Kay?" Becky said as she came to her feet, mindlessly wiping away dog spit. "You look a little sick."

"No. I'm not sick."

"Are you sure?" Matt's voice held a warning tone. "I think maybe you are sick. In fact, if you don't get to looking better pretty fast I think I'm going to have to send you home."

Kay gave him a drippy-sweet smile. "And miss taking care of my precious kitties? Why, Matt, I'd have to be on my deathbed first."

Matt narrowed his eyes, as if to say, *that can be arranged.*

Becky, though, missed Matt's reaction completely and gave Kay a cheerful grin. "It looks like you feel the same way about cats as I feel about dogs. Matt was lucky to find you."

"Yeah," Matt said, still glaring at Kay. "Lucky me."

After Becky left, Matt gazed at Kay admonishingly. "Kay, do you want everyone to know why you're really here?"

Kay twisted her mouth in frustration. She would have loved to have stuck her nose in the air and say she didn't care, but the truth was that for some reason, she did. She gave him a halfhearted shrug. "Not particularly."

"Then can you at least try to fake it a little? It doesn't have to be an Oscar-winning performance. Just try to keep your face from screaming 'yuck' all the time."

Kay sighed. "Sure, Matt. I guess I can fake anything for a hundred hours—no, wait. Ninety-four."

"What is it with you, anyway? Every time you get near an animal you act like you've been shoved into a leper colony."

The truth was on the tip of her tongue. She wanted to tell him that she didn't actually hate animals, she just had this...well, aversion. But once again she decided it would be wiser to stick with dislike and forego any mention of fear.

"I just don't like animals," she told Matt. "Is that so difficult to understand?"

He smiled. "I'm a veterinarian, Kay. Of course it's difficult to understand."

His tone was joking, but Kay wasn't buying the levity. Deep down, she knew he really meant what he said.

The phone rang. Matt went to the front desk to answer it, Chester hobbling along behind him. Kay headed back to the Cat Room, wishing Matt would stay off the subject of how she felt about animals. She was punctual, she worked hard and she didn't cheat one minute on her time. What more did he want?

A few minutes later, as she was dishing up cat chow, a little tiger-striped kitten put both paws up on the side of his cage and mewed plaintively. Kay eyed him speculatively, then peered around the door. Matt was still on the telephone.

Looking back at the kitten, she had to admit he was kind of cute, like a fuzzy little plush toy. What if she just held him for a minute? She was a whole lot bigger than he was, so what was the worst that could happen?

She watched him for a long time before finally going to the kitten's cage. She opened it up and extracted him, holding him at arm's length, amazed at how he weighed less than nothing. Then she eased him against her chest and stroked his head. The kitten arched against her finger in delight. Then she felt a tiny rumble in his throat and realized he was purring.

"See? Now is that so awful?"

Kay spun around to see Matt at the doorway. In a reflex action she pulled the kitten away from her chest, but not before he hooked his claws into her shirt. Aghast, she pulled on him first one way, then the other, but no matter how much she manipulated the furry little body the kitten refused to let go.

Matt grinned. "Kind of like having a piece of bubble gum stuck to your shoe, isn't it?"

"The little monster's clawing me, for heaven's sake!"

"Yeah, he's a monster, all right. All eight ounces of him."

"Matt! Do something!"

Matt ambled forward, wrapped his hand around the kitten and surveyed the points of attachment. He frowned, as if this was indeed an insurmountable problem. "Gosh, Kay. He's really stuck, isn't he? Would you consider wearing him until he falls asleep?"

"Get this cat off me!"

Matt finally bent to the task, unhooking the kitten's claws from her chest, one by one, *very* slowly. Kay glared at him. "I guess you think this is pretty funny."

"Absolutely not," he said, looking offended. "Kitten attachments are serious business. In fact, if I can't get him loose, we'll have to call 911. They'll bring the jaws of life—"

"Just get him off!"

As Matt returned to his task, Kay shifted awkwardly and tried to look over his shoulder. Instead, though, her gaze wandered compulsively back to his hands—strong, capable, dexterous hands that were hovering way too close to her body for comfort. As he manipulated the kitten's claws, the back of one of his hands brushed lightly across her breast, spurring fantasies about those hands touching her in far more intimate ways.

Finally she closed her eyes in self-defense, not knowing which bothered her more—the cat stuck to her chest, or her inability to stop thinking about Matt's hands as he extracted the cat from her chest.

It seemed like hours before he finally removed the last claw and pulled the kitten away. Kay took two reflexive steps backward, brushing her hands across her T-shirt. "Why wouldn't he let go?"

Matt pulled the kitten against his chest and tickled him under the chin. "Maybe he likes you."

"No. No way. Animals don't like me, especially cats."

"Oh, please! You act like the entire cat population got together at their annual meeting and decided to hate you."

Kay eyed the kitten warily. "I'm not so sure they didn't."

"Oh, come on, Kay," Matt said, flashing her one of his most devastating smiles. "Everyone knows it's no longer cat policy to blackball a human. Now they pretty much leave it up to the discretion of the individual cat."

That smile of his almost made her forget she was standing in a room full of felines. Then she got a whiff of cat poop and it all came back to her. "Look, Matt. As cats go, I'm sure he's very nice. He'll make somebody a wonderful pet someday. Now put him away, will you?"

Matt sighed with resignation and turned to put the kitten back in the cage. But as he pulled the kitten away from his chest, those tiny claws latched onto his shirt. To Kay's delight, the kitten clung to Matt as resolutely as he'd clung to her.

Kay crossed her arms, enjoying every moment of his predicament. "Well, well. Looks like the cat's on the other chest now, doesn't it?"

To her surprise, though, Matt simply reached down, gave each paw a gentle squeeze, and miraculously the kitten was detached. He returned him to the cage, and as Kay stood there with her mouth hanging open, he smiled at her and winked. Then he turned and left the room, whistling nonchalantly as he went.

A FEW DAYS later Kay still hadn't forgiven Matt for using that kitten to deliberately embarrass her. As she grabbed a broom from the supply closet in the Dog Room, she told herself it was a good thing he wasn't around right now. A real good thing. If she had to be subjected to that amused grin of his one more time she'd probably end up slapping it right off his face.

She heard the back door open and close, and turned to see Ashley and Mandy dragging Rambo and another smaller dog back from a walk. After watching the two teenagers for several days now, Kay knew why they'd been assigned the brainless task of dog walking.

After putting the little dog away, Mandy looked out the door toward the front desk. All at once she let out a strangled gasp.

"Oh my God! Ashley! There he is!"

"Where?"

"There! He just came in the front door!"

Ashley stuffed Rambo into his cage and gave the gate a quick bump with her hip to close it. She hurried to stand next to Mandy, whose palm fluttered against her chest as if she were on the verge of cardiac arrest.

"Move over," Ashley whispered. "I want to see."

"Wait! I haven't gotten to look yet!"

As the girls jockeyed for position, Kay's curiosity overtook her. Who in the world were they ogling? She looked past the girls to the front desk, but remained confused. The only person of the opposite sex she saw there was Matt.

Matt?

"Look at that smile!" Ashley let out a little sigh. "Have you ever seen anything so totally awesome in your life?"

"Never. And he's so *mature*."

"He's thirty-two," Ashley said. "I asked Hazel."

Mandy spun around, horrified. "Ash! He's old enough to be our father!"

"Only if he had us when he was really young."

"Never mind." Mandy lifted her chin. "I don't care. I just decided I prefer older men."

"Even if he's divorced?"

"Divorced? No way."

"It's true."

Matt? Divorced? Kay hadn't even considered that. But then, it only made sense. An attractive man like that couldn't possibly make it to age thirty-two without some woman—

Stop it, Kay. You sound like them.

"I'm going to talk to him," Ashley said. "Are you coming?"

Mandy drew back. "Oh, no! I'd just die if he spoke to me!"

Just then Matt turned and saw them at the doorway. He flashed them a brilliant smile and waved. "Hi, girls."

Both girls waved weakly, then ducked around the doorway and clasped each other in an attack of wild teenage euphoria. Ashley repeated her plea that they actually speak to Matt, while Mandy continued to insist that it was absolutely out of the question.

Mandy finally won, dragging Ashley away and coaxing her to get another dog to walk. Kay ducked inside the supply closet until they left, then peered toward the front desk. Matt stood talking to Hazel who, as usual, had a crossword puzzle book in her lap.

Kay might have thought twice about what she was getting ready to do, but because of the kitten incident she didn't even hesitate. She left the Dog Room and walked to the front desk.

"Well, hi there, Kay," Matt said, that amused grin creeping over his face again. "How are things going today? Any more...sticky situations?"

Kay smiled sweetly. "Why, no. Not at all. Things are going well. Thank you very much for asking."

Matt's smile evaporated. Something was up, and he knew it.

"So, Matt," she said, brushing some imaginary dust from the countertop. "Tell me. Whose heart is going to get broken?"

"Excuse me?"

"You can't have them both, you know."

Matt looked befuddled. "What are you talking about?"

"Mandy and Ashley. The hormone twins."

His blank expression never wavered.

"Come on, Matt. Haven't you noticed them staring at you?"

"Staring at me?" He looked down at himself, as if he expected to see catsup on his shirt, or his fly unzipped. "Why would they be staring at me?"

Kay assumed a breathless, besotten teenage voice. "Because they like older, more *mature* men, of course."

It took a moment for light to dawn on Matt, and when it did, an expression of utter disbelief overtook his face. "Oh...you have *got* to be joking."

"Nope. And you'd better be careful. If you smile at those girls again like you did a minute ago, one of them is going to faint dead away. Then you'll end up giving her mouth-to-mouth resuscitation, and before you know it she'll be spray-painting your name on water towers and asking you to the prom."

Matt's pained expression intensified. He was so clueless that for a moment Kay almost felt sorry for him. Then she thought of the kitten incident again and her sympathy vanished.

"I thought you needed to know," she said, dropping her voice dramatically. "I mean, what if some irate father storms through the door toting a shotgun and asks you what your intentions are?"

"Intentions? They're sixteen years old!"

"Precisely! There are laws against that kind of thing!"

Matt had the glazed, wide-eyed look of a deer staring into the headlights of an oncoming truck. Kay couldn't remember the last time she'd had more fun rubbing something in. At the same time there was something endearing about the fact that he hadn't had a clue those girls suffered from a major case of the hots for him.

"Okay, Dr. Ramsey," Matt said, still flustered but trying not to show it, "since you've so brilliantly diagnosed this problem, tell me what I need to do to treat it."

He was so dead serious that Kay almost laughed out loud. Instead she maintained a somber expression and leaned toward him.

"It'll take care of itself."

"Huh?"

"Look, Matt. Teenaged girls swap their affections the way they swap their clothes. Give it a few weeks. One morning they'll wake up and see you for the crusty old man you are and fall in love with some varsity football star two lockers down."

"She's right, you know."

That verification came from Hazel, who never looked up from her crossword.

Matt turned to Hazel with disbelief. "So you noticed it, too?"

"Of course I noticed it."

"Why didn't you *tell* me?"

"Figured you knew. Everyone else does."

Kay hadn't counted on Hazel adding insult to injury, and Matt's expression of complete distress delighted her.

"But don't worry," Hazel added. "Like Kay said, in a couple of weeks they'll forget all about you. You'll be invisible." Then, for the first time, the old woman peeked over the top of her crossword. "To everyone except Kay, that is. She's logged more time staring at you than Ashley and Mandy put together."

5

A RED-HOT FLUSH started somewhere around Kay's breast-bone and filtered up to her face, and suddenly she wished the ground beneath her feet would open up and swallow her. Hazel's words held so much truth that no matter how much she begged her brain to formulate a comeback, it flatly refused to comply.

Hazel lowered her head and put her pencil to her cross-word again as though completely oblivious to the fact that she'd just lit a powder keg. Kay stood speechless, bracing herself to take whatever Matt was getting ready to throw at her, because after what she'd just put him through it was inconceivable that he'd let this one go.

But instead of pouncing on the opportunity, the smirk she expected to see was nowhere in sight. They stared at each other a long time, their gazes glued together. Matt's mouth hung open, as if words were forming in his mind he couldn't quite verbalize, and Kay knew she had to be wearing the same dumb expression. Seconds ticked away as something unspoken passed between them she couldn't identify and certainly hadn't counted on.

Finally Matt cleared his throat and said something to Hazel about having to get some paper for the printer. He came around the counter and brushed past Kay, then went into the back room and closed the door behind him.

Kay glanced back at Hazel, who never looked up from her crossword. Good God, had she been that obvious? She made a mental note that when Hazel was around, she shouldn't even sneeze in Matt's direction.

Kay slunk out of the reception area and returned to the Cat Room. She picked up the pooper-scooper and dug into her job with a vengeance, repeating to herself all the reasons why any kind of relationship with Matt Forester would be a match made in hell. Number one, he was a veterinarian. Number two, like Robert, he was intent on making her life miserable.

And number three, he was a veterinarian.

LATER, on his way out of the shelter, Matt stopped at the counter where Hazel sat. "I think you embarrassed Kay earlier," he said offhandedly.

"Like she didn't embarrass you?" Hazel gave a little snort of disgust. "I just thought it was about time she got a taste of her own medicine, that's all."

"So," he said, with as much nonchalance as he could muster. "She's been staring at me, too?"

Hazel's gaze slowly panned up to meet his. "Good Lord. Don't tell me you've been doing some looking of your own?"

Matt stood very still for a moment, then forced a smile. "No. Of course not. I just wondered, that's all."

He wondered, all right. He wondered why Kay hadn't denied Hazel's accusation. So far she hadn't hesitated to let it be known if she thought she'd been wronged. Instead she'd looked up at him wordlessly, those blue eyes wide, a pink flush rising on her cheeks. If only she'd denied it he might have been able to tease her about it, and then eventually they'd have tossed a few snide remarks at each other and let it go at that.

But she hadn't denied it. Instead she'd just stood there,

staring at him, until the moment grew so uncomfortable that he'd done them both a favor and extricated himself.

She's been thinking about you, too.

That thought brought on instant fantasies involving Kay in ways he'd prohibited himself from thinking about up to now. Then he took a deep breath and forced himself to look at the situation logically. She was one of the few young, attractive, unattached women who'd crossed his path since he'd become legally and morally free to look, so of course he was going to sit up and take notice. But he reminded himself that this particular woman was off-limits. Period. If he got involved with her and Hollinger found out, Matt was pretty sure he could kiss the grant goodbye. He issued himself a set of marching orders: *Run the shelter as if its survival depends on you, and treat Kay as if its survival depends on Hollinger.*

"You don't like Kay much, do you, Hazel?"

"Something's wrong with people who don't like animals."

"I caught her petting a kitten a few days ago. I think maybe there's a heart in there somewhere."

"Doc, you perform surgery, and I'm pretty sure even you couldn't find her heart."

That might be true. Still, he couldn't shake the feeling that maybe he'd like to give it a try, anyway.

KAY DRAGGED a bag of trash through the Dog Room toward the back door, eager to dispose of the final remnants of tonight's Cat Room cleaning. She glanced at her watch. It was nearly six forty-five. She had just enough time to get home, shower and plop in front of the tube with Sheila for the final evening of *Dirty Little Lies.*

Just as she put her hand on the doorknob to go outside, she looked down and saw Chester lying in his cage. He glanced up at her with that ugly bulldog face, then rested his chin on his good paw and let out a little doggy sigh.

Kay felt that uncomfortable twist in her stomach again. How did Matt expect to find this mutt a home? A lot of decent-looking animals had been here for weeks, some for months. At least most of them had *something* going for them. Chester had nothing.

Well, okay. He didn't bark a lot. That was a plus. Or maybe he realized the futility of it since he'd never be heard over Rambo, who at this moment was yapping away for absolutely no reason at all. And from what she'd seen, Chester's personality seemed fairly sedate and agreeable, as dogs went. But who was ever going to look past the paw thing?

Kay dragged the trash bag out the back door, leaving it ajar as she crossed the yard to the back fence. The rickety gate leading to the alley squeaked painfully as she swung it open. She removed the lid from the trash can, but just as she was about to give the bag a final heave-ho, something big and black streaked past her. She spun around to see Rambo bounding down the alley.

"Rambo!" She stared at him a moment, dumbfounded. He circled and sniffed, then galloped away from her in blissful, bounding leaps. How in the world had he got out?

Ashley. She'd been so wrapped up in gawking at Matt that she hadn't latched his cage. Again.

Kay watched him frolic down the alley, knowing she couldn't possibly chase after that monster. He was like a bulldozer, mowing down anything that got in his way. Mega-dog. Supersized dog. Dog to the tenth power. No way could she even think about going after him.

She started to go inside to tell Matt and Hazel what had happened, but then she realized Rambo was already at the end of the alley and was making a right onto Gibson

Street, and all at once she imagined him running out in front of a car and getting hit. Then she imagined the look that would be on Matt's face when he found him. She'd been around here long enough to know that he loved every one of his animals, even a brainless maniac like Rambo, and he'd dedicated a huge part of his life to keeping them safe. How could she stand here and let one of them get away?

Kay took off running. When she reached the end of the alley, she spied Rambo three houses north, cavorting around a lawn sprinkler. For the next half hour she hop-scotched after him, nearly catching him a dozen times, only to have him slip from her grasp at the last minute.

She chased him down streets, across yards and through alleys, sharpening her vocabulary of four-letter words the whole way. Finally she saw him engaging in an intense sniffing contest with a little brown rag-mop of a dog through a chain-link fence. She tiptoed up behind him, clamped her hand onto his collar, then dug her heels into the grass and held on as he tried to take off again.

She yanked her belt from around her waist and looped it through Rambo's collar, muttering really nasty things under her breath. She proceeded to drag him, leaping and panting, back toward the shelter, trying to pretend she really didn't have a hundred pounds of canine hurricane on the end of a very short leash. The sun hovered low on the horizon as she finally pulled him through the gate into the backyard. About to drop from exhaustion, she climbed the back steps and reached out to open the door.

It was locked.

She beat on the door, calling as loudly as she could. No one answered. A feeling of foreboding oozed through her. Everyone was gone for the day.

Hadn't they noticed she was gone? What about Rambo?

How could they possibly have missed the fact that *he* wasn't there?

In desperation she pulled Rambo through the backyard and headed next door to Matt's clinic. Her panic escalated when she saw that no lights shone through the windows either upstairs or down. She banged on the front door. No response. Had he stepped out for a few minutes, or would he be gone the whole evening?

Finally Kay slumped onto the bench beside the front door, with Rambo panting wildly beside her. "I can't believe this," she muttered, staring dumbly ahead. "I simply cannot believe this."

She looked at her watch. It was twenty-five minutes until *Dirty Little Lies*. Missing the last night of a miniseries was not even an option.

She dragged Rambo down the steps to her car and hustled him into the back seat, thankful she'd thrown her purse in the trunk and had her car keys in her pocket. She slid into the driver's seat and glared at the dog in the rearview mirror.

"Now, listen up, dog. I can't sit here all night, so you're coming home with me. You're going to go into my kitchen like a good little monster, where you're going to stay until I get a hold of Matt. You are to keep your paws to yourself. Do you understand? You are to—"

Rambo took a flying leap into the front seat and slurped his tongue the length of Kay's face. She shoved him away with disgust. He spun around and slimed the passenger window with his wet nose, then let out a bark that reverberated inside the car like an atomic explosion.

Kay started the car. "This is a bad idea," she muttered. "A very bad idea."

MATT STOOD at the makeshift podium in the cafeteria of Thomas Jefferson Middle School, wrapping up his address

to the ladies of the McKinney Metropolitan Ladies' Club
Over the past year he'd been asked to speak to a variety
of groups about the shelter, which was good because i
usually resulted in a few donations, and bad because h
detested public speaking.

"...and as I said before," Matt said, "you're welcome
to drop by the shelter anytime and see how we help these
animals. And please consider volunteering some of you
time, either at the shelter itself or as a temporary foster
parent for one of our animals. Or adopt a pet yourself
We've got plenty to pick from." *Oh, boy, do we.* "Ther
are lots of ways to get involved, to make a difference."
Matt flashed the most sincere smile he could muster. "The
animals thank you, and so do I."

As the ladies applauded, Mrs. Flaherty, the short, stou
president of the McKinney Metropolitan Ladies' Club
stepped up beside him, laid an envelope on the podiun
and leaned into the microphone.

"Dr. Forester, I know I speak for all of us when I sa
that we find your establishment of the Westwood Anima
Shelter worthwhile both to the animals and the citizens o
this community. In light of that, we'd like to present yo
with a small donation."

Small? Lord, he hoped she was just being humble.

"Dr. Forester, please accept this check from the Mc
Kinney Metropolitan Ladies' Club in the amount of..
twenty dollars!"

Matt blinked with disappointment and groaned in
wardly. Twenty dollars? Would the bank notice if he
added a couple of zeros?

He forced himself to smile as Mrs. Flaherty handed hin
the check, then thanked her profusely, which led to an

other round of applause, and Matt wishing he was anywhere else.

By the time he extricated himself from the horde of
chattering women and headed out of the building it had
started to rain. As he ran through the downpour to his car,
all he could think about was getting home, getting out of
this suit, and maybe using the twenty-dollar check as a
bookmark.

Twenty bucks. Damn.

He put the key into the ignition, then stopped and sat
in silence for a moment. He had to stop this self-pity stuff.
It wasn't their fault he couldn't say no to any misbegotten
animal that wandered up to his door. And it wasn't their
fault his ex-wife was living it up on her income and half
of his. Twenty bucks beat nothing, which is what he'd
have gotten if he'd sat at home, cracked a beer, then fallen
asleep on the sofa watching that trashy miniseries.

Minutes later he turned onto Porter Avenue and headed
down the street toward home. As he drew closer, he saw
a car in his driveway. He pulled up behind it and got out,
ignoring the rain that had settled into a warm drizzle.

The evening thus far had been pretty boring, but as he
looked toward the house there was no doubt in his mind
that the excitement level was getting ready to pick up considerably.

Kay was sitting on his front porch—holding Rambo.

6

MATT WALKED warily up the porch steps. Kay stood up, took a few steps forward and thrust the leash at him, which he could see now wasn't a leash at all but a leather belt. At the same time Rambo leaped up and slapped his muddy paws against Matt's chest.

"Rambo! Hey, buddy!" Matt scratched the dog behind the ears, then glanced at Kay and felt a twinge of dread. Something was terribly wrong here, and from the homicidal expression on her face he could tell he was about to bear the brunt of it.

"Where have you been?"

Matt recoiled, wondering what in the world he'd stepped into. "Well...was there someplace I was supposed to be?"

"Yes! You were supposed to be here two hours ago so you could put this mutt back in the shelter where he belongs!"

Matt glanced around, bewildered. "How did he get *out* of the shelter?"

Kay took a deep, angry breath and swiped her limp blond hair away from her face. "I took out the trash at the end of the day. He got loose. I went after him. He led me halfway across town before I finally caught him again. And when I got back to the shelter—guess what? Everyone was gone, including you."

"You've been waiting here with him all that time?"

"No. Unfortunately, I took him home with me."

Matt glanced down at Rambo, who danced brainlessly at the end of the makeshift leash. "Hope you've got a big backyard."

"I don't have *any* backyard! I live in an apartment—a beautifully restored 1930s apartment with arched doorways and plaster walls and wood floors and stained glass—" Kay's fists tightened at her sides, and he thought for a moment she truly intended to use them. "He got me evicted. That monster got me evicted from my apartment!"

"Evicted?" Matt cringed at the image that came to mind—piles of rubble and settling dust, with Rambo cavorting in the aftermath. "What happened?"

Kay's eyes narrowed with fury. "He broke a vase."

"A vase?" Matt had expected something a little more structurally undermining. "That's it?"

"Oh, it wasn't just any old vase. It belonged to my landlady. It sat on a little mahogany table in the entry hall. Mrs. Dalton's Great-Aunt Helen shipped it to the States during the London Blitz in the Second World War so it wouldn't get broken. Did you hear that, Matt? *So it wouldn't get broken!*"

"Still, it's just one vase—"

"One eight-hundred-dollar vase!"

Matt winced. "Oh, boy."

"I know what it's worth because Mrs. Dalton told me. Repeatedly. With tears in her eyes. You'd think it held her dead husband's ashes or something, the way she was going on. I'm already way behind on my rent, and with the eight hundred—" She paused, and for a moment Matt thought she was going to cry. "Mrs. Dalton suggested that perhaps it would be best if I moved out."

A twenty-dollar donation, and now this. Matt's evening was complete.

"And I had no idea where you were or when you'd be back," Kay went on. "For all I knew you had a date—" she paused and eyed him speculatively "—and you weren't planning on coming home at all."

Matt had to smile at that one. He only wished his love life was as active as she seemed to think. "You're right. I did have a date. In fact, I was surrounded by women all night. I'm a pretty popular guy, you know." *With the over-sixty crowd.*

Kay stared at him for a moment as if she half believed him. Then she waved the thought away with a sweep of her hand. "Never mind. I'm not the least bit interested in your love life. All I wanted to do was watch—"

She stopped suddenly, her anger momentarily suspended. Then she dropped her gaze and looked away.

"Watch what, Kay?"

She let out a disgusted breath, then turned back around with her chin raised defensively. "Something on television."

"Television? You mean you dragged this one-dog destruction team home with you so you wouldn't miss a television show?"

"It wasn't just any television show! It was a miniseries!"

"Like that makes a difference?"

"I already had three nights invested in that show, and I wasn't about to miss an episode just because of that dog!"

"So you got kicked out of your apartment instead?"

Kay's lips tightened. She glared first at Rambo, then at Matt. Finally an expression of complete disgust flooded her face. "Oh, all right! It was a stupid thing to do. But that doesn't lessen your liability in this situation."

"Excuse me? My liability?"

"Yes! He's your dog!"

"He's not *my* dog! He's—" Matt stopped. She was right. Rambo was part of the shelter, for which he had total responsibility. "Okay, technically he's my dog, but he didn't get to your apartment building by himself, did he?"

Kay took an angry step forward. "Look, I'm not going to foot the bill for something *your* dog did. My sister's an attorney, and a pretty wicked one at that. If I have to—"

"Oh, will you stop it? Is that the only way you people know how to solve problems? By dragging someone to court?"

"Don't you understand? I don't have eight hundred dollars! I barely have *eight* dollars! When I move out, Mrs. Dalton will keep my deposit as a down payment on the eight hundred and the rent I still owe, but that means I won't have any money for a deposit on another apartment. Before this is all over with, I'm going to be sleeping at the bus station!"

Even though she had the approach of an attack dog, Matt was beginning to feel sorry for her. After all, she'd taken responsibility for Rambo instead of letting him run loose, which was a pretty big step for a woman who feels about dogs the way the average person feels about rattlesnakes.

But what about the eight-hundred-dollar debt Rambo had incurred? He thought of the twenty-dollar check in his pocket and almost laughed out loud. Maybe it would buy him a ticket to that mythical place where money grows on trees.

"Kay, I'd really like to give you the money."

"Good. Then we don't have a problem after all."

"But I don't have eight hundred dollars." He collapsed on the bench beside the front door and yanked his tie from around his neck. "Do you know where I was tonight?"

"I told you before. I'm not interested in your love life."

"Oh, would you get off that? I didn't have a date."

"But you said you were with women—"

"Yes. The members of the McKinney Metropolitan Ladies' Club. And not one of them was under age sixty. They invited me to speak about the shelter." He tossed his muddy tie to the bench beside him, then reached into his shirt pocket, pulled out a check and held it up. "The ladies were kind enough to make a donation. Twenty dollars."

"That's very nice. But it's seven hundred and eighty short."

"Right now, it's just about all I've got."

"Oh, come on, Matt. Surely—"

"I'm not joking, Kay. What my ex-wife didn't take, the shelter has used up."

Then Kay remembered. He was divorced. Suddenly her anger gave way to a little curiosity. "Do you mind if I ask…how long were you married?"

"Eight years." Matt's voice took on an unmistakably bitter tone.

Kay shoved Matt's muddy tie aside and sat down beside him. "So what happened? I mean, why did you…?"

"Get a divorce? Because my ex-wife wanted an uptown address and her name in the society pages, and she finally figured out that wasn't going to happen as long as she was married to me."

Matt put his elbows on his knees and clasped his hands in front of him. Kay sat in silence, listening to the rain pelt the bushes beside the porch steps. She'd come here ready to do battle with Matt, only to find herself hopelessly sympathetic with the enemy.

"And then there's the shelter," Matt went on. "I bought the place next door so I could take in strays. It's something I've wanted to do ever since I was a kid. We were pretty broke back then, so I never had pets, but I thought when I grew up...." His voice faded away, his face falling into a disillusioned frown. "Now I'm broke again, and I've got thirty-some mouths to feed."

Kay remembered the way he'd sweated over that rattle-trap air conditioner, with grease from head to toe, and now she knew why. So he wouldn't have to call a repairman.

"I'm sorry, Kay," Matt said. "I have no idea why I told you all that. You've got enough problems of your own to think about." He rubbed his eyes, then let out a weary breath. "I guess I just wanted you to know that I'm really not..." he glanced at her, then looked away again "...a tightwad."

Kay remembered that insult she'd hurled his way and cringed at how petty it sounded now. He looked so forlorn sitting on the paint-chipped bench, wet and rumpled, holding that twenty-dollar check, that she regretted every word she'd uttered about that stupid cat litter.

"Do you have any friends who can put you up for a while?"

Sheila came to mind, but Kay couldn't possibly horn in on her and Jim. They'd only been married a few months. And she couldn't move back into the apartment building she'd just been evicted from, anyway. Unfortunately, she had no other friends she'd feel comfortable staying with more than a day or two.

"No," she told Matt. "I don't."

"Relatives?"

"I have a sister, but I'd rather sleep at the bus station."

"Could she at least loan you—"

"No. I can't ask her for money. She already thinks I'm incompetent." She sighed softly. "I'll think of something."

After another long silence, Matt finally stood up. "Well. I guess I'd better get Rambo back to the shelter." He removed Kay's belt from the dog's collar and handed it to her. Then he got a thoughtful look on his face. He glanced up at the second floor window, then back to Kay. "You know, this is a big house. I have a spare room. It's a mess right now, but I can clean it up."

"What?"

"You can put most of your stuff in storage and bring the necessities here. After a few months you'll have enough money for another apartment."

"You mean, you want me to move in?"

"Why not?"

Kay stared at him dumbly, at a total loss for words. "Well, because I...I can't just *jump* right into something like that. I mean, I barely know you."

"When do you need to move?" Matt asked.

"Uh, Saturday if I can. But—"

"Okay. I'll have the room cleaned out by then."

"Now, wait a minute! Hold on! I never actually said yes!"

"Oh, yeah. You've got all those other options to consider."

She had *no* other options to consider. But move in with Matt?

All at once she realized how dangerous that could be. He seemed to be making the offer in the most platonic way possible, but sitting here with him on this bench with nothing else present but the moonlight and a very large dog, Kay forgot for a moment that he was a veterinarian and saw him only as a man. A very attractive man. A very attractive man who would be just down the hall if she moved in with him, tempting her to think about him even more than she already did when she needed desperately to *stop* those thoughts. He was clearly the wrong man for her. A broke veterinarian—how mortified would her family be if she brought home one of those?

She'd only completed eighteen hours at the shelter, and she was going to have to save up a lot of money before she could look for another apartment. If she moved in with Matt, it might be a long stay. She decided right then: no matter how much her body said *yes,* it was time for her brain to say *no.*

"You don't know me either, Matt," she told him, trying a different approach. "I'm a pain to live with. Really. I stay up late. I eat dinner in front of the television. I clean house only when the mood strikes. I leave my underwear soaking in the sink, and I sing in the shower. Show tunes. Loud. And I'm so nasty first thing in the morning even Willard Scott won't talk to me."

Matt smiled broadly. "Me too. See you Saturday."

He turned and dragged Rambo through the rain toward the shelter, leaving Kay standing dumbfounded on the porch.

So there it was. She was moving in with Matt.

GOOD LORD, Forester, what were you thinking?

Matt gave Rambo a quick towel dry and put him back in his cage, all the while lambasting himself for the incredibly stupid thing he'd just done. With painful clarity, he imagined the leap in logic Robert Hollinger would make if he found out he and Kay were living together. He'd assume they were having an affair. Hollinger's plans for revenge clearly didn't include such a thing, because that might imply that Kay wasn't being punished enough. It didn't matter if they were actually involved or not. If Hollinger even thought they were, the Dorland Grant was history.

If only he'd had the good sense to keep his mouth shut and let Kay fend for herself, he wouldn't be in this mess right now. But she'd looked so helpless standing there on his front porch, telling him she was broke and had no place to go. The invitation had been out of his mouth before he even realized it. She was the one woman on earth he needed desperately to avoid, and he'd just invited her to move in with him. How incredibly stupid was that?

Well. He'd just have to make sure Hollinger never found out.

Unfortunately, Robert Hollinger wasn't his only worry right now. What about the room he'd promised Kay?

Returning to the house, he headed for the spare bedroom and squeaked the door open, hoping it wasn't as bad as he remembered.

It was worse.

By Kay's description of her apartment he knew she was used to something considerably more elegant than the cracked windows and dingy walls he now saw before him, not to mention the decade-by-decade collection of old furniture and other garage-sale items left by the house's previous owners.

He scanned the room, looking for something to give him hope. Maybe the old brass bed would be salvageable. And the dresser, too, if he could find the missing drawer. And there were a few items up in the attic he might be able to resurrect....

Then he slumped against the door with a heavy sigh. Who was he kidding? There was no way he was ever going to make this room habitable by Saturday.

No way.

KAY CALLED IN a few favors from friends she'd helped move over the years and managed to get the majority of her possessions from her apartment into thirty-two-dollar-a-month storage space at Stor-Ur-Self. Then she filled her car with the bare necessities—clothes, toiletries, portable television. It had nearly torn her heart out to leave her beautiful apartment, and when she closed the door for the last time and handed Mrs. Dalton the key, she truly thought she was going to cry.

She swallowed her tears and headed for Matt's house. It was just before noon when she got there. Somehow she thought the clinic would be a little more plush than the shelter, but that hope evaporated the moment she opened the door.

In the waiting room were the same electric-orange plastic chairs she'd seen at the shelter. A bulletin board hung on one wall, sporting ads for local pet-related businesses, a cartoon or two, and a collage of cat and dog photos—evidently Matt's patients. Pale gray walls and a white tile floor rounded out the utilitarian decor.

She heard voices and saw Matt coming down the hall alongside an older woman carrying a tiny white poodle with red ribbons on his ears. "But he threw up twice," the woman said, her voice quivering. "Twice in an hour!"

"He's all right, Mrs. Feinstein," Matt told her. "It's just a little stomach upset." Then he saw Kay. He pointed up the stairs. "Last door on the left. I'll be up there as soon as I can." He nodded surreptitiously toward the old woman and gave Kay a tiny shrug that said it could be two minutes or two hours.

As Matt gently admonished the old lady about letting her dog snack on Twinkies and fish sticks, Kay went up the creaky oak stairs. When she reached the second floor and looked through the first doorway she came to, she realized that even Matt's living quarters left a lot to be desired.

At one time the room had been a large bedroom complete with fireplace. Now a few chairs, a coffee table and a ratty old sofa qualified it, barely, as a living area. The beige paint on the woodwork had peeled, displaying a moss-green layer below it, and the faded wallpaper looked to be original turn-of-the-century. She had a passion for vintage homes, but lack of tender loving care made this place look just plain old.

With great trepidation, Kay continued down the hall toward the room Matt had designated as hers, expecting more of the same tired old decor as in the living room. But when she peeked around the doorway, she was astonished at what she saw.

Centered on the back wall between two windows sat a brass bed, a little dinged-up but brightly polished, draped with a well-worn double wedding ring quilt. A Tiffany-style lamp rested on a bedside table, its shade intact except for one tiny pane missing at its crown. An old oak dresser was missing a drawer but was polished to a warm glow and topped with a lace runner. An eclectic assortment of framed items hung on the walls, from old photographs to seafaring maps. White lace-trimmed curtains graced every window, and while their edges were tattered, when Kay drew one toward her face and inhaled, she smelled fabric softener.

But most surprising was that the walls had been painted a clean, fresh antique white, the faint odor of latex paint still lingering in the air. The only drawback seemed to be an enormous white cat lounging in the middle of the bed, but right now she didn't even care about that. The rest of the house might look old and tired, but this room was pretty and charming and so much more than she expected that she stared at it with wonder. *It feels like my apartment,* she thought, as an overwhelming wave of contentment swept over her. *It feels like home.*

And her next thought was: *He did this for me.*

MATT MANEUVERED Mrs. Feinstein out the door, hoping she would take his advice and give Andre's shaky gastrointestinal system a rest. He shut the door and put the Closed sign in the window, then looked up the stairs, wondering if he should go up there at all.

He'd half expected Kay to come marching back down the moment she got up there, her face screwed up with distaste at the sight of that room. But he hadn't heard a sound from the second floor. Maybe she was waiting for him to come up before she told him how really awful it was.

He climbed the stairs and walked down the hall toward the spare bedroom. The door stood open. He peered inside and saw Kay sitting on the bed with her back to him, staring around the room, absentmindedly running her hand across that tattered old quilt he'd found to put on the bed. He knocked softly on the door. She spun around and stood up.

"I see you've met Marilyn," Matt said.

"Marilyn?"

He nodded to the cat stretched out on the bed.

"Oh, yeah," she said. "The cat."

"I guess I should have shut the door."

Kay just shrugged.

"Is everything...okay?" he asked her.

"Okay?" She said the word with disbelief, and as she glanced around the room again his heart sank.

"Kay, about the room. I know you're used to something a lot better than this. These odds and ends were all I had. This whole house needs a complete overhaul. One of these days—"

"No!" she said suddenly, taking several quick steps toward him. "It's perfect! Just...perfect."

He stared at her with disbelief. Perfect? This old stuff?

"I was so upset about moving out of my apartment. But then I saw this...how you'd fixed everything up..."

She took another step toward him, closing the gap between them, then rested her palm against his shoulder and kissed him on the cheek. "Thank you," she murmured. "Thank you for doing this for me."

Her feather-soft whisper against his ear sent warm shivers down his spine. This was totally unexpected. He'd learned to deal with the belligerent side of Kay. That was familiar ground. But this sweet, vulnerable side of her was uncharted territory. Without even thinking, he rested his hand against the small of her back. She froze, her cheek hovering a scant inch from his.

"I'm glad you like it."

The moment the words were out of his mouth he knew he'd made a mistake. Not because of the words themselves, but because of the way they came out—low, sultry...suggestive. Her hand tightened against his shoulder, and he knew he'd started something he shouldn't even consider finishing. So why didn't he back away?

Why didn't she?

Suddenly everything about Kay filled his senses, from the cool texture of her white cotton shirt beneath his hand to the last subtle notes of the floral fragrance that lingered at the pulse point behind her ear. Then her hand glided over his shoulder, and he took in a quick, silent breath as she shifted her body and leaned into him.

Oh, boy.

His brain screamed at his body to *do* something, but the moment Kay touched him his muscles had gone so weak he was surprised he could still stand up. She exhaled softly just beneath his right ear, circled her hand around his collar, and dropped her lips against his neck in a gentle kiss.

He couldn't move. He couldn't speak. All he seemed able to do was feel—and what a feeling! He closed his eyes as her lips moved along the angle of his jaw, his heart going wild as she traced a slow but definite path of kisses toward his mouth.

He had to stop her. In about three seconds her lips were going to reach their destination, and if they did, he knew he'd be lost. It had been too damned long since he'd held a woman, and he knew if he didn't push her away right now—

Too late.

7

AS KAY'S LIPS fell against Matt's in a warm, soft, amaz
ingly seductive kiss, the last of his sanity slipped away
Gently at first, then more persuasively, she molded he
lips against his with a proficiency that astonished him. He
hands fluttered like dandelion fuzz against the back of hi
neck, teasing him toward her, making him want to wrap
his arms around her and—

No!

Something snapped inside Matt's head and sanity came
rushing back. He jerked away from her, took her by the
shoulders and held her at arm's length. Her eyelids flut
tered with surprise.

"No, Kay. We can't do this. Not while you're—" He
paused, then let out a long breath. "We just can't do this
That's all."

She stared at him a long time, as if awakening from a
dream. Then an expression of pained realization crep
across her face. She put her hand against her mouth an
her eyes dropped closed. Her voice became a whisper
"Oh, God. I've made a fool out of myself, haven't I?"

Matt came very close to grabbing her by the shoulder
again and kissing her just to prove how wrong she was
He hated that she felt embarrassed about doing somethin
he would have wanted as much as she did, if circum
stances had been different. But how was he supposed t
tell her that?

"Kay, I promise this has nothing to do with you. I've just got some other...problems I need to work out, and I shouldn't be complicating things."

At least that was somewhat true. Still, he could tell his words did nothing to ease her discomfort. Finally he said, "I think we both just got a little carried away."

Kay's gaze inched up to meet his, her cheeks flushed red. "Not both of us," she said quietly. "Just me. But you don't have to worry. It won't happen again."

"Kay, it's all right." He told himself to smile, but he wasn't sure his lips got the message. "It was no big deal."

Kay still looked mortified, and Matt kicked himself for not having the good sense to turn and run the moment she touched him. "Look, why don't I help you move your things in?"

"Maybe you'd rather I didn't."

"What?"

"Maybe I should find another place to live."

He saw so much misery in her eyes that he almost told her the whole truth. Fortunately he managed to swallow the words while they were still on the tip of his tongue. "No. That's not what I want. Please don't leave."

She still looked embarrassed, and he hated himself for letting it happen. Finally she nodded. After they moved her things in, she thanked him for his help, then disappeared into her room and closed the door behind her.

Matt went to the living room, telling himself he'd done the only thing he could have done. Kay living with him he might be able to explain away. But if their relationship became something more—no way.

Up until five minutes ago, he'd been doing a pretty good job of thinking of Kay as just a roommate. But the moment her lips met his, he was doomed.

He tried to look at things logically. Maybe getting this

lust thing out of the way right up front was the best thing
that could have happened. Any kind of relationship with
her would jeopardize the most important thing in his life
right now, and he couldn't let that happen, no matter how
wonderful her perfume smelled. No matter how warm and
intriguing her touch had been. No matter how expertly she
used those soft, sweet lips of hers....

Oh boy.

Matt collapsed on the sofa, chastising himself for letting
his body rule over his brain. Even without Hollinger in
the picture, the picture was all wrong, anyway. Since she
didn't like animals, she'd never understand his passion for
the shelter and his dedication to keeping its doors open.
Sooner or later, just like his ex-wife, she'd wonder why
he chose to spend more money than he made trying to
give a few helpless animals a chance at some kind of life.

And then she'd be gone.

AT TEN-THIRTY that night, Kay lay awake in the cozy
brass bed in that perfect little room, staring at the freshly
painted ceiling, her stomach still in knots from the stupid,
impulsive thing she'd done.

If only she hadn't actually kissed Matt. If only she'd
backed away before she'd lost her head, she wouldn't be
lying here feeling silly and hurt and embarrassed beyond
belief. But she'd been overwhelmed by the sweet, wonderful thing he'd done for her by fixing up that room, and
her gratitude had gotten all tangled up with the incredible
fantasies she'd been having about him. All at once she'd
desperately wanted to touch him in ways she'd only
dreamed about, and, before she knew it, the compulsion
to make it happen completely engulfed her. And then...

And then she'd made a fool of herself.

Claire was right. She never thought about a damned

thing before she did it. She'd got engaged to Robert when she didn't love him. She'd had his dogs shaved when she knew he'd go ballistic. She'd taken Rambo home with her when she knew he was a disaster waiting to happen. She'd agreed to move in with Matt, the last man on earth she should tempt herself with. Then, the whopper of them all, she'd made the wild assumption that maybe he was as attracted to her as she was to him.

That had been stupid. *Stupid.*

She turned over and pulled the covers up to her chin, wishing she could crawl under a rock somewhere and die. What had made her think Matt would ever be interested in her? She'd made his life miserable from the moment she'd shown up here with all her whining and complaining. She steered clear of animals at every opportunity, the very thing he'd dedicated his life to. And every chance she got she made it clear to him that she was counting the hours—the minutes—until she could kiss this place good-bye.

Still, in spite of all that, when she'd needed help he'd offered her a rent-free room, then gone out of his way to make her comfortable in it. She didn't deserve it.

And she certainly didn't deserve him.

WHEN KAY ARRIVED at the shelter on Monday she ran into Matt. Literally. He came out the door as she was coming in, and he had to grab her by the shoulders and steady her to keep from knocking her flat.

"I—I'm sorry," she told him. "I wasn't watching where I was going."

"No. I was the one who barrelled out the door without looking."

"No. It was my fault—"

"Kay, I almost knocked you down. It was my fault."

All this excruciating politeness was about to make her sick. She wanted so badly to laugh with him about how they'd both nearly ended up on their fannies on the porch, but all they seemed to be able to do was shuffle around and apologize. Then Matt yanked his hands away from her shoulders as if he suddenly realized he was touching toxic waste. She slipped past him and went on into the shelter.

As Kay went into the Cat Room, she saw Becky putting a little black dog into a cage across the hall.

"Another one?" Kay asked.

Becky came into the Cat Room. "Yeah. This one had a viral infection. He's better now. I predict he'll be adopted before the week's out."

"Really?"

"Yeah. He's small, he's cute and he's friendly. He can't miss." Then Becky glanced back to the Dog Room and frowned. "How's Chester getting along? Has anyone looked at him?"

Kay felt that funny twinge in her stomach again. She figured it wouldn't hurt to stretch the truth. "A few people, I think."

"Kay? Will you do me a favor?"

"Uh...sure."

"Will you give Chester a little extra attention if you get the chance? I think he's going to be here for a while."

Kay felt a knot in her throat. The truth was that she *had* gone into the Dog Room to see Chester a couple of times, and once she'd even brought him a dog biscuit. Now she decided she'd make sure to do it every day. "Yeah. I will."

"Thanks. That'd make me feel a lot better." Then she sighed. "Poor guy. If someone would just get to know him a little, I know they'd take him home."

Just then a big orange-and-white cat jumped up on the table beside them. Becky scratched him behind the ears. "Hi there, Harpo." She tickled her fingernails down the cat's back, and he fell on his side and blinked with delight. "Has he meowed yet?"

"Not a sound. Matt says its possible that he's got some congenital abnormality or something."

"I think maybe he just doesn't have anything to gripe about. This place has never looked better. You spoil these cats to death."

Spoil them? That was a joke. She was just doing her job. She had to admit it wasn't as bad around here as she'd first thought, but taking care of twenty-some cats still wasn't her recreation of choice.

In the past few days, though, she'd found it far more comfortable to be around the cats than around Matt. How could she get through the next couple of months if she couldn't even be in the same room with him without feeling the same way Chester had to feel: completely and utterly rejected.

THE NEXT AFTERNOON after Matt closed the clinic, he made a quick run over to the shelter to drop off a dog he'd treated for worms. He could hear Kay in the Cat Room next door, but just talking to her had become a chore so he passed by without speaking.

The past several evenings at home she'd come through the back door with takeout food and slipped upstairs to her room. If he hadn't heard her shuffling around in the bathroom once in a while, he would have sworn she wasn't even in the house.

He told himself that was a good thing. The only way he was going to be able to get through the next few months was to keep his distance from Kay—far enough away that his brain would rule his body instead of the other way around. Somehow he had to pretend that she didn't want him as much as he wanted her. Pretend she wasn't blond and beautiful. Pretend he hadn't seen something in those gorgeous blue eyes besides bad attitude.

Pretend her bedroom wasn't ten paces from his.

As he started to leave the shelter, a big, burly man walked in, a clipboard in his hand.

"Lookin' for Dr. Forester."

"That's me."

The man called over his shoulder, out the door. "Okay, Harry! This is the place!"

A moment later another man wheeled a dolly through the door and deposited two big boxes on the floor. Matt circled the counter.

"Wait a minute! What's this?"

"The cat litter you asked for."

"Cat litter?" Matt looked out the window and saw the truck they were unloading from. Across the side it read, Super Scoop Cat Litter.

"Hold on!" he said. "I didn't order any cat litter!"

"Well, someone did," the man said, checking his clipboard. "Someone named...Kay Ramsey."

Matt's mouth fell open in disbelief. Kay couldn't have ordered this cat litter. She couldn't have.

Wait a minute. What was he thinking? This was a woman who took revenge on her fiancé by having his dogs shaved.

"Kay!" he shouted. "Kay, get in here!"

Kay flew out of the Cat Room at the sound of Matt's voice, then skidded to a halt when he met her with a furious expression.

"What have you done here?" he demanded.

When Kay saw the boxes her face lit up like a kid at Christmas. "Oh! It's here! It's finally here!"

She grabbed a pen from the counter and slit open one of the boxes. She pulled out a container of Super Scoop and gave it a big, noisy kiss.

"Kay!" Matt shouted. "Put that back!"

The deliveryman brought in another dolly-load of litter and deposited it beside the other boxes.

"No!" Matt said. "Take it back! She had no authority to order this stuff!"

The man looked at his clipboard. "But it says right here—"

"I don't care what it says! I'm not paying for it!"

"It's all right," Kay said to the deliveryman. "Go ahead. Give Dr. Forester the bill."

The deliveryman looked confused. "Lady, there isn't any bill. This is a gratis shipment."

Now Matt was completely lost. "Huh?"

"A freebie. You're a nonprofit animal welfare something-or-other, aren't you?"

"Yeah…"

"The company does this once in a while. It's good for PR."

As Matt stood there speechless, Kay headed back to the Cat Room with a bounce in her step he'd never noticed before. And as she disappeared around the corner, she tossed him a sly smile that said it wouldn't be wise to underestimate her again.

LATER THAT EVENING when Kay came through the back door into the kitchen, Matt was standing at the stove stirring something in a big pot. It smelled wonderful, whatever it was. A whole lot better than the double cheeseburger she was getting ready to take up to her room. She murmured a hello and started toward the stairs.

"Kay. Wait."

As she turned back, Matt set the spoon he held down on the counter. He paused for a moment, then let out a long breath. "Look, about the cat litter. I didn't give you a chance to explain. I yelled at you when I should have been thanking you."

Surprised at the sudden, heartfelt appreciation, Kay felt a blush rise to her cheeks.

"Every buck I save on supplies keeps the doors to the shelter open a little longer. How did you do it, anyway?"

"It was nothing. Really. A couple of years ago I worked for Promos—uh, a public relations firm. I found out you can get a whole lot of stuff just by asking. They used to drum it into our heads—don't ever pay for something if you can get it for nothing."

Matt smiled. "Well, since zero dollars is about the only price tag I can live with right now, I guess it's lucky for me you came along."

Matt's approval made Kay feel as if sunlight was warming her all the way down to her toes. When she'd initially concocted her plan, all she'd been interested in was finding a way to get rid of that awful, smelly old litter. But she wasn't thinking of herself now. She was thinking of helping him. And it was the best she'd felt in a long time.

"Oh, and another thing." Matt stepped quickly over to her, grabbed the burger sack from her hand and flung it into the trash.

"Matt! What the—"

"You cook the spaghetti noodles while I finish the sauce. They're in the cabinet."

Kay just stood there, staring at him.

"I don't like having a roommate I never see. I want

you to have dinner with me. Do you have any objection to that?''

Objection? To having dinner with Matt? "No. No objection."

"Fine. Now move it on the noodles. The sauce is about done."

Fifteen minutes later they sat down to a meal of spaghetti and garlic bread, and Kay decided it had been a long time since she'd had a dinner that tasted so good. Actually, the food was pretty average, but she felt so wonderful about what had happened with the cat litter that every bite she put into her mouth tasted like cuisine from a five-star restaurant.

"From now on let's just split groceries and take turns cooking," Matt said. "How does that sound?"

Kay winced. "Pretty good in theory. But I'm a lousy cook."

"Don't worry about it. I'm a pretty rotten cook myself. But there isn't much I won't eat. And if either of us really goofs something up we can always order a pizza."

After dinner, Matt washed the dishes and Kay dried them. She was just putting the last dinner plate away, when all at once something big and white leaped onto the kitchen counter next to the sink.

Kay instinctively yelped and leaped backward, her hand fluttering against her chest. Marilyn sat down nonchalantly, giving Kay a look that said one of the humans in her midst had just lost her mind.

"Marilyn! Get down!" Matt scooped up the cat. He deposited her on the floor, then looked back at Kay. "Kay? Are you all right?"

As Marilyn strolled out of the kitchen, Kay took a deep breath and let it out slowly. "I'm sorry, Matt. I didn't see her coming...and then suddenly she was there...and..."

"It's all right. Marilyn is harmless. I promise."

"I know she is," Kay said quickly. "Really. I'm sure she's a very nice cat. I was just…you know. Surprised. That's all."

She tried to sound like it was no big deal—and it really wasn't—but she still felt as if she was babbling, and Matt's confused stare confirmed that fact.

He took the last plate from her hand and put it away. "Okay. Dinner's over. Now it's playtime."

"Playtime?"

Matt grabbed a neon-green Frisbee from his office beside the kitchen. He led Kay out the front door and toward the park across the street, Buddy trotting at his heels. The park ran the length of the block, an idyllic, tree-clustered island in a sea of turn-of-the-century residential homes and small businesses.

When they reached a wide-open space, Matt handed Kay the Frisbee. "Throw it."

"Huh?"

"I said throw it." He pointed toward the clearing. "Out there. Hard as you can."

"Excuse me, but isn't someone supposed to be at the other end to catch it?"

"Just throw it."

Something was up. "Is this a practical joke? You suggest something stupid just to see if I'll do it, and then you laugh your head off? Is that it? Because if it is—"

"Will you just *throw* the damned thing?"

She knew she was going to regret this, but she took a few steps forward and hurled the Frisbee as hard as she could. And she couldn't believe what happened next.

The moment it left her hand, Buddy exploded from beside Matt and shot into the open field as if his tail had suddenly caught fire. She watched in awe as he raced beneath the spinning disk, then leaped off the ground with all four feet. As the Frisbee descended, he met it in mid-air and snapped his jaws around it. The moment his feet hit the ground he spun around and raced back to Kay. To her complete disbelief, he sat down, the Frisbee between his teeth, his eyes meeting hers with an expectant twinkle.

Kay looked at Matt, dumbfounded, then back to Buddy. "How did you teach him to do that?"

"I think he was born knowing how."

"Will he do it again?"

"He'll drop dead doing it."

She reached down gingerly, took the Frisbee from between his teeth and wiped the dog spit off on her jeans. She threw it again, and Buddy took off. Almost immediately a gust of wind caught the Frisbee and caused it to veer sharply to the left and hurtle toward earth.

"Oh no!" Kay said. "He can't—"

"Watch."

Buddy screeched to a halt and doubled back. He zeroed in on the falling Frisbee, and with a huge horizontal leap he plucked it out of the air before it hit the ground. He brought it back to her. She took it from his mouth and reared back to throw it again.

"Uh-oh," Matt said.

"What?"

"You forgot to wipe off the dog spit."

She waved the Frisbee at him in a gesture of feigned disgust, then wound up and threw it again. Later, Kay couldn't have said whether she remembered to wipe off the dog spit every time or not. But as she threw the Frisbee again and again, she couldn't remember the last time she'd had so much fun.

When it looked as if Buddy was indeed going to drop dead, Matt motioned to a park bench. He and Kay sat down, while Buddy collapsed at Matt's feet. The warm evening breeze swirled around them, containing only a hint of the oppressive heat they'd endured that day. A feeling of contentment settled over Kay like a warm, fuzzy blanket.

She glanced down at Matt's hands, and for a long, unguarded moment she imagined lacing her fingers through his, then inching over to rest her head against his chest, feeling its rise and fall and listening to the beat of his heart. He looked so strong and solid and comfortable that the thought of lying in his arms went from passing fancy to near-compulsion, until finally she had to force her gaze away. If she stared at him one moment more she might forget that looking might be permitted, but touching wasn't.

"Think you could do it again?" Matt asked.

"Do what?"

"Get some more donations."

Kay hadn't considered that, but how difficult could it be? She shrugged. "Sure. If one company would donate, why wouldn't others?" She said it nonchalantly, but she felt a little shiver of delight at the thought of doing more to help him.

She glanced down at Buddy, who had rolled to his side and lay motionless, as if he'd gotten mowed down by an eighteen-wheeler. All in all, as dogs went, he wasn't that bad to be around.

"Uh-oh. I think I killed him."

Matt smiled. "Don't worry. He'll come back to life by tomorrow night."

Tomorrow night. The prospect of spending her evenings with Matt sent something warm and wonderful flowing through her. It was also probably the dumbest feeling she could possibly have. He'd spelled out quite clearly what the boundaries of their relationship were the day she moved in, but the concept of Matt as just a friend was growing harder for her to hold on to. And the more time she spent with him, the farther that concept was likely to slip from her grasp.

A few minutes later they got up to go home, walking side by side across the park as evening edged into night. Matt noticed that Buddy was trailing at Kay's heels now, probably because she was the one holding the Frisbee. The little dog was a sucker for good time. It looked as if Kay was, too.

He thought back to how she'd reacted in the kitchen when Marilyn had jumped onto the counter, as if a monstrous spider had crawled up her leg or a snake had slithered across her shoe. That's when it had dawned on him. Kay didn't just dislike animals. She was afraid of them. For some reason, though, she seemed determined to hide that fact. So instead of confronting her with it, he'd decided to show her a side to pet ownership she might not have experienced before. A fun side. And judging from the smile on her face when Buddy brought that Frisbee back to her again and again, he'd succeeded.

Now he'd like to take Hollinger apart, limb by limb.

The guy had to know that Kay was actually afraid of animals, yet he'd gleefully sent her to her own personal hell so he could soak up a little revenge. How much lower could one man sink?

Then he remembered. He was doing a little sinking of his own.

He glanced at Kay, feeling a ripple of apprehension that somehow she was going to find out about the deal he'd made with Hollinger. And he was surprised at how desperately he wanted to keep that from happening.

All at once Buddy reached up and snatched the Frisbee

from Kay's hand. She swung around, her fists on her hips, glaring at him. She lunged for the Frisbee, but Buddy backed away.

"You goofy little dog! Give that back to me!"

She took off after him, but he managed to stay one step ahead of her, his little doggy smile curling around the Frisbee. Thinking Kay might be getting a little angry at Buddy's antics, Matt started to intervene. Then he heard the most beautiful sound.

Kay's laughter.

It filled the twilight like a soft, lilting melody, chasing away every memory he had of the wary, confrontational woman who'd first shown up at the shelter. And he had a feeling that from now on, whenever he thought of Kay, this is what he would remember.

"YOU GOT a dozen *what?*"

Matt had caught the last few seconds of the phone conversation Kay had been carrying on at the reception desk at the shelter, the umpteenth one she'd made in the past few weeks, and he wasn't sure he liked what he had heard. She spun around from the phone with a big smile. "Kitty-Tees."

Matt grimaced. "What in the world is a Kitty-Tee?"

Kay rolled her eyes. "Don't you keep up? They're what the well-dressed cat is wearing this season, of course. They're from Pet Palace. They come in long-sleeved, short-sleeved, small, medium and large, and they're fifty-fifty poly-cotton so they won't shrink up to nothing in the dryer. They're sending over three lime green, three electric blue—"

"Wait a minute! You seem to be telling me you're going to dress the cats up in T-shirts. Is that right?"

Kay smiled dreamily. "Won't they just be the cutest things?"

Good God, he'd created a monster. For the past couple of weeks Kay had been like a human vacuum cleaner run amok, sucking up all the pet-related items she could get her hands on. Up to now he'd approved wholeheartedly. But cats wearing T-shirts?

"The Super Scoop was great," he told her. "And the Tasty Cat. And the grooming brushes and the Kitty Yum-Yums—"

"And the Port-a-Pets. Don't forget those."

"They're great, Kay. Really. I'm glad you found them. I'm glad you found them for *free*. But just because something's free doesn't mean we ought to take it. Cats in T-shirts—"

"Oh, will you hush a minute? I swear your sense of humor is melting away before my very eyes." Kay pointed toward the Cat Room. "Look. You've got two cats back there who've had part of their coats clipped— one because of a skin problem and the other because of mats. Nobody will look at them right now, even though their hair will eventually grow back in and they'll be good as new. But don't you think if I put them in cute little T-shirts it'll cover up the problem until someone can get to know them a little? They might find out there's a potential pet under those bad haircuts."

Matt was astonished, and not just because of the irony of a dog shaver catering to cats with raggedy coats. This seemed to be a step above basic necessities. After spending forty hours at the shelter, had her feelings changed? Was Kay actually going out of her way to help a few unfortunate animals find a decent home?

"After all," Kay added, "that's the point, isn't it?

Moving some of these creatures out of here before the next ones show up?''

Matt felt a flush of disappointment. Kay saw the shelter as a conveyor belt moving a product through a warehouse. He realized now that just because she'd grown less fearful of the animals didn't mean she'd suddenly started loving them. She was scrounging donations only because it beat cleaning cat boxes. It was nothing more than a game to her, a fun little exercise in negotiation to see just how much free stuff she could come up with and how many deals she could make. Still, he'd liked thinking, if only for a moment, that maybe she'd done it for the animals.

And for him.

8

THE NEXT MORNING Kay raced toward the elevator in the lobby of the Cauthron Building, wedging her hand between the closing doors until they popped open again. She wiggled her way onto the elevator, breathing heavily, then punched the button for the fourteenth floor. When the doors opened, she ran through the elevator lobby, flung open the glass doors of Breckenridge, Davis, Hill, Scott & Wooster, then sprinted to her desk.

She checked her watch and breathed a sigh of relief. It was eight o'clock straight up. If there was one thing Mr. Breckenridge insisted on, it was punctuality.

That's when she saw the red rose.

Kay's heart fluttered a little as she sat down, eased the rose aside and opened the card that accompanied it. She saw only two words written there: Dinner tonight?

She turned the card over. Nothing else.

"I made reservations at Rodolpho's."

At the sound of the deep male voice, she looked up to see Jason Bradley, a high-flying junior associate in the firm, leaning against the doorway. Disappointment oozed through her. For a fleeting moment she'd hoped that somehow Matt had found his way into her office, come to her desk—

"They have the best Italian food in town," Jason said.

Kay shook her head. "No. I don't think so."

Jason's smile dimmed. "You don't like Italian?"

"I love Italian."

"Too short notice, then. Maybe this weekend—"

"No. I'm sorry, Jason. I'm just not interested in dating anyone right now."

"Ah. I see." He had a look on his face that said, *Girls line up around the block to go out with me, so what's the matter with you?* He walked over to her desk, placed his palms against it and fixed his gaze on hers. "Did you know I've never lost a court case?"

"As I understand it, you've only tried two."

Kay knew her barb hit home, but he recovered admirably. "That's right. And both times I got what I wanted." He gave her a calculating smile which was intended, she knew, to warn her of his considerable male prowess. "Keep that in mind."

As Jason sauntered out the door, Kay shook her head and tossed the note card into the trash. Truthfully, Jason really wasn't such a bad guy—yet. He was blessed with good looks, a privileged background and a knack for playing the game of law. But his complete inability to process the word *no* pretty much put him at the bottom of her list of men she wanted to date.

Actually, she'd told Jason the truth. She didn't want to see any other men right now. What would be the point, when all she'd be thinking about was Matt?

With a regretful sigh, Kay loaded more legal-size paper into her printer, trying to put her mind where it belonged right now—on her job. She'd assumed that working six weeks at Breckenridge, Davis, Hill, Scott & Wooster would be sheer torture, and at first it had been. Mr. Breckenridge was stern and demanding, and though he never actually said it, Kay always felt as if he disapproved of everything she did. Still, once she learned to read his moods, to give him what he wanted instead of what he asked for, and to yield to his stone-age idea that it was her responsibility to insure he had his two cups of Colombian decaf every morning, things ran pretty smoothly.

Now, with her six-week assignment nearly up, she'd been surprised when he'd asked her to continue for two more weeks while his secretary took a longer maternity leave. She'd said yes immediately. The temporary pay was pretty good, and her savings were starting to mount up. In fact, it wouldn't be long before she could start looking for an apartment.

An apartment. A permanent place to live. By herself.

She rested her chin on her hands, staring mindlessly at her pencil cup. She couldn't stay with Matt forever. Once she was out of the shelter and out of his house, she'd be out of his life. And the thought of that was almost intolerable.

"Miss Ramsey?"

Kay spun around to find Mr. Breckenridge staring at her over the tops of his bifocals.

"I was told that you volunteer some of your free time at an animal shelter. Is that correct?"

"Uh—yes, sir. I do."

"Perhaps you can help me. I'm considering getting a dog. My wife died a few months ago, and I was thinking perhaps a dog—" He stopped, looking a little flustered, then cleared his throat. "Do you find this shelter of yours to be a quality place to obtain a pet?"

"Oh, yes! Absolutely! We have at least a dozen dogs over there right now. Some puppies, too. Any one of them would make a great pet." She held up her finger. "Just a moment."

Kay reached in her lower desk drawer, pulled out her purse and found one of Matt's business cards. She handed it to him. "Come by anytime. I'll introduce you to Dr. Forester. He's the one who started the shelter."

Breckenridge eyed the card. "The Westwood Animal Shelter? I understand that it's up for the Dorland Grant."

Dorland Grant? Robert had something to do with that. She had no idea Matt had applied for it.

"The Dorland Grant? That's a lot of money, isn't it?"

"Twenty-five thousand dollars."

Wow. Why hadn't Matt told her?

"Well, I know Dr. Forester works hard to keep the doors open. He deserves all the help he can get." She pointed to the card. "Be sure to come by sometime soon. I know you'll be able to find a nice dog."

"Yes. Well. I'll give it some thought." He tucked the card into his coat pocket. "Oh, and Miss Ramsey?"

Kay smiled. "Yes?"

"There were grounds in the last pot of coffee you made. See that it doesn't happen again."

As he strode back into his office, Kay ignored his negative assessment of her coffee-making ability, surprised instead by his interest in the shelter. Unlike Robert, Mr. Breckenridge didn't appear to want a dog as a status symbol. He wanted a pet. And he was actually considering coming to the Westwood Animal Shelter to find one.

Kay smiled. In spite of the fact that he was a slave-driving perfectionist with antiquated ideas about boss-secretary relationships, all at once he didn't seem like such a bad guy.

MATT SAT at his kitchen table thumbing through a veterinary journal, hoping the aroma emanating from the bucket of chicken on the table beside him was enough to mask the smell of the hamburger-noodle casserole he'd just incinerated. He'd warned Kay what a lousy cook he was, and in the time she'd been living with him he'd demonstrated that fact more than once. She came through the back door a few moments later, crinkling her nose and glancing around anxiously as if searching for a fire extinguisher.

"How bad was it this time?" she asked.

"My casserole got a little singed around the edges."

"Did the smoke alarm go off?"

"They probably heard it in Cleveland."

"Good. The wiring in this house looks like a plateful of spaghetti. At least now we know when it finally goes up in flames we have a shot at getting out alive."

She pulled the lid off the bucket of chicken, fished out a wing and dropped it to one of the paper plates Matt had set out. "Just what I need—a few more clogged arteries."

Matt dug around for a chicken leg. "Then it's a good thing I asked for extra cholesterol."

She put the cardboard top back on the bucket. "You didn't tell me you'd applied for the Dorland Grant."

Matt almost choked on his chicken leg. Where had *that* come from?

"Uh—yeah. About three months ago." He gave her a shaky smile. "Who wouldn't? It's twenty-five thousand dollars. Have you looked around the shelter? I could *use* twenty-five thousand."

"Mr. Breckenridge, my temporary boss, told me about it. I guess his firm is part of the Dorland Group, too, like Robert's."

Matt's throat tightened at the mention of Robert's name. He was never going to get this chicken leg down. "It's a long shot, Kay. Don't get your hopes up."

"Well, I'd offer to use my influence with Robert to help you get that grant, but as you well know, I don't have any."

Matt figured he had enough for both of them.

He breathed a little easier as they ate, realizing Ka knew he'd applied for the grant, but that was all. Wha would she say if she knew he'd made a deal with Rober behind her back so he could pocket that twenty-five thou sand?

She hated Robert, and if she knew what he'd done she'd hate him, too.

As THE DAYS passed, Kay's evenings with Matt took o a deliciously warm, comfortable tone. She soon discov ered his social life rivaled hers for sheer boredom. H didn't seem the least bit averse to spending time with he whether they were goofing around in the park or jus lounging in front of the TV.

No matter what old movie she suggested they watch he'd already seen it half a dozen times and didn't min seeing it again. If she cooked something barely identifiabl for dinner, he told her he liked trying new things. If sh flooded the basement with suds because she put too muc detergent in the washer, he helped her clean it up and sai the floor needed washing anyway.

"This is it," Matt said one evening, as they watche *Psycho* for the umpteenth time each. "She's heading fo the shower."

Kay pulled a pillow against her chest and settled int the sofa, which was approximately the size of the *Titanic* With Matt sitting on one end of it and her on the othe they were barely in the same room.

Matt nodded toward the television. Janet Leigh wa turning on the shower. "She's done this, what—about million times? Surely this time she'll see him coming."

Kay smiled automatically, but her mind was elsewhere She closed her eyes, not because she didn't want to se

Janet Leigh slashed to death one more time, but because the scene in her mind was so much more entertaining. She saw Matt wrapping his arms around her and pulling her close, whispering meaningless, intimate words to her, looking at her with a desire that melted her heart. Then he was kissing her—deep, drugging kisses that left her breathless—and telling her how incredibly blind he'd been to have denied his feelings, to have ever thought the two of them didn't belong together.

"Kay? Are you all right?"

She blinked her eyes open. Janet Leigh was history, and Matt was staring at Kay as if she'd grown an extra nose.

"Yeah. I'm fine. It's just that…well, it's the blood. I never did like the sight of blood."

"It's a black-and-white movie."

"I've got an overactive imagination."

And it was a good thing she did, because it looked as if in her imagination was the only place she and Matt would ever share anything more than an old Hitchcock movie and a beat-up sofa, and she desperately wanted more.

She had to stop this. He didn't see her like that. He saw her as a friend, or a roommate or—

Or maybe it was the animal thing.

Kay sighed. The way she felt about animals wasn't something she could hide that easily. She had to admit that she no longer regarded cats and dogs with the same distaste as alligators and tarantulas, but if she tried to tell Matt she loved them as much as he did, he'd know she was lying.

A FEW DAYS later, Matt closed up the clinic at five-thirty and headed over to the shelter as he usually did, only this time he found himself surveying the huge backyard that sprawled behind the big prairie-style house. He stopped and stared at it a long time, imagining how he might be able to use that space to build some outdoor dog runs, or maybe even add onto the shelter itself. He could accommodate a lot more animals with just a little bit of expansion. A lot of the work he could do himself and save money, but still it would take money, and—

And it all came around to Robert Hollinger.

Disgusted, Matt yanked his thoughts out of the clouds and back down to planet Earth. He had no business spending that money before he even had it, or for that matter even counting on getting it in the first place.

As he came through the back door of the shelter, the first sound he heard was the soft mechanical screeching of the air-conditioning unit. Forget expansion. He couldn't even maintain what he already had.

As he came into the reception area, he started to say a quick hello to Hazel, but before he could speak she put her finger to her lips, then nodded toward the Cat Room.

Intrigued, he tiptoed toward the Cat Room and peered around the doorway. Clyde's cage door was open. Kay stood beside it, a box of Kitty Yum-Yums in her hand. She placed one of the cat treats at the very edge of the cage. Clyde's ears flicked forward with interest.

"Look here, Clyde," Kay said, a musical singsong to her voice. "A Yum-Yum. Liver and egg flavor. You like Yum-Yums, don't you? They're yummy, yummy, yummy..."

As Kay sang that ridiculous commercial jingle, she scooted the Yum-Yum further into the cage with the tip of her finger. Matt watched in awe as Clyde took one step forward, then another, finally stretching his neck out and snagging the Yum-Yum between his teeth. He backed away as he chewed it, one watchful green eye on Kay at all times.

"Good stuff, huh?" Kay said. "Do you want another one?" She pulled another treat from the box and placed it at the edge of the cage. As Clyde stretched toward it, she reached out her forefinger to stroke his head. Startled, Clyde yanked his head back and raised a forepaw into the air.

"Kay! Be careful!"

Clyde spun around at the sound of Matt's voice, then flattened his ears against his head and hissed. Matt took three quick steps into the room, clanged the cage door shut and latched it. Clyde slapped his paw against the cage and spit wildly.

Kay spun furiously on Matt. "What did you do that for?"

"Do you want to lose a finger?"

"He wouldn't have bitten me!"

"Don't bet on that."

"We were getting along just fine! I give him Yum-Yums every day and he hasn't bitten me yet!"

"Then you're even crazier than I thought. There's nothing meaner on this planet than an angry tomcat!"

"He's not a tomcat anymore. You fixed that, remember? And he wasn't angry—at least not until you showed up!"

"Hey! Don't you think I know what a cat who's getting ready to lose it looks like?" Matt pointed to his right cheek, to the faded scar that had once been bright red claw marks. "See that? Where do you think I got that? From your friend, Clyde. That's where!"

"So he doesn't like you. He's just a dumb cat, so whose fault is that?"

Kay stared up at him hotly, her fists planted against her

hips, standing resolutely between him and that godfor-
saken creature who would turn into a lap cat about the
day hell froze over. And all at once it struck Matt what a
fool he was. Kay was defending Clyde, *defending* him,
and he was arguing with her.

He looked over at Clyde, who sat glaring at him as if
he were the most vile human who'd ever drawn breath.
Then he turned to Kay, whose expression bore a striking
resemblance to Clyde's. Matt gave her a tiny shrug. "I
just thought you were going to get hurt. That's all."

The rough edges of Kay's anger melted away. "Well,
I wasn't. I know what I'm doing."

"Yes. I can see that."

"He may be here a while," Kay said. "He's just a
stupid cat, but do you see any reason he has to be miserable?"

"No. I don't."

"Are you going to tell me not to give him any more
Yum-Yums?"

"No. I don't think I am."

"Good. Now, why don't you go home and start dinner?
Clyde and I haven't finished our conversation."

"Be happy to."

"If you make Beanie Weenies again, I'm burning the
kitchen down."

"Gotcha."

He slipped out the door, then stopped and leaned
against the wall as Kay resumed her talk with Clyde. He
told himself that taming this particular tiger was nothing
more than a challenge to her, like scrounging donations
for the shelter. But as he listened to her murmur honey-
laced words of endearment to that decrepit old cat, he
wondered if maybe she was losing her heart to an animal
after all.

"GOOD NEWS," Matt told Kay when she got home from the shelter. "No Beanie Weenies. Tonight we're getting a decent meal."

"What?"

"Becky just called. You remember her, right? She was the one who took care of Chester. Her husband, Jerry, got a new barbecue grill and she invited us for dinner. I told her we'd come."

"We? As in both of us?"

"Yeah. Is that okay?"

Kay stopped and stared at him. "I don't know Becky very well. Are you sure she wants me to come, too?"

"Positive. They're grilling steaks."

"Steaks?" Just the word made Kay's mouth water. "What time?"

"Seven o'clock."

"Good. I have just enough time to take a quick shower."

"Fine. But I'm right behind you, so don't you dare use up all the hot water again."

Kay flashed him a quick smile and trotted up the stairs. Then it occurred to her that if only he'd join her in the shower, they could use up the hot water together and forget about going to Becky's house at all.

9

WHEN THEY pulled up to Becky's house, Kay decided it looked just as she'd expected it to. The lawn was a little overgrown and scattered with kid toys, and a wreath on the door said "Welcome Friends."

Becky greeted them at the door with hugs, and Matt handed her the bottle of wine he'd brought. Then he caught sight of a droopy-diapered toddler hiding behind Becky's leg. He reached down and scooped him up with a flourish. "Hey, Bobby-baby! How's it going?"

The baby grinned and grabbed Matt's ear, practically yanking it off the side of his head. Matt countered with a tickle to his tummy, which made the baby squeal with delight. All at once Kay had a flash of Matt as a father. He'd be one of those guys who got down on the floor and played with his kids, who did the peekaboo thing and carried them around on his shoulders, who gave them heaping doses of love and encouragement and just the right amount of discipline. Kay had always been leery of motherhood, wondering if she'd be as cold and demanding to her children as her mother had been to her. But with a man like Matt, who clearly loved kids, she could actually see herself—

Good Lord. Where had that ridiculous flash-forward come from? In the span of thirty seconds, she'd pushed them out of the "good friends" category right into "married with children."

They followed Becky into the kitchen. She set the wine down on the counter, then opened the back door. To Kay's dismay, three big, hairy canines of questionable parentage squirmed into the house. Becky swept the baby from Matt's arms, and he greeted each of the dogs in turn. They sniffed and circled Kay, too, and she managed to pat each of them with at least a modicum of enthusiasm.

"Good job, Kay," Matt whispered as they followed Becky into the backyard. "I think they like you."

She rolled her eyes. He smiled broadly, then slipped his arm around her shoulders and gave her a little hug. A shiver of delight passed through Kay when he touched her, and despite the unexpected flurry of dog activity, she was suddenly very glad she'd come.

"Hey, Jerry!" Matt said, shaking the man's hand. "That's a good-looking grill you've got there."

"Yep. All the bells and whistles. Becky didn't think I needed a new one, but she'll change her tune once she tastes the steaks." He smiled at Kay. "So, Matt. You gonna introduce me?"

"Kay, this is Jerry Green. Jerry, Kay Ramsey."

Jerry wiped his hand on his barbecue apron and shook her hand. "Hear you're a volunteer over at the shelter."

"Yes. That's right."

"So is that how you two met?"

Kay glanced at Matt. "Uh—yes. I guess it is."

Jerry winked at Matt, and all at once something dawned on Kay. Becky and Jerry thought they were a couple, and that's why she'd been invited tonight. Suddenly Kay felt as if she was here under false pretenses. Matt, though, didn't appear to be giving their obvious misconception a second thought.

As it turned out, Jerry was right about his grill. The meal was perfect. The wine Matt had brought turned out to be pretty good, too, Kay decided, as she started on her second glass. When it got dark and the mosquitoes started to swarm, they went inside. Kay sat down on the love seat, and when Matt sat down beside her it struck her how small a piece of furniture it really was—very small and very cushy, with a definite little dip between the cushions.

Becky put the baby to bed and Jerry went in search of his new country and western CD. Matt draped his arm across the sofa behind Kay's head and settled back with a sigh of contentment.

"That was a great dinner," Matt said. "It's nice to have a real meal for a change."

"So you didn't like my macaroni and cheese last night? I think I'm insulted."

"Nonsense," Matt said. "It was delicious. My doctor says I should get more sodium and preservatives in my diet."

"Okay. So I'm not Julia Child. I suppose I should have asked you to give me your recipe for that masterpiece you created with Spam last week."

"No!" Matt held up his palm and shook his head, a look of horror on his face. "No. Let's stick with your macaroni and cheese. It's wonderful. And what a thrifty shopper you are. All the ingredients were right there in that little blue box for what—twenty-nine cents?"

"Twenty-three cents. I had a coupon."

Kay caught herself meeting Matt's eyes just a little longer than she really should. She tore her gaze away, only to notice that the love seat had forced them so close together that her leg rested against his. She shifted awkwardly in the other direction.

"Uncomfortable?" Matt asked.

"I thought you might be."

"Just relax, okay?"

Kay knew he was just being nice, as Matt always was, but the low, whispery tone of his voice made it sound like so much more. She took a deep breath and another sip of wine, feeling an incredible urge to shift back toward him again. Even with a few inches of space between them, she could feel the heat from his body mingling with hers.

Jerry and Becky sat down again, and the four of them chatted away most of the next hour. Matt told Becky and Jerry about the most recent donations Kay had arranged for the shelter, which made her blush with delight, and Becky added that the Cat Room had never looked better or the cats happier.

Unfortunately, as they talked, at least one of Becky's three dogs sat at Kay's feet the entire time, mugging for attention. One would scamper off, only to be replaced a minute later by another one, like some kind of canine tag team. *She's the one,* they were saying in silent dog language. *She doesn't like us. Let's see what we can do about that. I'll take the first shift.*

Surprisingly, though, as the evening progressed, Kay found her guard slipping, and once she even patted one of them on the head without thinking. And she knew it was because her attention was focused almost exclusively on Matt, her internal antenna tuned to every breath he took, every move he made, every brush of his leg or his arm against hers, no matter how insignificant. The wine was making her feel warm and a little woozy, or was that just because Matt was sitting so close he could have turned and kissed her? If she let her mind wander just a little, she could almost make herself believe that she and Matt were the couple Jerry and Becky assumed they were.

"Oooh! Dessert!" Becky hopped to her feet. "I almost forgot. Kay, would you help me?"

No. I want to stay right here, exactly in this spot, for the rest of my life.

"Sure." She got up obligingly and followed Becky to the kitchen. Becky cut a few gigantic pieces of cherry pie and put them onto plates. She handed Kay the ice cream and a scoop.

"You know," Becky said, "Matt looks great tonight."

Kay smiled, deciding it never hurt to speak the truth. "He looks great every night."

Becky laughed. "No. I mean he looks happy, relaxed. I haven't seen him like this in a long time."

"I think he just likes being around people."

"He likes being around you."

Kay froze. "Uh, Becky..."

"I watched him go through that divorce, you know. It was pretty wicked. I don't like to speak badly of anyone, but in his ex-wife's case, I'll make an exception. Matt's a great guy. He didn't deserve a woman like that." She smiled at Kay. "I'm glad he's finally found someone who makes him happy."

"Becky, I think you've got the wrong idea here. Matt and I are just friends."

Becky looked at her with disbelief. "But you're living together, aren't you?"

"Matt's just doing me a favor. I was a little short on cash and I had to move out of my apartment, so I'm borrowing his spare bedroom for a few months."

"Oh." Becky looked disappointed. "I'm sorry, Kay. I just assumed..." Her voice trailed off. She returned the knife to the cherry pie and cut another piece. "So," she said offhandedly, "have you ever thought about Matt... you know...like that?"

"No. Of course not."

"Not even a little?"

Good Lord. She couldn't remember a moment in time she *hadn't* thought of him "like that." Suddenly all the frustration she'd felt for the past several weeks bubbled up inside her until she thought if she didn't tell someone she would explode. She squeezed her eyes closed painfully, then let out a sigh of resignation. "Okay. Maybe a little."

"A lot?" Becky said.

Kay laid the ice cream scoop on the countertop. She glanced out to the living room and saw Matt still engaged in conversation with Jerry. She faced Becky. "Yes. All right. A lot."

"Well, thank God. I didn't think you were blind."

Kay sighed with frustration. "I think about him all the time, Becky. Matt's wonderful. He's sweet and he's kind and he's just about the most attractive man I've ever met."

"And don't forget sexy."

Kay looked at Becky with surprise.

"Hey, just because I'm married doesn't mean I can't look." She smiled. "So what's the problem?"

"He's not interested."

"I don't believe that."

Kay's heart leaped with faint hope. "Why not?"

"I've seen the way he looks at you."

"When?"

"At the shelter. And tonight. Pretty much all the time. Haven't you noticed?"

"Oh, I don't know. Sometimes I think maybe...and then..." Kay twisted her mouth with frustration. "If he really is interested, why doesn't he do something about it? It's not like he hasn't had the opportunity."

"Hmm." Becky shook her head, as if something just wasn't right. "Kay, I watched that man tonight. He's barely taken his eyes off you. He praised you to the heavens for the work you've done around the shelter. And you should have seen him follow your every little move when you got up to help me get dessert.'' Becky shook her head again. ''Nope. He wants you. I'd stake my life on it.''

''Then why doesn't he let *me* in on it?''

''Maybe you just need to give him a little more time. He went through the killer of all divorces, and he's under a lot of pressure right now with the shelter and all. Just give him some time.''

Time. If that's all she thought it would take, she'd wait for him forever.

''After all,'' Becky added with a smile, ''I don't think Matt's blind, either. You're perfect for him. You're smart, you're pretty and you're an animal lover. What more could he possibly want?''

IT WAS NEARLY ten o'clock before they said good-night to Becky and Jerry, and Matt wished the evening could have gone on forever. As the night wore on, that tiny love seat where he and Kay sat had seemed to grow tinier still. They gave up trying to keep a respectable distance and relaxed against each other, so close that Matt could smell Kay's peach shampoo, hear the soft jangle of her bracelets when she took a sip of wine and savor the warmth of her body next to his. And now, as they drove home, Kay's hand rested against the console between them, and it was all Matt could do to keep from reaching over to lace his fingers through hers.

He'd told himself when they'd arrived at Becky and Jerry's that they were just two good friends sharing an evening with two other good friends. That lasted right up to the moment Kay sat down in a lawn chair and crossed her legs, giving him an unrestricted view from her tanned thighs all the way down to her pink-polished toenails peeking out from her sandals. Then they landed on that love seat together, and it wasn't long before his thoughts had wandered into truly uncharted territory. Erotic territory. Territory one did not explore with a mere friend.

Kay gave him a lazy smile. "That was a fun evening."

"Yeah," he said. "It was. Maybe we can return the favor and have Jerry and Becky over sometime."

"If we plan on feeding them we'd better take out extra liability insurance."

"Why? So you can fix your macaroni and cheese?"

"No. So you can fix your Spam…stuff. Or we can cook together and make…" Kay started to giggle. "Spamaroni and cheese."

Matt laughed. "Now, *that* would be something to behold."

"Going down, or coming back up?" Kay giggled again. Then those giggles erupted into laughter, which made Matt laugh even harder. That led to the formation of other combinations of their respective specialties, such as tuna-noodle soup and wiener nachos and oatmeal pot pie, and soon they were laughing so hard that Kay got tears in her eyes and Matt came within inches of wrapping the car around a stop sign. By the time they made it home, Matt was basking in that feeling of relaxed euphoria he got whenever he laughed himself silly. And it didn't escape his attention how distant those memories were.

Matt unlocked the back door, and he and Kay stepped into the kitchen. The big old house was silent, with the only illumination coming from the full moon as it poured in through the window, casting a warm glow around the room.

Kay reached for the light switch near the wall phone. But instead of flipping it on, her hand hovered over it for a moment, then withdrew. Slowly she turned to face him.

In the pale glow of moonlight, her eyes took on a luminescent quality that mesmerized him. The silence of the big old house and the darkness and the late hour made it seem as if the two of them were a million miles away from the rest of humanity, and every other problem he had in his life all at once seemed totally insignificant.

"I really did have a wonderful time tonight," she said.

"Yeah. Me too."

Each second that ticked away seemed to draw them closer together, until the only thing that existed in the world was a dilapidated, turn-of-the-century house and the two of them staring at one another. Kay's gaze spelled out very clearly what was on her mind, and it was so close to what was on his mind that a shiver of raw awareness coursed through him. He had no business having these feelings. *Roommate, roommate, roommate,* he repeated to himself, doing that compartmentalizing thing that was supposed to keep friendly thoughts in one part of his brain and erotic thoughts in another. Unfortunately, with Kay standing there looking so beautiful, with moonlight warming her blond hair and her eyes a pair of perfect blue sapphires, compartmentalizing was pretty much out of the question. It would be easy, so easy, to lean closer, lay his hand against her cheek and—

Answer the phone.

The second it rang, they both jumped backward. Matt yanked up the receiver, resisting the urge to rip the whole damned thing off the wall.

"Hello?…Oh. Yes. Hello, Mrs. Feinstein." He rolled his eyes and shrugged.

Kay couldn't believe it. How did she know? How did Mrs. Feinstein know *exactly* the moment to call that would bother her the most?

While Matt talked, Kay went to the refrigerator and

opened the door, pretending to be searching for something but really wanting to feel a blast of cold air because it suddenly seemed so *warm* in here. Being close to Matt tended to raise her body temperature, and right now she could have popped the top right off a thermometer. Not that anything would have happened between them if Mrs. Feinstein hadn't called, no matter how long she stood staring at him in the moonlight. She'd hit too many dead ends with Matt already to think things were going to change now. But just for a moment there, she could have sworn...

She pulled a cola out of the fridge, opened it and took a long drink. The fizzy liquid took the edge off whatever alcohol high she had left and brought her back down to planet Earth.

"Maybe you'd better bring him on over," she heard Matt say. "No, it's all right. I'll be here."

"What is it this time?" Kay asked as he hung up.

"Seems Andre's running a bit of a fever."

"She actually took his temperature?"

"No. She felt his forehead."

"Can you tell a dog has a fever like that?"

"Nope." Matt smiled, then checked his watch. "It's only a little after ten. Would you like to stay up a while? Watch a little TV? It's Friday night."

"Sure."

"I shouldn't be long. There's bound to be something on TV later. You know, our usual stuff. A documentary, a news magazine, a sitcom—"

"Jerry Springer's doing 'My Brother's Wife Is a Lesbian Transvestite.'"

Matt grinned. "Now you're talking. I'll be up soon."

Kay went upstairs, and a few minutes later she heard Mrs. Feinstein's panicked little flurry of knocks on the front door. She flopped on the sofa and rested her head

on a pillow, then turned on a dumb sitcom to watch unt
Matt returned.

Until she'd moved in with him, she'd had no idea hov
much time he put into his work. Several times she'd see
him answer a page, and she'd often hear him on the tele
phone listening to problems and giving advice. And h
always took a few minutes in the evening to phone th
owners of some of the patients he'd seen that day, dog
or cats who'd had surgery or had been particularly il
Once the phone rang in the middle of the night and sh
heard him go downstairs, and she wondered how man
more times he'd done that and she hadn't realized it. An
he did all that in addition to seeing patients during hi
regular office hours and keeping the shelter running.

And more than once she'd seen him at the kitchen table
opening mail, going through what looked like bills. H
never discussed the specifics of the shelter's finances wit
her, but she knew by the look on his face and the wa
he'd toss the letters aside with a worried expression tha
things had to be bad.

She closed her eyes for a moment, wondering what els
she might be able to do to bring more money or mor
supplies into the shelter. Wondering what she could do t
make Matt think of her as more than just his roommate
Wondering how he'd react if he came back upstairs to fin
her lying naked on the sofa.

She blinked sleepily as she mulled over the possibilitie
The next thing she knew, a hand was on her shoulder. Sh
blinked her eyes open to find Matt staring down at her.

"Come on, Sleeping Beauty. It's time for bed."

Kay rose on one elbow. "What time is it?"

"Almost midnight."

Midnight? Matt had been downstairs almost two hours
"Wow. Her dog must have really been sick this time."

"No. He's fine."

Kay yawned, then sat up on the edge of the sofa. "Fever?"

"No. I finally convinced her he was all right."

Kay couldn't believe the things Matt put up with sometimes. If she'd been him, she'd have told the old lady to come back when her dog was really sick. Matt was pulled in ten different directions as it was, so why did he let people waste his time?

"Great," she said. "A hypochondriac pet owner. I bet that drives you crazy, doesn't it?"

"Oh, Mrs. Feinstein's okay. It's just that she lost her husband about six months ago, and her family doesn't have much to do with her. That poodle's about all she's got left, and she's afraid he's going to be next. I think sometimes all she wants to do is talk to someone. No big deal."

Kay just stared at him. No big deal?

Robert had once put off a hysterical client for two days because he couldn't stand the perfume she wore, and here was Matt taking huge chunks of time for a lonely old lady who didn't have anyone else to talk to. And he didn't think twice about it.

In that instant it was as if everything came together, and Kay understood. She finally understood that it wasn't just the animals Matt was so heavily invested in, but the lives of the people they touched.

And that was the moment she realized she loved him.

ON SATURDAY MORNING Kay hopped out of bed and made it over to the shelter by eight. She wanted to make sure she worked at least four hours—from eight to noon. She was closing in on completing her hundred hours, and she wanted to make sure she finished by the contract date. Robert would hold her to it—no doubt about that.

When she came through the door, Hazel handed her a courier package that had arrived late the day before. Kay noted the return address and smiled knowingly.

"What's in there?" Hazel asked.

Kay headed toward the Cat Room. "You'll see."

Twenty minutes later Hazel came to the doorway of the Cat Room, right about the time Kay buckled the last collar on the last cat. The old woman's gaze circled the room, going from one stray cat to the next, apparently unable to believe that every one of them was wearing a gaudy rhinestone collar.

"They're freebies from Cat's Meow," Kay said. "It's kind of like draping bag ladies in haute couture, but every little bit helps." Kay turned the Siamese and his stunning new collar around for Hazel's inspection. "What do you think? Pretty snazzy, huh?"

Hazel just stared.

"Wait till Matt sees them," Kay said, delighted at the thought. He'd roll his eyes as if it was the silliest thing he'd ever seen, then glare at her admonishingly. Then, when he couldn't keep up the stern facade any longer, his face would crack open into a smile as bright as the Fourth of July. It made her feel warm all over just to think about it.

If only she could feel that way forever.

Hazel turned her gaze from the cats back to Kay. "I've got to go over to the clinic for a few minutes. Will you watch the front desk for me?"

"Sure."

Hazel eyed the cats again, her eyes narrowing thoughtfully. "You know, maybe those collars aren't such a bad idea. Gives 'em a little attitude."

"So you like them?

"Yeah. Good thinking. And the bulletin board out front looks nice, too. Good job."

As Hazel walked away, Kay stared after her with astonishment. Had Hazel actually said she'd done something right?

Then she realized this was the third time in a week that Hazel had asked her to fill in at the front desk. And she rarely frowned anymore. In fact, she actually smiled once in a while. Hazel was a taskmaster, to be sure, but she never asked Kay to do anything she wasn't willing to do herself in a pinch. Kay felt a flush of warmth as she realized she was actually starting to like the old lady. Maybe Hazel was starting to like her, too.

She scooped up the packing peanuts and stuffed them along with the box into the trash. Then she went to the front desk, sat down and picked up Hazel's crossword puzzle. Fourteen down: a three-letter word for "ostrich cousin." She stared at the crossword a moment longer, then tossed it aside. All she could think about was the four-letter word for how she felt about Matt.

Could she really be in love with him? After her experience with Robert, as well as a few other ill-fated relationships, she wasn't even sure she knew what love felt like. She'd tried to put it out of her mind all day long, because it scared her to death to even think it. How pitiful was it to have those feelings for a man who felt nothing for her in return?

Kay heard a car door outside, bringing her thoughts back to earth. A minute later the door opened and a man came in, trailed by a kid about ten years old.

"We're thinking about adopting a dog," the man said.

Kay stood up. "You've come to the right place. As a

matter of fact," she told the kid, "we've got a very nice dog here I think you're really going to like."

Kay held her breath as she took the man and his son to the Dog Room and stopped in front of Chester's cage. Chester stood up and wagged his tail, pouring on what little charm he had, but Kay could tell he was coming up short.

"Him?" the kid said, screwing his face up with distaste.

"Yeah. He's a really good dog."

"But how's he supposed to play ball and stuff?"

"Oh, he can learn to play games. Maybe he's not as fast as the other dogs, but…"

The kid pointed to the cage next door. "Dad! Look at the big black dog! *That's* the one I want!"

Chester watched the kid a moment more, then limped to the back of his cage and lay down again. As Kay stared down at him she felt that funny twinge again, hating the way people dismissed him without so much as a second thought.

"I don't know, son," his father said, eyeing Rambo with great trepidation. "You think you can handle a big dog like that?"

"Sure I can!" The kid turned to Kay with an earnest expression. "Can you take him out? Can I play with him?"

Kay turned to the father. He shrugged helplessly.

Kay opened up Rambo's cage and he came shooting out. He headed straight for the kid, who wrapped his arms around his neck as Rambo slapped wild doggie kisses across his face.

"Dad, please! This is *such* a cool dog!"

"Our yard's really not that big—"

"I'll walk him every day!"

"I'll bet he eats like a horse."

The kid stood up and faced his father. "I'll pay for his food with my allowance. I promise. Please, Dad. Please!"

As the kid negotiated with his father, Rambo circled the small space. He sniffed everything in sight—the other dogs through their cages, the kid's shoes, the father's crotch.

The man's face reddened. He pushed Rambo away, then turned to Kay with a reluctant sigh. "Is he housebroken?"

"Housebroken? Uh, I'm sure that won't be a problem." Kay told herself that while her answer wasn't a no it wasn't exactly a yes, either, so she hadn't really fibbed.

"See?" the kid said. "Mom won't go ballistic as long as he's housebroken. And he's got short hair. She'll like that, too."

Rambo was still sniffing. He was sniffing so much, in fact, that Kay started to wonder why. And unfortunately, when he galloped over and started sniffing her, the light didn't dawn quickly enough. Rambo lifted his leg, and a second later Kay felt a warm trickle from her knee to her ankle.

"Rambo!" "Wow!" the kid said. "Look at that! He peed all over you!"

"I thought you said he was housebroken," his father muttered.

Kay didn't respond. She couldn't respond. As the distinctive odor of dog urine floated up to her nostrils, all she could think about was wrapping her hands around Rambo's neck and squeezing until his beady little eyes bugged out.

"Well, hello there, Kay."

Kay froze at the sound of that all-too-familiar voice. It couldn't be.

Slowly she turned around, and in that instant the indignity of the moment multiplied a hundredfold.

Robert.

10

ROBERT LEANED against the doorframe wearing a crisp Italian suit, a conservative silk tie and a self-satisfied grin that made Kay wish she could knock his mouthful of cosmetic dental work right down his throat. She glared at him. "What are *you* doing here?"

He shrugged nonchalantly. "I was in the neighborhood."

Mortified, Kay grabbed Rambo by the collar and shooed him back into his cage. At the same time the father shooed his kid out the door, apparently deciding this was not the day to go dog-shopping after all.

Kay strode past Robert out of the Dog Room. He stepped quickly out of her way, making a big show of giving her a wide berth. She went to the kitchen, retrieved a handful of paper towel and dabbed hopelessly at her leg. Robert stood at the door and stared at her, still wearing that insidious little grin.

"Do you do other impressions, too?" he asked her. "Or just fire hydrants?"

Kay gave up and tossed the paper towel into the trash. "The show's over, Robert. You can go home now."

He looked utterly distressed. "Why, Kay, is something the matter? I sense you're not having the rewarding experience I'd hoped for."

"Are you kidding?" she growled. "I'm having *exactly* the experience you hoped for."

Robert laughed. "No, I have to admit that even I didn't envision anything quite this humiliating. That big black mutt summed up all my feelings for you with one little lift of his leg."

Kay lunged toward Robert and almost had a double fistful of his lapels when an arm snaked around her and yanked her backward. Someone had grabbed her. Twisting around, she saw that someone was Matt. In the midst of her fury at Robert, she hadn't even heard him come in.

"Let *go* of me!" She struggled wildly against Matt, wanting nothing to come between her and her homicide target, but by now he'd wrapped both arms around her, trapping her against his body.

"Kay...?" Matt's voice was low and deliberate. "Maybe you'd better tell me what's going on here."

She pointed a furious finger at Robert. "I want him gone. No. Let me amend that. I want him dead!"

"Really, Kay," Robert said, folding his arms across his chest. "Isn't it about time you learned to control your temper?"

"You haven't even begun to see my temper, you slimebag!"

"Oh? And just what do you intend to do this time? You've already shaved every animal I've got."

While Kay continued to squirm in Matt's grip, Robert smiled broadly. "Well, Forester, I can see you've got your hands full, so I'll be going. It was nice chatting with you, Kay. I'll drop by again next time I'm in the neighborhood. I can't tell you how much I'm looking forward to it." Robert gave her one last nasty little chuckle, then turned and strode out the front door.

"Matt! Let...me...*go!*"

"Are you going after him?" Matt said.

"Yes!"

"Then I'm not letting you go."

Kay yanked vainly at Matt's forearm, then tried twisting left and right, but his grip was far too strong. "I'm not really going to kill him, Matt. I swear. I'm just going to make him *wish* he were dead!"

"Just calm down," Matt said in a disgustingly reasonable tone of voice, "and tell me what happened."

"You want to know what happened? Take a whiff."

He sniffed, then leaned away slightly to glance down at the leg of her jeans. "Uh-oh. Which dog got you?"

"Rambo. Robert showed up here to gloat just about at the time that canine cretin mistook my leg for a tree. Of course, Robert thought it was the most hysterical thing he'd ever seen. I hate him, Matt. I hate everything about him. I hate the way he looks, the way he walks, the way he talks—"

Matt pulled a kitchen chair away from the table and sat Kay down in it. She immediately tried to rise. He put his hands on her shoulders, shoved her down again, then pulled out a chair and sat down beside her.

"Kay? Can I ask you a question?"

She crossed her arms and fumed silently.

"Why in the world did you want to marry a guy like that?"

She met Matt's gaze, staring at him a long time. She hated to say it out loud, because it sounded so dumb. "As soon as I told my family that Robert proposed, you'd have thought I won the lottery, the way they went on. By the time they got through telling me how lucky I was, I figured they'd disown me if I turned him down. I think it was the first time in my life I did something they actually approved of."

Matt stared at her blankly for a moment, as if he hadn't

quite comprehended her meaning. "*That's* why you were going to marry him?"

"You don't understand, Matt. My parents are attorneys. My sister's an attorney. All I am is a legal secretary, and even that's pretty recent. Before that I was..."

Kay paused, feeling as if she was about to confess that she'd once been a streetwalker, and a pretty sleazy one at that.

"...a waitress."

She waited for that subtle twist of the mouth, the slight turning up of the nose she always saw on people's faces whenever she mentioned that word. But on Matt, she saw neither.

"There's nothing wrong with being a waitress," he said. "It's good, honest work."

Kay blinked with surprise. "I quit college my freshman year," she went on, knowing most people with advanced degrees thought dropouts were morons. Her family certainly did. But Matt just shrugged.

"College isn't for everyone."

Maybe he wasn't hearing her right. She shifted around and looked at him head-on. "I once got suspended from high school for toilet-papering the principal's house."

"I know a guy who went with his friends to his history teacher's house and lobbed raw eggs onto her skylights. It was a hundred and two degrees that day. They fried."

"What happened to him?"

"He graduated, went to college and became a veterinarian."

Kay smiled, even as her heart was breaking. As easily as her family made her feel inferior, Matt made her feel wonderful. Why couldn't he be more to her than just a friend?

"So what did you do in kindergarten?" he asked her. "Spray paint your ABCs on the schoolhouse wall?"

Kindergarten. She winced at the very thought of it. "No, but I once had to spend three days of recess time standing in the corner because I refused to color inside the lines."

Matt raised his eyebrows. "You really *were* a radical."

"Yeah. My teacher thought the world was going to end if I didn't get that red crayon in exactly the right place. My mother felt the same way, because the punishment didn't end with my nose in the corner at school."

"Conformity is overrated. Look at the way you solve problems. You wanted the cat litter. I wouldn't buy it, so you got them to donate it."

"That was no great accomplishment," she said, waving her hand. "Anyone with the gift of gab could have done the same thing."

"And you work hard at the shelter. The Cat Room looks like the Ritz Carlton."

"Big deal. Anyone with a strong back and a strong stomach could manage that, too."

"And for the first time in a long time," Matt said, his voice softening, "I don't hate the thought of coming home at night."

Kay closed her eyes, his words filling her with such warmth and comfort that the cold sting of her family's disapproval disappeared from her thoughts in a mental *poof*. Then frustration crept in again. Why was he saying such wonderful things? Didn't he know it made her want him that much more?

"Stop listening to your family," Matt said. "They'll make you crazy."

Hadn't Sheila told her that at least a hundred times?

Wasn't it time she started believing it? "I *don't* listen to them. I don't care what they think. Not anymore."

Kay's mouth moved with conviction, but she just couldn't get the rest of her body to follow suit. She bowed her head, then felt the tears coming. *Damn.* She was such a fool. Why else would she spend her whole life looking for approval from people she didn't even like?

She blinked quickly, feeling utterly ridiculous for crying over something she shouldn't even care about in the first place—especially in front of Matt.

"Okay," she said, sniffing a little. "So I'm not there yet. But I'm getting better."

At that moment Matt decided he hated every single member of Kay's family, and he'd never even met them. How could they do that to her? It infuriated him to think that someone could be as smart and capable as Kay, yet be told all her life she wasn't.

"So I guess it must have been pretty awkward when Robert broke your engagement," he said.

Kay's eyes widened. "Is that what he told you? That *he* broke our engagement?"

"Uh—yeah."

For a moment Kay looked positively homicidal. Then her expression settled into one of disgusted resignation. "I don't know why I'm surprised. If he'd have sex in his office with another woman three months before our wedding, he wouldn't think twice about lying about it, now would he?"

Matt's mouth dropped open. "He cheated on you? In his *office?*"

"Knowing Robert, he was too cheap to get a hotel room."

Matt couldn't believe it. All this time Hollinger had led him to believe that he was the noble one and Kay was the savage. Now that he knew the truth, Hollinger's stock had just plunged to an all-time low.

Kay sat in silence, staring down at her hands. To his dismay, he saw tears fill her eyes again. Then he had a thought that was completely intolerable. Could it be she still had feelings for Hollinger?

"Don't," he said softly. "Robert's not worth it."

"No," she said, waving her hand. "It's not that. Believe me. I don't give a damn about Robert Hollinger." She sighed. "It's just the whole idea of it, you know? Finding out you're less important to the man you're going to marry than a cheap brunette and three cocker spaniels?"

Matt thought he'd known what a jerk Hollinger was, but now he realized he'd only been seeing the tip of that iceberg. First her family, then her fiancé.

"Now I really know why you had those dogs shaved." He smiled. "Good for you."

Kay sniffed, then shook her head. "No. It's *not* good for me. I'm too impulsive and it gets me into trouble every time. If it wasn't for the fact that I did the dog-shaving thing, I wouldn't even be here."

Matt slid his palm against her face, brushing away a tear with his thumb. "And that," he said, "would have been my loss."

She froze, her blue eyes widening with surprise. Caught in her gaze, he couldn't look away. He trailed his thumb along her cheekbone, and slowly her surprise melted into a look of awareness, of expectation. She inclined her head to lean into his hand, closed her eyes and exhaled softly.

Oh, boy.

He couldn't remember the last time he'd wanted something as desperately as he wanted to kiss her right now. With her eyes closed he gazed at her leisurely, at the feathered lashes that brushed her cheeks, the delicate bone structure of her face and those warm, lush lips that were sending him a silent invitation to come closer. It was as if a thin, delicate thread was drawing him toward her, compelling him to kiss her so thoroughly and completely that it would make up for all the time he'd wasted not kissing her.

But he couldn't. Not yet.

And the reason he couldn't was because Robert Hollinger was a nasty, manipulative jerk who'd maneuvered him into a position where he had no choice but to act as if he was, at the very most, Kay's big brother or best buddy. And big brothers and best buddies couldn't even conceive of the thoughts that were running through his mind right now.

With great reluctance, he pulled his hand back and leaned away. She blinked her eyes open and stared at him, looking a little disoriented.

"I think I heard a car door outside," Matt said, his voice a little shaky. "Maybe it's a family with six kids and they all want a pet."

Kay blinked. "Yeah. Okay." She pushed her chair away from the table and stood up. "I'll tell them we're having a two-for-one special."

She managed a wobbly smile, then grabbed a paper towel on her way out of the kitchen and dabbed at her eyes. As she disappeared into the hall, Matt dropped his head to his hands and let out a long breath.

He kept telling himself she wasn't the right woman for him. That in the long run she wouldn't understand about the shelter, that she'd resent the money he spent just to take care of a ragtag bunch of animals. But the warnings he issued himself were only halfhearted, because now he knew that Kay hadn't gone looking for Hollinger. He'd just been the convenient fulfillment of other people's expectations, which meant her life goals probably didn't center around his-and-hers limos and a winter house in Florida.

She had less than fifteen hours left to work at the shelter. Once she'd put in her time, it wouldn't be long before she'd be moving out, and all at once he realized he couldn't bear the thought of her leaving. It had been so long since he'd had a warm, breathing human being beside him that he'd almost forgotten what it was like, and now that he remembered, he never wanted to be without it again.

Without her again.

How had this happened? It wasn't just loneliness, and it wasn't just lust. He'd blamed his feelings on those two things for quite some time now, but slowly his brain was admitting what his heart already knew. It wasn't just any warm body he wanted next to his. It was Kay's.

He didn't know how much longer he could play this game. Sooner or later she was going to see in his eyes how much he wanted her, and hear it in his voice, and he wouldn't be able to fool her anymore.

LATER THAT EVENING, Matt came in the kitchen door just in time to catch the ringing phone. As soon as he picked it up and heard the voice on the other end, he wished he hadn't.

Hollinger. Just hearing that smug voice, after what Kay had told him today, made his blood boil.

"I just wanted to let you know how pleased I am with the way things are turning out," Hollinger said. "That little show this afternoon was worth every string I've had to pull to get you that grant."

"Those things happen sometimes when you're around animals."

"Yes, they sometimes do. And seeing it happen to Kay made my day."

Matt was silent.

"I wanted to let you know, too, that the awards ceremony is in two weeks."

Matt froze. "Awards ceremony?"

"Of course. At the Fairmont Hotel. We're expecting two hundred people. And the press will be there—"

"Press? Now, wait a minute, Robert. You never said anything about—"

"What did you think was going to happen, Forester? Did you think I'd just send you a check in the mail?"

That's exactly what he'd thought. "No. Of course not. I just—"

"Two weeks from today at seven o'clock." Robert paused. "I assume there's no problem with that?"

"Uh—no. No problem."

"Good work, Forester," Hollinger said. "I knew I could count on you." The line clicked, and a dial tone droned in Matt's ear.

He hung up the phone, panic starting to set in. An awards ceremony? Two hundred people? The press, for God's sake?

When he thought of the measures he might have to take to keep Hollinger's involvement from Kay, it just about made him sick. Could he tell her the truth? Maybe now she would understand.

Oh, hell. Who was he kidding? After what had happened with Rambo today, her disgust with Hollinger had reached an all-time high. He pictured the look of betrayal that would spring to Kay's face if she found out what an underhanded deal he'd made with Hollinger, and he just couldn't bear it.

One way or another, he had to find a way to pick up

that grant money without Kay finding out the real reason he was getting it.

SEVERAL DAYS LATER, Kay sprawled on her bed, staring down at the checkbook calendar she held. A couple of months ago she'd circled the third Friday in September in red, looking forward to the day she'd be through at the shelter and Robert would be out of her life for good.

She slapped the calendar shut and rolled onto her back, staring up at the ceiling. As badly as she'd wanted to get the hundred hours over with in the beginning, that's how badly she now wanted them never to end. The thought of leaving Matt was unbearable.

Marilyn leaped from the windowsill and jumped up on the bed beside Kay. She stroked her absentmindedly, and the cat collapsed beside her, her purr reverberating through the silence of the room.

"Okay, Marilyn. You're a woman. And you've known him longer than I have. What am I doing wrong here?"

Marilyn turned to her with the arrogant expression of a feline sex goddess who could wiggle one paw and every tomcat within ten miles would come rushing to her side. *He's just one man,* those green eyes said, *and human at that. So what's the problem?*

"Great," Kay muttered. "Even the cat thinks I'm pitiful."

Ever since the day Robert had showed up at the shelter, Kay had held on to a tiny thread of hope that something might happen between her and Matt, something to bring back the warmth she'd felt as he touched her cheek and smiled at her and told her that her family was worthless but she wasn't. But nothing had. While Matt was still sweet and wonderful and the best company she'd ever had, the invisible wall remained between them. And it looked as if it would remain there forever.

She heard Matt's voice calling to her up the back stairs, telling her dinner was ready. She rose with a heavy sigh and trudged downstairs. Matt pulled a pair of chicken pot pies out of the oven and they sat down to eat.

"Well," Kay said, struggling for nonchalance, "I guess I have only a few more hours left to work at the shelter."

"Really?"

"Yeah. I think I'll go apartment hunting on Saturday."

"Don't hurry. You can stay here as long as you need to."

How about forever?

She knew he was just being nice, and she had no intention of prolonging the inevitable. The longer she stayed, the harder it would be to leave. And what if she stayed a few weeks longer, or maybe a month, and then one day Matt started to date someone? How could she deal with that? How could she sit by and watch some other woman have the man she wanted more than anything?

No. A clean break. It was the only way.

"It's okay," she told him. "I've got the money for an apartment deposit. I'll move out as soon as I find an apartment."

He nodded silently, and she wanted to cry. All Matt was losing was a roommate. Kay was losing the man she loved.

11

THE NEXT MORNING at work, Kay walked around in a daze, and it wasn't long until her state of mind translated to paper cuts and misrouted faxes and, right now, a spilled cup of coffee. As she stood in the kitchenette, pulling a wad of paper towels off the roll, she hoped Mr. Breckenridge wouldn't come wandering in and realize just how much of a klutz she'd become.

She swiped at the puddle of coffee on the counter, vowing to keep her mind on her work instead of on Matt. The woman she was filling in for would be coming back in a week, taking back the job Kay had actually grown to like. She intended to do the best job she could until then, hoping at least to get some kind of reference from Mr. Breckenridge that might help her find a permanent job after she left.

"Ms. Ramsey?"

Kay spun around, tucking the coffee-soaked paper towels behind her back. Mr. Breckenridge was standing behind her.

"Yes, sir?"

"May I see you for a moment, please?"

"Yes. Of course."

Kay didn't miss the ominous tone in his voice and wondered what was up. She followed him into his office. He motioned for her to close the door and sit down, his expression grim.

"Robert Hollinger. I understand you worked for him."

A rush of foreboding overwhelmed her. She'd assumed because she'd lasted several weeks here that Robert didn't know where she was working. But it looked as if he'd finally tracked her down.

"Yes, sir," she said. "I did."

"I spoke with him this morning. I must say he had some rather interesting things to say about your suitability as an employee. He told me—"

"You don't have to say it, Mr. Breckenridge," Kay said, feeling the reference she'd hoped for fly right out the window. "I know exactly how he feels about me."

"Then I'd like to hear what you have to say about him."

Had she heard him right? No one had ever talked to Robert and then wanted to hear *her* opinion on the matter. But here was Mr. Breckenridge, settling back in his chair, his fingers steepled in front of him, waiting for her reply.

A wave of hopelessness overtook her. What was the point of trying to defend herself? Kay knew whatever she said, she couldn't possibly counter whatever rotten things Robert had already told Breckenridge about her. He'd finally succeeded in forcing her to rock-bottom with nowhere else to go.

Then all at once her hopelessness was swept away by a wave of anger. If she let Robert continue to get away with this, she'd never work another day as long as she lived.

"Of course, Mr. Breckenridge. I'd be happy to tell you exactly what I think of Mr. Hollinger." She squared her shoulders, then met her boss's gaze head-on.

"Robert Hollinger is a manipulative, spiteful, self-centered man who lies as easily as he ties his shoes. Professionally, he's after the bottom line and doesn't give a damn whether justice is served or not. The longer I knew him, the more I realized there wasn't a kind, respectful or considerate bone in his body. All in all, I'd say he's pretty rotten excuse for a human being.''

Kay folded her arms across her chest, still fixing her gaze squarely at Mr. Breckenridge. He raised his bushy eyebrows with a hint of surprise. ''Well. I see.'' He took off his glasses and laid them on the desk in front of him. ''I appreciate your clarifying that for me. I don't know him well, but Mr. Hollinger's firm is a member of the Dorland Group, so I've worked with him on various projects through the years. I've always had an odd feeling about him, though. A sense that he was, shall we say...disingenuous? And when I spoke to him today, those feelings only grew stronger.''

Kay stared at Mr. Breckenridge with total disbelief.

''Under normal circumstances I'd be forced to take a reference at face value. But I've worked with you for quite some time now, Ms. Ramsey. And I must say that in that time, aside from your complete inability to make a decent pot of coffee, I haven't noticed any of the negative aspects of your character Mr. Hollinger was so quick to point out.''

Kay sat in a daze, unable to believe that a man like Mr. Breckenridge would take her word over Robert's. She felt a flush of pleasure that tickled her all the way to her toes.

''The reason I called you in here is to tell you that my secretary, the young lady you're filling in for, phoned yesterday to tell me she prefers full-time motherhood to working here. I was hoping you'd agree to take over her position permanently.''

Kay stared at him, dumbfounded. A full-time job? Here?

Then before she could recover from the fact that Mr.

Breckenridge had offered her a job, he mentioned a salary that was several thousand more than Robert had paid her, and she nearly fainted.

"Uh...yeah," she said, still in a daze. Then she composed herself as much as her shocked state would allow. "I mean, yes, Mr. Breckenridge. I accept your offer."

"See Ms. Hildebrand. She'll handle the necessary paperwork."

Mr. Breckenridge opened a folder in front of him and began to thumb through the papers it contained. Kay supposed that meant she was dismissed.

"Mr. Breckenridge?"

He looked up.

"I know what Robert must have said about me, and..." She paused, at a loss for words. "Thank you."

He looked back down at the folder on his desk. "There's no need to thank me. Hiring you is merely a good business decision."

Kay smiled at the compliment, feeling an overwhelming urge to kiss Mr. Breckenridge smack-dab on top of his bald little head. Instead she left his office with the decorum befitting the secretary of one of the most prominent attorneys in the city.

She went back out to her desk and sat down, still in shock. And that's when she had a stunning revelation. She actually liked being a legal secretary, panty hose and all. She liked the professional atmosphere, the respect she got from her co-workers, and the challenge that accompanied every task she took on. She was good at it.

And to her complete delight, Mr. Breckenridge thought so, too.

When five o'clock rolled around and she was getting ready to leave for the day, she looked up to see Jason leaning against the doorway, a knowing smile on his face.

"I assume you took the job."

Kay frowned. Apparently Mr. Breckenridge's intent to offer her a job was a secret only to her. "Yes. I did."

Jason eased toward her desk, wearing that look she'd grown so accustomed to in the past few weeks, as if he was going hunting and she was the prey. "I think this calls for a celebration, don't you? I've got a Jacquesson 1990 Blanc I've been wanting to try. Join me at my apartment at, say, seven o'clock?"

Kay assumed all those French words added up to a bottle of champagne, while all the rest of his words added up to a not-so-subtle proposition. And she didn't want to deal with any of it.

She wanted to go home. She wanted to tell Matt about her new job. He'd give her a big hug, then toast her with a can of cola, telling her all the while how fortunate Mr. Breckenridge was that she'd accepted his job offer. Then maybe they'd rent a movie and spend the rest of the evening on the sofa together.

Three feet apart.

Matt's gaze would be glued to the TV and her gaze glued to him. They'd snack a little, talk a little, laugh a little. And then...

And then nothing.

Kay almost cried at the hopelessness of it. Every imaginable door had opened between them, and Matt had refused to walk through any of them. He was sweet and sexy and one of the best friends she'd ever had. But they weren't lovers, and the way things looked, they never would be. She didn't know why Matt felt the way he did, but she did know one thing: it was time she stopped demeaning herself by desperately wanting a man who was never going to want her.

She sighed with resignation. Right now, the prospect of

spending one more night alone with Matt that led to nothing was even more painful than the prospect of spending an evening with Jason, and that was saying a lot.

"Okay, Jason," she said. "Pick me up at eight. Dinner at Rodolpho's. No champagne, and I don't even want to know where you live. Deal?"

A funny mix of emotions swam around on his face: elation that she'd finally agreed to go out with him, and annoyance that she was calling the shots. He looked left and right, then gave her a crooked smile. "Sure, sweetheart. Whatever you say."

She wrote her address on a sticky note, gave it to Jason and told him she'd see him at eight. That would give her enough time to finish her work at the shelter, then get dressed for dinner.

As he walked out of her office, she closed her eyes, feeling as if her heart had crumbled into a hundred tiny pieces. From the day she'd moved in with Matt it had been pretty clear they'd never have a future together, but this was the first time she'd actually made herself believe it.

MATT GOT STUCK at the clinic setting a golden retriever's broken leg, so it was nearly six-thirty before he made it over to the shelter. When he came through the front door he found the reception desk deserted. He figured Hazel was out back having a quick cigarette, and Kay was probably in the Cat Room. He stopped for a moment and looked around, and all at once it struck him how different the shelter seemed than it had only a few months ago.

Evidence of Kay was everywhere.

In the corner of the reception area sat a silk ficus tree she'd brought from her storage shed, a little worse for wear from dogs nosing it and cats batting at it, but definitely a nice addition. She'd organized and added to the bulletin board with Polaroid shots of animals going home with their new families, most notably two half-bald cats wearing Kitty-Tees. Looking at the desk, he saw that files were actually put away, a coffee mug had become a pencil cup and even the mail had its own little basket beside the telephone. And despite the mild yet distinct animal aroma in the air, if he closed his eyes he swore he could smell her perfume.

He went into the kitchen to grab a drink, and as he was closing the refrigerator door, he noticed movement out the kitchen window. Stepping closer, he couldn't believe what he saw.

In the long shadows of late afternoon, Kay stood in the backyard holding what looked like a brand-new hot-pink Frisbee in her hand. Chester sat at her feet. Matt watched as Kay showed the Frisbee to the dog, then backed away seven or eight paces. She tossed the Frisbee gently toward him. Chester leaped up with excitement as the disc approached, but in the end all he did was watch it fall to earth.

Kay picked up the Frisbee and showed it to Chester again, then tossed it, only to slump in frustration once more as both she and the dog watched it sail to the ground.

"She's been out there with him for the past half hour." Matt spun around to find Hazel standing behind him. He turned back to the window and watched in astonishment as Kay scratched Chester behind his ears, patted his side, then backed off again for another try. She caught his attention with the Frisbee, then tossed it again. It seemed to hover in midair for a long time before beginning its descent, only this time Chester actually raised up on his back paws and clamped his jaws around it before it hit the ground.

Kay let out a whoop of delight Matt could hear even through the closed window. She rushed over to Chester, took the Frisbee from him and praised him madly, patting him, scratching him and ruffling his ears. Chester got all excited and slurped his tongue across Kay's cheek, and she didn't even bother to wipe it off. Matt could see her lips forming the words *good boy,* over and over, and when she smiled at that misbegotten animal it was as if the clouds had parted and sunlight was streaming down from heaven.

"I overheard her talking to him when she took him out to the backyard," Hazel said. "She told him to pay attention, because if he could learn to play a game maybe some kid would want him."

In that moment any lingering thoughts Matt had about Kay not relating to animals shattered into a million pieces. This wasn't the Kay who'd come kicking and screaming into his shelter a couple of months ago. This Kay was sweet and compassionate with a heart the size of Texas, who'd grown to love an animal enough that she'd go out of her way to help him find a home. And looking at her now, he knew—she would understand. She would understand how much the shelter meant to him, because it was starting to mean something to her, too.

All at once he realized what an integral part of his life she'd become, so enmeshed in his everyday existence that he couldn't imagine tomorrow without her. She'd chased away the loneliness he'd felt for what seemed like forever. She made him eager to come home at night. And most importantly, she'd given him something he hadn't felt in a long time. Hope.

It was the last week of September. The air unit was still holding on. If it kept working another few weeks he'd have until spring to find a way to replace it. With fall here, his utility bills would drop dramatically. The donations Kay had gotten had lightened his financial burden just enough that if nothing else went wrong, he just might be able to keep things running. For the first time in a long while, he was actually looking forward to tomorrow.

He might even be able to get by without the Dorland Grant.

The moment that thought leaped into his mind, he froze. Then he examined it for a moment, playing it over, looking at it from all sides. All at once it didn't seem so incomprehensible. Why hadn't he seen it before?

If he turned down the grant, he'd be out from under Hollinger's thumb. He'd be free to tell Kay how he felt about her. And he'd never have to worry about Kay finding out what he'd done, because he'd never accepted that money in payment for anything. He strode to the front desk and started flipping through the phone book.

"What's going on, Doc?" Hazel asked.

He put his finger on Hollinger's number. "I'm going to tell Hollinger to forget the grant."

"You're what?"

He couldn't quite believe he'd said it, but now that the words were out of his mouth, they seemed to gain momentum. "I'm going to tell him to forget it. I never should have agreed to it in the first place. Things are better now. The donations Kay's gotten, the weather turning cooler…it's all going to work out. I don't need Hollinger."

Suddenly he felt wonderful, liberated. All he had to do was call Hollinger. Then he could go out into the backyard, sweep Kay into his arms, drag her back to the house and make love to her until neither one of them could stand up. He knew she wanted it as much as he did. He saw it in her eyes every day, in her smile, in the way she looked at him sometimes with such confusion, because they were so good together and she wondered why he didn't do anything about it.

It was time he did. His only regret was that he wouldn't see the look on Hollinger's face when he told him to shove it.

When he picked up the phone, though, he felt Hazel's hand on his shoulder. "Doc—stop."

He turned around, and she handed him an envelope.

"What's this?"

He looked down and saw the return address—Southern National Bank. The envelope wasn't thick enough for a statement, and the address label was individually typed, not bulk mail. He slid the letter out and read it, and when he did, it was as if the whole world had come crashing down around him.

The bank was giving him until the end of the month to bring the mortgage on the shelter current. If he didn't make up the back payments, they were going to foreclose.

Matt stared at the letter as if it was a death sentence. He closed his eyes, feeling that tight, burning sensation in his stomach again. He'd thought he had time. He'd thought the bank would work with him a few months longer, but now—

If he didn't take the grant, the shelter would close forever.

He spun around and headed toward the front door.

"Doc? Where are you going?"

He didn't respond. He left the shelter and got into his Jeep with Buddy and started to drive. He didn't know where he was going, and he didn't care. For safety's sake, it just had to be anywhere Kay wasn't.

For the next hour he made needless trips to needless places. He stopped by the hardware store for a washer to fix a leak in the kitchen sink, the drugstore for razor blades and aspirin, then went to the grocery store and dropped items almost randomly into a shopping cart. He spent a much-needed five or ten minutes in the frozen food section, not buying a thing but cooling off a lot.

Then somewhere between the ice cream and the frozen vegetables, he started to look at things logically. He told himself all he had to do was go to the awards ceremony, bank the money, get the shelter back in the black and then he could hold on to Kay forever.

He felt better as he drove home. Calm. In control. As long as he didn't think about Kay playing with Chester, about how her smile had lit up the whole neighborhood, he'd be just fine. He just might be able to keep his hands to himself until that money was safely in the bank.

When he pulled into his driveway, he was surprised to see a black Mercedes parked in front of his house. He came through the front door into the clinic waiting room, carrying his odd array of packages. He saw a man sitting in a waiting-room chair wearing a charcoal-gray suit, starched white shirt and silk tie, reading a copy of *Dog Fancy*.

Matt slowly closed the door. "Can I help you?"

The guy looked up. "I'm waiting for Kay. You're the vet, right?"

"Uh...yeah."

The guy's gaze circled the room, his nose crinkling as if he'd just smelled something rotten. "Interesting place you've got here."

Matt didn't respond. The man nodded down at the magazine. "Don't suppose you've got a *Wall Street Journal?*"

Matt eyed him suspiciously. "No. Afraid not."

The man looked back down and kept reading. Confused, Matt swung through the kitchen, dropped the sacks on the kitchen table, then headed up the back stairs. As he stepped onto the second floor, Kay's bedroom door opened. And the moment he saw her, the breath left his body.

In jeans and a T-shirt she was a knockout. In the conservative suits she wore to work she'd stop traffic. But the shimmery black slip of a dress she wore now showed off her anatomy to its full advantage. He thought he'd mentally catalogued every curve she had, but now he was seeing a landscape of hills and valleys he'd never even known existed. Her hair cascaded over her shoulders like a golden waterfall, and her perfume filled the air between them like a soft floral cloud.

He approached her slowly, blinking in awe, hoping his eyeballs weren't going to pop right out of his head.

"Kay?" His voice sounded funny, as if he'd swallowed something wrong. He cleared his throat. "Who's the guy downstairs?"

"Jason Bradley."

"Who?"

"We have a date."

Matt felt as if she'd slapped him. A date? Kay was going on a date?

She turned her back to him. "The zipper. I can't reach it. Do you mind?"

She swept her hair aside. Matt's gaze slid downward, from the smooth, pale skin of her neck, across her lacy scrap of a bra, to the zipper parked halfway down her back.

He took the zipper between his fingers and slowly pulled it upward, mourning the disappearance of one inch of beautiful skin after another. As the zipper reached its limit, his fingers brushed against the baby-fine hair at the back of her neck. For a wild, fleeting moment he saw himself kissing her there, teasing her with his lips, then easing that zipper slowly back down again...

"Thanks." Kay turned around, sweeping her hair over her shoulder again, shaking Matt back to reality. She disappeared into her bedroom, then reappeared with a small black handbag, tucking a tube of lipstick inside it.

"Where did you meet this guy?" Matt asked.

"At work."

"I don't like him."

Kay blinked with surprise. "You don't even know him."

"He wears wingtip shoes."

"He's a lawyer. It's part of the uniform."

"A lawyer?" Matt rolled his eyes. "Come on, Kay. Haven't you learned that lesson by now?"

Kay's lips tightened. "Jason's not Robert."

"Give him a few years. Where's he taking you?"

"Rodolpho's."

Matt winced at that little twist of the knife. It wasn't the most expensive place in town, but he distinctly remembered three little dollar signs beside its review in the newspaper. He'd be lucky to be able to take Kay to McDonald's for a Big Mac.

Kay started down the stairs. Matt followed, torturing himself by watching the provocative back and forth shift of her hips inside that shimmery little dress. When they reached the first floor, an expression of wolfish delight sprang to Jason's face the moment he caught sight of her. He stood up and gave a low whistle. "Now that," he said, "was worth the wait."

Kay smiled at him, and Matt wanted to die.

Jason took her arm and started for the door. Matt stood there helplessly, desperate to think of some way to stop her. Jason was clearly one of those guys who couldn't wait to carve another notch in his bedpost. How could Kay even think of going out with someone like that?

"When will you be home?" Matt asked, then kicked himself. He sounded like her father.

Jason got a solemn, obedient look on his face. "Don't worry, sir. I'll have her home by ten o'clock. Unless, of course, the sock hop runs late, or we decide to go necking under the bleachers."

Smart aleck. Now he really did feel like Ward Cleaver.

"Ready to celebrate?" Jason said, opening the door for Kay.

"Celebrate?" Matt said.

Jason turned back. "Old man Breckenridge offered her a job. Didn't she tell you?"

Matt felt sick. No. She hadn't told him.

"I didn't get the chance," Kay said. "I—"

Before she could say anything else, Jason took her arm and hustled her out the door. Then he stuck his head back in, a sly grin on his face. "Don't wait up."

Jason clicked the door shut. Matt peered through the blinds, watching as he walked down the porch steps with Kay, his hand resting with way too much familiarity against the small of her back. A slow burn of jealousy started in the pit of Matt's stomach and spread through the rest of his body. Kay had gotten a job, and she was celebrating with *him?*

Then he had a really horrible thought. What if the worst happened? What if she came home late, a little rumpled, with a smile of ecstasy on her face?

What if she didn't come home at all?

He watched Jason walk Kay to his car. Once she turned and looked back toward the house, and Matt's heart stopped. But then she continued on, into Jason's Mercedes and probably out of his life for good.

He let go of the blinds with an angry clatter. What could Kay possibly see in a guy like that?

Oh, hell—why *shouldn't* she want a guy like that? He could support her in style. She wouldn't have to eat macaroni and cheese from a little blue box, use pizza coupons or live in a turn-of-the-century monstrosity that hadn't seen updating since World War II. If it was between a guy like that and a broke veterinarian, who was she going to pick?

And Jason was just the kind of guy she could take home to meet Mom.

For the next three hours, every time Matt thought he heard a car door he muted the TV, leaped up and went to the window, only to discover it was a neighbor's car, or someone rattling a garbage can lid, or absolutely nothing but his own imagination kicking into overdrive. Tired of getting shoved out of Matt's lap so many times, Buddy finally crawled under the coffee table and fell asleep.

Matt had just collapsed on the sofa for the umpteenth time, reaching the conclusion that Kay wasn't going to come home at all, when he heard the crunch of tires on gravel outside. He ran to the window again. Jason's Mercedes swung into the driveway.

He tore out of the living room, took the stairs three at a time, then screeched to a halt at the front door, lucky he hadn't tripped over anything in the dark. He flicked a slat of the blinds and peered out.

Jason got out of his car, circled around and open the door for Kay. He took her hand and helped her out, the pale glow of the streetlight tossing their shadows down on the sidewalk. He leaned in and said something to her when she stood up beside him. She laughed, and Matt's heart dropped to his toes.

They walked toward the porch. Matt reprimanded himself for not thinking to turn on the porch light earlier. It was dark out there. Things happened in the dark that might not happen in the light. But he couldn't do it now or they'd know he was watching.

They climbed the porch steps, and Jason didn't waste any time. He eased his hand around Kay's back and pulled her against him. She didn't meet him halfway, but she didn't stop him, either. And when he leaned over to kiss the woman Matt wanted more than anything in the world, the slow tremor of jealousy he'd felt all evening exploded into a full-blown earthquake.

He flipped on the porch light, yanked open the door and glared at Jason. ''What do you think you're doing?''

Kay spun around, staring in disbelief. Jason's eyes widened, but he kept his surprise in check. He merely focused his attention on Kay again, then smiled. ''Well, if you must know, I was thinking about kissing Kay goodnight.''

''Think again.''

In one smooth move, Matt grabbed Kay's arm, pulled her from Jason's grasp and hauled her into the house. Then he poked his head back out the door.

''Sorry, fella. Date's over.''

He slammed the door, locked it, then flipped off the porch light. Jason tried the door, then started banging. ''Hey! Open up!''

''Matt!'' Kay gaped at him. ''What are you doing?''

Ignoring her protest, Matt slid his hands along either side of her neck, his fingers cradling her head. She took a reflexive step backward, bumping into the wall, her eyes wide with astonishment. He moved closer and tilted her face up until he was looking directly into her eyes. Every bit of the desire he'd suppressed for the past several weeks welled up inside him until he felt like a volcano ready to blow. He'd crossed the line, and there was no going back. To hell with Robert Hollinger. He needed Kay desperately, and he needed her now.

"You want a kiss," he whispered.

Slowly her gaze fell to his lips, hovered there a moment, then rose to meet his eyes again. "Yes."

"From him?" Matt gave a nod toward the door, then dropped his head toward Kay's, so close he could feel her breath against his lips. "Or me?"

Kay stared up at him, her china-blue eyes shimmering in the moonlight, and all at once the invisible wall that had stood like a fortress between them crumbled into dust.

"You," she whispered. "It's always been you."

12

As soon as the words were out of Kay's mouth, Matt's lips fell against hers in a kiss that was so hot, so hungry, so passion-filled that for a moment all she could do was melt in his arms and let it happen. After all these weeks of wanting him so desperately, she was finally in his arms, and he was kissing her as if he couldn't get enough of her. She clutched blindly at his shirt with one hand and clung to his shoulder with the other, trying to get her bearings, her world having suddenly, joyfully, turned upside down. Then she realized she didn't want any bearings, any solid ground, any direction at all. She wanted to stay lost in his kiss forever.

Jason banged on the door again, and they both jumped. "Hey!" he shouted. "This date's not over until *Kay* says it's over!"

Kay pulled away from Matt, barely able to catch her breath. She leaned toward the door, fumbled with the lock, then opened it slowly. Jason stared through the crack like a wounded bull.

"Thank you for the dinner, Jason, but...the date's over."

When he simply stared at her speechlessly, she said a quick good-night and closed the door, then locked it with a sharp *click*. Matt pulled her back instantly and kissed her again, teasing his tongue against hers in a dance of pure, slow seduction, and she was so lost in the feeling that she barely heard Jason stomping down the steps and the purr of his Mercedes as it disappeared down the block.

Kay didn't remember exactly how they made it up the stairs, only knew that Matt had stopped halfway up to pull her against him again, his lips trailing hot kisses beneath her ear, along her throat, in the hollow of her neck. At the same time his fingers curled beneath the hem of her dress, inching it upward until his palm rested against her thigh. She moaned softly, deep in the back of her throat, and Matt tightened his hand against her thigh and found her lips with his again. Mindless waves of pure pleasure washed over her until her heart was beating so wildly she seriously wondered if her body could withstand the assault.

At the head of the stairs Matt wrapped his arms around her again, but this time he found the zipper of her dress and drew it slowly downward.

"That's better," he murmured, his hands caressing her back. "Zipping it up earlier—that's what nearly killed me."

Kay's brain surfaced momentarily. He clearly hadn't wanted her to go out with Jason. So why hadn't he said something? And why hadn't he told her how he felt about her during one of the hundreds of other opportunities he'd had? Why had he driven her crazy with wanting him and never given her anything in return?

She pressed her palms against his chest. "Matt—stop."

He stared down at her.

"I have to know."

"Know what?"

"Why."

He stared at her blankly for a moment, as if he didn't know what she was talking about. Then a look of understanding came over his face. Still, he didn't respond.

"I've wanted this for a long time," she whispered. "So long. But I didn't think you did."

"I did want it, Kay, more than you'll ever know."

She looked at him with surprise. "But all this time—"

"I know." He closed his eyes. "I know. Don't think about that. Think about this." He brushed his lips against hers. "No matter what happens, this is exactly where I want to be. The rest will just have to work itself out."

She started to ask him what the "rest" was, but then he curled his hand around the back of her neck and pulled her into another kiss so hot that any misgivings she had slipped away like sand through her fingers.

I did want it...more than you'll ever know.

Kay still didn't understand, but she held on to those words like a drowning man clinging to a life preserver. All that mattered right now was that Matt had wanted her as much as she wanted him. She'd worry about the why later.

He pulled away slightly and eased her dress off her shoulders. She shimmied a little, and the dress fell in a pool at her feet. She tugged the hem of his T-shirt from his jeans, and he yanked it off impatiently, then pulled her against him again, the lacy cups of her bra teasing his bare chest.

"Bed," he whispered.

That single word sent Kay's emotions into chaos. She'd fantasized about this so many times that she was actually shaking when she took his hand. As she led him into the darkness of the pretty little room he'd created for her, she realized that dreams really *did* come true.

In the pale moonlight filtering through the lace curtains, the rest of their clothes seemed to melt away between them. Matt stretched out beside her on her cozy brass bed, enveloping her in his arms and pulling her against him, whispering nothing words against her ear until warm shivers ran down her spine. She was delighted to discover that he was the same here as he was in the rest of his life—kind and sweet and generous—at the same time showing her a repertoire of erotic talents that set her senses on fire.

Then Kay eased Matt onto his back, wanting to embark on a slow, sensual exploration of her own. She dropped featherlight kisses against his jaw, his throat, his chest. At the touch of her lips he closed his eyes, his breath coming faster, his muscles tensing as if she was bringing every nerve ending to life. She touched him everywhere, hungry for the feel of him, moving over his body with a boldness she'd never felt with any man before. And she knew it was because she'd never wanted any man the way she wanted Matt.

As the moments of the night slipped away, he took everything she gave to him and gave her even more in return, driving her crazy with pleasure, crazy with need, crazy with the knowledge that this was really Matt she was with, and that *his* hands and *his* lips and *his* soft-spoken words pushed her inch by inch to the edge of ecstasy.

When he finally slid inside her, she thought she'd die from the pleasure of it. Locked in an intense embrace, they found a hot, hard rhythm, moving together so spontaneously she felt as if they'd made love a thousand times before. Kay whispered his name over and over, urging him faster, harder.

Then all at once the world exploded around her in a hot, blinding rush. She let out a soft, strangled cry, and seconds later Matt clutched her tightly, groaning with satisfaction as he rose to the peak of the same tidal surge that had already washed over her. As they rode the waves of pleasure together, Kay felt as if he were showing her a sweeping, panoramic view of a secret paradise she'd barely even glimpsed before.

For a long time afterward they clung to each other, exhausted, Matt's breath hot against the hollow of her neck. Then his breathing became softer, more measured, and he rolled to one side and pulled Kay against him. In the cool darkness of her bedroom, she relaxed in his arms, her soft curves fitting deftly into the hard planes of his body. Kay felt delightfully alive and nearly dead from exhaustion at the same time.

"You're not going near that guy again," Matt said, lacing his arms protectively around her.

"No," Kay whispered. "I don't think I am."

"If you do, I'll have to neuter him—without anesthesia."

Kay laughed softly. "You'd be doing womankind a favor."

"If you don't like him, why did you go out with him?"

Her smile faded. When it came to her feelings for Matt, she never intended to hide them again. "Because I couldn't stand the thought of spending one more night next to you on that sofa when I wanted so badly to touch you and couldn't."

Matt sighed gently. He rolled her onto her back and stared down at her. "That won't happen again," he said, brushing a stray strand of hair away from her cheek. "I don't want to go five minutes without you touching me."

He met her lips for yet another long, lazy kiss, and Kay decided she'd do everything she could to make sure the five-minute mark was never reached. Even before Matt had touched her tonight, she'd already known she was in love with him. But now as his kiss sent her back into blissful oblivion, another thought fluttered through her mind, then floated downward until it lit gently on her heart.

He loves me, too.

A LITTLE before seven the next morning, a whisper of daylight filtered through the curtains of Kay's bedroom, nudging Matt awake. Kay lay beside him, tangled in the sheets, her back to his chest. He rose on one elbow and looked down at her, and decided he'd be content just to stare at her forever. He rested his hand lightly against her hip, then traced a path down her thigh to her knee and back up again, relishing the warmth of her silky skin beneath his hand. She stirred, then settled even closer to him, and he felt himself getting aroused all over again.

He'd thought he knew what it would be like to spend the night with Kay, to make love for hours, to hear her soft breathing and feel her move beneath him. But he hadn't had a clue. As vividly real as his fantasies had been, not one of them had even approached what they'd shared last night.

Then he thought about the little dance of deception he was going to have to do to keep Kay from finding out about the deal he'd made with Hollinger, and a wave of guilt hit him hard. He wished he could ease her awake, tell her the truth and take whatever came. But he couldn't. The truth could drive her away forever, and he couldn't stand the possibility of losing her.

He had no choice. He'd have to find a way to go to that awards ceremony without her knowing. He couldn't risk her coming along and finding out even a hint of truth from Hollinger.

He squeezed his eyes closed and shoved those thoughts from his mind. He leaned over, intending to kiss Kay awake and pick up where they'd left off last night, when all at once he heard the muffled sound of tires on gravel. He breathed a soft curse. This early, it had to be a patient. An emergency.

He slipped away from Kay and eased out from beneath the covers. She stirred a little, then was still again. He went to the window and looked out, and apprehension swept over him like a hurricane-force wind. The door to a white Lexus opened, and Robert Hollinger stepped out.

No, no, no!

Matt leaped into his jeans and yanked on a T-shirt, praying Kay would stay asleep. He flew out the bedroom door and down the stairs, hitting the bottom step at the same moment Robert rapped loudly on the door.

Stay asleep, Kay. Stay asleep.

Matt stopped for a moment with his hand on the door-knob, trying to get a grip on his respiratory system so he wouldn't sound like he'd just run a marathon. He opened the door, slipped out onto the front porch and pulled the door shut behind him.

"Robert," he said, trying to sound nonchalant and failing miserably. "What brings you out so early?"

"I was in the neighborhood."

Matt didn't like this, not one bit.

Hollinger turned and leaned against the porch railing, his arms folded over his chest, staring at Matt long and hard. "You'll never guess who I met at my club last night."

Matt eyed him warily.

"Jason Bradley. Name ring a bell?"

Matt nearly choked.

"Yes. He dropped in to drown his sorrows. It seems he'd spent a lovely evening with a woman, only to have her shove him aside for—of all things—a veterinarian. We had the most interesting conversation."

Slowly Hollinger's mask of phony congeniality melted away, exposing an expression of barely concealed fury.

"How long has Kay been living here?"

Matt stared at Hollinger, his mind spinning like crazy. What was he supposed to say? Denying it was foolish—

Jason knew better, and he clearly hadn't hesitated to enlighten his lawyer buddy.

He met Hollinger's gaze, trying to keep up his shaky facade of nonchalance. "Kay was low on money. She needed a place to stay. That's all."

"How charitable of you to open up your home to her."

Matt said nothing. Robert's expression turned wicked. "Now tell me how long you've been sleeping with her."

"I'll answer that."

Matt spun around when he heard the voice behind him, shocked to find Kay standing at the door. And she was wearing—oh, God—one of his shirts.

She stepped out onto the porch, but instead of approaching Hollinger, she walked toward Matt. He wondered why—until he saw a faintly seductive smile cross her lips. In one smooth move, she slipped her arms around his neck and kissed him—a deep, sensual, last-night-was-wonderful-can't-wait-for-tonight kind of kiss that left absolutely nothing to the imagination. If Hollinger wondered about their relationship before, he wasn't wondering now.

Kay pulled away slowly, languorously. "Just one night," she said, "and it was *wonderful.*"

Under any other circumstances, Matt would have been delighted by the compliment. Unfortunately, Kay's timing left a bit to be desired.

"Matt," Kay said softly, her arms still draped around his neck and her gaze still fixed on his, "tell this jerk that your personal life isn't any of his business."

"I beg to differ, Kay," Robert said. "It's very much my business. I've got twenty-five thousand dollars that says it is."

Matt squeezed his eyes closed, praying for an earthquake, or a tornado, or maybe a sudden thunderstorm complete with golf-ball-size hail—anything to distract

Kay from the pronouncement Hollinger had just made. But when she turned to face Hollinger with an expression of guarded curiosity, he knew even a volcanic eruption couldn't save him now.

Kay's hands slipped away from Matt's shoulders. "Twenty-five thousand dollars?"

Hollinger turned to Matt. "Oh, my. Have I spoken out of turn? I thought surely by now you'd told Kay the real reason you allowed her to come to the shelter."

"Real reason? What are you talking about?"

"Dr. Forester applied for a grant with the Dorland Group."

"Yes. I know. So?"

"Did you also know that he was absolutely guaranteed to get that grant?"

Kay shot Matt a look of surprise.

"Dr. Forester and I made a deal when you came to the shelter. I told him that as chairman of the selection committee, I could insure that the money was as good as in his pocket, if only he would do me one small favor."

Hollinger's eyes narrowed with wicked anticipation. He paused a long time, letting the moment grow larger and more treacherous until Matt couldn't stand it any longer.

"He had to agree to make your life miserable for one hundred hours."

Kay looked at Hollinger with the blank stare of someone who'd been struck with a bat but had yet to feel the pain. Then, as astonishment and disbelief rose on her face, she turned to Matt.

"Is that true? You let him bribe you?"

The look of betrayal on Kay's face was like a knife through Matt's heart.

"He bribed you to carry out his revenge? To make life miserable for me?"

"Try to understand," he told her. "I didn't even know you then. I didn't—"

Kay inched closer to him, dropping her voice. "But you do now. Why didn't you tell me?"

Matt was speechless. He wanted desperately for Kay to go inside, let him handle Hollinger, and then he could explain everything later. But he wasn't going to get that opportunity. Kay wasn't going anywhere.

"Don't take the money."

Her voice was an intense whisper, and the imploring look in her eyes cut straight to his heart. "Tell Robert to forget it, Matt," she whispered. *"Please."*

All at once he felt smothered, as if every atom of oxygen had suddenly been obliterated from the atmosphere. The two most important things in his life were hanging in the balance, and it was as if he had a huge, muddled mess in his mind that he couldn't possibly sort out. He met Kay's eyes again, and they stared at each other a long, shaky moment.

"Matt..?"

Matt opened his mouth to speak, but nothing came out. He didn't know what to say that wouldn't tear a huge, irreparable hole in the fabric of his life. He didn't know what to say that would keep those thirty animals at the shelter alive and well and keep Kay in his life at the same time. He didn't know what to say to make a spiteful jerk like Hollinger disappear from the planet forever and take his impossible dilemmas with him. He just didn't know what to say.

So he said nothing.

Kay spun around and headed for the door. Matt caught her arm. "Kay, wait—"

She yanked her arm from his grip. "Don't!"

"Uh-oh," Hollinger said. "Looks like we've got a lovers' spat."

"I can't do this, Matt. If you want to let yourself be manipulated by scum like Robert, that's fine. But I don't want any part of it."

Matt felt a flash of anger. Couldn't she see the position he was in? "Look, Kay. I've got thirty-some animals over there depending on me. And what do I tell people who bring me more? Do I tell them to take them to the pound, where I know they'll eventually die? Is that what I'm supposed to do?"

"You don't need that grant! Things are better now. I'll help you any way I can. Just please don't—"

"I got a letter from the bank yesterday. If I don't make up the back payments on the shelter they're foreclosing."

He saw her swallow hard, but the accusatory look in her eyes never faded. "Then take it, Matt. Go ahead. But what about the next time you need money? Whose game will you play then?"

She brushed past him, but he caught her arm again. He pulled her around to face him. "Kay. Please!"

He wished he could make her understand why he'd done it, but she refused even to look at him. The only thing she could see right now was that he'd entered into a shady deal with the man she hated most on earth, and there was no way she'd ever forgive him.

She closed her eyes, then eased out of his grasp, and he had the sudden, desperate feeling that it was the last time he'd ever touch her. "I don't want to lose you," he whispered.

A single tear slid down her cheek. "I think you already have."

She went into the house, leaving the door ajar, and as she disappeared up the stairs, Matt felt as if his heart had been yanked right out of his chest.

"I don't understand it," Hollinger said as he peeked

innocently into the house, shaking his head with bewilderment. "Kay seems a little distressed." He turned to Matt. "Does she seem a little distressed to you?"

Matt barely heard Hollinger's words. All he could think about was the look of betrayal on Kay's face, a look that washed away his memory of everything they'd shared last night.

"Well," Hollinger said jovially. "Looks like we're full-steam ahead on the awards ceremony, doesn't it?

Matt turned around slowly. "You're a bastard, Hollinger."

Robert laughed. "Some people think so."

"I want you to sign off on the agreement with Kay. She's still a few hours short, and I don't want her owing you any three thousand dollars if she doesn't finish."

"Now, why would you think I would give a damn now about all that volunteer crap? After all," he said with a wicked grin, "I got what I wanted."

All at once the malicious artistry with which Hollinger had manipulated the situation struck Matt full-force. He'd got what he wanted, all right. Revenge. It hadn't come quite the way he'd planned it, but he'd got it just the same.

"I'll see you at the awards ceremony Saturday. Seven o'clock. Don't be late."

Hollinger headed for his car, leaving Matt standing alone on the porch trying to decide who he hated more—Hollinger for driving Kay away from him, or himself for letting all this happen in the first place. He'd thought he'd known what Hollinger was capable of, but nothing had prepared him for this.

The devil had come to collect Matt's soul, and he'd handed it over without a fight.

13

THREE EVENINGS LATER, Kay sat on a lawn chair on the patio of Claire's condominium, staring at the city lights glimmering through the twilight. She thought about the apartment she'd put a deposit down on—a white-walled, beige-carpeted, characterless apartment she'd found the day after she left Matt's house. She could have searched longer and found something more aesthetically pleasing, but that would have meant staying with Claire several days longer and she wasn't sure she could tolerate that. The apartment would be ready next week and she'd be out of there.

All at once the sliding door behind Kay whooshed open and Claire strode onto the patio. "I'm telling you, Kay, you've got to do something about that cat."

Kay smiled furtively. "Oh? Why is that?"

"He *spat* at me!"

"Come on, Claire. Clyde's in a cage."

"Yeah, and last night he reached a paw out of that cage and practically took my arm off! And the way he stares at me sometimes, like some kind of feline serial killer..." Claire shuddered. "I tell you, it's creepy."

"You're not *afraid* of Clyde, are you, Claire?"

"Hell, yes, I'm afraid of him!"

Kay rolled her eyes in a perfect imitation of her sister. "Will you grow up? You're an adult now. The big bad kitty won't get you."

Claire twisted her mouth with disgust, apparently not

enjoying the irony of the situation half as much as Kay was. "What's *with* you, anyway? A few months ago you couldn't stand the sight of a cat. Now you're inviting one to live with you—in *my* condo!"

"It's only for a few days until my apartment is ready."

"No. He's got to go. Like I told you when you showed up with that mountain lion, this is a no-pets building. Legally speaking, my landlord has every right to—"

"Claire!"

Claire stopped short, her eyes wide at her sister's commanding tone.

"Do me a favor, will you? Just once, would you put all that attorney stuff on hold?" She pointed to a lawn chair. "Just...*sit*."

Claire's jaw dropped halfway to the ground. Then slowly she put her jaws back together and sat down where Kay had directed her to. It was the first time Kay could remember her sister relinquishing control to her, and it felt pretty damned good.

"Well, at the risk of bringing up more 'attorney stuff,'" Claire said, "I got the signed agreement from Robert today in the mail. I guess you're a free woman."

Kay felt a glimmer of relief that it was really over—that she wouldn't have go back to the shelter. She knew if she gave Matt half a chance he'd sweep her back into his arms with a heartstopping smile and a kiss that would render her temporarily insane, and for a while she would forget what he'd done. But she couldn't forget. She knew if she stayed with him she'd never feel strong and steady and anchored in his arms. She'd feel like a rowboat being tossed around in a storm with no land in sight, because she couldn't say for sure what he'd do the next time he needed money.

She felt Claire's gaze on her. She ignored it, staring ahead at nothing. She'd done a lot of that since she moved in with her sister—staring at nothing. It was something she generally did when she was trying really hard not to cry.

Claire let out a frustrated breath. "You know, I don't get it. You weren't anywhere near this broken up when you lost Robert, and you were engaged to him."

"Robert lost *me,* Claire. It's about time you got that straight."

Claire opened her mouth to respond, but this time she closed it again before words came out. They sat in silence, staring ahead at the city lights sparkling through the dusk. A bright half-moon hovered near the horizon.

"I guess you really liked the guy, huh?"

The sarcastic edge to Claire's voice had disappeared, catching Kay off-guard. She blinked, her stony facade starting to crumble. "I loved him, Claire."

That confession slipped out before Kay really realized what she'd said. She expected Claire to sit up straight, give her a figurative rap on the knuckles and tell her to snap out of it. Instead her sister dropped her gaze to her lap and sighed gently.

"I'm sorry, then. I'm sorry it didn't work out."

This unaccustomed sympathy from Claire only intensified Kay's misery. She thought about Frisbees, old movies, tiny love seats, bad cooking and the man she'd thought she loved. The man she still loved. The man she was going to have to learn not to love.

"I guess the cat can stay," Claire said, as if that hadn't already been decided, "but in your room. *Only* in your room. If I catch him anywhere else, I'm feeding him to the rottweiler down the street. Got that?"

Kay figured it would be more like Clyde eating the rottweiler. She smiled a little. "Got it."

Claire stared at Kay a long time, her gaze softening. "Hey, Scarlett," she said. "Tomorrow's another day."

Kay nodded, acknowledging the closest thing to a pep

talk she was likely to get from her sister—exactly five words more than she'd ever got before.

Claire went back inside, and Kay returned her gaze to the city lights. How long would it take before she could look at a dog, or a cat, or even a box of macaroni and cheese, without thinking of Matt? A long time, she figured.

Maybe forever.

ONE MORNING a few days later, Kay looked up from her computer screen to see Mr. Breckenridge standing in front of her desk.

"I just heard some good news, Ms. Ramsey."

"Good news?"

"Yes. About the Westwood Animal Shelter. I've just been notified that the selection committee has designated it to receive this year's grant. Since you volunteer there, I thought you'd be interested in knowing."

Kay felt as if a barely healed wound had just been ripped open again. "Yes," she said, forcing a smile. "That's wonderful."

"The awards banquet is Saturday night. I was wondering if perhaps you'd like to come along."

Kay felt a flutter of panic. No *way* could she go to that ceremony. "I'm sorry, Mr. Breckenridge. I couldn't possibly—"

"You can come as my guest. With your being a volunteer at the shelter, I can't think of anything more appropriate."

Kay wanted to tell him she wasn't a volunteer any longer, but that would seem a little odd since she'd been so enthusiastic about the shelter only a few weeks ago. Then she'd have to say *why* she wasn't a volunteer, and....

It was just best not to go there at all.

She started to tell Mr. Breckenridge that she already had something planned for that evening so she couldn't come.

But before she could decide which direction to go with that particular excuse, he sat down in the chair beside her desk and lowered his voice.

"Actually, Ms. Ramsey, you'd be doing me a favor."

"A favor?"

"Yes." He sighed a little. "You see, as president of the Dorland Group, I'm obligated to attend this event, but I must admit that I'm not looking forward to it. As you know, my wife died several months ago, and I haven't ventured out socially since then. We were married for over forty years, so it feels a little odd...." He got a faraway look on his face for a moment and his eyes got a little misty. Then he cleared his throat. "I thought perhaps you'd come along to keep me company."

No! I can't do it! But even as Kay's brain set up a flurry of wild protest, she got a little dewy-eyed herself. How must it feel to be alone after forty years of marriage?

"I'm just not up to enduring the condolences of minor acquaintances who feel the need to address my loss as a social necessity." He managed a small smile. "Perhaps if I have a beautiful young woman by my side, those people will spend their time gossiping instead of consoling."

Kay couldn't imagine anyone suggesting anything improper about Mr. Breckenridge's behavior under *any* circumstances. Kay sighed. It looked as if she was going to at least make it possible for them to try.

"So you don't mind being gossiped about?" she asked.

"At my age, Ms. Ramsey, I'd consider it a compliment."

Kay gave him a tiny smile. "Of course, Mr. Breckenridge. I'd be happy to go with you."

"Wonderful. It's at the Fairmont Hotel. Cocktails at six-thirty, ceremony at seven. Semiformal." He leaned closer and dropped his voice. "And when you choose what you're going to wear, young lady, please remember—I have a pacemaker.''

He rose from the chair and went back to his office. Kay felt a warm glow at the thought of doing something to help Mr. Breckenridge after all he'd done for her. But watch Matt accept that grant? How was she ever going to deal with that?

ON SATURDAY NIGHT at six forty-five, Matt stood at the mirror in the men's room of the Fairmont Hotel, yanking at his tie. No matter how many times he tied the damned thing, the knot was still crooked. What kind of sadist had invented these things? Even when they weren't choking you, they were hanging there crooked, waiting to pick up a good gust of wind so they could slap you in the face. And who really needed a silk spaghetti-sauce magnet, anyway?

Finally he stopped messing with the tie, placed his hands on the edges of the sink and bowed his head, letting out a long breath of frustration. It wasn't the tie that was the problem. It was that he was here in the first place. *That* was the problem.

Slowly he looked up and stared into the mirror, and he didn't particularly like the guy looking back. He hated himself for what he'd done to Kay. She would never forgive him. Some wounds went too deep to repair, and this was one of them. She was gone now and nothing was going to bring her back.

He couldn't help but recognize the irony of it. He'd denied his feelings for Kay partly because he'd feared she'd desert him just as his ex-wife had. Yet he was the one to blame for driving her away.

He couldn't forget her look of betrayal as she'd walked out of his house for the last time. Or the look of regret on Hazel's face when he'd told her Kay was gone. Or, for that matter, the pitiful look on Buddy's face as he held that Frisbee in his teeth and wondered where his favorite playmate was. The moment she'd left, it was as if every corner of the house suddenly turned cold and the four walls echoed with emptiness. Without Kay to bring the old house to life, it was nothing but an empty shell. And so was he.

At least he could save the shelter. It had been his dream since he was a kid, and he couldn't let it go now.

Then he thought about other dreams. Adult dreams. A wife, a family...

No.

He closed his eyes, willing those thoughts away. He'd made a decision, and there was nothing he could do to change it now.

Matt checked his watch. Ten to seven. In just a few minutes he was going to gain twenty-five thousand dollars and lose his self-respect. And the only thing he was thankful for was that Kay wouldn't be there to see it.

When Kay stepped inside the hotel ballroom, she was astonished at the size of the crowd. At least two hundred suits and cocktail dresses flowed around dozens of linen-draped tables aglow with candlelight. Up front sat a small portable stage with a podium in the center. To her great relief, she didn't see Matt.

She'd already decided that if she happened to meet his eyes, she'd just turn away. And when he got up to receive the grant, she'd just pretend he was someone else. Someone who ran an animal shelter that needed money. Someone who hadn't made a deal with her slimy ex-fiancé behind her back. Someone who hadn't broken her heart.

Mr. Breckenridge ushered Kay around, introducing her as his friend, which pleased Kay immensely. At least for his sake, she was glad she'd come. And in talking with people, she discovered that the general consensus seemed to be that there was no more deserving grant recipient than Dr. Matt Forester. Either they'd read Matt's application and knew what a wonderful place the shelter really was, or Robert had done one hell of a sales job.

"Kay! What a surprise!"

Kay spun around. Robert was standing behind her wearing a big, phony smile, and she felt an instantaneous rush of loathing.

He sidled up next to her. "What brings you here tonight?"

Mr. Breckenridge moved up beside Kay. "I do, Mr. Hollinger. Do you have any objection to that?"

"Why, of course not! Kay has been a volunteer at the shelter. Of course she'd want to see Dr. Forester receive the grant." He turned to her with a snide little grin. "Isn't that right, Kay?"

Kay just stared at him, remaining calm, refraining from wrapping her hands around his neck. Just how Sheila would have reacted.

"I'd like to meet our guest of honor," Mr. Breckenridge said. "Is he here yet?"

Robert checked his watch. "Uh...I'm sure he's arrived." He glanced around the ballroom, looking a little nervous. "I just haven't spotted him yet."

Kay felt a rush of hope. Could Matt have decided to stay home after all? To forego the grant? Was it possible...?

"Ah!" Robert said, looking toward the door. "There he is."

Kay glanced around to see Matt standing at the door of the ballroom, wearing a dark gray suit, white shirt and silk tie. He looked even more handsome than she remembered, and she felt a rush of longing so powerful it hurt. What had ever made her think she could do this? What had made her think she could see Matt again and not have the pain of his betrayal cut through her like a knife?

"There's a table up front for you and Kay," Robert told Mr. Breckenridge. "I'll bring Dr. Forester over."

Kay's heart beat wildly as Mr. Breckenridge escorted her to the table Robert indicated. She wanted so badly to leave. She wanted to walk out of here and forget this night had ever happened. But what would Mr. Breckenridge think?

A minute later Robert arrived with Matt, and it was clear he was every bit as shaken to see Kay as she was to see him. Then he turned to Robert, his surprise becoming an accusatory stare.

"Don't thank *me*," Robert told Matt, as if his discovery of Kay at the ceremony was something to be celebrated. "I had nothing to do with it. It was Mr. Breckenridge here who had the foresight to bring Kay along. There's nothing like having one of your volunteers here to see you receive this award, is there?"

Mr. Breckenridge extended his hand to Matt. "Hello, Dr. Forester. I'm Albert Breckenridge, president of the Dorland Group. I'm delighted that your shelter is receiving this grant. Ms. Ramsey has told me what a wonderful service you're providing the community."

Matt's shook his hand. "Uh...thank you. I appreciate that."

Robert glanced at his watch, then gave Matt a congenial grin. "Well, Dr. Forester. Looks like it's showtime. Mr. Breckenridge will give some opening remarks, and then I'll go up to introduce you."

Mr. Breckenridge pulled out a chair for Kay. Matt took his seat beside her, looking at the table, at his watch, at the chandelier overhead—clearly focusing on anything to avoid looking at her.

Mr. Breckenridge welcomed the crowd, then began a little talk about the Dorland Group and its history of philanthropy. Robert sat down across the table from Kay, his expression at least twice as smug as usual. She'd thought she already hated him to the greatest degree that was humanly possible, but tonight he'd swept her past that point by a mile.

Finally Mr. Breckenridge introduced Robert. He rose from his chair and went to the stage while Mr. Breckenridge returned to the table. And as Robert told the audience about this year's recipient of the Dorland Grant, Matt's attention was focused exclusively on the stage as if Kay weren't sitting next to him at all. As if she meant nothing to him. But all the while his finger tap-tap-tapped against the tabletop in a nervous rhythm.

"And now I'd like to introduce the man who's behind the Westwood Animal Shelter, a man who you all will agree is a worthy recipient of this year's Dorland Grant—Dr. Matt Forester."

The applause began, but instead of rising to his feet, Matt turned around and looked at Kay. His sudden attention startled her, but as she stared into those dark, mesmerizing eyes that had caught her attention from the first moment she saw him, all at once she instinctively knew his thoughts were the same as hers. He was thinking about the wonderful life they'd built together in such a short time, and about how two people who never should have fallen in love fell in love, anyway. But was he also thinking, as she was, that it was just too precious a thing to lose?

Then he touched her hand, and for a few sizzling seconds she had this wild idea that he was going to change his mind. He'd reconsidered taking the money. He was going to lean toward her, wrap his arms around her and—

"No," he said abruptly, looking away. "I can't do this."

Before the applause had even died down, he pulled his hand away from hers, rose from his chair and headed toward the stage.

14

I CAN'T do this.

As Matt's words echoed over and over in Kay's mind, tears welled up in her eyes, hot and insistent. How could she have thought that Matt might change his mind? He was here for one purpose tonight, and one purpose only. Didn't she know by now what was most important to him? Didn't she *know* it wasn't her?

I can't do this.

What he couldn't do was love her more than the shelter.

The applause that brought Matt to the stage faded away, and he stepped up to the microphone. Kay felt as if she'd stepped outside her body and was watching every terrible moment unfold in excruciating slow motion.

"First of all," he told the crowd, "let me tell you how much I appreciate being chosen for this honor. Your group has a remarkable history of providing aid to organizations that couldn't continue to exist without your help."

Kay was dying inside. Little by little, she felt her life draining away.

"I'm proud of what we've done at the shelter. It's become an asset to this community. A place where helpless, homeless animals can get a chance at a decent life. A place where animal lovers can find a pet to make their lives a little brighter."

Matt paused, looking out over the crowd, as if gathering his thoughts.

"I started the shelter because of a vow I made as a child, and it came to be an obsession. For the past two years I've lived my life for it, struggling to keep it alive and growing. It was the most important thing in my life, and I can truthfully tell you that there's nothing I wouldn't have done to make sure the doors stayed open."

He paused again, and a faint smile appeared on his lips. "Until now."

His gaze fell squarely on Kay, his expression intense and unwavering. She stared back at him, dumbfounded. What was he saying?

"I've come to realize that living in the past has put me in danger of destroying my chance at happiness in the future. You see, I've found something I love even more than the shelter. And I have Robert Hollinger to thank for that."

There was a moment when Kay's brain didn't quite catch up to Matt's meaning, and when it finally did, tears of joy sprang to her eyes. She couldn't believe it. The hundreds of people in the audience might not know it, but Matt had just said he loved her—more than the shelter.

And that meant more than anything.

"I know you're not going to understand this," Matt told the audience, "and I'm not going to try to explain it. But as generous as this grant is, and as much as I appreciate being chosen to receive it, I'm afraid I can't accept it."

For a moment, Kay couldn't breathe. Right before her eyes, the man she knew, the sweet, sexy, wonderful man she thought was lost to her forever, had suddenly reappeared.

I can't do this.

Why hadn't she heard what he'd really been saying? What he couldn't do was take the money if it meant losing her.

People started murmuring among themselves, and soon a crescendo of protests arose. Matt ignored all of it. He left the stage and walked toward the table where Kay sat.

Robert gaped at Matt, his expression thunderstruck. Kay could tell his conniving little mind had never believed that anyone would think that she was more important than money. For probably the first time in his life, he was speechless.

Without missing a beat, Matt took Kay by the hand and pulled her to her feet, barely giving her a chance to excuse herself to Mr. Breckenridge. He led her out of the ballroom and headed for the lobby of the hotel, moving so quickly that Kay had to trot to keep up. He continued past the front desk toward a bank of pay phones inset into their own secluded little room.

Without saying a word, he pulled Kay around the corner, tucked her head in the crook of his arm and kissed her—a deep, hard, insistent kiss that made her forget the grant, forget this evening, forget her own name. All she could remember was the words he'd spoken on stage, and how much she loved him for saying them.

Slowly Matt eased away and took her face in his hands. "I'm sorry, Kay. I never should have made that deal with Robert. It was wrong. *I* was wrong."

"Matt—"

"Just listen to me, okay?" His hands tightened against her face. "I can't live without you. I can live without the shelter, but I can't live without you. I love you, Kay, and I'm not letting anything get in the way of that ever again."

Kay stared at him, tears clouding her eyes. She couldn't believe it. He wanted her, not the money. And he wanted her forever.

"I don't know what's going to happen with the shelter, but it doesn't matter. You're what matters. I miss you.

Hazel misses you. Chester misses you. And Buddy...
Good *Lord,* if that dog brings me that Frisbee one more
time with that look on his face—"

"I love you too, Matt."

Matt stopped in mid-sentence. Then one of those heartstopping smiles of his spread across his face, and he
dropped a gentle kiss against her forehead. "Thank God.
Can we go home now?"

"Not so fast, Forester."

Matt and Kay spun around to find Robert staring at
them, his eyes tight little slits of anger. "You can't just
walk out of here. You have to take that money!"

"No," Matt said. "I don't believe I do."

Robert got right up in Matt's face, spitting fire. "But
that was our deal! You can't just back out now!"

"Back out of what, Mr. Hollinger?"

Robert spun around, his eyes wide. As he continued to
search for his tongue, Mr. Breckenridge glared at him with
unconcealed disgust.

"I've never been particularly fond of you, Mr. Hollinger. I never could put my finger on the reason for that,
until you lied to me about Ms. Ramsey's suitability as an
employee."

"I didn't lie! She was a lousy secretary. She—"

"Impossible. She's the best secretary I've ever had."
Then he turned to Kay. "I intend to get to the bottom of
this eventually. But right now, I just need to know one
thing. To your knowledge, did Mr. Hollinger attempt to
redirect the funds of this organization in an underhanded
manner?"

Kay had to tell the truth. "Yes, sir. He did."

"I see."

Robert's mouth fell open. "You're taking her word for
it?"

"Of course I am. You see, we've already established the value of *your* word."

Robert just stood, speechless once again. Twice in one night. This had to be a record.

"I'm going to recommend to the board that your firm be expelled from this organization. And rest assured that I'll make it clear to the membership why that decision was made."

"But he agreed to take the money!" Robert said, pointing at Matt. "He's just as much at fault as I am!"

"So you *did* try to give Dr. Forester the grant in exchange for some kind of personal gain?"

Robert paused a moment, shell-shocked. "Well...*no!*"

"Yes," Kay said quietly.

"You shut up!" Robert said, pointing an angry finger, then turning the same finger on Matt. "If I go down, you're going down with me!"

"Excuse me," Mr. Breckenridge said, "but I believe Dr. Forester just turned down the money. You, on the other hand, had every intention of seeing this deception through to the very end."

Robert just sputtered, his face an unattractive shade of puce.

"There'll be more discussion on this matter, I assure you," Mr. Breckenridge said to Robert. "But right now, I believe it would be in your best interest to leave the premises."

All at once Kay realized a crowd had gathered behind them, a crowd of people who were clearly wondering why the man Robert had pushed so hard to receive this honor had just tossed it right back in his face. When Robert saw he had an audience, he swallowed hard and started to back away.

"You can't do this, Breckenridge."

"Watch me, Mr. Hollinger."

Robert spun around and strode angrily out the front door of the hotel. Matt looped his arm around Kay's waist, and she leaned into him with a silent sigh of relief. Just when she thought this evening couldn't get any better, it had.

Mr. Breckenridge turned to Kay. "There's one more thing I'd like to talk to you about before you go."

"Yes?"

"You told me you have several dogs at the shelter that might be suitable for a pet. Would it be possible for me to drop by tomorrow to have a look?"

"Oh, yes!" Kay said. "Absolutely!"

"Excellent. I'll see you in the morning."

As Mr. Breckenridge walked off, Matt whispered in Kay's ear. "Come on. Let's go home."

Home.

Home to a monstrosity of a house with a pretty little storybook room where dreams come true. Home to a Frisbee-catching mutt and a feline sex goddess. Home to a ratty old sofa the size of a doomed ocean liner that might as well have been the size of Becky's love seat, because curled up in Matt's arms that's about all the space she figured they'd occupy. Home with the man she loved. And she couldn't wait to get there.

TRUE TO HIS WORD, Mr. Breckenridge showed up at the shelter the next morning promptly at nine o'clock. But before surveying the canine population for a pet, he had news for Kay and Matt.

"After you left last night," he said, "I held an emergency meeting of the board of directors and the selection committee. A poll of the committee members indicated that the shelter was a few votes shy of the number needed to receive the grant, which means that after Mr. Hollinger tallied the votes, he misreported the outcome. When the board heard about this, he was unanimously voted out of the Dorland Group.''

"So another organization actually won the grant?" Kay said.

"Yes. And that organization will receive twenty-five thousand dollars." He pulled an envelope from his pocket and held it out to Matt. "But so will the Westwood Animal Shelter."

Matt stared down at it with a look of total disbelief.

"Take it, Dr. Forester. With our blessing."

Matt accepted the check Mr. Breckenridge placed in his hand. "I don't know what to say."

"You don't have to say anything. Your actions last night spoke louder than words, as did Mr. Hollinger's. He's getting what he deserves. And so are you."

Kay felt as if she were flying. They could make up the back payments on the mortgage, buy a new air unit, maybe even expand a little to take in more animals. The shelter was going to survive. And she and Matt still had each other.

They escorted Mr. Breckenridge to the Dog Room, where he did a thorough evaluation of every dog in the shelter, but it wasn't an easy choice. One was too big, the next one too small. One was too hairy, another too loud. And a puppy was out of the question—he couldn't possibly deal with all that *activity*.

Who would have thought a three-legged bulldog would be just right?

Kay sniffed a little when she filled out the paperwork, got tears in her eyes when she handed Mr. Breckenridge the leash and cried like a fool when she hugged Chester goodbye. And Matt couldn't stop smiling.

An hour later Mr. Breckenridge phoned back to say that his niece had expressed interest in getting a dog, too, but she was afraid that the average dog might have trouble maintaining his sanity around her four wild, uncivilized sons. Since Rambo had no sanity to lose and could clearly hold his own in any uncivilized situation, another match was made.

"Those were the tough ones," Kay told Matt later, as they lay in bed, bathed in moonlight. "The rest will be a piece of cake, particularly since Clyde's living with us now."

Matt closed his eyes. "Heaven help us."

"No. Heaven help *you*. You're the one who neutered him."

Matt teased a fingertip along Kay's cheek. "You're not afraid of the animals anymore, are you?"

"Afraid?"

"You don't hate animals, Kay. You're afraid of them. I've known that for a long time."

That surprised her, but only for a moment. There wasn't much about her that Matt *didn't* know, when it came to important stuff, anyway. He still didn't know she ate the middles out of Oreos and actually liked Barry Manilow songs. She smiled. All in good time.

"You're right. I was afraid. But you know what? I don't think I am anymore."

"I don't think you are, either. You're crazy about every one of those animals. And they're crazy about you."

She felt so lucky, so happy, so loved that she almost couldn't stand it. And for some reason, the word *niche* came to mind.

She'd finally found a place where her family's opinion didn't matter. All that mattered was that she and Matt were there together. "You're right. I want all of them to get homes. And I'm not going to stop until that happens."

"God help the next poor soul who comes in. You'll send him home with a whole menagerie."

"That's right. If one's good, five must be better."

All at once the bedroom door squeaked open. Buddy nosed his way in and jumped up on the bed. Kay looked at Matt pointedly.

"Buddy," Matt said admonishingly. "Go on. Get out of here."

Buddy scooted toward them on his stomach, probably thinking that if he did it really slowly they wouldn't notice. He reached Kay and stuck his nose under her hand, his tail thumping against the sheets. She looked at Matt as if it was the most disgusting thing she'd ever seen, then rolled her eyes and petted him anyway.

"This dog is spoiled rotten."

"Nah. He's just trying to stay on your good side. See, he never knows when you might pick up a pair of dog clippers, flip those suckers on—"

Kay grabbed a pillow and smacked Matt across the face. Laughing, he yanked it out of her hand, tossed it aside, then pinned her against the bed and kissed her—a deep, delicious, languorous kiss that knocked the fight right out of her. When she came to her senses again, Matt was staring down at her.

"I want it to be like this forever," he whispered.

The man she loved was offering her forever. Did it get any better than that?

Matt pulled her close, tucking the antique quilt around them. She melted against him, enclosed in a cocoon of warmth and caring and love. As she drifted off to sleep, her last thought was that sometimes the oddest things happen.

How was she to know that she'd come here for a hundred hours and end up staying a lifetime?

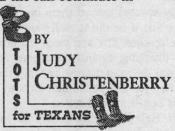

**Don't miss
an exciting opportunity
to save on the purchase of
Harlequin and Silhouette books!**

Buy any two Harlequin or
Silhouette books and save
$10.00 off future Harlequin
and Silhouette purchases

OR

buy any three
Harlequin or Silhouette books
and save **$20.00 off** future
Harlequin and Silhouette purchases.

*Watch for details
coming in October 2000!*

PHQ400

HARLEQUIN

Duets™

#35

THE DEPUTY'S BRIDE by Liz Ireland
Lone Star Lawmen: Book 2

Trouble with a capital *T*... That stands for Ruby Treadwell!
Heartbreak Ridge's wildest woman has deputy sheriff Cody Tucker
ready to throw in his badge. First she finagles a few free nights in his
jail, then she proposes marriage to the blushing lawman. Cody insists
that Ruby leave town before he falls prey to her tempting charms...
even if the only way is to whisk her off on a honeymoon!

SITTING PRETTY by Cheryl Anne Porter
It Could Happen to You...

Jayde Green is in one heck of a fix. After landing a job house-sitting
for tycoon Bradford Hale, she should've been sitting pretty. She'd
finally be able to help her parents out financially. Only, she never
expected to have to lie in order to get them to take the money. And
she definitely hadn't intended to fall for her gorgeous employer! It
couldn't get any worse—until her family showed up to meet Brad,
their new son-in-law...?

#36

FIT TO BE TIED by Carol Finch

Devlin Callahan is ready to read the riot act to his neighbor—the
fruitcake female who turned her forty-acre ranch into a blasted zoo!
Jessica Porter's exotic animals are scaring his cattle and sheep and
sending them stampeding everywhere. But when Devlin confronts
Jess, the gorgeous warmhearted blonde leaves him tongue-tied. Does
Devlin really want to run her out of town when she's got him all tied
up in knots?

THE LYON'S DEN by Selina Sinclair

Lyon Mackenzie couldn't afford to lose Miss Hammond. But his
seemingly robotic assistant was resigning—to get married, of all
things! When Liv realized her beastly boss was in a bind, she agreed
to stay on temporarily. Only, she hadn't counted on playing mommy to
her godson for that week, or on playing wife to Lyon when their
biggest client caught them in a compromising position!